SAFE HARBOR

"This is a strange place to be," said Ewna. "Perhaps you did see these things in a vision, Mara. But we did not."

Mara understood then. Deep down, her people had still been hoping to return to the lands that they loved. But she had finally given up hope of ever returning to the Village by the Lake. Mara realized that she no longer yearned for a place that held more painful memories than good ones.

She climbed to the top of the mesa, bracing her back against one face of rock and pushing herself up with her feet. Mara sat back and smiled. Here was a little world of her own. Across the vast plain was the canyon that they had walked along—a zigzag line, disappearing into the haze. There was a special grandeur to this place that excited her even while it soothed her spirit.

True, Graum might still be out there, searching for her. But for the time being, she felt safe.

PEOPLE OF THE MESA

PEOPLE
OF THE
MESA

▼▲▼

Charlotte Prentiss

AN ONYX BOOK

To John Silbersack,
who deserves no less and
may even deserve a bit more

ONYX
Published by the Penguin Group
Penguin Books USA Inc., 375 Hudson Street,
New York, New York 10014, U.S.A.
Penguin Books Ltd, 27 Wrights Lane,
London W8 5TZ, England
Penguin Books Australia Ltd, Ringwood,
Victoria, Australia
Penguin Books Canada Ltd, 10 Alcorn Avenue,
Toronto, Ontario, Canada M4V 3B2
Penguin Books (N.Z.) Ltd, 182–190 Wairau Road,
Auckland 10, New Zealand

Penguin Books Ltd, Registered Offices:
Harmondsworth, Middlesex, England

First published by Onyx, an imprint of Dutton Signet,
a division of Penguin Books USA Inc.

First Printing, February, 1995
10 9 8 7 6 5 4 3 2 1

PART ONE
▼ ▲ ▼

Portents

Chapter 1

For three days and three nights, she ate nothing. Her body felt frail and light, as if it barely belonged to her. She sat naked now on the ceremonial chair near the center of the Spirit House, close to a great crackling fire of pine logs, while the elder women of her tribe knelt on the hard earthen floor and chanted the Song of First Blood. The sound filled Mara's ears, steady and rhythmic, like the sound of blood in her veins. She clung to the rough poles of the chair, forcing herself to sit motionless. She felt dizzy, thirsty, and scared.

Lizel, the old priestess, had donned her lion skin—the sacred costume which she only wore when a girl came of age. She was moving around the big fire, now, crouching, snarling, and leaping, then freezing for long moments and staring into midair as if there were creatures there which only she could see. She called to the Spirit of the Sun; she called to his wife, the Moon; she called to all the animal spirits, and she shook her talisman—a sheep stomach that had been hardened with glue from the hooves of bison and filled with small stones. The rattling was a sharp sound, so sudden that it seemed frightening amid the gentle tones of the women's voices.

Lizel stooped and picked up a leather bowl. She threw water from it onto hot stones that had been ranged around the fire, and steam hissed and billowed up till the whole house was filled with warm, damp mist. Mara felt it on her face, and the mist seemed to make it more difficult for her to breathe. She gulped air, feeling anxious that she might faint and disgrace herself. Somehow, she told herself, she would endure. It would not be much longer now. She was almost a woman.

*   *   *

Lizel stopped her dance, and the women stopped their singing. For a long moment, it was ominously silent in the round, windowless Spirit House. Lizel bowed to the fire and stood for a moment in contemplation. Then she walked toward Mara and crouched low, less than an arm's length away.

The priestess was a frightening sight, with the lion skin draped across her back and its head concealing hers. Its fangs were bared, and pebbles of quartz were set where its eyes had been. They glowed dimly, as if they had somehow trapped some light from the Moon.

Steam still rose from the stones around the fire, casting halos around the yellow flames. The house was so hot that Mara was sweating now, despite her nakedness.

"I am a great mountain cat," Lizel said. Her voice had changed; it was low and guttural, as if the spirit of the cat really had invaded her body. "Its spirit lives with mine," she said. "Its voice speaks with mine. Its strength is in my flesh. With its power, I call upon Mother Moon. Look kindly on this girl. Today she will be a woman. Tonight, a bride."

There was a gentle murmuring from all the women gathered around.

Lizel leaned closer to Mara—so close, the lion mask almost touched her face. "Speak your name."

Mara's mouth was painfully dry. She swallowed, and she felt as if the skin inside her throat was cracking. "I am Mara of the Lake People," she said.

"Speak your clan! Louder, now!"

"My clan is the clan of Ternees. Ternees, my mother, is the Chieftain of our tribe."

There was another low murmur of assent.

"Good. It is time now to meet your spirit." Lizel picked up a small leather sack which had been painstakingly ornamented with drawings etched into the skin. "Breathe the fragrance of the land where all creatures make their home. Breathe deeply, and let the land tell you whose spirit is yours."

The mouth of the sack was pressed tight over Mara's face. She inhaled and almost choked on the pungent fragrance of herbs, dried flowers, and grasses. She breathed again, and felt herself getting dizzy. The crackling of the fire started moving away from her, as if her own spirit was escaping her flesh. Her vision darkened. She felt herself swaying.

"Breathe deeply!"

The air grew so dark, all Mara could see were the gleaming quartz lion-eyes. As if in the distance on a grassy plain, she heard an animal scream—and yet, it was more than a scream. It seemed like a voice, talking to her now, telling her of the life it led roaming the wild country, hunting through the tall grasses.

"Cat," she muttered, as the bag was taken from her mouth. "Bobcat."

"Ah." Lizel's voice sounded close, yet far away. "The bobcat is quick, fierce, and strong." Once again she pressed the leather sack to Mara's face. "Now, your journey."

Mara took quick, panting breaths. She felt her body trembling. She had very little strength left. Once again, her vision darkened. Sounds grew deeper in her ears. Everything around her seemed slow and dim.

She lost all sight of the lion mask and the house where the fire lit the faces of the waiting women. She seemed to be standing out on the grassland. A crescent moon was in the sky, and there was a group of low, mounded silhouettes in the distance—a village, she realized. Her village, the home of her people, by the Great Lake. There was a feeling of deep peace and tranquillity.

And then, suddenly, it was transformed. The village was in flames. The whole land was burning. There was a roaring sound. The heat hit her face. A black shape came running toward her, as if it meant to strike her down. It was a huge black bear, its teeth bared, its body towering over her.

Its fur was matted with fresh, thick blood.

Mara screamed.

She found herself slumped in the chair. It seemed as if a whole day had passed, although she knew it had only been moments. Lizel's hands were shaking her by the shoulders. "Tell, Mara. Tell what you saw."

"A bear," Mara gasped. Should she say more? No; what she had seen was too terrible. It would disrupt the ceremony. She shouldn't talk of it—not now, maybe not ever.

"A bear." Lizel turned to the audience of women. "The strongest, most powerful hunter. Mara's life journey will bring her strength. She, too, will be strong." Lizel stepped back, reached under her lion skin, and pulled out a long flint knife. Then she squatted down in the birthing position. She put her free hand between her legs and gave a loud yell, a cry of exultation, a cry of life itself. Suddenly something was in her hands, as if she had dragged it from inside her body. It was a small furry shape, a rabbit so freshly killed that it was not yet stiff. She brought the flint knife around in a quick, scything motion, and blood welled up amid the fur.

Lizel leaped up. The rabbit's belly had been slit wide open. She wiped it across Mara's bare torso, from her neck, down between her breasts, all the way to her thighs, where Mara had bled for the first time just seven days ago. Then Lizel reached with gnarled hands inside the furry form and dragged out the liver, glistening so dark that it seemed black. "Eat!" she cried, pressing it to Mara's lips.

After her three days of fasting, the taste was almost too intense for Mara to bear. She choked, but finally managed to chew and shallow.

Lizel stepped back. "Mara is a girl no longer," she proclaimed. "She is a woman now. I say it, and it is so."

Suddenly there was a yelling so loud, Mara feared her skull would break. All the women in the Spirit House were on their feet, shouting their approval. They started flinging tiny stones, a hailstorm of gravel. Mara shielded her eyes. Her whole body stung and burned as the stones hit her. She felt overwhelmed—with pain from this new ordeal, and gladness that she was a woman now, and pride that she had endured the ceremony with the courage that was expected of the Chieftain's daughter.

At the same time, she trembled. As she pressed her

hands over her eyes, the darkness seemed to light up with dancing yellow shapes, and once again she saw flames engulfing the buildings of her tribe.

Mara found herself being dragged onto her feet. The women were lining up to embrace her. Her mother, Ternees, came first; then her older sister, Shani; then her aunts, Elmay and Jorno and Tamra; then the other female relatives in her clan; and finally, the remaining women of her tribe. Mara felt so dazed, she didn't really see their faces, and she barely heard their words. They hugged her and patted her, and one by one, they left.

Finally there was no sound in the Spirit House but the crackling of the fire.

Lizel had set aside the lion's head. Gently, she led Mara to a bed of willow boughs, where she sat her down. She turned to Trifen, a thin, dowdy orphan boy who helped her in the Spirit House, and she told him to bring some hot soup to break Mara's fast.

The smell of the soup made Mara's hunger leap inside her, and she found herself drinking greedily from the leather bowl that was placed in her hands. Lizel muttered a command, the bowl was refilled, and Mara drank again.

"Was it . . . right?" she said, looking up at Lizel, when she had drunk her fill. "Did the spirits smile on me? Was it the way that it's supposed to be?"

Lizel touched Mara's shoulder. The old woman's face was heavily wrinkled, and her deep-set eyes were almost lost in shadow. She seemed bent and frail, and yet even now, Mara sensed the strange power inside her. "It was good, Mara," Lizel said. "You are a woman now." She paused for a moment. "Of course, there is more to come."

"The pairing ceremony?"

Lizel looked solemn. "The pairing." Once again, she touched Mara's shoulder. "Rest, now."

The command seemed to have a power of its own. Mara felt a wave of drowsy warmth spreading out from her belly, making her limbs swollen and heavy. She found herself slumping down on the bed. There was an apprehensive moment as she wondered if sleep might torment her with more visions of fire. But her fears couldn't stave off the sleep that swept over her as dark and sudden as the fall of night.

She dreamed, but not of omens. She found herself standing amid snowy mountains, watching a young hunter running toward her through the drifts. His furs were flapping around him, and his feet were kicking up white powder that glittered in the sunlight. He smiled at her and raised his arm in greeting.

"Kormor," she cried. "Kormor, I'm here!"

She woke, speaking his name.

"You'll be with him soon enough." It was Lizel's voice. She was sitting close by, wearing different clothes, now—a gray robe stitched together from wolf pelts, with a necklace of mammoth teeth. Her white hair hung almost to her waist. Her face was brown from the sun, the wind, and the passing seasons. "Bring the meat over," she called to Trifen.

Mara smelled the aroma of roasted rabbit, and her mouth started watering reflexively. The soup and her sleep had merely sharpened her hunger. She found that some sheepskins had been laid over her. She pulled them tighter around her.

Trifen came over holding a board laden with chunks of rabbit meat. He was a shy, thin, serious-faced boy, and he never spoke. Indeed, he had no voice at all, and people said that a sparrow had slipped down into his throat and stolen it while he slept in his crib on the day he was born. He lived with Lizel, helping with all her chores. Since he could not speak, the secrets of her rituals and potions were safe with him.

He kneeled and placed the meat in front of Mara, respectfully avoiding her eyes. Mara seized the food and feasted on it greedily. The taste was so pungent, so aromatic, it brought tears to her eyes.

Once again, in her imagination, she saw Kormor. "Have you been outside at all, Lizel?" she asked. "Have you seen him?"

Lizel smiled faintly. "Today I shall not leave the Spirit House. This is where my power lies."

Mara turned to Trifen. "What about you? Have you seen Kormor?"

He looked at her uneasily. He never seemed to like it when people spoke to him. Finally, reluctantly, he nodded.

Mara tensed forward. "Did he seem happy?"

Once again, Trifen nodded his head.

Mara lay back on one elbow. Soon, now, she would be paired, and Kormor would be hers. *He would be hers.* She had spent so much time imagining this day, how it would feel, and what it would mean to her, it was hard now to believe it was finally happening. She was a woman, she reminded herself. She was entitled to a mate. It would be so.

She seized the rest of the rabbit meat and ate it greedily, not caring that the juices ran down her chin.

"Trifen, bring more," said Lizel.

The boy hurried back to the fire.

Mara looked across at the flames, and the sight of them took away the brief pleasure she had felt. Once again, she saw the village burning and the bear stained with blood. She shifted uneasily. She was not the kind of person who normally had visions. She was practical; she wasn't a dreamer. When there was a problem, she always wanted to take the simplest path to solve it, and she was never very interested in contemplating the mysteries of life. She lived for the present, not the future.

"Something is troubling you," said Lizel.

Mara looked up quickly. She found that the old woman had walked closer to her, moving as silently as a shadow. She was looming over Mara, now, and staring down at her. "If you have questions, you should ask them, Mara. If you have doubts, this is the time when they should be spoken."

Mara shook her head quickly. "It's nothing," she said.

Lizel opened her mouth to speak again—but then she paused. There was a faint rustling sound from the doorway of the Spirit House, where doubled panels of mammoth hide shut the world outside. A footstep sounded on the packed earth floor.

Lizel's face changed. Her expression of thoughtful concern was replaced by one of anger. "Who enters this house?" she called out, turning away from Mara. "This is the Resting Time." She stepped toward the door. "We must not be disturbed."

A figure came into view, touched faintly by the firelight. A tall woman stood there, dressed in pale antelope hide. She stood with calm self-assurance, as if Lizel's words meant nothing to her and this house was hers.

Mara looked at the intruder, and she felt a new, sick sense of foreboding as she recognized Ternees, her mother. "With respect," Ternees said, "I must speak with my daughter."

Lizel put her hands on her hips. "You know that this is not customary."

"I know." Ternees's voice was low-pitched and gentle. But Mara knew how deceptive that gentleness could be. Ternees ruled the tribe with compassion, but she never tolerated dissent. "I must speak with her all the same," she said. She nodded to the priestess. "You will excuse us, please."

Mara saw Lizel's profile, thin-lipped with disapproval. Abruptly the priestess turned away. She strode to the fire and sat down near Trifen, turning her back.

Ternees came over to Mara, moving gracefully, as she always did. She seated herself on a tree stump beside the bed of willow boughs, and she clasped her hands on her knees. In all the times Mara had seen her mother, Ternees had always seemed like this, calmly in control, expecting other people to yield to her authority.

Mara was still exhausted from her days of fasting. She was half naked, and her skin was still daubed with blood from the ritual. She felt in no state to deal with her mother. "Why are you here?" she asked.

Ternees watched Mara for a long moment. Her face was enigmatic.

Mara shifted uneasily. "Mother—"

"You are a woman now," Ternees spoke.

Mara nodded.

"So now you can make your own decisions," Ternees went on. "As is our custom."

Mara felt her stomach tensing. She had learned to

dread these times when her mother watched her steadily and began speaking in this gentle, reasonable voice. Always, Ternees wanted Mara to do something, or be something. And always, Mara found herself fighting a battle to hold on to her own self, her own spirit, her own needs and desires.

"Still," Ternees was saying, "you are not yet paired with Kormor. Not until tonight." Ternees's dark eyes were unblinking. No doubt she cared for her daughter and wanted her to be happy. But from the outside, Ternees seemed unrelievedly stern, devoid of weakness. "I have told you before," she said, "that I disapprove of this pairing."

Mara felt a warmth growing in her chest, and then she felt her face growing hot as the anger spread through her. "Mother, please, this is not the time—"

"I have come here now," Ternees went on, "because my conscience won't let me rest unless I suggest to you once more that you should abandon this plan. There is still time, Mara."

"No!" The word escaped from her with far more force than she had intended. It echoed in the big house.

Ternees didn't flinch from the sound. She watched Mara as calmly as before. "You have always been the willful one, Mara," she said. There was regret in her voice, now. "You're always too restless to wait, too angry to compromise. But think: It can be hard and lonely to choose a path that leads away from your family. I know that it hasn't always been easy for you in the Clan House. But I tell you this, Mara: If you will postpone this pairing just for a few months, to give yourself a little more time to think—why, all of us will make a special effort for you in our House."

Mara closed her eyes. There had been other times like this when her mother had tried to tempt her. Sometimes Mara had yielded—yet in the end, it had never brought her happiness. She always seemed to find that to fit in, she had to surrender. "Thank you, Mother," she said, "but no."

Ternees made an impatient sound. "You're a woman now. Doesn't that give you the confidence to take your time instead of rushing to be paired? This man is from outside our tribe. I don't believe he'll make you happy, Mara. I worry for your future. Even now he still doesn't fully respect our customs—"

Mara struggled up onto her feet. "Mother, I have chosen him!" She felt herself trembling. "And I will be paired with him. Tonight. Please!"

Ternees pressed her lips together. Slowly, taking her time, she stood up opposite Mara. "He shows respect, but he doesn't feel it. This much I know. Do you dispute it?"

Mara pressed her fingers to her temples. It felt as if her mother was trying to chip away at her, to pry her apart bit by bit, until she could reach inside Mara and seize her spirit and break it. "Please," Mara muttered.

"He throws a spear farther than other men," Ternees went on. "That's the only thing he has to be proud of. Still, he's arrogant, as if he has more to boast about than we do."

Mara couldn't stand it any longer. "Stop it!" she shouted. "Please, I can't stand it." She shook her head, and she found tears in her eyes. "Why can't you let me be the way I want to be?"

Ternees studied her a moment. "I see you haven't changed," she said, with a touch of sadness in her voice. She sighed, and the fierceness faded in her. "So be it, Mara." She wrapped her robe around her, stood up, and took a step back. "I will conduct the pairing ceremony. You will have the man of your choice, since that is our custom." She looked at Mara just once more, and this time she even seemed to feel sorrow. "I warn you, though, if this pairing fails, it will disgrace our House."

Mara wiped her tears away on the back of her hand. She hated the way her mother had the power to rouse such emotions in her. "Soon I won't be *in* your House," she muttered.

Ternees grimaced. "That, too, is your decision. But if you leave our clan, it will not be easy for you to come back." She turned to the door—then hesitated. "One more thing: If your pairing fails, I will disown you, Mara. Do you understand that? If you break your bond with

Kormor, I will tell our people that you are unfit to take my place as Chieftain, if I die and if Shani dies before you."

She turned, then, and walked stiffly away.

Mara sank down on the bed, shivering under the sheepskins. Her thoughts were incoherent. It was wrong, she told herself. It was cruel, and it was unfair. But she wasn't even sure exactly what she meant.

Lizel came over to her. She sat down beside Mara on the bed of willow boughs, and she took Mara's hand. "Is this truly your path?" she asked softly.

Mara nodded. "It is." She looked up at Lizel. "Do you think my mother is right?"

"This is not a simple thing, Mara." She was thoughtful for a long moment. "I will give you advice. It is customary, before your pairing. But first, I think, you should rest some more."

Mara felt so upset, she didn't see how she could go back to sleep. And yet, as the emotions gradually subsided inside her, she realized she felt completely drained. Her exhaustion had a power of its own.

With a great act of will, she drove her thoughts out of her head, and she lay down again, pulling the sheepskins up around her face.

Chapter 2

She woke to the sound of drums—a deep, resonant thrumming from outside the Spirit House. Much time must have passed, she realized with a shock. She heard the distant voice of old Lorm, the News Teller, as he went from one home to the next, calling people out, though there was little need for that now. The time of the pairing ceremony was near, and most people in the tribe would already be gathering in the Meeting Place.

Mara blinked and looked up from where she lay. Charms and fetishes had been hung above her, protecting her while she slept. She saw a bird made from sparrow feathers embedded in a rounded piece of clay; a fossil shaped like a snail shell, dangling from a string of woven grasses; a fragment of deerskin on which the outline of a deer had been drawn; and a turtle shell inscribed with markings that were mysterious to Mara, though Lizel would have known their meaning.

Heavy wooden poles—pine logs, each nearly twice the height of a man—stood four-square, supporting the domed roof of the circular Spirit House. The roof was made of birch branches, with willow laid across them and a layer of hard clay on top of that. The underside of the roof was dark brown, almost black in the flickering fire-light. Through the smoke hole at the center, Mara saw that the sky had faded from blue to purple. Outside, people would be lighting torches, getting ready for the celebration.

"Mara, it is time," said Lizel. She came over, with Trifen following behind her carrying a large leather bowl of water, which he set down with elaborate care.

Mara stood up, letting the sheepskins fall away. Trifen

moved forward and started washing her, using a square of fine, rare bear hide. The water had been warmed by the fire, and it was scented with herbs. It felt good on Mara's body, and she was glad to see the sacrificial blood being rinsed away.

Lizel watched with her arms folded, still wearing her cloak of gray wolf pelts. The drumming outside began growing louder, as more men started pounding on the skins in the Meeting Place. So it was really happening now, whether her mother wanted it or not. For a moment Mara felt true, deep sadness that it had to be done in defiance of her mother and her clan. The rift had been bad enough before; after this, it would be far wider.

Still, if she was to be true to herself, she had no choice. And she was convinced that if she followed her path, she would find new happiness.

Mara told herself that this was a special moment. She looked around, trying to memorize all the details and refusing to think anymore of her frightening vision or her fears for the future. Surely she would want to look back on this time often, throughout her life.

She waited while Trifen dried her with the sheepskins that she had slept under. Then she sat once again in the ceremonial chair. Pigments had been mixed on a slab of stone: red clay, white chalk, and dark berry juices. Mara stared straight ahead, trying to calm herself while Trifen began braiding her long black hair and Lizel began the painstaking task of painting the bridal patterns on Mara's face.

Outside the house, the rhythm of the drumming became more insistent. Mara imagined she could feel it through the earth under her feet. She heard people in the Meeting Place chanting now, praising the Sun as it sank behind the mountains beyond the lake, and welcoming Mother Moon as she claimed the land below for her own.

While Lizel used brushes fashioned from grass and reeds to spread cool, wet pigment across Mara's cheeks, Mara found herself thinking again of Kormor. Where was he now? What was he thinking, and what was he doing? She knew he would be making preparations of his own, with the elder men of the tribe, and she wished she could watch them. She still remembered, with complete clarity, the first time she had seen Kormor, just a year ago, when he first arrived at the village.

He had come from a tribe in the North Lands, where the sea was rising, food was scarce, and people were warring with each other. Kormor's people had made the great journey south across the jagged, icebound mountains, but it had cost them dearly. Two score people had started out. Only Kormor had survived. The others—Kormor's parents among them—had been lost in a rockslide that swept them into a crevasse. Only luck had saved Kormor, and only his exceptional strength had sustained him through the rest of the journey on his own.

He was a powerful young man, tall and massively muscled. He had thick, unruly black hair, and eyes that were shrewd, always alert. He seldom spoke, and he seemed to measure every gesture, moving cautiously, conserving his strength.

He had arrived among the Lake People frostbitten and exhausted, and full of silent anger—at fate and at himself, as if it had been his fault that so many had died. As soon as she'd seen him, Mara had wanted him.

She hadn't been the only one. Shani, her older sister, had eyed Kormor with obvious interest, and at first he seemed to respond. Mara decided that this was one time when she could not bear to let her sister take something from her. She pledged herself to win Kormor, and she did everything in her power to achieve her goal.

She noticed that he often walked alone by the lake early in the morning; so she went out before him and bathed in the shallow water, bare from the waist up, where he would be sure to see her. Another time, in the heat of the summer, she saw him walking up into the hills alone. She managed to find a path that took her ahead of him, and when he found her, she was lying naked in the grass, sunbathing. She gave a little cry of surprise and covered herself—though she couldn't conceal her guilty smile as she saw the look in his eyes.

Attracting his attention had been easy enough. Restraining her own desire had been much harder. She had always been headstrong, and her natural inclination was to let her feelings guide her. When he started walking with her, and then hunting with her, it had taken all her willpower to hold herself back and wait till she came of age.

Abruptly, Mara realized that Lizel had stepped back. The old woman was looking at Mara with her eyes narrowed, assessing her handiwork. Finally, she gave a curt nod.

Trifen came forward, holding a large square of black slate. He gently placed it on Mara's knees, then picked up a bowl of water and poured some of it onto the stone.

Mara leaned forward so that she could peer at her reflection in the slate. She had large, dark eyes and a full, proud mouth. Deep down, she had never been quite satisfied with the way she looked. Shani was more of a beauty, with a face that wasn't so broad and cheekbones that were more clearly defined. Also, Shani had inherited her mother's way of moving with calm elegance and poise. Mara always felt impetuous and clumsy by comparison.

But she was far too proud ever to admit that. And now that she saw herself in the wet, black slate, she felt deeply pleased. Her hair had been beautifully braided, with small bones, feathers, and wildflowers woven into it. Her face had been elaborately painted, with her cheeks highlighted in red, and delicate thin lines of white and black scribed around her eyes and mouth. Truly, she was a beautiful bride.

She looked up at Lizel. "Thank you," she said.

The priestess nodded slowly. "It is good," she said. She turned to Trifen. "Take the slate away. Bring the bridal robe."

Mara stood up, and she felt soft deerskin being draped around her shoulders. It had been whitened with chalk, and drawings of animals and birds had been etched into it by the women of the tribe. They had colored their drawings with the juice of wild berries, and they had woven porcupine quills in elaborate patterns. Mara waited while Lizel fastened the thongs at the sides of the robe. Then she sat down again so that Trifen could fit sandals of beaver skin to her feet.

Then there was only one more thing. Lizel proffered a thong with a single round, white stone bound into it. "This, Mara, you must put on for yourself."

Mara took it from her. There was a slight tremor in her hand as she raised it over her head. More than anything else, it was proof that the pairing was imminent. It was her Bonding Stone, which custom had forbidden her to wear till this night.

Mara placed it around her neck, and she felt the weight of it between her small breasts. She realized she had been holding her breath, and she let out a little sigh.

Lizel turned away for a moment. When she turned back, her face was hidden by her wolf mask. Several sections of skin were stitched together around the open jaws, so the face seemed huge. Lizel started chanting in a harsh northern tongue, and something about it made Mara shiver. At times like these, she felt the animal spirits close by. That, of course, was the way it should be: to have them in this sacred place, and beg them for their strength. Yet still her skin prickled. A current of air touched the back of her neck, and she imagined that it was the breath of a wolf upon her.

She shivered and closed her eyes. Lizel's voice merged with the singing and the drumming outside the house, and the sounds invaded Mara's mind, calming her.

After a long time, Lizel stopped chanting. Mara felt a spot of something wet and warm being placed upon her forehead. A drop of dove's blood, she realized, to give her its virtues of peace and tranquillity, which her people valued above all else.

She opened her eyes. Lizel stood before her, unmasked. "You are ready now," the old woman said. She smiled. For a brief moment, the hard lines of her face seemed to soften, and Mara saw into Lizel deeper than she had ever seen before. She imagined Lizel fifteen years old, like Mara herself. Perhaps Lizel had been just as filled with apprehension and uncertainty then—though it seemed hard to imagine.

But then the moment was gone. Lizel turned and

flicked her hand at Trifen. The young boy quickly retreated to the door. The panels of mammoth hide opened
just wide enough for his thin body to pass between them.
There was a shout of recognition from outside as he
joined the people who had gathered there. Everyone
knew now that the preparations were complete.

Lizel took Mara's hand. The old woman's skin was
rough and dry, like parched earth. "Now, Mara, is the
time for advice, if you wish to receive it."

Mara nodded. "Yes. Please."

"Come, then." Lizel led her over to the fire, and they
sat facing one another in the light of the flames. "So,"
said Lizel, settling herself. "What is it you would like
to ask?"

Mara felt suddenly self-conscious. She seldom confided
in other people. She had long since learned that her
mother was not a sympathetic listener, and Shani was so
competitive, she simply couldn't be trusted. As for the
other young girls of the tribe—some of them were
friendly, but they never seemed to accept Mara as one
of them. Maybe she was too outspoken and willful, as
her mother said. Or maybe the girls were too much
aware that Mara was the Chieftain's younger daughter.

Mara realized that the moment of silence was growing
longer. "I would like to know," she said, forcing the
words out, "if you think I have ... made an unwise
choice."

Lizel nodded slowly. Her face looked grave. "He's a
proud young man, Mara," she said. "And in some ways,
that can be troublesome. He's been biding his time, you
know, waiting for you. He may be more ... difficult,
when the waiting is finally over."

Mara felt disconcerted. She'd expected Lizel to offer
advice on domestic life, children, and the everyday business of sharing with a man. "I don't think—"

Lizel silenced Mara with a stern look. "This is my
advice, girl. Pay attention, now."

Mara felt her cheeks redden under the bridal paint.
"I'm sorry," she muttered.

Lizel turned stared into the flames without blinking.
"So, now. He is strong, and that may be troublesome,

but still his strength is good, because I sense we will need men who are strong."

Mara leaned forward. "How so?"

Lizel frowned, still watching the dancing flames. "I sense a time of changes, girl. I have seen portents." Without warning, she turned and looked directly into Mara's eyes. "During the Ceremony of First Blood, when I told you to see your journey, you were not happy with what you saw."

Mara blinked and drew back. She had the sudden eerie sense that Lizel had looked into her mind. "I saw the bear—"

"Yes." Lizel's eyes were still on her, sharp as a bird's. "And what else?"

Mara felt flustered. This was still not the time to speak of such things. And yet she felt as if Lizel already knew. "There was something else," she finally admitted. Haltingly, then, she described the burning village and the bear's fur drenched in blood.

Lizel nodded slowly. The corners of her mouth turned down, and the shadows seemed to deepen under her eyes. She rocked to and fro for a moment. "I came to your people sixteen years ago, just before you were born, Mara. I came from the North Lands, where I had seen men turn their spears against each other, and people dying from starvation, and even the ones who survived were all the time living in fear. I came here, and I saw that this village was a magical place. Your people had built these great houses, and they had laid down a code of peace and sharing, and they were determined that it should always be so. Well, now, that's a wonderful thing, is it not?"

"Yes," Mara whispered. She felt a new chill inside her, now—an uneasiness far deeper than anything she had known before.

"But still," Lizel went on, "it goes against the way of the world. There is always birth and death, the changing of seasons, the rhythm of years. Nothing stays the same forever."

Mara felt a great need for Lizel to stop talking this

way. "Lizel, why are you saying these things? This is supposed to be a time of happiness and hope."

Lizel suddenly reached out and seized Mara's wrist. She held it tightly. "You must be strong. You must be vigilant and always prepared. Then, maybe, you'll have something to hope for, and a chance to be happy. Are you listening to me?"

Mara wanted to pull away, but Lizel's grip was amazingly tight. Reluctantly, Mara nodded.

"You *are* strong," Lizel went on. "Strong enough to defy even your mother, our Chieftain. So if there are dark omens, and if there's a time of change, you will have your strength to sustain you."

This was all so different from what Mara had expected. "I don't understand," she said.

"Your people are weak, like children," said Lizel. "Remember what I say! Your sister, and even your mother—they have never had to fight for anything. When the time comes, you must stand up and speak out and do what must be done, even when others lack that courage. Will you remember that?"

Mara nodded dumbly.

The old woman released Mara's wrist. She stood up, turned away, and started walking toward the door.

"Wait!" Mara called to her.

Lizel didn't answer. She pulled aside the panel of mammoth hide.

The crowd outside let out a roar of approval. Mara jumped to her feet, feeling panick-stricken. She took a shaky step. A feather fell from her hair. She hesitated, wondering whether to pick it up. One feather didn't matter, did it? Or did it? Was it an omen? Her thoughts were chaotic, like startled birds fluttering across the sky.

Through the doorway, she glimpsed flaming torches and grinning faces, the crowd waiting, eager to see her. This was the moment, and even though she'd been looking forward to it for almost a year, she felt confused and disoriented. She hurried forward and ducked through the opening, and the drumming and the shouting closed in around her.

She tried to regain her composure. Morro and Joquar,

two strong young hunters, were waiting right beside the door, holding between them a seat made of poles lashed together. They were being jostled by the crowd. One of them almost lost his balance.

Trying to move with dignity, trying to capture some of her mother's poise, Mara turned and perched on the seat. She straightened her bridal clothes and placed one hand on each shoulder of the men on either side of her, and they raised her up.

The seat tilted under her, then steadied. She looked out over the heads of the throng. The domed roofs of the Clan Houses were all around. Some people had climbed up there and were calling and waving to her. She smiled uneasily and raised her hand.

Her bearers took her between the houses, toward the Meeting Place. That was where the men were drumming, and that was where the biggest crowd had gathered. All the men were bare-chested, their skin gleaming in the torchlight. The women were decked out in feathers, and everyone's face was painted.

The night air was cool on Mara's cheeks as she was carried above the crowd, but nervous perspiration broke out on her forehead. Finally she was in the Meeting Place itself, and her bearers were setting her down, lowering her back into the warmth and noise. Her feet touched the ground, and she stood up. The ground seemed uneven beneath her sandals. She was buffeted by the bodies pressing close around her.

Her bearers opened a path for her, and she moved forward, stepping cautiously. To stumble would be a terrible embarrassment; to fall was unthinkable.

Her mother was standing up on the Speaking Stone at the far side of the Meeting Place, outside the House of their clan—the biggest House of all. She was holding a mask of whitened doeskin in front of her face, trimmed with dove feathers. It looked as if Mother Moon herself had come down from the sky to shine here on Her people.

Mara's sister, Shani, was standing to one side. She was wearing a simple costume—a shawl of rabbit pelts, and a skirt woven from grasses—but still she looked elegant, as she always did. Mara felt a twinge of anger, then suppressed it almost instantly. There was no way that Shani would spoil this most special night. After all, Shani was still unpaired, even though she was a year older. Mara was the one who had claimed Kormor for her own.

And there he was, standing just the other side of Ternees. Mara felt a leap of pure pleasure. In him, at least, there were no bad portents. He was staring straight ahead, as custom demanded, but she sensed that he wished he could be looking at her. His long, black hair fanned out to his shoulders. He seemed so calm and strong, his strength was contagious.

Mara look her place on the other side of her mother, and she, too, stared ahead, over the faces of the crowd. Their eyes were bright, their teeth were gleaming, their voices were shouting while the drumming reached a crescendo.

Then Ternees raised her arms, and all the sound stopped.

Mara's ears rang in the sudden silence. Gradually, she started hearing the sounds of the night. Somewhere, an owl screamed. Closer, there were snapping, sizzling noises coming from the cooking fires, and a baby crying in one of the Clan Houses. But those were the only sounds as the people stood massed together, silently showing their respect.

Ternees drew herself up to address them. "People of the Great Lake," she said calmly, gently, "this is a special day."

There was kindness in her voice, and love. Ternees genuinely loved her people, and she loved her daughter, too—or so Mara liked to think. No one would have guessed, from her tone, how deeply she had been opposed to the pairing that they had gathered to witness.

"Many years ago," Ternees went on, "the First Mother of my clan came to this place. Her name was Laena of the Panther People."

There was another gentle murmuring as everyone acknowledged the familiar words.

"She was the first of all people to make the great journey from the north, across the frozen mountains, in search of a bountiful land where people would not harm each other and there would be food for everyone." Ternees paused. "This is that land."

The villagers let out a sigh of assent.

"We were the first to build our homes in this new land. We still govern ourselves as Laena taught us. Here, men and women share equally, and each person is free to follow her path—*no matter what it may be.*"

Maybe, Mara thought, there was an edge of anger to those last few words. Yes; they were intended for her, there was no doubt of that, and she felt momentarily stung by them. *Please,* she thought, *just pair us and be kind to us. This is no time to be harsh.*

"We welcome all strangers," Ternees said. "Our tribe is a haven and a resting place, and always it shall be so."

Mara had heard the words so many times, and instinctively she believed them, just as she believed that the sun would rise each day. She looked out at the domed houses, so big and proud, rooted in the land, built to last forever. How could it be possible for such a place to be destroyed? Suddenly she doubted Lizel's words, and her own vision—or at least the meaning she had put upon it.

"Mara," said Ternees, turning toward her. "Who have you chosen as your mate?"

This, then, was the real moment, which she had rehearsed in her head so often. She was anxious, but the anxiety was in her belly, not her head. Her thoughts suddenly seemed very clear. She turned toward the crowd and took a deep breath. Would her voice fail her?

"I choose Kormor!" she cried. And the words were clear and loud, edged with a triumph that she couldn't conceal.

Ternees turned to Kormor. "And you, Kormor, who have you chosen?"

"I have chosen Mara." He didn't hesitate before he spoke. He made it sound so simple, so obvious, it hardly needed to be said. Mara suddenly wondered how he could seem so casual. Didn't he understand the importance of this moment? Wasn't this as important to him as it was to her?

But then Ternees was gripping her left wrist and pulling her arm across till her hand touched Kormor's. His skin felt warm and real, and it calmed her. His hand clutched hers tightly, and she clutched his in return.

"You will exchange your Bonding Stones," Ternees said.

With her free hand, Mara took hold of the thong that carried the plain white stone. She lifted it up over her head. Kormor, meanwhile, was doing the same thing, taking off the stone that he wore. Looking quietly satisfied, he placed his stone around Mara's neck. Then he bowed his head so that she could reach up and give her Bonding Stone to him.

"Good," said Ternees. "Now, listen. You will live as one and you will share as one. Let everyone see, here, you are one. You are equal parts of the whole. You are paired."

Mara realized there were tears on her cheeks. All the anticipation, all the fighting and struggling flowed out of her in a rush.

"Go now!" Ternees cried. "Go to the Coupling Tent. This is your time. Go!"

Mara glanced at Kormor. He was grinning at her. He looked happy and proud. And so he should, she thought to herself. She had sacrificed so much for him. She was risking her place in her clan, even her birthright in the tribe, for this pairing.

Everyone started cheering. The crowd opened a path for the couple. Kormor ran forward and Mara went after him. People were touching her, slapping her shoulder, shouting their good wishes. The noise was harsh in her ears.

Then she was out of the Meeting Place, running with Kormor, past the round Clan Houses, through the muddle of tents and huts on the outskirts of the village. Cool night air flooded her lungs. Her white deerskin robe fluttered around her. The cheering receded behind her and the darkness of the night closed in as Mara ran and ran, feeling triumphant now, while she plunged forward into the darkness.

Chapter 3

They ran till they reached the hills at the eastern edge of the wide, shallow valley. From here, the flaming torches in the Meeting Place were a tiny yellow glow almost lost in the great sweep of the land, and the lake was a slender streak of silver beneath the moon.

Kormor led the way up a rough slope. They reached a shelf in the hillside—and here was the Coupling Tent he had set up for her, in the custom of her tribe, using mammoth skins stretched across poles. It was half hidden amid a copse of cottonwood trees, with a stream running close by.

Mara stopped and rested a moment. It had been a struggle for her to run in the long robe, and Kormor's legs were much longer than hers. "It's perfect," she told him as she got her breath back and looked at the tent, at the hillside, and then at him, standing to one side, so strong and proud. Suddenly she felt so happy, she couldn't help laughing. "Kormor, it's wonderful."

"I worked hard," he said. "Look inside."

She hesitated. Part of her wanted to stay out here, savoring the intense happiness that made her skin feel hot, like the embers of a fire. When she walked into that tent . . . things would be different. The taboos of her tribe, which protected all women who were not paired, would no longer apply to her. There would be nothing to prevent him from having her. And how would that feel? So often, she had tried to imagine it. The thought of it scared her. One of her aunts had warned her that it would be painful the first time.

She glanced quickly at Kormor. He was so much bigger than she was, and he was staring at her in the moonlight with an avid intensity that made her want to hide herself, even while it excited her.

He stepped forward. He unlaced the door flap of the tent, and then he peeled it back, holding it open for her.

So there was no turning back. *Be bold,* she told herself. She stepped forward, ducked through the flap, and went inside.

Two spears stood just inside the door. A small fire was glowing in a pit lined with round white stones. Kindling had been stacked beside it, and freshly roasted meat was set out on a sheet of birch bark. There was a bed of bison skin stretched across a wooden frame, and when she looked down, she found that he had brought rushes from the lakeside and had spread them over the floor.

Kormor's northern tribe would never have built tents like this. Wood was too precious in those icebound lands. Tent building was a skill he had learned from the Lake People, and he had learned it well. "It's nicely done," she said as he entered the tent behind her.

"It had to be fit for a Chieftain's daughter," he said.

"Yes," she said, "and it is." She suddenly felt foolish, staring at the tent skin and the poles, trying to avoid meeting his eyes. This was not the way it should be. He was her mate now. He was the one she would trust and depend on, more than anyone else in the world.

She looked up at him and smiled. "Thank you, Kormor," she said.

He didn't smile back. His eyes were wide as he stared down at her, and his lips were tightly pressed together. She saw his nostrils flare as he breathed deeply. His wedding robe had fallen open, exposing his muscled chest and his deerskin breeches. He reached out and took hold of her shoulders.

She jumped at the physical contact, then smiled with embarrassment. "You seem so fierce," she whispered.

He ran his palms down from her shoulders, slid his fingers under her arms, and dragged her forward till he could link his hands together behind her back. "I have you now." He spoke slowly, as if in a reverie.

"We have each other," she corrected him.

He held her against him, and she felt the hardness of

his body against hers. He bent his head and kissed her. Sometimes, during their courtship rituals, she had allowed him to do that. But his kisses then had been very different—fleeting, tantalizing, sometimes playful. He was pressing his mouth more insistently now. He pressed harder, till it actually hurt. Instinctively she tried to pull back—but he raised one of his hands behind her head, so that she couldn't turn her face away.

His strength was exciting, yet Mara was beginning to feel smothered by him. She felt his other hand reaching down, fumbling with the ties at the side of her robe. Then, with a shock, she felt his palm hot against the skin of her waist. He was reaching up, across her belly. He was grabbing hold of her breast.

She made smothered protests and started to struggle. This was too fast for her. She hadn't even had a chance yet to take account of the fact that she was paired with him. She needed to sit with him, and she needed him to be gentle—

His fingers clenched tight. Too tight.

She gave a muffled cry of shock and pain. She pulled her arms up against his chest and tried to force him away from her. He resisted, and he was much stronger than she was, but she struggled harder, and finally she managed to wrench herself free.

She stood there, gasping for breath, feeling confused and shaken. "Kormor! You hurt me!"

He just stared at her. "I want you," he said.

She laughed uneasily, trying to make light of it. "I want you, too. But you know the ways of my people. Women and men must be equal. Come here to the bed; let's sit together."

He reached for her.

"Wait!" she told him. She took a quick step back.

He shook his head. His shoulders were bunched, and he was flexing his fingers impatiently. She could see a vein pulsing quickly at the side of his neck. "I had to wait for months. Almost a year. There's no more waiting now." He reached out and started tearing at the ties at the side of her clothing.

"Kormor!" she cried. "Show some respect! This is my wedding robe!"

He made an impatient gesture. "Then you take it off."

The look in his eyes actually unnerved her. Clumsily, she undid the thongs. As she let the robe fall away from her body, he stared fixedly at her. She raised one arm across her breasts and dropped her other hand over her crotch. "You now," she said, still trying to sound a little playful. "Your turn to undress."

He stepped forward, seized her wrist, and pulled her hand away from her breasts.

"Stop!" she shouted at him. "Don't be so rough!"

He gave a grunt of annoyance and threw her onto the bed of bison hide.

She landed facedown, and started to push herself up. But he fell on her from behind, pinning her. She felt his weight squeezing the breath out of her. "No, Kormor!" she shouted. She tried to reach behind, to grab hold of him, but she was helpless. He seized the back of her neck and held her that way while he forced his knees between her thighs. His breath was coming in little gasps. She could feel him trembling.

Mara screamed with anger and distress. She thought of all the daydreams she'd had about this first night in the Coupling Tent, when they would discover each other's secret pleasures, savor each other, and indulge all the desires that had been pent up for so long. This was a travesty of what she'd imagined. She felt tears coming to her eyes.

She screamed again, even though she knew there was no point in it, because they were totally alone out here on the hillside. She squirmed, trying to throw him off, but she was tiny compared to him. Her face was forced into the bison skin. Its pungent odor filled her nostrils. She felt him groping between her legs and then suddenly, incredibly, he was pushing himself into her.

It hurt far more than she'd ever expected. It was a pain where no pain had ever been before. "Stop it!" she cried. "Kormor, it hurts!"

His hips lunged once, twice, and a third time. Then he gave a great shout. He fell onto her, squashing her. A shudder went through him, and then slowly his grip on her relaxed.

Mara felt a moment of disbelief. The whole thing had ended as quickly as it had begun. Could it be over?

Then she felt a wave of fury. "Get off!" she screamed. His head was close behind hers; she could feel his breath against the side of her neck. Quickly, she reached up. She grabbed his long hair and pulled on it with all her strength, twisting her wrists as she did so.

He yelled and reared back.

Instantly, she rolled off the bed. She fell down onto the floor and scrambled around the fireplace on her hands and knees. Then she sprang up onto her feet and grabbed one of the spears by the tent flap. She crouched down, gasping for breath, her heart fluttering in her chest. "Don't come near me!" she shouted at him.

He sat up on the bed, staring at her, looking too surprised to speak.

She swallowed hard, trying to calm herself. Her hands were shaking. There was a warm wetness between her legs. She was bleeding from where he had forced himself into her. The thought of it roused her anger all over again. "How dare you! How dare you treat me that way!"

He still stared at her in disbelief. "What are you talking about?"

Well, at least he no longer seemed a threat to her. She raised the spear and thrust it down into the ground with all her strength. The shaft stood there, vibrating. She pointed to the blood trickling down the inside of her thigh. "You hurt me! Can't you understand that?"

He looked down, then up at her face. "You're supposed to bleed," he said. "It proves no man has had you before."

He was like a stranger, here in the tent with her. She felt dizzy. She sat down hard on the ground, and she held her head between her hands, trying to think clearly. "I know a woman may bleed the first time," she said. Maybe if she could explain herself calmly and clearly, then he would understand. "I know it may hurt the first time," she went on. "But Kormor, you treated me cruelly." She looked up at him. "You think this is how people make love together? You just grab a woman and throw her down and force yourself into her?"

He folded his arms across his bare, broad chest and tossed his long hair back behind his shoulders. "I did what any man would do," he said. "And most women would want it that way."

This was so terribly wrong, she didn't know how she could even begin to make sense of it all. Her tribe had been founded by a woman, and it had always been governed by women. They deeply believed in kindness and equality among all people, men and women alike, before and after they were paired. "Kormor," she said, trying hard to be patient, "this isn't the way you approached me before we were paired. Why are you treating me this way now? Don't you even remember all the times we laughed together, and flirted with each other, and played together?"

He paused. Was he thinking about what she said? He seemed to be. And yet, at the same time she saw the pride in his face. What was it that Lizel had said? Suddenly the words came back to Mara: *He's a proud young man, and in some ways, that can be troublesome. He may be more . . . difficult, when the waiting is finally over.*

Mara felt apprehension growing inside her. She tried to force the feeling away. Kormor cared for her; she knew that. He must be able to understand and respect her needs.

He leaned forward, resting his elbows on his knees. He looked at her steadily. "A spirited woman enjoys a man's passion," he told her. "They say only a cold woman wants a man to take his time."

"But who says that, Kormor?" she asked him. "The boys you hunt with? If your friends tell you that women like to be treated like animals, that just means they know nothing about women, and nothing about the ways of our tribe."

He grunted, and she saw his anger stirring. "In the North Lands—"

"You are not in the North Lands now!" Her voice was shrill.

"Don't scold me, Mara." He stood up. "It's not your place to do that."

She scrambled up onto her feet to face him. "Then what am I supposed to do when you hurt me?"

He shook his head dismissively. "I didn't hurt you. You're just not used to it, that's all. Maybe if we do it again—"

"No!" Her voice was a scream. She seized the spear that she'd stabbed into the soft soil, and then pulled it free. "Wait in here," she said. "Don't follow me outside. Do you understand?"

He just stared at her.

She turned and ducked out of the tent, into the night.

Chapter 4

She climbed a little farther up the rocky hillside and sat naked in the cold air, resting the spear across her knees. She reached behind her and started angrily pulling the flowers and feathers out of her braided hair, flinging them down into the grass. She unraveled the braids and shook her hair free, scattering the rest of the ornaments around her. Then she pressed her hands over her face as tears started to flow.

She sat there for a long time, weeping and shivering. She wished she could go back to the village; but that was unthinkable. People would see that she had abandoned her pairing on the very first night. First they would be shocked, then they would be outraged, and then they would shun her. She would become an outcast in her own tribe. So her choice was clear: Her pairing must be made to work. There was no other way.

Perhaps, she thought, she had made a mistake trying to reason with him. Maybe the only way to deal with him was to stand up to him. After all, it was just as important to him that their pairing should endure. If she refused to be intimidated by him, then sooner or later he would simply have to compromise.

But what a terrible disappointment this was, to be battling her loved one on the first night of their pairing. She walked slowly down the rocky hillside, picking her way from one clump of grass to the next in the clear light of the Moon.

She entered the tent and set the spear to one side.

The fire had burned low and was barely flickering. In the dim red light she saw him lying on his side on the bed, almost hidden in shadow. He was completely naked, and she couldn't stop herself from pausing a moment and studying his body. She remembered all the times she had been tempted to touch his private places when she had been flirting with him. Even now, despite what had happened, she felt an instinctive urge to do so.

Then she saw his eyes gleaming faintly in the gloom, and she realized he was awake and looking at her. She felt suddenly embarrassed. She crouched down by the fire and fed some of the kindling into it, till flames started dancing. She pulled her bridal robe around her shoulders and held out her hands to embrace the warmth.

Still he lay there, watching her, saying nothing. Evidently it was up to her to decide what to say. "You and I have a lifetime to share," she said. "There is no way around that."

He didn't answer.

"We must find ways to get along with each other," she went on. "Otherwise we won't be happy together. You do want to live happily with me, don't you, Kormor?"

"Of course," he said.

"Very well, then." She stood up. She gathered her courage, walked to the bed, and sat on the corner of it as far from him as she could. "Let me explain now the way you should treat me when we couple together."

He made an angry sound at the back of his throat. "You think because you're the Chieftain's daughter, you can order me around?"

"No, Kormor! I think that you are a man, and I am a woman, and we are paired with each other." She paused for a moment, and an idea came to her that was so bold, it scared her. "We should try to please each other," she went on. "And perhaps—if you don't know how—I can show you."

She saw him clench his fist. He smacked the side of it, then, against the bison hide.

"Think about what I'm saying," she insisted, forcing herself not to be intimidated by the power of him. "I don't just mean that you should learn to please me. I think I can learn to please you."

He gave her a suspicious look. "What do you mean by that?"

Now, at least, she had roused his curiosity. She combed her fingers through her hair, making him wait for a moment. "I've talked to my Aunt Tamra about the ways of men and women," she said quietly. It was strange to be speaking so openly about things that were so private, but she saw no alternative. "She told me several things a woman can do to give pleasure to a man."

"Your aunt." He grunted. "What does she know about men?"

"Tamra has a husband. Peigor, remember? The two of them have been paired for a score of years, maybe more. I think she may have learned something in all that time."

Kormor had no answer to that. He said nothing, but she could sense his sullenness.

"So I'll show you what Tamra told me," she said, sounding far bolder than she felt.

He was silent for another long moment. She tried to imagine what was going on in his mind. Suspicion, curiosity, caution.

"Describe what you mean," he said.

She shook her head. "No, I have to show you. Unless you're afraid of what I might do."

He let out a scornful laugh. "Of course not."

She knew that much about him: that he would never back down from a challenge. "All right, then," she said. She moved farther up the bed so she was sitting on a level with his hips. She had to pause for a moment, to look inside herself again for her courage. Then, boldly, she reached out and placed her hand on his chest. She ran her fingers gently across his skin. And despite feeling angry with him and hurt by him, she liked the contact. She didn't want to be fighting with him like this. She needed him.

She closed her eyes for a moment, gently learning the contours of his chest and his belly.

She felt him shift on the bed, and she opened her eyes just in time to see him reaching for her. Quickly, she took hold of his wrist with her free hand. "No," she said. She remembered the pain she'd felt when he had grabbed her breast. Part of her still hated him for the way he had treated her, but that was something she would have to deal with later. "I don't want you to touch me now," she said, making her voice a little more gentle. "This is my time to touch you."

Reluctantly, he dropped his arm back onto the bed.

She moved lower. Mustering all her courage, she took him in her hands. She had seen men's genitals, but to do this gave her a dizzy feeling. She marveled at the change in him as he became hard under her touch.

He squirmed on the bed. "Mara—"

"Does that feel good?"

"This isn't what a woman should do."

"You mean it doesn't give you pleasure?"

He was silent.

She kept on caressing him. "It does please you, doesn't it?"

"Yes." His voice was tight. He was breathing quickly.

"Well, then. It pleases me, too. So there can be nothing wrong with it." She started touching him faster and more purposefully. He reached to stop her, then seemed to lose his willpower. He rolled onto his back, groaned, pushed his hips up—and suddenly he reached his climax.

When it was over, she smelled the essence of him on her hand. A sweet, strange smell. She was trembling—with shock at her own boldness, and relief that it had worked. Silently, she thanked her aunt for her wisdom.

Kormor rolled over, turning his back to her. He was breathing heavily.

"Was it nice?" she asked him.

He grunted noncommittally. "How did you know how to do that?"

"I told you. It was described to me."

He gave her a quick, suspicious look. "You haven't practiced it with other men?"

She felt hurt. "How can you say such a thing?"

He sat up, still looking at her suspiciously. "It just seems strange that you know how to do that." He fell silent, and he remained silent for a very long time, sitting there on the bed with her in the little tent. "I think you should wait for me to tell you," he said finally, "if I ever want you to do that for me again."

She looked at him, trying to understand. Was he too

proud to face the fact that it was within her power to please him? "If I must wait for you to ask me to please you," she said, "then I suppose you should wait till I ask you to couple with me again."

He swung his legs over the side of the bed and stood up, clenching his fists. "Mara—"

She faced him. "We should be equal, Kormor, you and I. That's the way of my tribe. You learned that long ago."

He made an angry sound, grabbed his breeches, and pulled them on. It was his turn to seize hold of a spear and leave the tent.

Watching him go, Mara remembered all the times they had spent together during their courtship, practicing with their spears, sharing the game they had killed, or just sitting quietly and watching the land around them as shadows from the distant mountains spread across the valley. He had been kind and generous to her then. She couldn't let herself think that there would be no more moments like that.

And then, suddenly, she understood. As long as she had been out of his reach, he hadn't dared to do anything that might displease her. He had kept his fierceness and his desire for her in check. That had excited her, to see how dangerous he was, and to know that in a certain sense she had the upper hand. She'd never stopped to think that the balance could shift after they were paired, and her control over him would be gone.

He was gone for a long time, and she managed to sleep a little, despite her unhappiness.

Much later, she felt him on the bed behind her. "Mara," he called to her softly. He shook her shoulder.

She turned over, half afraid that he might try to force himself on her again. She looked at him warily. "What is it?" she asked.

"I've thought a long time," he said. He sounded calm, now—more like the Kormor she knew and trusted. "You're right that we must find a way for our pairing to endure. I understand that."

She wasn't sure whether she should let herself feel hopeful. "I'm glad," she said tentatively.

"I also understand that things are different here, compared with the North Lands." He paused. "But still, a woman should show a man respect."

She was still muzzy-headed from sleep. She tried to concentrate. Was there a trap in what he had just said?

"So," he said, "this is what I've decided. When we are seen together, you should be respectful of me. You mustn't defy me. Otherwise, I won't be respected by other men."

She tried to consider what this might actually mean— but already he had started talking again.

"When we are alone together," he went on, dropping his voice, "that will be different. When we're alone, I've decided, I'll listen to what you have to say. And if there's something worthwhile that you can teach me, in that case, I'll learn it from you."

She realized that the words were hard for him to speak. She told herself to encourage him, even though it seemed so obvious to her that any man or woman should be willing to learn from another person. "Thank you, Kormor," she said. "I'm glad."

"But you'll never speak of this to anyone." His voice was sharp now. "You must promise. You will never tell anyone; do you agree?"

Suddenly she felt too weary to argue with him anymore. "All right," she said, "I'll do as you suggest."

"You will?" He sounded cautious.

"Yes." And then her spirit reasserted itself. "But just for one year. After that, we'll talk again."

Finally he nodded. "Good enough," he said.

There was a long silence between them. Wood hissed in the fire. The night wind ruffled the panels of the tent.

"I don't want to fight with you," he said.

"I don't want to fight with you, either," she said.

He grunted. "Well, that's as it should be. A woman shouldn't fight with her mate." He stretched out on his back. "We should sleep."

She waited to see if he would touch her, or kiss her, or say something kind. But no; he just folded his arms across his chest, and he closed his eyes. In his mind, apparently, everything had been resolved.

Chapter 5

Mara looked down at her hands. They were streaked with red clay, white chalk, and black charcoal. She rinsed them in the quick, cold stream that flowed in front of her, then bathed her face again, and again, till no more color came away and the designs which Lizel had created with such care had been erased forever.

Mara combed her fingers through her hair, feeling a moment of regret that she had unraveled her braids during the night. Some women wore their bridal braids for a week or more.

She stood up and picked her way across the hillside, back to the tent. Kormor was standing near the tent with his back to her, looking out over the valley, although there was not much for him to see. Heavy clouds had blown in from the south and were trapped now between the hills that bordered the wide, shallow valley, as tended to happen in the late spring season. The valley floor was mottled with pale mist. It was thickest in the far distance, where it lay like a great white pool that covered the lake and hid the village completely.

"Did you quench the fire?" she asked him.

He gave a curt nod.

"Then we should go. My family will be expecting us."

Kormor started down the hillside without a word. She watched him walking away from her, then gave a little grunt of irritation as she followed. She had honored his wishes last night; so why did he have to be so grim and silent this morning? Had it really wounded his male pride so much?

She followed him for a while, tracing a zigzag path into the valley. And then, abruptly, he stopped. His eyes

were alert, and she saw him sniffing the air. For a moment she put her feelings aside. She had long since
learned that his hunting instincts were sharper than hers.
"What is it?" she whispered.

"Bear." He pointed far ahead. Divots of grass had
been strewn around as the beast had dug up a rabbit
hole with its powerful claws.

She drew a slow, deep breath, keeping her lips slightly
parted so that she could taste as well as smell the air. "I
don't catch his scent," she whispered.

He shook his head. "Nor do I." He walked forward,
squatted down, and touched the earth that had been
turned over. "The soil isn't fresh," he said. "Maybe he
was here yesterday." He stood up. "All the same, we
should be careful."

Mara was silent, remembering her vision of the bear
drenched in blood. She shivered. The morning seemed
colder than before.

She continued walking, and she found herself gradually
increasing her pace. It suddenly seemed very important
for her to see the village again, with all the people in it
alive and well. Finally she couldn't contain her anxiety
any longer, and she broke into a run. Her wedding robe
dragged through the tall, wet grass, so she gathered it up
around her hips, clutching the deerskin in one hand while
she held her spear in the other.

Soon the first tendrils of the mist were settling dank
and cold on her skin. Then, as she ran deeper into it,
the mist became a thick fog. She found her view of the
world reduced to a circle of grassland that moved as she
moved. Beyond it and above her, everything was blank,
uniform gray.

She heard Kormor's footsteps receding as he lost sight
of her. "Mara!" he shouted.

She ignored him. The air was moist and cold in her
lungs as she forced herself to run faster. Finally she came
to a path, and she recognized it as the one that ran south
from the village. She started along it, leaping across pud-
dles, still holding her robe up around her hips, though
her hand was cramping and her arm was aching with the
effort. Faint shapes loomed up ahead of her, and she

realized that she was among the outlying huts. Here they were, the same as always, and suddenly she realized that her fears had been groundless. The village was no different from before.

She let go of her robe and leaned on her spear, breathing hard from her long, fast run. Kormor came running up, and he almost fell over her in the fog. "Mara! Why did you run away like that?"

She looked up at him and couldn't think what to say. How could she tell him that she had feared the whole village would be burned to the ground?

"That was dangerous." He gestured behind them. "The bear could have been out on the grassland. In the fog, you would never have known."

She swallowed hard and managed to catch her breath. "I had my spear," she said.

He looked at her irritably. "No hunter fights a full-grown bear on his own, if he has a choice." He shook his head. "I could have lost you, Mara." Abruptly he fell silent.

He had been concerned for her safety, she realized. He had been afraid that she could be taken from him, just as his tribe and his family had been.

Impulsively, she touched his arm. "I'm sorry," she said. "You're right. I acted recklessly."

He looked doubtful. Then, as he saw that she was sincere, he reached out and touched her shoulder. Stiffly, he smiled at her.

She moved closer to him. But footsteps sounded on the path ahead. A man emerged from the fog, walking toward them with a fishing spear slung across his shoulder. It was Wabin, one of the oldest men of the tribe, a thin, hunched figure in a hooded robe, with wisps of white hair showing around his wrinkled face. He had been a fine hunter in his day. He wasn't strong enough to run out across the grasslands now, but he still enjoyed fishing. "Greetings," he said. And then, recognizing Mara, he bowed. "Good fortune to you, Mara! May your pairing be long and happy!"

"Thank you," she said, feeling embarrassed. "Good fishing to you, Wabin."

He laughed as he walked on by. "There'll be no fish to see on a day like this. But sometimes, you know, the sun breaks through soonest over the water." He walked on, then, and disappeared into the grayness.

"Mara." Kormor touched her sleeve. "Let's look at our new home."

She hesitated. "My mother will be angry that we're late."

He made a dismissive gesture. "This will only take a moment."

It was always easy for him to convince her to do something with him, instead of with her family. She smiled. "All right."

They left the path and cut through between the dwellings. This outer region of the village was where the newcomers lived—immigrants from the North Lands who still preferred to build homes in the styles of their former tribes. Some dwellings were nothing more than pits covered over with mammoth hide. Others were little houses of sun-baked clay. Still others were built from reeds thatched across branches.

On a morning like this, few people were venturing away from the comfort of their hearths. Mara smelled wood smoke from cooking fires, and fresh meat roasting.

Then she heard water lapping, and she found herself at the lakeshore. When she had been younger, she had often come here in search of solitude. At times when her sister had teased and mocked her, or her mother had scolded her, she would sit here on the grass and stare out over the lake, wishing she could somehow leave the world she knew, and live under the water where she could be queen of the water kingdom, with the turtles and the fish serving as her people.

After she met Kormor, they started coming out here together. It had seemed a fine idea to build their own little home on the shore, even though it was traditional in her tribe for the man to be brought into the woman's Clan House and become part of the extended family.

Kormor had set up a permanent tent for the two of them just a few days ago, in the style used by his people. And here it was, in front of her. Two rows of mammoth ribs were planted in the ground, meeting at the top to form a natural arch. Fresh-cured hide from mammoths and mastodons had been stitched together and stretched across the ribs, and Kormor had etched designs into the thick leather—of hunters carrying spears, deer and elk and sheep among the mountains, and Mother Moon shining down, bestowing good fortune on her people. A small figure stood near a shape that was meant to be the lake, and Kormor had told Mara that the figure was her, waiting for him to return from a hunt.

Staring at it, she felt tugged by waves of conflicting emotion. She had been so excited, watching him working with his young friends, taking such care to anchor the ribs firmly and grease the seams to make them watertight. She had imagined herself cooking game that they hunted together, and curing hides, and sleeping curled up beside him, listening to the water lapping at the shore. But now that she was standing here beside him, she felt anxious. He had promised to learn how to please her, but could he keep his word? Would he lose patience and be cruel to her again?

"It's a beautiful tent, Kormor," she said, turning away. "But now, you know, we really must go. My family will be waiting."

There was a great shout of welcome as she entered the Clan House with Kormor by her side. Everyone clustered around, hugging her, grabbing her hands, pulling her to the center where a big fire was burning and fresh meat and dried fruits and pine nuts had been set out.

Suddenly she found herself face-to-face with her mother. Ternees's face was stern, and her eyes narrowed as she noticed Mara's unbraided hair. But she ritually took Mara's head between her hands and kissed her on the forehead. "Welcome, Mara," she said. "And welcome, Kormor." She inclined her head to him. "We were beginning to wonder when you would get here."

"Mara's been busy," one of Mara's uncles shouted out.

"That's right," another man said. "Kormor made sure of that."

There were waves of laughter. Mara felt her cheeks

turning red. She'd often seen this kind of teasing on the day after a pairing, but there had been so much on her mind, she hadn't thought twice about the welcome she'd receive in her Clan House. As the laughter echoed around her, she felt nonplussed. How could she possibly respond?

"With a big fellow like Kormor, it's a wonder she got here at all," someone else shouted out.

Mara glanced at Kormor—and saw, with dismay, that he was grinning broadly.

In sudden confusion, she strode quickly to the food that had been set out. She stared down at it, hoping that her hair would hide her flushed cheeks. How could he smile like that, as if he was proud about what had happened between them? How could he take pleasure in something that had been so crude and painful for her?

"She's shy!" someone said, and there was still more laughter, though not as loud as before.

"I'm just hungry," she said, a little more loudly than she'd intended. She seized a piece of roasted bison and started gnawing it, though in truth her stomach was churning, and all she really wanted was to turn and run out of the house.

The men were gathering around Kormor, congratulating him. The women began gathering around Mara.

"Sister." It was Shani's voice, from close behind. "You didn't greet me."

Mara turned quickly. "I'm sorry," she said.

Shani embraced her for a moment, then stepped back, holding Mara by her shoulders. "I'm so happy for you." She reached into a fold of her robe and handed Mara a small object—the shape of a fish carved out of a fragment of pine wood. "I made this for you. I know how much you love the lake, so ..." She shrugged. "I thought this would remind you of it."

Mara stared at the crude little carving. "Thank you," she said, though it was hard for her to utter the words. She wasn't sure exactly what she'd expected from her sister, but she'd seen other brides receiving beautiful necklaces that had taken weeks or months to make. Certainly her wedding clothes had been made with that kind of care by her aunts and the other elder women of the tribe. Mara had never seen anyone insulted with an ugly little token like this, and she couldn't imagine why Shani had done such a thing.

"You're really going to move out of our house?" Shani was saying. "You haven't changed your mind?"

Mara nodded blankly.

Shani patted her cheek. "Well, we'll miss you. But you'll come and visit, won't you?"

"Of course," Mara said.

Other women were pressing forward, impatient to greet her. Everyone had a gift, but Mara soon realized that all the gifts were small and simple. Gradually, she began to understand. Ternees had disapproved of this pairing. Ternees had made it clear that no one should honor it extravagantly. And of course, everyone had obeyed.

After the gift-giving, the clan gathered around the fire for singing and storytelling. Mara sat beside Kormor, but she was hardly aware of him—hardly aware of anything in the big house. The voices and the laughter around her were familiar, reminding her of all the other family rituals she had known, but there was no comfort in the sense of community, now that she knew how they felt about her.

After a while, she excused herself and went to her sleeping area. Beds were ranged all around the edge of the circular house, with panels of hide hanging between them to provide a little privacy. In a bleak frame of mind, she started packing up her clothes and possessions. There was a winter coat of sheepskin, the hood lined with wolverine. Moccasins of buckskin. Winter boots of bison hide. Necklaces of wooden beads and wolf teeth. She wrapped them all in a big deerskin, then paused, looking across at everyone still sitting in the center of the house. Kormor had started telling a hunting story, while three of the younger children ran around, chasing each other, playing tag, and Ternees sat in her usual place on a chair made from pine branches, presiding over the gathering. This, here, was Mara's home. And yet, she had never felt less at home in it.

She was distracted by a movement near the door. Someone was entering the house. It was Trifen, she realized, Lizel's mute helper.

Mara went quickly over to him. "This is a family time, Trifen," she whispered.

The boy looked up at her with his large, dark eyes, and he nodded to show that he understood. But he didn't leave.

"What is it?" Mara said.

He tugged at her sleeve and gestured toward the door.

Mara hesitated. She glanced at the group by the fire. Several people were looking across at her questioningly. "He wants to show me something," she said. She turned then and followed him outside.

The fog had gone, chased away by the midday sun. Mara blinked in the sudden brightness. She shaded her eyes. There was a small crowd of people coming into the Meeting Place, with a big man leading the way, dragging something behind him.

Mara moved forward. The big man was a stranger; she'd never seen him before. And then she saw what he was dragging, and a chill went through her. It was the body of a bear, lashed to a framework of tree limbs. The bear's head was tilted back, with its eyes staring and its jaws gaping wide. Its arms were spread out, tied with thongs. Its black fur was matted with blood from a dozen wounds in its chest and belly.

There was shouting and commotion now as more people came out of the Clan Houses and stared in awe at the spectacle in front of them. The tall stranger was almost as big as the bear himself. There was a short woman with him, and a thin, sickly-looking young man. Together they lifted the travois till it stood on end and leaned back against one of the Clan Houses at the side of the Meeting Place.

Mara found the beast facing her. She hardly heard the voices of the villagers as they gathered around. She stared at the bear, and the air seemed to freeze around her. With the animal's forepaws raised high, lashed to the wooden frame, there was no longer any possible doubt. This was the vision she had had in the Spirit House.

Chapter 6

The strangers stood on either side of their prize, and the villagers talked excitedly, touching the bear, sniffing it, tasting its blood. Then Ternees came out among them, and they quickly moved aside, deferring to her.

"Welcome," Ternees said, spreading her arms as she faced the strangers. She repeated the word in several of the northern dialects. "I am Chieftain of this village. We are the Lake People. We bid you welcome."

The leader of the group stepped forward. He was truly the biggest man that Mara had ever seen, not only tall but wide, with a barrel chest, a fat belly, and arms as thick as a normal man's thighs. He wore a hat and cape made from a dozen assorted furs stitched together, like a history of all the assorted animals he had hunted. His face was fat and ugly, marred with scars. He had thick, broken lips, and several of his teeth were missing. His eyes were small, almost lost above his plump cheeks. His hair was stringy, matted with dirt, and gathered back in a thong so that it hung between his shoulder blades. His size and his ugliness were equally fearsome.

"You're the Chieftain, eh?" He looked at Ternees. The doubt was audible in his voice.

Ternees inclined her head. "No doubt you're from the North Lands. There the Chieftain of a tribe is always a man. Here, our customs are different."

There was a flicker of interest in the man's eyes. Then his face widened in an ugly grin. "So, we're honored to be here in such a fine tribe as this." He glanced at the big Clan Houses and the many people crowding around him. "My name is Graum," he shouted out, so that everyone could hear. "This is my wife, Dira." He gestured to the short, fat woman who stood close beside him. Her looks were little better than his. Her frizzy black hair was matted and tangled, her nose was wide and flat, and her mouth was so wide, it seemed to split her face in half.

"And this is my son, Joh," Graum went on, gesturing to the thin, unhealthy-looking young man. He looked about Mara's age. He was thin-shouldered and hollow-chested, dressed in ragged skins that hung loosely on his bony frame.

Graum raised his spear and dug the tip of it into the neck of the bear, turning its head. "And this," he said, "is our gift. For your fine village." He grinned again, and his fat lips pulled back from his damaged teeth.

"A fine gift indeed." Ternees stepped forward and made a polite show of examining the trophy. Then she turned back to Graum. "So, you are in need of a place to stay."

"Well, yes, that's so." Graum spread his hands. "My boy and my wife, they work hard. And when it comes to hunting . . ." he glanced at the bear, "I can do my share."

There was a murmur of approval from the crowd. Ternees clapped her hands. "Good. All travelers are welcome here. We have skins and poles, if you need to set up a tent. We're peaceful, generous people, Graum, and everything that we have, we share." Ternees turned and gestured to Mara. "My daughter will show you where you can make your home, and she can tell you some of the ways of our tribe. She has no trouble speaking the northern dialects."

Mara found herself looking directly into her mother's face. She still felt unnerved by the figure of the bear before her, and it took her a moment to respond. "Mother . . ." she began.

People were turning and looking at her. On the day after her pairing, she should be honored, not given chores. Mara moved forward stiffly, barely able to believe that this was happening. "This is not right," she said in a tense, low voice, when she was less than an arm's length away. "You are shaming me, Mother."

Ternees made a little impatient sound. She took

Mara's arm and squeezed it sharply enough to hurt. "Graum, this is my daughter Mara."

The big man stared down at her. "Mara, eh?" His gaze lingered a moment longer than was polite, and she had the uneasy sense that he was studying the shape of her body under her robe. But then he turned back to Ternees, and he was grinning again, humble and polite. "I'll take my son and set up a tent," he said, "while my wife stays here to help skin this." He gestured toward the bear with his thumb. "If that's all right with you," he added.

"Certainly," said Ternees.

People started pressing forward. Everyone wanted to touch the bear for good luck, before it was butchered. Mara turned to Graum, thinking that if she had to do this chore, she should get it done as soon as possible. "This way," she told him coldly as she pushed through the crowd.

A knot of villagers trailed after her as she led Graum and his son between the Clan Houses. Men and women alike were staring at Graum with frank curiosity.

"I have a question," said Tiear. He was a calm, thoughtful man who had arrived among the Lake People only two years previously. He was well liked, though some said he was too strict with his children. "If you don't mind me asking," he went on, "which tribe in the North Lands are you from?"

"Whitefoot People," said Graum, glancing at him briefly.

Tiear frowned. "I've never heard of that tribe."

"We made our home on the far north shore," said Graum. "Till we were forced to move south. Nothing to eat in the North Lands now."

Mara glanced at his bulk. "It seems as if you haven't gone hungry."

He grinned as if amused by what she'd said. But now that she was able to see his face more closely, she realized his grin wasn't as friendly as it seemed. When he bared his teeth, he looked more like an animal than a man—an animal that had been challenged and was ready to fight.

"I'm a fine hunter," he said. "Even when game is scarce, my family never goes hungry."

"I've seen many people come over the mountains," someone else said. It was Yacor, the elder chief of the hunters. "They're always hungry. There's no game up on the ice, least of all in the winter months."

Graum turned, and his grin grew wider. "We stopped for a few weeks on the plains after we came down from the ice," he said. "That's where we got our strength back." He stared steadily at Yacor, waiting for him to reply.

Yacor shook his head. "Even so, I'm surprised you and your family survived such a journey." There was grudging respect in his voice.

"No one has ever come over the mountains in the winter months," one of the younger hunters said. And there was a murmuring of agreement.

Graum nodded to them, acknowledging their admiration. He turned back to Mara. "Tell me, are there other tribes near here?"

"To the south," she said. "The Silver River People. Each year, we meet them for a festival. They give us fine flints for our spears, and we give them dried fish that we gather from the lake."

"Flints as fine as this?" Graum turned his spear around and held the point where everyone could see it.

The men clustered around. The flint was not white, streaked with black, like the ones they knew. Instead, it was a pale, delicate pink. Yacor placed his own spear beside it and tested the point of each one with the side of his thumb. "As sharp as ours," he said reluctantly.

"But much harder," Graum said. "So hard, it cuts bone." He set the base of his spear down on the ground. "A flint knapper in the North Lands taught me the secret." He eyed the men who were gathered around him. "If there's any of you thinks he has the skill to learn it, maybe I'll share it with you."

Several of the young men shouted that they were willing to try. The older ones glanced at each other and said nothing.

Graum turned back to Mara. "These River People in the south . . . are they warlike?"

"No," said Mara. "Why should they be?"

Graum shrugged. "Human nature."

Mara shook her head decisively. "You're from the north, where people have to fight for their share of food and land. Here there's more than enough for everyone. No one needs to steal from his neighbor."

Graum frowned. "What about men who steal or fight just for its own sake? I've known a few of them."

Something about this big, ugly man was making her uneasy, but she wasn't sure whether her feelings were sensible or whether she was just unnerved by the trophy he had brought into the village. "There are no thieves in this tribe," Mara told him as decisively as she could. "And if a man fights with another man, he is shunned. No one speaks to him. He becomes a stranger among his own people—for days or even months."

Graum nodded seriously. "That's good," he said. "I'm glad to hear that." He glanced at everyone around him. "I'm honored to be here with people as decent as this."

"The honor is ours," said Tiear, "to have such a hunter in our village."

There was a murmur of agreement, and Graum smiled.

Mara took him to the huts where supplies were stored. Old Man Hopwa was there, as he always was, keeping track of the inventory and making sure that everything was properly in its place. With simple pride, he showed Graum the different kinds of woods that were kept here. There were long, straight poles of hardwood that had been cured and dried, ready to be turned into spears. Thicker pine branches had been chopped into sections as tall as a man, to support tents. Then there were stacked logs for firewood, piles of hides, and caches of food so that the tribe would never be cold or hungry.

The caches were deep pits lined with dry grass, tightly covered with flat rocks. Dried meat was in one, dried fish in the next. Others were filled with dried fruit—wild strawberries, blackberries, black currants, and plums. Some contained pine nuts.

"You eat this?" said Graum, holding a handful of the pine nuts.

"It comes from a tree," Hopwa told him. "The tree has a wooden cone, but inside, the nuts are good to eat." He grinned encouragingly. "Try them."

Graum threw the nuts back into the food cache. "Not enough game around here, eh?"

"We have plenty of game," said Yacor. "But we have many people. If everyone eats meat all the time, then the game will be hunted so much, it will be gone."

Graum grunted. "In the North Lands—"

"In the North Lands, everyone eats meat," Mara said, "because there isn't enough of anything else." So many times she had been through this conversation with travelers from the north. "The South Lands are different. Our customs are different."

Graum gave her a long, thoughtful look. Then, without answering her, he turned to his son. "Joh, set a tent there." He pointed to a patch of land beyond the most recent settlements. "See where I mean?"

The boy nodded. There was a slackness in his face, making him look half-witted. "I see," he said.

"I'll come and check on you in a while," said Graum. He clapped his hands and rubbed them slowly together. "Seems to me that bear of mine should be ready for roasting soon."

The men followed him as he turned back toward the Meeting Place. Mara watched them go. She hadn't had a chance to tell Graum how to dispose of his refuse in the huts they kept for that purpose, or how the chores were arranged, with men and women taking turns, some hunting game, others gathering from the land. Well, someone else could tell him.

She stood for a moment, watching Joh pulling out tent poles, while Old Man Hopwa fussed around him. "Do you need help?" she asked.

John turned and stared at her. "Help?"

She wondered what was the matter with him. "Can you do this on your own?" she said, speaking slowly.

"Yes," he said. He turned his back, then, and went on with his work.

Mara shrugged. She had made her offer. She owed him nothing more. She started back toward the center of the village now—but not to the Meeting Place. Her destination lay elsewhere.

All was quiet as Mara made her way into the Spirit House. In fact, it was so silent, she thought it must be empty. There was no sign anywhere of Trifen, but finally Mara saw Lizel in her wolfskin robe, hunched like a shadow beside the fitful light of a tiny fire.

"Lizel?" Mara called softly. "May I speak to you?"

The old lady said nothing. She sat motionless.

Mara hesitated, then moved forward, stepping as quietly as she could. When the house was still like this, she was afraid of making a sound. Were the spirits here? Was Lizel speaking with them?

She crouched down opposite Lizel and waited. Faintly, from outside the house, she heard shouts from the direction of the Meeting Place. A feast of bear meat was a rare treat indeed, and everyone would want to help slice it and roast it. Mara could imagine them all clustering around, and Graum amid them, giving directions. The kill, after all, had been his.

Mara sighed. This day felt so strange, so unexpected, after her pairing and the Ceremony of First Blood that had gone before it. She could still remember how she had felt, full of trepidation and excitement, as Trifen had held the wet slate and she had looked at the reflection of her face. Why, that had been just over there in the chair near the fire. And yet already the memory was fading, eclipsed by everything that had happened since.

"So, Mara," said Lizel.

The old woman's voice was pitched low, but even so, it made Mara jump.

"You have come," Lizel went on, "because of your vision of the bear. And the trophy in the Meeting Place."

"Yes," Mara whispered.

Lizel grunted. She closed her eyes and bowed her head so that her face was almost hidden by the hood of her robe. "Mara, a vision is a personal thing. No one can be sure what a vision means."

"But the beast in the Meeting Place is exactly the way I saw it," Mara said.

"I have no doubt of that." Lizel straightened up. She took hold of a dark polished stick which she used as a cane, and she clasped both her hands over it, pushing herself onto her feet. She grimaced, massaging her hips. "The spirits are silent, Mara. Today they tell me nothing." She looked down at Mara's upturned face, and her eyes narrowed. "But was your vision the only reason you're here? Is there something else, now?"

Mara turned her head quickly away. Was her unhappiness so obvious, anyone could see it?"

"You should tell me," said Lizel.

And suddenly Mara did want to tell her. She was afraid of Lizel, and she had never felt close to the old woman; yet since the ceremony, there was an intimacy which had never been there before. "Last night was not what I expected," Mara said in a low voice. "With Kormor. He was ... cruel. He hurt me."

Lizel sighed. "Young men like him, so full of their fierce pride. And so many of them in the tribe now." She went to a slab of wood where dried bullberries had been set out, with a little pemmican. She squatted down and started picking at them, chewing them with difficulty, since many of her teeth were gone. "The women perish in the journey over the mountains," she went on. "Or the men leave them in the North Lands because they think they're not strong enough to make the journey."

"Yes," Mara said.

"Still," Lizel went on, "women have their own strength. Our muscles may be weaker, but we can be strong-willed, Mara, and we can endure." She wiped her hands and turned away from the berries.

Mara suddenly felt impatient with the priestess. She scrambled up. "But why, Lizel? Why should it be such a struggle?" She gestured helplessly. "My sister, my mother, and now my mate—I thought all the fighting would end when I became paired."

"Mara, Mara." The old woman shook her head. "Men

have a fighting spirit, you know that. Women are most constant, more cautious. That's why women should plan before men may act. Women have to guide the men's strength."

Mara had heard these words before. This was one of the principles—maybe the most fundamental principle—on which her tribe was based.

Lizel waved her away. "This is a difficult time for you, but it will pass." She moved back to her place by the fire.

"Is that all?" Mara said. Somehow she had imagined that Lizel would have some secret to tell her, some answer to her problems.

"Well," said Lizel, picking up a small stick and tossing it into the fitful flames, "there is one thing."

Mara paused. "Yes?"

"You will be stronger, Mara, when you find the spirit that chose you. The bobcat, I mean. Tonight or tomorrow night, you must go to the forest. There, I think, you will find what you need."

Chapter 7

That evening there was dancing and laughter in the Meeting Place. It was a smaller party than had been held for Mara's pairing, but the Lake People were always eager for an excuse to celebrate, and some of them had never tasted fresh, pungent bear meat before.

Mara sat on her own through most of it, feeling thoughtful and withdrawn, while Kormor laughed and sparred with his young hunter friends, and the children played in the shadows around the Clan Houses, and the women sang songs, and the men joined in.

Graum took a place of honor, sitting with Ternees on the Speaking Stone. His wife, Dira, sat on the ground beside him. Mara noticing how attentive she was to Graum's needs, passing him food when he wanted to eat and water when he wanted to drink. Each time she looked up at him, her mouth curled in a happy smile, as if just being near him made her contented.

But when Joh helped himself to a portion of meat before Graum had sampled it, Dira's smile vanished. She spat an admonishment at the boy and cuffed him around his ear. The blow was powerful enough to rock him backward. He hunkered down, shrinking away from her, though he didn't seem surprised by the treatment.

As the night grew dark, some of the women left the Meeting Place to go to their homes and put their children to bed, and some of the men started telling hunting stories. Yacor was wearing his finest robe, made from the hide of a white lion. Graum asked about it, and Yacor told the story of how he had speared it when he led an expedition into the mountains that lay far to the east.

Graum nodded, studying Yacor intently, as if the man was just as interesting as the story he told.

Finally Ternees turned to Graum. "We have all been waiting," she said, "to hear your own story. How did you kill the prize that you brought here?" She gestured to the bearskin, stretched across a wooden rack where it had been scraped and now stood ready for curing.

Graum was silent for a long moment, looking around the fire, eyeing each person in turn. "There's more than one way to kill a big, ugly beast like that," he said. He spoke softly, so that his voice was almost lost in the crackling of the fire. Kormor had seated himself beside Mara, and she saw him leaning forward to catch the words. All the other young hunters were doing the same.

"A bear runs faster than a man," Graum went on. "And he's twice as strong. So you can't just spear him. Likely as not, he'll get angry, pull the spear out, chase you, and rip your head off."

"We know this," Yacor said. "All hunters know this."

Graum turned to him. For a moment he looked annoyed at being interrupted. But then, slowly, he grinned. "Of course you do," he said. "A fine hunter like you, Yacor—I don't need to tell you about the ways of bears. But still, you're wondering how I killed that one with just my wife and son to help me, eh?"

Yacor shifted uncomfortably. "I told you my story," he said. "It is your turn to tell yours."

"Well, maybe so." Graum shrugged. "But frankly, I'd rather not. Killing bears—that's a secret I'll keep for a while, if you don't mind. Takes a lot of cunning and courage, that's all I'll say for now. Maybe another time, when I know you all better, I'll say how it was done."

There was an uneasy silence. Yacor turned to Tiear, and the two of them exchanged a glance that Mara couldn't interpret.

"I think you should understand, Graum," said Ternees, "that in our tribe, it's our way to be open with each other. We have no secrets here."

Graum rubbed his jaw. "Well, all right, there's other things I'm willing to tell. Assuming you want to know of them."

"I'm sure we are all interested," said Ternees. There was something in her face now that hadn't been there before. She had pulled back from Graum, and her mouth was stern.

Graum looked around the circle of faces lit by the fire. "Maybe we can put together a hunting party tomorrow," he said. "It's always better to learn by doing than learn by telling."

One young man stood up—Ulmei, a boy who had not yet come of age but was always eager to prove himself. "I'll go," he said.

Immediately other young men were on their feet. Mara saw that Kormor was among them.

Graum held up his arms. "Wait, wait. There's too many of you." He glanced around at all the eager faces, and he chuckled. "So many men in this tribe ... seems we're going to have to pick and choose a little here." He rubbed his palms slowly together. "How about if we pick the ten who are strongest and bravest?"

The men looked at each other uneasily.

Ternees turned toward Graum. "This is not our way," she said. Her tone was cold. "We share equally here, Graum. Men and women alike. And we know that wisdom counts as much as bravery."

He blinked at her, and he frowned. "Well, now, no offense," he said. "I always respect another tribe's customs, 'specially if it's so big and it's been established so long."

Ternees gave him a stiff smile. "Thank you."

Graum held up one hand. "But," he said, "it stands to reason a hunting party can't be so big it scares away the game. And this will be my own little expedition, yes? So I have to pick and choose somehow. And since I'm a strong fellow, I'd like others who are strong and brave like me. That way they won't hold me back."

Yacor leaned forward. "What are you getting at, Graum? What is it that you want?"

"Well." He slapped his hands on his knees. "Where I come from, there's a little game we used to play. We take some hot stones from in the fire—just pebbles, no more than that. Pull them out from the flames with pairs of sticks, then each man picks up a stone in his left hand and holds it in his fist. And the ones who dare to hold on to it the longest are the ones who come along with me."

The youngest men were glancing at each other, obviously willing to try this game.

Ternees stood up. "Let this be known," she said, and her voice cut through the still night air. "We are free people. Any man may do as he pleases here. But I see no point in a challenge if it doesn't serve a man or his tribe. And I see no shame in turning away from it." She eyed her people briefly, then turned to Graum. "You are a brave hunter, and I thank you for the gift you brought us. Now I will bid you good night." She turned, then, and walked away from the fire, into her Clan House.

Several of the older men looked at each other. There was a long, uncomfortable pause. Finally Yacor stood up. Immediately the other elders joined him. They nodded politely to Graum, then walked away out of the firelight, back to their homes.

Mara nudged Kormor. "Shall we leave?" she whispered.

He shook his head. He said nothing.

A score of men and a couple of women still remained around the fire. Graum eyed them, and he grinned. "Seems some people don't like my little game," he said. "And it makes me wonder why. Maybe it's because they don't want to be tested." He eyed the young men who were still gathered around the fire, facing him. "Be embarrassing, wouldn't it, if one of the older hunters was beaten out by a young one?"

There was something sly in his tone. Mara felt angered by it. She looked around, wondering if anyone else would speak; but no one did. They seemed impressed by the big man and his great trophy standing in the shadows behind him. And he was trading on that.

Impulsively, before she really knew what she was doing, she stood up. "Graum," she said, "your game doesn't test the skills or the strength of a hunter. Holding a hot stone tells you nothing about the way someone holds or throws a spear. I think my mother was right. This challenge of yours means nothing."

People looked up at her in surprise. There was an uneasy silence.

"Well," said Graum, with his little eyes glinting in the firelight and his head tilted to one side as he examined her, "now, what would a young woman like you know about that?"

"I can cast a spear, like anyone in our tribe." She returned his gaze steadily, though she felt a tightening in her belly.

He gave her his grin, and his eyes became little slits. "You cast a spear, eh? But it takes a lot more to kill a beast like that." He gestured again at the bearskin stretched across the frame behind him. Then he leaned forward. "It takes courage."

Mara drew a breath to answer him, but Kormor took hold of her wrist and squeezed it hard. She glanced down at him and saw him giving her a stern look. He turned, then, to Graum. "Let's begin," he said.

"Good!" Graum clapped his hands. "Gather around, now. Each man get a pebble out from under the flames." He turned to his wife and son. "You two, walk around, see no one cheats." He chuckled.

Kormor moved forward, but now it was Mara's turn to seize his shoulder. "Please," she told him. "Don't do this."

He gave her a look of surprise. Then all the muscles in his face tightened. "I will do as I please," he said in a low voice.

"Kormor—"

He turned his back on her. He pushed forward, taking his place beside the fire.

Mara stared at him, feeling helpless. He had no reason to play this stupid game. Everyone already knew that he was one of the strongest, bravest men in the tribe, and a fine hunter.

The men were using sticks and twigs to flick stones out from the fire. One of the stones bounced onto a man's deerskin coat, and there was a sudden scorching smell. When he shook the stone off, a dark circle showed where the stone had been.

"All right," said Graum. "Now!"

As Mara watched, a score of hands reached out and took the pebbles. There were grunts of surprise and pain. Men's faces contorted. Their jaws clenched. Two men gasped and dropped their stones; then two more. They blew on their palms and shook them, laughing uneasily.

One by one now, the rest of the men quickly gave up and threw down their stones. Some cursed. Some grunted in pain.

Only Kormor was left with his fist still clenched. He was kneeling with his back straight, his face rigid, his eyes staring steadily at Graum.

Mara moved forward. "Kormor!"

He ignored her. Sweat was breaking out on his forehead. His arm was trembling. But still he held the stone.

She grabbed his wrist. "Kormor, let it go!" she shouted. "Please!"

He wrestled his wrist free from her, then lashed out with the side of his arm, knocking her away from him. She found herself thrown backward, sprawling in the dirt.

She lay there for a moment, feeling stunned. Calmly, silently, Kormor turned away from her, stretched out his arm, opened his hand, and dropped the stone back into the fire. He nodded to Graum, then rested his hand back by his side.

Mara glimpsed his palm. It was black where the skin had been charred by the heat.

She let out a little cry of anger as she got back up onto her feet. She looked at Graum, then at Kormor, then at all the young men gathered around. Her feeling of injustice was so strong, she couldn't speak. Then she noticed Dira watching her, giving her a strange smile. Mara had the creepy feeling that the woman was actually enjoying Mara's distress.

With tears starting in her eyes, Mara turned and ran from the fire, away among the Clan Houses, toward the lake.

Later, she lay alone in the new home Kormor had built. Finally she saw a brief flash of moonlight as Kormor pulled aside the door flap. She heard the rustle of his robes and she smelled the scent of him as he slid inside. Faintly, in the darkness, she saw him shucking off his clothes. Then the bed of bison hide creaked under her as he added his weight to it.

She waited, lying with her back turned to him. What would he say?

"We made an agreement last night, you and me." His voice sounded low and angry.

"Agreement?" This wasn't what she'd expected. She turned over, trying to see his face in the darkness.

"Yes," he said. "You agreed that in public, you would show respect."

It made her head ache, trying to understand him, trying to see things as he saw them. Had she really broken the pledge? Perhaps, in a way, it was true. She should be willing to admit that she might be at fault. "I'm sorry," she blurted out, "if you feel I didn't honor our agreement. I just didn't want you to hurt yourself, Kormor! I didn't want you to damage your body playing that ugly man's stupid game."

She sensed the tension in him as he lay beside her. He seemed so full of anger, it scared her. But when he spoke, his voice was still low and tightly controlled. "It was my decision," he told her. "It wasn't yours. You had no right to interfere."

"Well, I said I'm sorry." She got up on one elbow. There was only the faintest outline of his profile in the gloom. "And I truly am. But even so—how could it give you the right to hit me?" She shook her head violently. "It's always wrong for a man to strike a woman. It's a taboo."

There was a long silence. He didn't reply.

"Kormor!" She reached out and shook him.

Angrily, he knocked her hand away. "You shamed me earlier, too," he said. "In front of your family, when you turned away from me."

She paused, trying to understand this new accusation. "You mean when they were making those awful jokes? Kormor, I couldn't stand the look on your face! You looked as if you were *proud* of what—what you did to me last night."

Suddenly he leaned closer, and his breath was on her

face. "I was proud, yes." The tension was growing still greater in him. His voice had a scolding edge to it. "I was proud to be paired with the Chieftain's daughter, and proud to be the first to lie with her and take her for my own. But you can't let me have that pride. You want me to do whatever you tell me. You want to give orders, just like your mother."

Mara felt sudden outrage. "Don't you *ever* compare me with her!" she cried. "How can you say such a thing?"

"There's a lot you don't understand." His voice was low and grim. "I think perhaps I have to teach you."

She felt him groping for her. He touched her shoulder, then seized her arm. He gave a sudden twist, pulling her elbow out from under her. She thumped down onto the bed. He went on twisting, forcing her onto her stomach. "No!" she shouted. "I'll scream—"

Something was forced into her mouth. It was a piece of sheepskin which he used to clean his spear. It tasted of mud and dried animal blood. She tried to spit it out, but his hand was wrapped around her face.

She felt outrage so strong, it swept her up like a hot, fierce wind. How could he dare to do this? She struggled, but he was lying on her, pinning her with his weight, just as he had the previous night. Once again she heard his breath coming in little urgent gasps. His knees forced her thighs apart. She fought him with all her strength, but it was hopeless. He forced himself into her.

She screamed into the sheepskin. She had not yet healed from his previous abuse, and the pain was hot and sharp. She tried to reach back and grab his hair as she'd done before, but he was expecting that, and he held his head out of reach. His hips moved, and he thrust into her three times, four times—and then he stiffened and grunted and fell down onto her, gasping.

She struggled and finally managed to free one hand. She reached up and pulled the stinking sheepskin out of her mouth. "Get off me!" she screamed at him.

She felt him moving off the bed. She squirmed around, with her heart racing, her whole body shaking. Her face was wet with tears, though she hadn't realized she was crying.

She heard the sound of the tent flat being opened. Was he leaving? No; she saw his silhouette as he sat just inside the flap, looking out at the night.

"You want me to be like that woman, Dira," she shouted at him, with a mixture of scorn and despair. "You want me sitting at your feet, grinning like a fool."

He turned and looked at her. "I'd like you to show some respect. As we agreed."

"What about *your* respect for *me*?" Her voice was shrill.

"You'll have none of that, so long as you act like a spoiled child who needs to be taught a lesson."

She shook her head, unable to understand, feeling overwhelmed by the hopelessness of her situation. "You're the child. You and that stupid game. I saw your hand. You hurt yourself terribly."

"My left hand," he said quietly.

"Oh. Oh, so you still have your right hand to hit me with?"

"Yes, and if you provoke me again, I may have to do that."

She jumped up, grabbed her hunting coat, and threw it around herself. She seized her spear. "Out of the way," she told him.

"Don't speak to me that way, Mara." His voice was a warning.

"Out of the way!" she screamed. Her voice was so loud, she saw him recoil from the sound.

She seized the moment, pushed past him, and scrambled through the tent flap.

"Where are you going?" he called after her.

"Away from you." She started striding between the tents and houses, under the bright light of the moon.

He didn't try to follow her. Suddenly she was on her own, alone among the silent homes of the tribe. But then she saw a flicker of movement up ahead, and she heard a footstep.

For a moment Mara forgot her outrage and despair. She froze, listening. She caught the faint sound of someone moving quickly, running away from her. Could it have been Shani? Could she have been listening outside the tent?

Mara started running. She sprinted as fast as she could, taking the shortest path toward her Clan House. Along the way, once again, she saw a faint shape moving. But when she reached the Meeting Place, everything was silent and still. The area was empty, with just a faint flickering flame where the fire had burned earlier.

Mara paused, trying to quiet her own heavy breathing so that she could listen. But there wasn't the slightest sound. If Shani had been there, she was hiding now.

Mara tightened her grip on her spear, then strode out of the Meeting Place, moving purposefully, now, toward the grasslands beyond.

Chapter 8

Mother Moon was almost full, high in the sky. The night was so clear, Mara felt as if she could see every single blade of grass. She moved swiftly across the wide, shallow valley, pausing often, sniffing and tasting the air. She saw droppings from sheep and musk oxen, most of them old and dry. She saw the footprints of bison in a hollow where there was damp, bare earth. But none of these things interested her.

She came to a small stream which flowed down a cleft in the land, making its way eventually to the lake. She smelled raccoons here, and wolves. But the scent she wanted was not in the air.

Bobcats were hard to find. Often they stayed in woodland, where they could hunt mice and climb to safety from predators.

Many years ago there had been thickets of willows near the river, and groves of young juniper and balsam fir scattered across the valley. But those trees had been cut down by her people long ago, and there was no longer any underbrush to hide small animals. She would have to roam farther, to the eastern slope of the valley, where the pine forests grew.

She paused to drink from the stream, moving cautiously in case some large animal should be nearby. Graum had killed one bear, and where there was one, there could be more.

When her thirst was satisfied, she sat on the riverbank for a moment and stared up at the Moon, praying for power. More than any of the other spirits, Mother Moon guided Mara's people. The Moon Spirit touched every woman, causing her to bleed and renew herself each month. When the Sun was tired and slept behind the horizon, the Moon was still dutiful, guiding hunters to their prey.

Feeling calmer now, Mara moved on across the valley. Her body was weary, but she refused to acknowledge that. Her eyes were alert, probing each shadow. Her feet in their buckskin moccasins made no sound as she picked her way across the grassland.

She came to the edge of the pine woods and stopped. The forest was dark and ominous, and she was reluctant to venture in alone. She hefted her spear, trying to decide what to do. Then she remembered a huge boulder that stood nearby on the slope of the hillside. If she climbed it, she could be safe from bears and mountain lions, and she could lie in wait.

She ran quickly around the edge of the forest, then scrambled up a steep slope. The boulder loomed above her. Some people in her tribe said it was enchanted and called it the Rock that Moves, because every spring, after the snow melted and heavy rains washed the hillside, the boulder seemed to move farther down toward the valley. Mara herself wasn't sure what to believe, but she stopped for just a moment and faced the boulder, paying it her respect and begging it for its power before she went up to it and began to climb, wedging her feet in a fissure that ran up one side.

Soon she was safe on top of it, where the stone was still slightly warm from the sunlight that it had gathered during the day. She stretched out on her back with her spear beside her, and she lay in complete silence, staring up at the Moon, waiting and listening.

For a long time she heard nothing. Her mind started wandering, and she found herself reliving events from years ago. She remembered the first time she'd tried to use a spear, and had flung it at a squirrel that chattered insults at her from a tree. The squirrel had leaped away, and the spear had gone far beyond its target, lodging in some high branches. She'd had to climb up to retrieve it, and Shani had laughed at her. But Mara had made a grim vow to prove herself. She had practiced hard, and a year later she had finally managed to spear a squirrel, which was hard to do, since squirrels were so small and moved so fast. Shani had not been able to laugh at her then.

Other memories called to Mara: her first mammoth hunt, where she had slipped and fallen and sprained her ankle; and her second hunt, where she had taken a risk, running forward and casting the killing spear when the beast still had some of its spirit left. Her father had chided her for that, but then, her father had always been a timid man, happier spearing fish than mammoth. In fact, his lack of courage and ambition had always bothered her, and she'd found it hard to respect the way he constantly deferred to Ternees. He had died just two summers ago, after a long sickness, and Mara still had mixed feelings about him. She certainly felt his absence, even now.

She blinked, feeling suddenly confused. The Moon had shifted. The night air was colder. She was shivering. She had fallen asleep, she realized. Feeling angry with herself, she sat up. Then she stopped and listened. There was a rustling sound in the foliage below the rock. Was that what had woken her?

Cautiously, she peered down. At first she saw nothing. Then she made out the faint shape rooting around in dead leaves near the bottom of the boulder.

Was it a bobcat? Suddenly she was sure that it was.

She picked up her spear, careful not to make a sound. She stood, moved to the edge of the boulder nearest the hillside, then jumped down.

She hit the ground harder than she had expected. It was impossible not to make a sound. The cat heard her and ran. She went after it, leaping down the slope with the wind on her face.

The cat veered into the forest. Mara didn't hesitate. She plunged in among the trees, crashing through deadwood, springing over rocks and brambles, slapping thin branches out of her way. There was a small clearing just ahead. She saw the cat's shadow as it raced away. Mara ran forward—and cried out as she found the ground falling apart under her.

There was a cracking sound. Her feet shot out and she

plunged down. She flung out her arm and managed to seize a sapling. The sapling bent over and her hand slid along it, ripping leaves away, tearing her skin. She clenched her fist with all her strength, and finally her grip held.

For a long moment she hung there, blinking in the semidarkness, feeling frightened and trying to understand what had happened. There was a pit, she realized. Her legs were dangling into it. She hadn't seen it because someone had covered it over with thin branches and leaves.

Bit by bit, she brought her fear back under control. She managed to pull herself back up onto the forest floor, looked at her palm, and saw a thin smear of blood, dark in the moonlight that filtered through the trees. It wasn't a serious wound—just a graze.

The cat was long gone, but it no longer concerned her. She wanted to know what had almost happened to her. She stooped and dragged some of the branches aside so that the pit was more clearly revealed. Then she peered down. The pit was deeper than she was tall, and it was wider than she could jump across. She looked around and saw heaps of excavated earth nearby, and she wondered why anyone would have done such a thing.

She pulled more of the covering of branches away, and then she understood. There were sharpened stakes at the bottom of the pit, pointing upward. It was a trap.

She placed her spear across the edge and carefully lowered herself, holding the spear for support. As soon as her feet touched the bottom, she caught the familiar smell of bear. She peered at the sharpened stakes, and they were stained with blood. So this was the brave hunter's secret. No wonder he hadn't wanted to share it.

Mara seized one of the stakes and started working at it, wrenching it to and fro. It was deeply seated in the ground, but finally she managed to pull it free. She reached up to her spear, then, and hauled herself out.

Suddenly she realized it was no accident that she had found this place. The bobcat had woken her, and it had led her here.

She muttered a fervent prayer of thanks to the spirit of the cat, which had served her so well. And then, gripping the bloody stake in one hand and her spear in the other, she marched out of the forest.

Chapter 9

When she reached the village, the first light of dawn was changing the sky from black to purple above the mountains in the east. Mara felt giddy with fatigue, but this was no time to stop and rest.

The village was silent around her. All its people were still sleeping as she strode among the dwellings to her own Clan House. As she walked inside, she breathed the familiar smells of wood smoke, meat, animal hide, and human flesh, and she felt touched by an unexpected pang of nostalgia. She saw the people sleeping in their beds around the perimeter, each in its little curtained niche. She saw spears leaning against the wall, clothes hanging from the wooden beams, and bags of dried delicacies and provisions ranged around the fire. To her surprise, she found that she missed her mother and her aunts and all her other relatives—even the ones who had been at odds with her. So many times she had felt unhappy here; yet now that she had left, it called her more powerfully than she would have believed possible.

She shook her head, trying to dispel the emotions and restore her sense of purpose.

She crept across the floor of hard, packed earth to the bed of Lorm, the News Teller. Lorm was a solitary man, too slow-witted to be a hunter, too shy to be paired with a woman. He did chores around the Clan House, and he did them with a smile; but telling the news was what he lived for. It seemed to give him a sense of importance to walk around the village, announcing the rituals or the festivals, or calling people out of their homes if Ternees wanted a meeting.

Mara bent over him and shook him gently. "Lorm," she whispered. "Lorm, wake up."

He opened his eyes and blinked at her. For a moment he seemed not to recognize her. Then his eyes widened in surprise. "Mara, what are you doing here?"

"Shh," she told him, pressing her finger against his lips. "Come with me. Quietly, now."

He struggled out of bed and shuffled after her, outside into the Meeting Place.

"Listen carefully," she said. "Something important has happened. I must tell everyone in the tribe. You must call them all here. Do you understand?"

He looked at her uncertainly. "Something important?"

"Yes," she said. Would he obey her? She was the Chieftain's daughter, after all; but she was the younger daughter, and Ternees had obviously spoken against her to the people of her clan.

Lorm looked uncomfortable. "Maybe I should waken Ternees," he said.

She caught his arm. "No, Lorm. This is my meeting. I am a woman now. I can call a meeting if I wish."

It was true that anyone in the village could call people out, if an event was important enough—if mammoth were seen nearby, for instance, and it was urgent to organize a hunt. Still, Lorm looked at her doubtfully.

"Start at the houses at the outside of the village," she told him. "Bring the people with you, to the center, here." That way there should be the least chance of her mother interfering.

"Start at the outside?" He still sounded doubtful.

"That's right." She tried to make her voice authoritative. "This is very important, Lorm. Just tell everyone to come to the Meeting Place. That's all."

"Well, all right, Mara." He turned and shuffled away, repeating her instructions to himself.

So there was no going back now. She had set something in motion. To prove she was right? To take out her anger? For a moment she felt unsure of her own motives. But then it was clear to her. The bear had been a terrible omen, and Graum had arrived with the bear. She felt deep inside her that he was a threat to her people.

Now that she knew that he had lied to them, wasn't it her duty to tell them all? It had to be done quickly, before the young hunters set out with him today and he had a chance to impress them even more than he had last night.

She climbed up onto the Speaking Stone, the very same place where her mother had stood in the pairing ceremony. She tried to summon her courage and calm herself. She told herself that this was her duty, for she alone had been chosen by the bobcat to learn the truth.

She heard Lorm's voice in the distance, shouting for people to wake and come out of their homes. Mara closed her eyes for a moment. This, she decided, was a bigger test of strength than holding a pebble that was hot from the fire.

A few villagers started walking into the Meeting Place, looking bleary-eyed and puzzled. They shouted questions at her.

"I'm waiting," she said, "for the strangers. For Graum and Dira. This concerns them."

Gradually the place filled with people. They stared doubtfully at Mara and turned to each other, asking what had happened. She ignored them as well as she could. Then her relatives started emerging from their Clan House, and finally Ternees appeared. She stood in the doorway, frowning at Mara in the dim morning light, as if she couldn't believe what she saw. "What's the purpose of this?" she called out.

Mara searched the faces that filled the Meeting Place. Suddenly she saw Graum at the back of the crowd. "I am Mara, daughter of Ternees," she shouted, as loudly as she could. "I call this meeting here."

Everyone turned to face her. They looked ill-tempered. It was not a common thing for a meeting to be called this way. It was even less common for someone so young to stand on the Speaking Stone.

Mara sensed their hostility. It made her still more nervous. But clearly there was no going back. "Yesterday, strangers came to our tribe," she shouted out. "Their leader, whose name is Graum, is here in the Meeting Place. He claimed to be a great hunter, and he brought with him the bear that he had killed."

Graum started pushing forward, heading toward her. She was still holding the stake that she had dragged out of the pit in the forest, but she was keeping it behind her back so that he wouldn't know what she had discovered.

"Graum refused to tell our hunters how he killed the beast," Mara went on. "He said it had taken a lot of courage." She drew a deep breath. "I say to you that he lied."

There was a murmur from the crowd. Graum reached the front and stopped still, staring at her. His wife pushed through and stood beside him, giving Mara a look of pure hatred.

Mara felt queasy, faced with their anger and the resentment of the crowd. But she forced herself on, because there was nothing else, now, that she could do. "Last night," she said, "I found a pit that had been dug in the pine forest. It's close by the Rock that Moves. Any of you can go there and see it for yourselves. The pit was covered over with branches and leaves. When I pulled the branches aside, down at the bottom I found sharp stakes. Like this." She brought it out and held it high. The sky had lightened enough so that everyone could see that the pointed end was dark with blood.

"Graum didn't kill the bear," Mara called out. "The bear killed itself! Graum placed meat in the pit to lure it there, and it fell on the sticks and bled to death." She turned and faced the big man. "Last night, he challenged our hunters to show their courage. My own husband burned his hand badly, and many others also hurt themselves, for no good reason. Graum insulted our elder hunters, implying that they weren't worthy of learning his hunting skills. But he is the one who is not worthy. He lied to us all."

"Get down from there!" a voice shouted out. It was Dira, stepping forward, reaching out to grab Mara.

Quickly Graum seized her shoulder, holding her back. "No need for that," he said.

"Mara." It was Ternees's voice. She was walking forward, approaching the Speaking Stone. "It's no small thing to question a man's word and his skill as a hunter."

Mara felt herself trembling. It was hard enough, standing

up in front of the crowd and facing Graum. She wasn't sure she could sustain her courage if her mother turned against her. *Please,* she thought, *please don't be cruel and severe.* "It is no small thing, Mother," she said, trying to keep the tremor out of her voice, "for him to mislead our young men, and insult our elders, and lie to us all."

"Yes," Ternees agreed slowly, "that is so." She moved to the front of the crowd. "Graum, what do you have to say about this?"

The big man turned and looked around at all the people who had gathered in the Meeting Place. If he was worried, he showed no sign of it. He seemed relaxed, and he took his time. "I lied to no one," he said.

"You lie to us still!" Mara shouted back.

Ternees glared at Mara. "Quiet," she said. She turned back to Graum. "I think you should explain."

The big man shrugged. "I said last night, I chose not to tell my way of killing that bear. And none of you knew how, did you?" He shrugged again. "Takes cunning, which is what I said. Takes courage, too, because you never know what a bear may do. You dig the pit and place the bait, but the bear may not fall, or he may not get hurt too badly, and he may climb right out and come after you. So you heard what I said last night. I said there's more than one way to kill a big, ugly beast." He waited for that to sink in. "I didn't lie. And there's nothing to be ashamed of when it comes to setting a trap. Like you said yourself, Ternees, wisdom counts as much as bravery. A good hunter uses his head as well as his strength. He doesn't risk his life more than he needs to." He paused again. "I think we can all agree on that."

There was a murmur of assent from the young men in the crowd. It took Mara a moment to realize that they were siding with Graum. But why? No matter what he said, obviously he had deceived them last night, letting them imagine he had speared the beast with great bravery. But then she saw it from their point of view: She was a young woman who had only just come of age. And she was telling them that Graum had made fools of them all. That was an insult to their pride. She could see in their faces, they were resenting her, rejecting her words.

Was it already too late? Mara searched for Yacor's face. She saw him near the center of the crowd, and that gave her new hope. "Yacor," she cried out. "You were by the fire last night. You left when Graum insulted your pride. Isn't that true?"

Yacor was a tenacious hunter, but he was quiet and modest in his dealings with other people. In any dispute, he always looked for a compromise. "I had a difference of opinion with Graum," he said. He spoke slowly, reluctantly. "Seemed to me he was playing a game with our young hunters, which I didn't entirely approve of."

Mara looked around at the crowd of villagers. Were they listening? They respected Yacor. Surely, if he supported her, they would be swayed by him. "Graum misled everyone," Mara called out to Yacor, "don't you agree?"

Yacor looked uncomfortable. "He let us believe what we wanted to believe," he said. "Most men will do that sometimes, when they tell hunting stories. But he didn't tell any actual lies that I recall."

"Thank you, my friend," said Graum, turning and nodding to Yacor. "You are an honorable man."

"Yacor wasn't your friend last night!" Mara shouted, clenching her fists. She could sense the moment slipping away from her, and she sensed that her strength would not be enough to pull it back. "After Yacor left the fireside, do you all know what Graum said? He said Yacor was afraid to test his courage against the young hunters. That's what he said!"

Graum shook his head, looking deeply offended. "Never. I never said that."

"All right." Ternees stepped forward, holding up her hands. "This is accomplishing nothing, now." She turned to Mara. "Step down, please."

Their eyes met. Mara felt herself weakening. Her mother was doing what she had so often done: giving the orders, putting Mara in her place, taking everything away. Mara felt her knees trembling, but she didn't yield.

"I am your Chieftain." Ternees glared. "You have called your meeting. You have made your speech. Now I will talk to my people. Step down."

Mara blinked. She looked around, not knowing exactly

what she was searching for. Kormor? If he was in the Meeting Place, she didn't see him, and anyway, he wouldn't approve of her behaving this way. Was there no way out of this? She felt unsteady and confused. She had been so sure that this was the right thing to do. Had the spirit of the cat tricked her? Had she not understood it? Was it all her fault?

Clumsily, almost losing her balance, she stepped off the stone.

Her mother climbed up and took her place. She looked out over the crowd. "Graum," she called out, "I said last night, if a challenge doesn't serve a man or his tribe, then I see no point in it. All men here must listen to this. Graum's way of testing a man's worth was not the way of our people."

She paused to let that be understood.

"But I also said," she went on, "that people should be free to follow their own paths. Anyone who feels he can learn something from Graum may do so. Did he let us believe, last night, that he is a more daring hunter than he really is? The truth of that is easily tested. Graum, weren't you planning to take some of our young men on a hunt today?"

He nodded.

"In that case," Ternees went on, "our young men will see for themselves. If you are a fine hunter, you will earn their respect. If not, you will earn their scorn."

There was a murmuring of agreement from the crowd. They looked relieved, now. Somehow, Ternees had resolved the situation. They didn't need to worry themselves with it any further.

And yet, Mara thought, nothing had been resolved. Graum had escaped her challenge. And what if the young hunters who went out with him were as foolish as they had been last night? Obviously their judgment couldn't be trusted.

"Does anyone wish to speak?" Ternees called out. "If so, I will yield the Speaking Stone."

No one moved forward. Mara felt sick inside. She no longer had the will to stand up and talk to the crowd.

"Then this matter is settled," said Ternees, climbing

down. Calmly, ignoring Mara, she turned her back and walked into her Clan House.

Suddenly everyone seemed to be talking. The young men of the tribe pushed forward and gathered around Graum, nodding to him, showing their support. The older hunters held back, exchanging words, shaking their heads. Many of the women were staring at Graum, murmuring to each other. Some were eying him with interest, others with doubt.

A hand seized Mara and whirled her around. She found herself suddenly staring into Dira's face. The little woman gave a shout of anger and scythed her arm, lashing out at Mara, slapping at her with her fingers curled, so that her nails drew blood. Mara's head was turned by the blow, and she had to step back to keep her balance. Dira paused, breathing hard, then spat. The spittle hit Mara in the eyes.

"Hey! Stop that." It was Graum, grabbing his wife, pulling her back.

Mara wiped her face furiously. To be shamed like this, in front of everyone—

"She's very loyal to me," Graum was saying. "When someone speaks bad of me, she can't stand that."

"I spoke truly!" Mara shouted.

Graum gave her a measuring look. "Well, like your mother said, we'll let the facts speak for themselves in the days to come, eh?" He glanced again at the people around him, then turned back to Dira. "You should understand," he said, "this young girl here may have her own problems. You know, when a woman's not happy at home, she often takes it out on other people."

"How dare you!" Mara shouted at him. She looked around. Surely her people would support her now. But Graum had pitched her voice low enough so that only she and Dira had heard him.

Mara gave a cry of frustration. She turned away. There was no point in staying here, being attacked and humiliated. She stumbled out of the Meeting Place, avoiding people's eyes, shaking away the hands that reached for her.

She hardly saw the village as she walked among the dwellings. Moments later she found herself outside the tent that Kormor had built. And there he was, emerging from it, dressed in his hunting coat, pulling a pack up onto his shoulders.

He paused as he saw her. For a moment they stared at each other, and neither said a word.

She needed him, she realized. Even though he had been so awful to her, he was still her mate, and now, more than ever, she had no one else in the world to turn to. "Kormor—"

"I heard you," he said. "You took a bad situation and you made it worse."

"But Kormor, I said nothing about you!" Her voice was plaintive, and she hated the weakness she felt inside her, but she had used up all her strength. "I had to speak out."

Kormor shouldered his pack with quick, jerky movements. "When I come back from hunting with Graum, tomorrow or the next day, I'll have made up my own mind, without any more of your outbursts to embarrass me." He seized his spear.

"Kormor!" She grabbed his free hand.

He yelled and pulled it away from her.

It was the hand he had burned, she realized. She felt a sudden pang.

He was shuddering. His face was contorted with pain. She saw that he had wrapped a scrap of sheepskin clumsily around his palm, and she had loosened it. The wound was exposed now. She looked at it in horror. The skin had been completely burned away. She could see the tendons beneath. Pink fluid was oozing out.

He quickly turned it away from her. "It will heal," he said shortly.

"I can't believe you did that to yourself!" she cried. "And now you're going out on a hunt?"

"Yes," he said. He wrapped the piece of sheepskin around his hand again, then tied a thong around it and tightened it with his teeth. He gave her a last hard look.

He turned, then, and walked away.

Chapter 10

Exhausted, she slept through the morning. When she finally woke, it was early in the afternoon, and she heard the busy daytime sounds of the village through the tent's roof of mammoth hide. There were men and women wading in the lake, splashing water and laughing, happy that summer was coming and the days were growing warmer. A woman in a nearby home was chanting one of the old songs, trying to calm her crying baby. Two boys ran past, shouting something that was lost in the wind.

Mara sat up, feeling muzzy-headed and confused. For a moment she couldn't understand where she was. She blinked, wondering why she didn't see the high domed roof of her Clan House, with the people of her family nearby.

Then the events of the past two days came back to her in a rush of memory, and she lay back down, feeling overwhelmed. She had always been headstrong, and sometimes, in the past, she had taken sudden, rash actions that caused trouble for her later. But there had never been a situation like this.

Even now, she couldn't quite understand how it had happened and what had gone wrong. Hadn't Lizel told her to stand up and speak out and do what must be done, even when others lacked the courage to do so? She had followed the old woman's advice, and she had been guided by the bobcat and by the portent of her vision. Why had fate been so unkind to her?

There were no answers. And now, more than ever before, there was no one to help her. Should she go back to Lizel again? No; she no longer trusted the priestess's advice.

Mara rolled out of bed and realized that she was hungry. She stood up and bumped her head against one of the curving mammoth ribs that supported the roof of hide. Would she ever feel comfortable living here, after everything that had happened? The thought troubled her. She pushed it away.

There was no food in the tent, so she put on her hunting coat and moccasins, picked up her spear, and ventured outside.

The lake shimmered silver in the afternoon sun, and children were kicking up spray in the shallows. Mara would have liked to join them—to throw off all her cares for a moment and act like a child again. But there was no time for that. She turned and walked into the village.

A woman came toward her, humming to herself, carrying a basket on her head. It was her aunt, she realized. Aunt Tamra. Instinctively Mara felt happy to see her. Tamra, after all, had always been the friendliest of her aunts—the one who had taken the time to tell her about the ways of men, and how a couple should give each other pleasure. "Hello, Aunt," she said, giving her a hopeful smile.

Tamra paused. She reached up and steadied her basket. "Mara, dear." She didn't return the smile. She looked ill-at-ease.

Mara found herself unable to think of anything to say. "I ... was just thinking about all of you, in the Clan House," she said.

Tamra hesitated. "Well, we miss you, Mara." The words sounded forced. "But you know, if I may give you some advice, dear—you should be a little more thoughtful. Perhaps listen to people, instead of expecting them always to listen to you."

Mara blinked. She looked down at the ground. "I'm sure you're right," she said.

"Well, I must be getting along." Tamra moved on a couple of steps, then hesitated. "Are you all right, Mara? I heard that you and Kormor ..." She trailed off.

Gossip always moved rapidly through the village, and

Mara had certainly given everyone enough to gossip
about. Without a doubt, there would be some wild exag-
gerations circulating by now, especially if someone really
had been listening outside the tent last night. "I'm all
right," Mara said. She forced another smile, then hurried away.

There were two more encounters like that, in quick
succession. Both times, Mara tried to make herself sound
untroubled. It was a terrible effort, and she felt her spirits sinking.

Finally she reached the food caches. Old Man Hopwa
was there, ready to scoop out provisions for people who
needed them or receive new food from those who had
it to spare. Women brought pemmican that they had
made by pounding meat and marrow fat till it was hard
and powdery. Men carried fish that had been smoked in
little tents of rawhide or dried on racks in the sun. Hopwa's leathery face turned from one person to the next,
always smiling, always good-natured.

Mara waited till a couple of villagers had concluded
their business with him. Then, when she could be sure
of a moment alone with him, she moved forward.
"Hopwa, I need pemmican for a two-day hunt," she told
him. "And dried bullberries." She handed him the bag
that she always took with her when she went hunting.

"Running short in your house, eh?" he said as he
fussed around, nudging a cover off one of the caches
and using the shoulder bone of a bison to measure out
the berries.

"I'm no longer living in my Clan House," she told him.

He squinted at her. "No longer? Why, it's Mara, of
course. Yes, someone said something about that. Now,
isn't that a strange state of affairs." There was nothing
judgmental in the way he said it. He sounded honestly
puzzled.

"My mate, Kormor, has built us our own home," Mara
told him.

His simple face opened in a smile, exposing the meager
brown remnants of his teeth. "Yes, yes. It comes back
to me now. You know, Mara, my memory—"

"It's all right, Hopwa." Mara found herself feeling

oddly touched. He was simpleminded, but he was always friendly, always kind. He managed to do in daily life what Ternees merely talked about. He was tolerant of everyone, he accepted everyone as a friend, and he never passed judgment on anyone's conduct. Impulsively, she put her arm around his stooped, bony shoulders and gave him a hug. "Thank you," she said.

"What for?" he asked her, looking puzzled.

She wasn't sure what to say. She took the bag containing the food she'd asked for, and then, feeling embarrassed, she hurried on.

Soon she was outside the village, heading across the valley, following the same direction she had taken during the night. In the distance, she saw tiny figures climbing the zigzag path up the cliffs which walled the northern end of the valley. There was a rocky plateau up there, where an agile hunter could sometimes kill mountain sheep. And beyond the plateau, the northern mountain slopes held other game, though none of it was as easy to hunt as the animals that grazed down here in the grasslands of the valley.

Ahead of Mara, the land was empty. She felt glad of that. Her goal, now, was one which she could not share.

The pine forest looked very different from the way it had seemed during the night. Shafts of sun slanted down, dappling underbrush that was dotted with tiny wildflowers. Insects hummed to and fro, and the smell of pine sap was heavy in the air.

Mara came to the open pit. She walked carefully around it to the opposite side, sniffing the air. She crouched down to study the soil. There was a faint footprint, barely visible in the dry, powdery surface. It was the small paw mark of a cat.

Tentatively, she delved into the foliage. She moved back and forth, looking carefully; and she found a tiny shred of gray fur snagged on a thorn. She picked it up and rubbed it between her finger and thumb. It felt silky, almost oily. It couldn't have been exposed to the weather for more than a couple of days.

Cautiously now, she pushed ahead, with her spear

raised and her left hand stretched out for balance. She walked with her knees bent and her feet placed well apart, ready to jump at the slightest sound.

She came to another paw print in a brown band of soil. And now, as a faint current of air wafted among the trees, she could smell the cat. Its lair must be very close by.

A thicket of brambles lay in front of her, and behind it was a large fallen tree. The tree looked old and rotten. It could easily be hollow. Mara crouched down. Sure enough, there was a gap under the brambles, with more little shreds of fur dangling from the thorns.

Slowly, cautiously, Mara reached with her left hand and tugged at some of the tangled vegetation. She peeled it back, a little at a time.

A screech shattered the peace of the forest. It was wild, piercing, shrill enough to raise the hairs on the back of her neck. Instinctively, she leaped backward. She stopped still, then, with her pulse beating fast. She stooped down, and this time she saw the cat. It was crouching under the brambles with all its fur raised and its mouth open wide, its ears flattened, its muscles bunched up, ready to spring.

She hesitated. A bobcat was small game, but it could lacerate a careless hunter with its claws. Mara judged the distance carefully, knowing she probably had only one chance. She braced herself, and she flung her spear.

There was another screech, but it turned into a terrible yowl. Mara's aim had been true; the spear had pieced the animal's chest. She ripped the brambles out of the way, moving swiftly now. She drew her flint knife. The bobcat saw her looming over it and it halfheartedly raised a paw with all its fearsome claws extended. But life was already fading from its yellow eyes. Mara muttered a quick prayer to its spirit: an entreaty and an atonement. Then, grimly, she cut the neck to let the blood flow. The cat stiffened and it died.

Mara crouched beside it for a moment, touching its tawny gray and brown fur. "Thank you," she whispered, "for giving me your spirit, with all its strength." She unfurled a small piece of doeskin and rolled the cat into it. She turned, then, and found a clear patch of soft earth. Quickly she started digging into it with her knife, pausing to scoop away the loosened earth with her hands. After a little while, she had dug a hole that was deep enough.

Gently she placed the cat into the ground. Once again, she said a short prayer to its spirit. Then she shoveled the earth back into place, and she trod it down.

She stood up and cleaned her hands as well as she could, using a clump of grass. It felt wrong to bury the game that she had killed, instead of eating it. But her people believed that the animal's spirit would be stronger if its body was left intact. And Mara needed strength more now than ever before.

She wondered why the cat had chosen to stand its ground instead of running away from her. She paused a moment, frowning. And then, cautiously, she crept back toward the hollow log where the cat had stood.

She stopped and listened. Faintly, she heard a high-pitched cry. She turned her head, trying to focus on the sound. Definitely, it came from the log.

Mara pushed farther into the brambles and hacked at them with her knife till there was room for her to squat among them. There was a hole in the log, just as she'd suspected.

She used her knife to widen the hole. She peered in, and there, among the yellow, crumbly rotten wood, she saw a single kitten. It was huddled against the back of its lair, mewing plaintively.

So the mother cat had been defending its young. Mara felt mixed emotions as she looked at the little one. Nothing could be more natural to her than hunting for game and eating the animals she killed. And yet, as she stared at the kitten, something in its eyes stirred her. It was an outcast now. And so was she.

She reached out, feinted, then seized the kitten by the back of its neck. She lifted it out and held it up. It was very small, perhaps only three weeks old.

The kitten stuck its front legs out as if it wanted to seize hold of her. Its back legs kicked feebly. It stared into her face, crying out in its tiny voice.

With her free hand, Mara groped for her food bag.

She emptied out the pemmican and berries, then thrust the kitten inside and closed the top of the bag so that it wouldn't escape. She hesitated, not wanting to leave the food on the forest floor. But perhaps that was the right thing to do, as a sacrifice for the mother cat that she had killed and the young one she had taken.

She turned, then, and strode back the way she had come.

During the first part of Mara's journey, the kitten kicked and struggled and pressed its nose to the neck of the bag, trying to claw its way free. But as she continued on her way, it gradually quieted down. In fact, she eventually became concerned in case it had suffocated. But when she opened the bag a fraction and peeked in, she saw two luminous eyes peering up, seemingly without fear, as if the animal had resigned itself and was now placing its trust in her. That made her feel uneasy, for she didn't really know what she was going to do.

Daylight was fading by the time she approached the village, and the sun lay hidden behind the mountains beyond the lake. Mara saw no one else walking on the floor of the valley, and she realized they would be back in their Clan Houses by now, eating their evening meals, talking about the things they had done that day. Some of them would be doing chores, perhaps playing with their children—except for the young hunters, of course, who were out with Graum.

Mara continued on her way to the village—and she saw two people coming toward her.

She stopped, feeling puzzled. Why would anyone be leaving the village on a journey this late in the day?

Then, with a new feeling of concern, she recognized the travelers. Lizel was in the lead, hunched forward under the load of a bundle strapped across her back. Trifen was coming after her, clutching two poles under his arms. The poles slanted behind him, trailing in the grass, and on this small travois was a second bundle.

Mara felt a deep sense of wrongness. "Where are you going?" she called, moving quickly toward them.

Lizel paused as Mara came close. She grunted and set

her burden down. It made a heavy thump as it landed on the grassland.

"Why are you leaving the village?" Mara asked, feeling the tension growing inside her. "What's happened?"

The old woman eyed Mara, then looked past her, contemplating the way south. "Nothing has happened," she said.

"But are you leaving?"

"Yes." Lizel's voice sounded strange. It lacked its usual strength, and her face was sad. She looked, in fact, as if someone near to her had died. Finally she seemed to make up her mind about what she wanted to say. She turned to Mara. "You mustn't speak of this."

Mara nodded quickly, though she felt confused by the idea that Lizel would choose to confide in her.

Lizel narrowed her eyes, looking around at the darkening landscape as if she hoped to see something that she had been looking for. "The spirits have not spoken to me," she said, "ever since your Ceremony of First Blood. All my life, as long as I can remember, the spirits have spoken to me. But now there's silence. So I must search for a sign. I will spend some time out here, Mara, under the guidance of Mother Moon, who is the most sacred spirit of all."

Mara blinked, finding herself at a loss. She had always felt in awe of Lizel, respecting her and fearing her. And now Lizel was just a woman, old and bent and weary.

Lizel focused on her again. "Tell no one, Mara! No one in the tribe should know that my powers have gone."

"But maybe they haven't gone. This is a turbulent time, Lizel—"

"Oh, yes. Yes, it is. There are portents."

Mara hesitated. She felt a sudden impulse—and surely she should have learned by now that her impulses couldn't be trusted. Still, she had to ask. "Can I . . . come with you?" The idea suddenly seemed immensely appealing. Surely it would solve all her problems.

Lizel looked at her and slowly smiled. "Run away, you mean." She gave a weak, dry laugh. "No, Mara. You must stay with your mate and your people. They may need you."

"Need me?" Mara grunted in disgust. "They don't even like me, Lizel. They look on me with doubt. They hate my outbursts. And in any case, they have my mother, and if she should ever fail, they have Shani—"

"No!" Lizel seized Mara's shoulder and gave her a little shake. "I told you once before, your mother and your sister never had to fight for anything. They have never been truly challenged. Do you understand?"

Mara wanted to pull back. She felt unnerved by Lizel's sudden intensity. "No ones *dares* to challenge my mother," Mara said.

"Hah." Lizel sounded scornful. "Remember, Ternees doesn't believe in fighting. She lets each person follow her own path, yes? But there's another problem, girl. What if that path is wrong? And what if people are too stupid to understand that?" She pushed her face even closer to Mara's, till Mara could see every line and wrinkle, and Lizel's breath was on her.

And then, abruptly, Lizel pulled back. She let go of Mara and hugged herself against the chill evening air, and once again she seemed just a forlorn old woman. "I saw how you stood up to Graum in the Meeting Place. I was at the back of the crowd, but I saw. That was a brave thing you did, Mara."

"But I failed." It was painful for her even to think about it.

"You failed this time. But you learned. Next time, you may not fail." Lizel glanced at her thoughtfully. "Did you look for your spirit?"

"I found it," Mara said, "just this afternoon. The spirit of the cat is in me now."

"Ah. Good." Her eyes shifted. "But what's in that bag, there?"

"The bobcat was defending a young one," Mara explained. She slung the bag off her shoulder and opened it a crack for Lizel to peer in.

"Well," said Lizel. "Whatever are you going to do with that?" She was no longer fierce. She sounded surprised.

Mara paused. She didn't know what to say. "I don't

know. I just ... wanted it, for my own." She took the bag back.

"So you have a living spirit now, as well as the one from the mother cat," Lizel said, half to herself. "Well, now, isn't that a strange thing. And maybe it's a wise thing, too. Wiser than you realize." She gave her a challenging look. "Where will you keep it? What will you feed it?"

"Well, Kormor has a trap that he made of wood, to catch foxes. I thought I might keep the little one there. And I'll get scraps of meat—"

"No, no." Lizel spoke sharply. "I've seen the way animals raise their young. They're like us—they must have milk till they're half grown." She paused for a moment. "You know Vola?"

"The woman whose baby was stillborn?"

"Yes. Go to her. Her breasts may still make milk, even though her child didn't live. Squeeze the milk into a leather cup, then take it back to your little spirit." She nodded toward the leather bag. "And if Vola questions you, tell her I said to do it. In fact—tell her that the little cat is to be kept alive for me, till I return. Do you understand? Tell her I'll be displeased if it isn't done." She gave Mara a sly smile.

"So—you *will* be coming back?"

The smile vanished. "Tell Vola that I will. Tell anyone else the same thing." She glanced at Trifen, who had been standing a few paces away, watching them solemnly. "Are you ready, boy?"

He nodded.

Lizel reached down for her pack.

"Here," said Mara, "let me help."

Lizel waved her away. "I need no help." She raised the pack, grunting with the effort, and settled it across her shoulders. "Remember everything I've said! It was no accident, meeting you here."

Mara nodded. Then she turned to the boy. "Goodbye, Trifen."

Unexpectedly, he stepped forward. He hugged her quickly, then moved back, avoiding her eyes.

She watched as the old woman started walking, picking

her way slowly across the grassland, and the young boy started dragging his travois after her. Mara stood there a long time, staring after them, waiting to see if either of them would look back at her, and hoping that they would, but neither of them did. And then the gathering darkness claimed them, and they were gone.

Mara turned, clutching the kitten in its sack. She continued on across the grassland toward the village, thinking about what Lizel had said, feeling anxious now, and wondering what might lie ahead.

PART TWO

▼▲▼

The Storm

Chapter 11

The kitten was almost a cat, now. Its body was longer than Mara's forearm, and its claws were fearsome. She woke with a start as it leaped onto her chest. She could see its silhouette against daylight filtering around the edges of the door flap, and she could hear its purring as it trod rhythmically on the sheepskin under which she slept.

She reached out and ran her fingers through the bobcat's thick, tawny coat. It nuzzled her wrist, licked her skin, then moved forward till she felt its breath on her face. It sniffed her and made a guttural "Rrrrow?"

It was a male cat, and sometimes it seemed to act as if it was her boy-child. This was all very strange to her, and even stranger to other people in the tribe. The Lake People looked on animals as wild spirits, to be worshiped for their strength or killed as food. To tame one and possess it as a pet had never been attempted, as far as anyone could remember. It seemed taboo.

She had named the cat Claws, and she thought of him as hers now; but when she saw his ungoverned strength and his powerful killing instinct, she knew that she could never truly own him, no matter how much her nurturing had put her in the place of his mother. He had grown from a helpless little scrap of fur to a fierce hunter with claws that sometimes drew blood even when he didn't intend to.

Two months ago, his wild spirit had made him desperate to roam, so she'd released him and watched him slink out through the door flap, never expecting to see him again. When she woke the next morning, he hadn't returned; but the morning after that he pushed his way into the tent, bring her a white-footed mouse that he had caught and killed out on the grasslands.

That had been a source of wonder to her—that he should bring her the mouse whole, instead of eating it. It seemed he was making a sacrifice to her, just as a hunter might sacrifice a deer to the Moon Spirit, praying for better hunting to come. But the mouse had turned out to be the first of many trophies that Claws brought back. In the end, she decided it was his way of repaying her for sparing his life.

Every night now he went out to roam and hunt; and every morning she found him staring at her with enigmatic golden eyes, nestling up against her and purring softly. Kormor thought it was unwise to allow such a wild animal to share their home, though he respected the bobcat as a hunter, and he even fed Claws once in a while. But the cat never trusted him as he trusted Mara.

The bed beside Mara was empty this morning. Kormor had gone on a four-day hunt with Graum and the other young men of the tribe. That had been happening more and more often as the long, hot summer ran its course. Mara valued her time alone, because it meant she wouldn't have to cope with his grim moods, his criticism of her, and his outbursts of anger. Still, after a while the solitude made her melancholy. Her only friend, really, was this half-wild animal, lying against her now and purring so loudly that it made her skin tremble.

"So what have you brought me this morning, Claws?" She gently pushed him aside and sat up on the edge of the bed. She reached for the door flap and opened it a little wider, admitting a wedge of yellow sunlight. The packed earth floor of her home was littered with odd items that she somehow never put away—a stray moccasin, a hide scraper, some spear heads, some lengths of thong—but there were no trophies today from his night-time hunt.

"So you must be hungry," she said. She went to the food cache that she had dug in one corner, and she moved the flat rock that served as its lid. Claws was there in a moment, nuzzling her ankles, then pressing his nose to the gap between the lid and the pit beneath. Impatiently, he reached in with his paw. Mara gently nudged him aside, then delved into the cache and extracted a strip of dried venison which she dropped in front of him.

He seized it in his jaws and dragged it away into the corner as if he was afraid she might try to take it back from him. He started working on it there, turning his head to one side, hunkering down and flattening his ears and making little growling sounds while he gnawed the meat.

She watched him, thinking that it felt good to give a living thing such pleasure. Also, he was handsome to look at. His body was striped in shades of gray and brown, while his legs were mottled in a spotty pattern which extended up across his stomach. His silky kitten fur was gone now, replaced with a dense, shaggy pelt. His paws seemed huge, as if he was wearing his own set of round, furry moccasins. His ears were tufted, and more tufts of fur hung down each side from his wide cheeks.

Mara heard a sound behind her. She turned in surprise, and Claws seized his breakfast and bolted with it under the wooden frame of the bed.

There was someone outside the tent, peering in. "Mara?" It was a young woman's voice. "Mara, are you in there?"

It was her sister, Mara realized. She blinked, trying to refocus her thoughts. She spent so much time alone, it confused her to be interrupted like this. "Shani?" She pushed her hair back from her face and gathered a deer-skin robe around her shoulders. "Is that you?" She opened the tent flap and shaded her eyes against the light. "Do you want to come in?"

Her sister stepped down into the small home, ducking her head beneath the arched mammoth ribs. She glanced around, cautiously at first, then narrowing her eyes in disapproval.

Months had passed since Mara had moved here, but through all that time, Shani had never visited. Now that she was suddenly here, without explanation or warning, Mara felt flustered. "Sit," she said. She went to a tree stump and cleared away some spear points which she had been reflaking. She felt suddenly embarrassed by the smallness and the clutter of her little home. And then, just as quickly, she felt annoyed with herself for feeling that way. Shouldn't she be free to live in any way she chose? And why should Shani's disapproval matter to her? "This is such a surprise," she said, retreating to the bed. "What brings you here?"

Shani was still looking around, taking in every little detail. "It seemed about time," she said, "that I should see where you've been hiding yourself away."

"Is there something you want?" Mara reached down to the food cache and took out some more dried venison, some pine nuts, and some dried berries. She placed them on a strip of bark and put it near her sister.

Shani picked up a handful of the pine nuts and nibbled them without much interest. "I was wondering about you," she said, shrugging one shoulder. "So many months it's been since you left our house. You used to come and visit, but we haven't seen you in weeks." She straightened her robe, then clasped her hands nearly in her lap. Every movement was precise and graceful. "Are you well?"

Mara hesitated. Basically she was healthy enough, yet she didn't feel well. More and more, in the past few weeks, she had suffered from aches and pains and a general feeling of lethargy that she never quite managed to shake off. "I have no complaints," she said.

"But you seem to spend so much time in this little tent. I never see you at the washing place, or in the evenings, around the big fire. Sister, you almost seem to have abandoned your own tribe."

Was Shani showing genuine concern, or was she being critical? Mara honestly couldn't tell. Shani seldom came straight out and said what was on her mind. She would sit and chat, sounding friendly, as she did now—and then, much later, Mara would sometimes realize that there had been quite a different meaning behind her words.

Mara felt torn. In a way, she was glad that her sister had come here. Still, she found it hard to trust her motives. "I didn't abandon my tribe," Mara said, trying to keep her voice neutral. "I feel as if my tribe abandoned me. Surely you remember what happened in the Meeting Place?"

Shani looked momentarily puzzled. "With Graum, you mean?" She gestured dismissively. "Mara, you can't possibly hold a grudge just because everyone didn't do what you wanted."

"But that wasn't how it happened," Mara protested. "I tried to help my tribe. And . . . they turned away from me." As she said the words, she found herself reliving the embarrassment and humiliation. The emotions surged up in her, almost as strong as four months ago. "Graum lied to our people," she reminded Shani. "He went against our customs, and he misled our young hunters. Now he acts like a father to them, and they follow him blindly." As she said the words, she felt a powerful sense of injustice. "Sister, surely you must see that what I say is true."

Shani looked unconcerned. "Perhaps there's truth in it," she agreed, "but does it matter? Young men are always foolish and reckless. They follow Graum now, but in a year or two they'll find something better to do. In the meantime, Graum doesn't rule our tribe."

"I think he'd like to," Mara said sharply.

Shani laughed. "Really? I've seen no sign of it. But even if you're right, it makes no difference what he wants. Ternees is quite happy to continue as our Chieftain, and our people are happy to follow her."

Mara sighed and rubbed her temples with the tips of her fingers. She had a headache, she realized, and the conversation was making her feel queasy. Really, there was no way she could justifiy her fears to Shani. She thought of her vision of the bear and the burning buildings; but there seemed no point in telling Shani that. "You should remember," she said, "Kormor is one of Graum's admirers now. In fact, he's Graum's closest companion. And through him, I hear the things that the men say among themselves. I tell you, Shani, they have no respect for the traditions of our tribe."

"Oh, really?" Shani sounded amused. "So Mother was right about Kormor all along."

Mara clenched her jaw. She told herself not to lose

her temper. "There may have been some truth in what Mother said." It was an effort for her to speak the words, but it was a matter of pride for her always to be honest. As she thought about her situation, though, her strength failed her. It had been so hard, trying to live with Kormor and sustaining herself during these past months. She blinked. Unexpectedly, she suddenly felt like crying.

Shani's smile faded. She frowned at Mara. "You're not happy, sister. Do you regret leaving our House?"

Mara shifted uncomfortably. She didn't like being quizzed this way, and she still wasn't convinced that Shani was genuinely concerned. "My relatives all wanted me gone," she said. "You yourself wanted me gone." She couldn't keep the bitterness out of her voice.

"Oh, come now, it wasn't as bad as that." She said it idly, as if it had been a small matter. "You know, Mara, you can be a difficult person to get along with. That's all."

So it was Mara's fault, and Shani was criticizing her, the same way Ternees always did. Shani was so comfortably wrapped up in her little world, presiding with her mother over the rest of the clan, Mara's problems were irrelevant to her.

Mara felt her distress turning to resentment. "So why did you come here?" she demanded.

Shani raised her palms toward Mara. "Sister, I thought you'd be pleased to see me."

Mara closed her eyes for a moment. "Just tell me why," she said.

Shani shrugged. "Well, I do have some news that I wanted to tell you." She gave Mara a strange, secret little smile. "I have chosen a mate."

"Ah." Mara lay back on the bed. She took a moment to adjust to this revelation. "I didn't know. I didn't even know you were in a courtship. Well! This is a surprise. Who is he?"

"He—" Shani broke off and looked down, frowning, as Claws crawled out from under the bed. He had finished eating and seemed curious now about this stranger in his home. He eyed her warily, then jumped up onto the bed beside Mara.

"I see you still have your animal," Shani said. Once again, her voice sounded disapproving.

"He's perfectly harmless," said Mara. She stroked Claws, trying to calm him.

Shani looked unconvinced. "Do you realize what people have been saying? They say that cat's an evil spirit, and there's something strange about the way it allies itself with you."

"Surely you don't believe that." Mara looked at her sister's face. "You don't, do you?"

Shani looked evasive. "Well, Mara, I don't know. It does seem ... unnatural, the way that it behaves with you."

Mara sighed. "This is just a cat that chooses to live here instead of in the forest. Now tell me, who it is you've chosen. That's obviously what you really came to talk about."

Shani forced her eyes away from the cat. She straightened her robe and clasped her hands back in her lap. "I've chosen Ipaw," she said.

Mara stared at her. There was a long moment of silence. Suddenly she laughed. "Your cousin Ipaw?"

"Yes." The muscles in Shani's face tightened as she heard Mara's tone of voice.

"But ... he's so timid. He doesn't even hunt. Shani, are you serious?"

For the first time during her visit, Shani's serenity seemed ruffled. She glared at Mara. "You're very impolite." She drew herself up. "There are more important things in a man than how well he hunts." There was a little tic at the side of her cheek. "Why, I should have thought you would have learned that by now."

"What do you mean?" Mara sat up. The quick motion startled Claws, who jumped away from her, flattening his ears.

Shani gave her a challenging look. "Why, everyone in the village knows how Kormor treats you."

Mara swung her legs over the side of the bed—then paused, feeling tension seize her stomach so tightly, it made her nauseous. "It's none of their business," she said, speaking the words with difficulty. "My life with my mate is a private matter."

Shani shook her hair back with an angry toss of her head. "But Dira has told everyone. Are you really pretending that you didn't know?"

Mara felt as if she had just been struck in the chest. She blundered past Shani, out of her home, into the bright sunlight. She took a few shaky steps, then dropped down onto her knees at the edge of the lake. She clutched her stomach, doubled forward, and vomited into the tall reeds.

Slowly the spasms subsided. Mara kneeled there for a long moment, taking slow breaths. She stared ahead, not really seeing the lake sparkling in the sun, not really hearing the voices of children playing in the water.

"Mara." It was a man's voice. "Mara, what's wrong?"

She turned and looked up. "Ipaw," she said, with dull surprise. He was tall and thin, with a round head that looked too large for his body. He was always smiling, always good-natured, but so shy, he never seemed able to look anyone in the eye. It was inconceivable, Mara thought, that Shani had really chosen him as her mate.

"What's wrong?" Ipaw asked again.

Mara struggled up. "Just ... feeling bad about something." She shook her head, trying to clear it. "It seems every time something bothers me, it goes to my stomach."

"You should get a remedy," said Shani, emerging from Mara's home. She paused and adjusted her deerskin around her. "Some chokecherry, or some mountain ash."

"Red elderberry," said Ipaw. "That always settles my stomach."

"Yes, thank you," said Mara, not wanting to see or talk to either of them anymore.

"You should ask Dira," said Ipaw. He nodded encouragingly. "She knows a lot about herbs."

For a moment Mara wondered if he was making fun of her. But no; that wasn't his way.

"Did you hear," said Shani, "Dira moved into the old Spirit House? Just two days ago. Mother suggested it." She eyed Mara calmly, waiting for her reaction.

"The Spirit House?" Mara stared at her in disbelief.

Shani shrugged. "Lizel has been gone for months, and it doesn't look as if she's coming back. Dira has been helping people for some time, now, and she does seem to have some skill. Why not take advantage of it?" She smiled faintly. "The woman has her uses—even if she does tend to talk a little too freely." She fussed with her hair, then turned to Ipaw and gave him a wide, radiant smile. "I'm sorry, Ipaw. I kept you waiting much too long. We can go now."

Ipaw looked at her, and his eyes shone. He shyly took her hand. "I didn't mind waiting," he said. "It's such a pleasant day."

"Good-bye, Mara," said Shani. "Take care of yourself."

"Come and visit," Ipaw added. But his attention was already shifting away from Mara. Once again, he looked at Shani with simple, wide-eyed love.

Mara stood and watched in silence as the two of them walked away along the lakeshore.

Chapter 12

A little later, she stood outside the Spirit House. The great bulk of the building, which had once seemed so full of excitement and mystery, now seemed dark and threatening. Once again, Mara felt a deep sense of injustice. It was a violation of all that was right for Dira to be in this sacred place.

Of course, she understood why Ternees had allowed it. Ternees believed that everyone had some goodness or some usefulness, and a leader should promote each person's gift so that it could benefit the whole tribe. If Graum lied, or Dira spread gossip, that was wrong, and Ternees would encourage everyone to show their disapproval. But she would never punish anyone, because that would cause resentment—negative feelings which could ultimately create harm. And she would never cast them out, because that would mean losing their usefulness.

Mara forced herself forward. She pushed the door flap aside and walked in.

Dira was sitting by the fire in the center of the house, talking to a man and a woman while her boy, Joh, worked silently in the shadows, pressing some wildflowers between two stones, one round, the other dish-shaped. Mara waited patiently near the edge of the house, saying nothing. She watched Joh pick up the dish-shaped stone with its puddle of sap and place it before the couple. The woman drank from it. Then the two of them thanked Dira, and they left, walking past Mara without seeming to notice her in the dimness.

Mara moved forward. "Dira," she said.

The little woman looked up, with her mouth widening in an ugly smile. But her smile vanished as she saw who it was. There was suspicion in her small, black eyes as she looked at Mara.

"I see you've made yourself at home here," Mara said.

Dira didn't answer her directly. "We've all been wondering about you, Mara," she said. "We haven't seen you in so long. Are you well?"

Mara squatted opposite the woman, trying to hide the emotions that she felt. She sensed that if Dira saw any sign of weakness, she would use it against her in some way. "I'm quite well," she said. "I just came here ... to see you in your new home." And really, that was the truth of the matter. She had wanted to see this with her own eyes.

Dira gave her an artificial smile. "How kind of you," she said. "I hope you understand, I don't ever imagine I could take Lizel's place. But I seem to have some talent as a healer, even though it's not what I really want. In fact it's really very tiring, coping with so many people's problems. I wish there was someone else to help them. But there isn't and so ..." she shrugged, "I do what I can."

The words sounded sincere, yet there was something about the sound of them that told Mara this was a speech that Dira had given many times before. What was its real intention? Why, it was meant to make people feel grateful to Dira for making such a noble sacrifice. It was meant to convince them that she was serving the tribe out of kindness and duty. And instinctively, Mara sensed that this was a lie. Dira was here for only one reason: it suited her purposes somehow.

Would anyone else in the village sense that about her? The Lake People were kind, generous, and naturally trusting. They were slow to judge, quick to forgive. If Dira said she was driven by a noble sense of duty, they probably believed her.

"So, is there something I can do for you?" Dira said, still with her fixed smile.

"No," said Mara, standing up. She took a step backward. "No, thank you. Not now." She turned, then paused. Faintly, from outside, she heard people shouting. There were cries of welcome.

"That must be my husband, back from the hunt," said Dira. Her smile shifted. Suddenly it was a genuine look of happiness. Quickly, she stood up. She pushed past Mara and hurried out of the House.

The young hunters were dragging their trophies into the Meeting Place. Each pair of men pulled a travois between them, and each travois was groaning with game. There were at least a dozen white-tailed deer, a couple of mule deer, some rabbits, a wolf, several mountain goats, and two bison. Graum was supervising, shouting orders while the hunters heaved the game off their sleds and laid it out in a long line. A couple dozen villagers were inspecting the animals, shouting congratulations to the hunters, while the bodies of the dead animals thumped down onto the packed earth and the hunters wiped sweat from their faces as they labored under the hot sun.

Ternees came out of her Clan House. She shaded her eyes for a moment, taking in the scene. Her face was composed; her expression was unreadable. If she was pleased by the size of the catch, she didn't show it.

Looking at her mother, Mira felt a sudden need to talk to her. It seemed so very long since they had last spoken. But then she checked herself. What was she hoping for, really? Acceptance, perhaps, or affection. But could she really expect to receive that? If she humbled herself, perhaps, and bent herself into the form that Ternees considered correct. Mara shook her head, feeling tormented by the problem that had haunted her for so much of her life. If she wanted her mother's kindness and attention, she would have to surrender her own self to receive it.

Mara turned away—and she noticed Yacor walking into the Meeting Place. The elder hunter stopped and shaded his eyes, assessing the game as Ternees had done. His face turned grim. He saw Ternees and strode across to her.

Mara was too far away to hear their conversation, but she saw Yacor making sharp, impatient gestures, and she saw Ternees laying her hand on his shoulder to calm him.

A moment later, the Chieftain walked to the Speaking Stone. She stepped up onto it and raised her hands. "Hear me," she called out.

The villagers in the Meeting Place turned toward her. The hunters paused in their work, and the noise quickly died down. Dust drifted slowly in the hot midday sun. Flies hummed to and fro and hawks wheeled silently above, attracted by the fresh meat below.

"Our fine young hunters have done well," Ternees said. She nodded to Graum and to the men near him. "We will eat generously tonight." She paused. "But let me speak plainly. There are some people who feel that you may be taking too much from the land."

The young hunters glanced at each other, then at Graum, automatically turning to him for guidance. Mara saw Kormor standing with his arms folded, close beside the big man. Kormor's face was streaked with mud. His bare forearms were smeared with dirt and dried animal blood. His long hair was dull with dust, and there were blades of grass caught in it. His hunting robe was torn, and his body was crisscrossed with scratches. But he was proud and he stood with his head held high.

Graum, meanwhile, said nothing, and his face showed nothing. He waited in silence.

"Graum," said Terness, "we shouldn't deplete the land. If we take too much this year, we may go hungry in years to come. We must never forget the terrible lesson of the North Lands. We must conserve our game."

"There's no comparison." It was Kormor who spoke. He stepped forward. "With respect, you have never been to the North Lands. It's nothing like this. We have a feast here. There's no shortage of game."

Ternees frowned at him, obviously insulted by his bluntness. "Even so," she said, "it's wise—"

Kormor gestured impatiently. "Yacor is the only one who wants us to hunt less. I saw him advising you there. With all respect, he was a fine hunter in his day, but that day has passed. He hates to see us bringing in so much game, because he knows he lacks the strength and skill himself. It shames him."

The silence in the Meeting Place was ominous now.

People glanced at Yacor. He was known to be patient, placid, friendly to everyone. But he was a fine hunter, and he had his pride. He glared at Kormor. "You have no right—" he began.

"I have a right to speak the truth," said Kormor, calmly and flatly. He gestured at Graum. "This man leads us well. He tracks game better than anyone we have ever known. We should be thanking him, not criticizing him, for the food that he's led us to."

Yacor took a step toward Kormor. "You listen to me." He paused, and Mara saw that he was trying to contain his temper. "You should know—you should all know— it's the way of our tribe to hunt no more than we need. We don't kill just for the sake of killing." His lips drew back from his teeth. "We are not boys trying to make ourselves look like men."

Mara felt the tension growing. People were looking worried now. This kind of conflict had always been rare, and they abhorred it. A couple of elders moved toward Yacor as if they feared they might have to restrain him.

"What's that on your hands, Yacor?" Kormor called out.

Yacor hesitated. The question seemed to throw him off balance.

"It's berry juice, isn't it?" Kormor shouted. "You've been picking berries with the women, Yacor. What right do you have to tell us about hunting?"

Now Yacor could no longer contain himself. He clenched his fists. "Boy, you'll apologize for that."

"No." The word came from Ternees, sharp and loud. "Hear me. Stop this."

Yacor ignored her. He took another step toward Kormor. The elders hurried over and grabbed his arms.

"Stop!" Ternees shouted.

Yacor glanced at Ternees, and his anger seemed to waver. Kormor, meanwhile, stood impassively, saying nothing.

"Yacor, this is not our way," Ternees said sharply.

Yacor blinked. He muttered something, glared at the young hunters, and spat on the ground.

"There will be no more insults," Ternees went on, eyeing Kormor, now. "Do you understand?"

Kormor looked up at her. He took his time, then nodded slowly.

"Good." Ternees paused. "Now, you will tell me clearly and truly, please. Is the game being depleted, or not?"

Kormor opened his mouth to speak, but Graum placed his hand on his shoulder and motioned him to be silent. "I agree with you," the big man said. "There's no need for unpleasantness here. You know how it is with young men. They feel a strong passion for what they do."

Ternees gave him an impatient look. "I merely want to know—"

He held up his hands. "I'll answer your question. There's no shortage of game. There's as much as you want—" he grinned at her, "if you know where to look for it."

Ternees studied him. She didn't return his smile. She turned back to Yacor. "Have you noticed fewer animals out on the land?"

He gave Graum a disparaging glance. "Yes," he said.

"Not true!" shouted Kormor. And suddenly all the young hunters were speaking out, yelling their defiance.

Graum turned and eyed them sternly. Within a few moments, they quieted down. "Now, let's show some respect," he said to them. "Ternees is our leader. She's just looking for the truth here, isn't that so?" He turned back to her. "Like I say, there's no shortage of game." He spread his hands. "In fact, I don't know what all the fuss is about."

Ternees was silent for a long moment. "The question is hard to answer," she said. "But I think we should be guided by the traditions laid down by my ancestors. When in doubt, we will exercise caution." She nodded to herself, reaching a decision. "This is the fruit-picking season. There's certainly no shortage of wild berries. For the next two weeks, Graum, you and your young men will do no more hunting. You will help on the hillsides, gathering berries. I have decided, and it is so."

There was a moment of surprised silence. Mara saw

the anger in Kormor's eyes, and she knew it well. She knew, too, that it wouldn't be easily quenched. Abruptly, he banged the blunt end of his spear down into the dirt. "This is wrong," he said.

The other young hunters started murmuring their agreement.

"Quiet!" Graum told them.

They looked at him in surprise. Almost at once, they fell silent.

"It's every man's duty to obey the leader of the tribe," Graum said. He turned back to Ternees. "Naturally, we'll do as you say." He inclined his head respectfully, although Mara sensed there was something other than respect in his quick, dark eyes.

"Thank you, Graum." Ternees stepped down stiffly from the Speaking Stone, and the tension of the moment was suddenly over.

Yacor strode past Mara with his shoulders bunched, his jaw set. He ignored the people around him as he left the Meeting Place.

The rest of the villagers were gathering into little groups, talking in low, urgent voices, glancing after Yacor, then looking uneasily at Graum and his men.

"You see," said a quiet voice, "Mother has no trouble keeping Graum in his place."

Mara turned and found Shani standing just behind her, with Ipaw close by, smiling shyly.

"Graum chose to back down," Mara said to her sister. "No one forced him to."

Shani looked at Mara as if she found her faintly amusing. "Do you really think anyone would have put up with him if he had defied her?"

Mara felt herself getting irritated. "There's no point in talking about this, Shani," she said. "We're not going to agree." She turned away. "Excuse me, please. I must speak with my mate." She walked across the Meeting Place, threading her way between the clusters of people. "Kormor," she called out.

He turned to her. As he looked at her, something seemed to close inside him. He became cautious and reserved. They had sparred so often in the past months, neither of them was very open toward the other anymore.

"You spoke well," she said to him, loudly enough for others to hear.

He nodded, but said nothing.

She took his arm and pulled him closer. "I'm told that Dira has been spreading gossip about us," she murmured into his ear. "It might help if we seem to be friendly in front of everyone."

She saw his eyes change as he understood her. But then, just as quickly, he shrugged her hand away. "It doesn't matter what people say," he told her. "And in any case, if you really want to stop them from gossiping, it's really very simple. You should give them less to gossip about."

He turned his back, then. He went over to the heaps of game and started shouting instructions to the other young hunters, arranging for the animals to be gutted and skinned.

Chapter 13

She was alone during most of the afternoon. Without a doubt, Kormor would have preferred her to be out there in the Meeting Place, helping to roast some of the meat, setting some of it out to dry, and smoking the rest. Maybe if she worked hard and followed his instructions as a dutiful wife, then he would be kinder to her—although secretly she doubted it.

She realized that she had the same problem with him that she had with her mother. Ternees and Kormor both wanted her to be meek and dutiful, without a will of her own. Why did it have to be that way? Did they find her so unappealing as she really was?

She lay with Claws on the bed, watching him doze through the afternoon. Sometimes he had little cat dreams that made his paw twitch and his lips draw back from his teeth, and she wondered if he was dreaming of hunting small creatures out in the grasslands. His life seemed so simple compared with hers. All he needed was to hunt, to eat, and to sleep. She found herself envying him.

Later, she heard Graum's young hunters shouting to each other and singing hunting songs as they washed themselves in the lake and dried themselves in the sun. Finally, as the sun dipped toward the mountains, Kormor returned home.

It seemed clear, though, he was not plannning to stay for long. He glanced at her and her cat, but he said nothing as he went to the corner where he kept his hunting supplies. Methodically, he started laying out crude sections of chert—glossy white triangles of flint streaked with faint veins of gray. These were blanks that had been traded to the Lake People by the Silver River People. One day, these blanks would be used to make spear points.

"What are you doing?" she asked, sitting up on the bed. Beside her, Claws had opened his eyes and was watching Kormor enigmatically.

"I'm going out," he said, selecting six of the blanks, bagging them, and putting the rest back in storage.

"At this time of day?" She frowned. He seldom liked to begin a journey at night. The tribe where he had grown up, in the North Lands, had been deeply superstitious about night creatures. They believed that bats and owls contained the souls of men who had died dishonorably and were condemned to roam forever through the darkness, never finding a resting place. Mara had dismissed this as a foolish fantasy, but Kormor was still deeply serious about it.

"It's time," Kormor said, "for Graum to show us how he hardens his flints." He pulled on a fresh hunting robe, then slung his bag over his shoulder.

"In the nighttime?"

"Yes. It can only be done in darkness, so we're sure of privacy." He left, then, without looking back.

Much later, before it was light, she heard him return. There were muffled sounds of movement, then the whisper of a firestick. She opened her eyes, rolled over, and saw him squatting near the door flap, which had been opened so that the moonlight flooded in. He was spinning the stick quickly between his palms, pausing to nudge small particles of tinder around the tip of the rod, then spinning it some more, till it glowed dim red where it pressed into its wooden socket. A yellow flame flickered, and Kormor fed wood shavings into it. Soon a fire was burning. He took a small twig, lit the end, then used it to light a lump of elk fat in a stone dish near the corner of the tent.

"What are you doing?" she called softly to him.

He glanced at her. "Working," he said.

She scrambled up and pulled a skin around her shoul-

ders. The tent never held much of the daytime heat, and
the air around her was chilly. Claws had gone, she realized; he was out hunting.

She moved over and saw that Kormor had once again
laid out the six rough triangles of chert. But they were
no longer white; they were pink.

Mara picked one of them up. The transformation was
eerie. She rubbed her thumb across the rough edge, then
scraped it with her nail. "It's no sharper," she said.

"But it's harder," he said. "Give it here." He held out
his palm.

In the flickering yellow light, she noticed the round
circle of scar tissue on his hand, puckered and ugly. The
wound had healed, as he'd said it would; but it had disfigured him, and his hand would never be as limber as
it had been before.

Reluctantly, she gave the chert back to him. "How was
it changed?"

Kormor shook his head. "I can't tell you that."

"You can't?" She sat back on the bed and drew her
knees up, hugging them against herself. "You mean you
don't know?"

He gave her an annoyed look. "Graum showed his
hunters the secret. But he made us swear to tell no
one else."

"Ah," she said. "So you are one of *his* hunters, now."

"Of course I am," he said.

She wrinkled her nose. "You make it sound as if he
owns you."

He glared at her and slowly flexed the fingers of his
right hand.

"Are you going to hit me again?" she said, lowering
her voice, watching him steadily, refusing to show weakness, even after all the times he'd forced her to yield to
him. "Everyone knows about it, Kormor. I told you in
the Meeting Place, Dira has gossiped about us. People
know that we fight with each other and you hurt me."

He pushed himself up, moving swiftly. He stood over
her. "I don't believe Dira told them. I think it was you."

"Ah," she said, understanding him now. "You think
I'm trying to embarrass you in front of my people."

"Yes." He glared at her.

"But you're wrong. I'm too ashamed to tell anyone. Shani said that Dira has been gossiping. I always knew that ugly little woman was like poison. Her and her husband." She stared up at him, trying not to flinch, waiting to see if he was going to seize hold of her, as he sometimes did.

She saw the anger growing in him, and even though it scared her, it gave her a small feeling of satisfaction. Really, the only power she had over him these days was to make him angry. But even that was better than no power at all.

He seemed to be fighting inside himself. Finally he grunted in disgust and turned away. "I've got no time for this. I have work to do." He went back to the corner where the flame burned.

Bit by bit, Mara felt the tension drain out of her. Then, without warning, nausea gripped her. She clutched her stomach and rolled onto her side. She retched feebly.

He paused and looked at her.

Another spasm caught her. She seized the piece of birch bark where she had laid out food for Shani. She spat a little bile onto it. And then, blessedly, her stomach quieted. "It's nothing." She wiped her mouth on the back of her hand. "It just happens when I'm upset."

He watched her for a moment more. "Instead of sneering at Dira, you might ask for her help."

"There's nothing wrong with me," Mara said sharply.

He settled himself cross-legged on the floor and turned away from her. He set one of the blanks on a piece of soft sandstone with a hollow that had been abraded in its center. Then he strapped a flat piece of birch wood across his chest, and he picked up a deer antler. He braced the broad end of the antler against the block of birch, then aimed the tip of the antler against the edge of the pink chert. He leaned slowly forward, using the weight of his body to bear down with the sharp bone tip. He grunted with the effort, and there was a faint *chunk* as the antler tip pried away a tiny flake of chert and jumped down into the sandstone block beneath.

Kormor leaned back, turned over the chert, reposi-

tioned the antler, and repeated the process. Judging from
the amount of strength he had to use, the chert truly had
been hardened. Mara wondered how it had been done.
But, she realized, that was the game that Graum
played—a game of secrets that seemed valuable just because they were secrets. And the secrets always had to
be earned in some way, usually involving sacrifice or
pain. Really, it wasn't important whether flint was white
or black or pink. Any spear head would pierce an animal's flesh. The whole thing was childish—and yet, her
husband seemed completely absorbed in it, as if it were
the most important thing in his life.

Mara placed her palms over her stomach, hoping that
the warmth would ease the last of the nausea away.
Could there really be something wrong with her? That
was an awful thought, because she didn't think she could
bear to ask Dira for a remedy.

She woke to the *clink, clink* of stone on stone. She
opened her eyes and blinked. Brilliant sun was beaming
in through the open door flap. Kormor was still sitting
in the same place, still working. He had chipped away
the chert with infinite care, giving it two gently curved
cutting edges. Now he was using a hammer stone to chip
larger flakes from the base, to make a gutter which would
fit into the slot of the end of a spear shaft. The spear
head was almost finished.

"Aren't you tired?" she said.

"Yes," he said flatly, without bothering to look at her.
She saw that his eyes were bleary and his face was pale
from lack of sleep. "Don't interrupt me. If I make a
mistake now, the point could be ruined." Carefully he
positioned a short, thin chisel stone. Then he raised the
larger, rounded stone that he was using as his hammer,
and he brought it down with precise force of the chisel.
He grunted with satisfaction as another flake of chert
was chipped away.

"I'm going out," she told him, "to help with the gathering." That would be better than lying here watching
him ignore her. It seemed so stupid, so wrong that they
should spend their lives like this, circling around each

other, bickering with each other. At first she had tried to be gentle and kind toward him. That worked—but only for a while. Sooner or later, she always disagreed with him over some little thing, and he couldn't stand that. Really, the only way to please him was to surrender her own self completely. And even though she would have cherished the peace it would bring, she simply couldn't do it.

"I'll be out on the hillside myself in a little while," he said without looking up.

"You will?" She looked at him in surprise.

"Of course. Graum gave his word. So we'll be there for the fruit picking."

There was a strange mood in the people who moved together across the hillsides gathering ripe berries. Mara remembered how they had been in previous years, men and women working side by side, singing together, stripped half naked under the late-summer sun, knowing that soon enough its heat would be gone and the land would be claimed by winter. Berry gathering was a happy ritual. The people delved into thickets and hacked branches off the bushes with stone tools, then dragged the branches out and shook the berries off, catching them in deerskins draped over poles.

But there was little singing this year, and no one spoke very much. The day was cruelly hot, and the heat was so damp, it made everyone irritable. Some of the older men were still grumbling about the way Yacor had been treated in the Meeting Place yesterday. Fathers were snapping at their children, complaining that they should work harder. Women complained at their husbands for being so short-tempered.

Graum's young hunters came out as he had promised, but they didn't appear till midday, and they seemed too tired to do any real work. They sat around in the shade of the pine trees, sometimes napping in the tall grass, sometimes picking arguments with people working near them. The young hunters complained that berry-picking wasn't even necessary. They had already spent long, hard days hunting game and bringing it back to the village.

The supply caches were almost full. There was no need for extra food.

Graum chose not to involve himself in any of the arguments. He spent most of his time supervising Dira and Joh, and he made sure they harvested a good share of the fruit. In some way that Mara couldn't pin down, he seemed to be biding his time.

As the day wore on and tempers wore thin, Mara half expected Ternees to talk to her people and scold the young men. But of course, that was not her way. She had already said what should be done. Now she would merely show the way and wait for others to follow of their free will. If someone was truly obstinate and went against the spirit of the tribe, that person would simply be ignored. Sooner or later, the weight of everyones's silent disapproval would become hard to bear—as Mara had found herself, many times. To be a rebel among the Lake People meant being shunned by one's friends, one's clan, and even one's closest family. Few people could stand that for long.

But Graum's young hunters just seemed to grow more defiant as the afternoon wore on. There was a feeling of growing unease, a sense of growing anger. Dark, towering clouds had gathered above the mountains around the valley, and it seemed as if a thunderstorm might dispel the oppressive heat. Yet the sky remained clear overhead, and there was no relief from the heat.

Then they heard a cry.

A tiny figure was running across the valley, coming from the tall cliffs that lay to the north. As he came closer, Mara recognized him. He was Lumo, a strange, solitary boy who often went away on his own, exploring the farthest trails that led into the tall slopes to the north. Sometimes he came back with a rabbit or a squirrel that he had snared. More often, he came back with nothing.

Today, though, he brought something far more valuable than any small piece of game. "Mastodon!" he was crying as he leaped through the tall grass. "Six! Up on the cliffs! Mastodon! I saw them!"

One by one, the villagers ceased their work and started picking their way down the rugged hillside, dragging their bags of berries behind them. Ternees hurried over to the boy, and Yacor and Tiear joined her. All the villagers came clustering around.

Yacor knelt beside Lumo. "You are sure, now?" he said. "Six mastodon. All of them together."

"I saw them!" Lumo's young face was deeply serious. "And they were mastodon. Smaller than mammoth. Thinner coat, brown, not gray."

"Yes. I saw two bulls, three females, and one little one."

"Explain to us where they were," Tiear said. "And tell us which way they were going."

Haltingly, Lumo described the path he had taken. It wasn't far; less than a quarter-day's journey. There was a narrow valley where the soil was too thin for trees to grow, and the grass was fresh and green, the way the big beasts liked it. Still, there wouldn't be enough there to feed them for long. Soon they'd be searching for fresh pastures, and they'd be gone. The villagers would have to act quickly.

"It's unusual," Yacor said, "for them to have climbed up there. I've seldom seen them off the valley floor."

"They're eager for food anywhere they can find it, this time of year," said Kormor.

Yacor glanced in his direction, barely acknowledging him. "I'm aware of that," he said.

"Very well," said Ternees. "It's been more than a year since we last saw mastodon here. This is an opportunity we shouldn't miss. Yacor, you will plan the hunt."

There were sounds of protest from the young hunters. But Graum held up his hand. "We'll be happy," he announced, "to put our trust in Yacor and follow his plan, whatever it may be. He's a wise man with great experience. He can count on our support."

Mara stared at Graum's fat, complacent face, trying to see what lay behind it. But he seemed for all the world to be amiable, respectful, and ready to do his part.

Chapter 14

At dawn the next day, Mara was out on the cliffs. The storm had still not broken and the clouds had sunk lower, obliterating the sun. The world was now a dim gray place, and the warm air felt so moist, it seemed to leave damp traces on her skin.

Mara picked her way up the zigzag path on the cliff face, following a line of toiling figures, with more climbing behind her. Almost every able-bodied person had come out for the hunt. Only mothers with young children had been left behind. Together the people made the climb, toiling in the humid heat, pausing often to wipe away sweat that stung their eyes.

Mara moved cautiously, probing the path with the end of her spear shaft, fearing that if she suffered another of her bouts of nausea and dizziness, it might kill her. The path was narrow and treacherous, with some of the footholds barely visible in the soft, crumbling rock. Legend had it that Laena, Mother of the Lake People, had carved this trail many generations ago after she came down from the high mountains to the north. Each time Mara came here, she thought of her blood link with Laena. She liked to imagine that Laena's spirit might still be dwelling up on these rocky heights, somehow watching over her.

Mara reached a turn in the path and glanced down. Far below, at the base of the cliffs, women were setting fires and lashing together simple wooden racks to dry and smoke the mastodon meat. Meanwhile, up above, the first of the villagers had reached the top of the climb. Mara saw the tiny black figures silhouetted against the lowering sky.

A little later, she was up at the top herself. Some people were sitting and resting. Others were pacing around, eager to move on. Mara sensed anticipation in her people, and yet the angry mood of the previous day remained unresolved. Few faces were smiling. There was little talking and no laughter. Frequently Mara saw people glancing apprehensively at the dark sky.

"Listen, now," Ternees addressed them, "Yacor will lead us around to the top of the narrow valley where the herd is. His scouts have already come back to us. They've placed smoke fires at the bottom end of the valley to hold the animals there. Our elder hunters are taking positions along the ridges on either side. Graum and his young men will move to the bottom of the valley, and they'll douse the fires when Yacor gives his signal. Do you all understand?"

No one spoke. The plan had been formulated the previous night, and everyone had heard of it by now. Describing it was a formality, to make doubly sure that there would be no mistakes.

"All right," Ternees said, "the rest of us will follow Yacor now."

Yacor surveyed everyone, then turned and started away from the cliff edge, across a rocky plateau dotted with clumps of grass and a few hardy, scrawny trees. At the northern edge of it there were steepening hillsides, and farther along, in one of the great furrows in the land, the herd of mastodon grazed.

Mara sensed someone near her. She looked around and saw Lomel, a girl she hardly knew. Lomel was Tiear's daughter; she had come over the mountains from the North Lands just two years ago with her father, her mother, and her brother, Arin, who had since become one of Graum's young hunters. Tiear's family had built themselves a sturdy house from heavy pine logs that they had dragged halfway across the valley. They were tough, hardworking people.

"Hello, Mara," Lomel said. "Do you mind if I walk with you? I've never been up into this part of the land before."

Mara looked at Lomel's face. It seemed honest and

open. She had clear eyes and a shy smile. "Of course you can walk with me," Mara said. "But didn't you come this way when you made the great journey over the mountains?"

Lomel shook her head. "We were farther east, I think." She squinted into the dim light. "It's hard for me to remember. I was so exhausted then. Arin had to carry me some of the way. You know my brother, don't you?"

"I've seen him with Graum's hunters."

"Yes," said Lomel. Her face clouded for a moment.

Mara looked at the girl a little more carefully. She wasn't tall, and she had a stocky build, with thick, powerful arms and legs. Her hair, too, was thick, tied back loosely so that it fanned down her back. Her face, though, was her best feature, very friendly and kind.

"You're fourteen now?" Mara asked.

Lomel nodded.

"So you were only twelve when you came over the peaks. Young, for such a great journey."

Lomel smiled, showing strong, even teeth. "My parents made sure I was tough enough," she said. "Tiear always gave me the heaviest chores to do."

Mara sensed something behind that statement—a life that might not have been happy, even though Lomel seemed philosophical about it now. "Does it bother you," Mara said, "that your brother has started hunting with Graum?"

Lomel looked cautious. "Why?"

Mara wondered what she should say. "Some of the young men," she said, "seem to have changed now that Graum's leading them. They're more aggressive, and they don't listen to anyone else. Don't you think?"

Now it was Lomel's turn to choose her words carefully. "I trust Arin," she said. "He's a good person. You know, he just came of age, and it's natural for him to want to prove himself." She fell silent, but she didn't seem to have finished. Suddenly she looked directly at Mara. "I saw you in the Meeting Place, on the day after Graum arrived in our tribe," she said.

Mara felt a little twinge in her stomach. She hated to be reminded of that time.

"You were brave, facing him like that," Lomel went on. Her face was very serious now. "I think our people should have supported you more."

Mara gave the girl a searching look. But there was no deviousness in the girl's eyes. She spoke simply and truly. "Thank you," said Mara, feeling surprised. Impulsively, she took Lomel's hand and squeezed it. Then she quickly released it, feeling foolish.

"Is something wrong?" Lomel asked.

Mara turned away. "Nothing's wrong. But ... there aren't many people who seem to feel the way you do, Lomel. I don't have many friends at the moment."

Lomel tilted her head to one side. "You're the Chieftain's daughter."

"Younger daughter." Mara felt like saying more, but she checked herself. She shouldn't pour out her feelings to this relative stranger. "We can talk more about this some other time," she said, "if you want."

Lomel shrugged. "As you wish."

They had almost reached the slopes at the inside edge of the plateau now. Just ahead, the land started rising steeply. Yacor was leading the way, with Ternees just behind him, and Shani and Ipaw following her. Mara watched for a moment, smiling faintly as she saw Ipaw moving clumsily, ducking and bobbing from one foothold to the next.

Yacor, meanwhile, was taking his time. He knew that many people in the party were less agile than he was. There were other men like Ipaw who lacked hunting skills. There were also some grandfathers and grandmothers for whom the pace had to be slow.

Mara started up the slope, picking her way from one boulder to the next. She settled into a calm, easy rhythm, concentrating mainly on the ground under her feet, while Lomel followed close behind her. It would have been a pleasant climb if it weren't for the hot, stormy weather. The dark clouds now seemed so close above, she felt as if she might be able to reach up and trail her fingers through the dangling wisps of grayness.

"No more talking," Yacor called back from the head of the party as they neared the crest of the first hill. His order was relayed to those at the rear. He moved cautiously now, turning away from the summit and starting along a horizontal ridge that led to the east.

There was an unexpected gust of wind, bending tufts of tall grass and swaying the branches of a nearby pine. A hawk cried out overhead, complaining in the rough air. Mara followed the people ahead of her, watching an occasional grasshopper leap out of the way of her moccasins as she gently set them down. The hillside was strewn with yellow blossoms and tiny purple wildflowers. But she hardly saw these things. In her imagination, she was already looking on the beasts in the valley that lay ahead.

When they finally reached their destination, the fierce gusts of wind had started coming more often, alternating from the west and the east. Mara's skin prickled. She sensed that the storm was near.

Yacor was peering over a rill in the land that lay just ahead. He directed half of the people to his left, half to his right. He waited, watching carefully while they spread out. Mara reached a place where there was a flat rock that she could stand on, and she stopped there. She glanced at Lomel, just behind her. The two of them grinned at each other. There was a good, tense feeling, now. Mara remembered all the other mammoth and mastodon hunts that she had known—maybe a dozen altogether. There was always a thrill of danger, even though the male hunters were the ones who took the greatest risks. There was always the excitement of confronting great beasts that were so much larger than the largest man, and hearing their snorting and bellowing and the thundering of their hooves when they were forced to stampede.

Mara reached into her shoulder pack and pulled out her noisemaker—a clapper made from two wide, flat pieces of well-dried wood. All along the ridge, her companions were bringing out bone whistles, bull-roarers, and clappers like her own. They hunkered down, watching Yacor, waiting for his signal.

Mara saw him murmur something to Ternees, who was crouched close beside him. She glanced up at the sky, then nodded her assent. And then there was a long pause.

Mara waited, feeling increasingly impatient. Suddenly she realized Yacor was waiting for the storm.

Lightning was already flickering around the peaks to the north. A slow, deep rumble came echoing across the landscape. The wind picked up, died down, then blew hard again. The hawk was gone from the sky, having taken refuge somewhere. The grasshoppers had stopped singing. The landscape was barren of life. Every small, wild creature seemed to have hidden in its burrow.

The lightning flashed again, closer than before. Mara saw dark gray columns beneath the clouds as rain was vented down onto the land.

Yacor held up his hand, warning the people to wait just a few moments more. Another burst of lightning— and this time the thunder came sooner, in a loud crash. Without warning, the clouds opened overhead. Mara was suddenly drenched, and the thunder crashed again.

"Now!" Yacor shouted.

All the villagers leaped up. They ran over the top, down into the valley that lay beyond, screaming, shouting, blowing their whistles, whirling their bull-roarers. Mara saw the mastodon herd before her, wheeling and bellowing in fear as the rain hit them and the thunder crashed again and the horde of villagers came charging down the steep slope, doing everything they could to add to the din.

The elder hunters had come out of hiding farther along the valley, and they, too, were running down into it. They started casting their spears, not with any hope of killing the huge animals, but to sting them into action.

Mara jumped from one foothold to the next, slapping her clapper against her leg, clutching her spear in her free hand, and shouting till her throat hurt. Down in the valley, the mastodons were stampeding in terror—and the smoky fires that had kept them from leaving the valley had been quenched as Graum's young men threw earth over the smoldering wood and leaves.

Now came the treacherous part. The beasts were running faster than any man, pounding out of the valley, while the elder hunters chased them and the rest of the villagers followed along behind. The young hunters had been hiding behind some boulders just beyond. They jumped up now and ran forward, confronting the mastodons, hurling their own missiles.

The mastodons veered away from this new, sudden source of danger. They milled uncertainly for a moment. Through the heavy rain, Mara thought she saw Kormor casting his spear at the big bull that was the leader of the herd. The bull turned and charged on toward the southwest. The villagers yelled in exultation. The beasts were heading on a path, now, that would inexorably lead them back to the plateau and the cliffs that rimmed it.

Mara's legs were covered with bramble scratches, her hair was plastered to her face by the torrential rain, and one of her moccasins had almost been torn off her foot when she'd stepped into a gap between two rocks. Rain was running down her body, under her robe, but she didn't care. She finally descended to the floor of the valley, and now she could run faster on the gentler slope, eager to see the ending of this chase. Everyone around her was doing the same, leaping across the grassland with their spears held high.

Mara emerged onto the plateau. The land was more treacherous here, sprinkled with loose stones and crisscrossed with fissures that were half hidden under tufted grass. She saw several people go down, shouting in surprise and pain as they lost their footing and fell flat on the hard ground.

The mastodons, too, had difficulty with the terrain. They were stumbling, jostling one another, showing the whites of their eyes as they raised their heads and trumpeted, peering back through the rain at the people chasing after them.

Another peal of thunder sounded. It seemed to come from directly overhead. One of the beasts panicked. It charged forward—and found, too late, that it had reached the edge of the plateau. It tried to stop and turn, but the others had been blindly following it, and they were still pressing ahead. The animal yelled in terror as it lost its footing and toppled forward.

Mara ran to the edge and looked along the line of the cliffs, just in time to see the mastodon going over. It plummeted down, waving its legs, venting a terrible high-pitched scream as it fell. It smacked into the rocks at the foot of the cliffs, and at that moment, its screaming died. From beneath its brown hide, blood started seeping out. The bright red flowed over the rocks, washed by the pouring rain.

The others in the herd were more dangerous now. They saw the threat of the cliff edge, and they backed away from it, turning to face their pursuers. The rain eased off a little, and Mara got a clearer view of the great bull who still led the herd. He was twice her height, with great curving tusks that almost met in front of his trunk. He stamped on the rocky ground, tossed his head back, and yelled his defiance.

"Get back!" It was Yacor's voice. "Back toward the north! Let them go!"

Some people obeyed—but others clustered close to the beasts, still trying to force more of them over the cliff.

"Back!" Yacor shouted again.

Mara saw a couple of young hunters making a last rush forward, hurling their spears, hoping to lodge one in a mastodon's eye. She was almost certain that one of the men was Kormor.

"Back, or you'll be killed!" Yacor screamed.

Finally the men obeyed, and the five mastodons saw their chance to escape. They charged forward.

Mara leaped aside and took cover behind a boulder. The beasts thundered toward her, scattering loose fragments of rock. The ground trembled as they charged past. She heard the great panting noises that they made, and she smelled the heady odor of their bodies. Then they were gone, back toward the grasslands from where they had come.

The rain began to diminish. The storm had moved south, and the light was brightening a little.

One by one, the villagers started picking themselves up from where they had thrown themselves on the ground. Many people were laughing, letting go of all the tension. But Graum's young hunters were clustering around the elder hunters, and Mara heard shouts of anger.

She hurried forward, joining the crowd that was swiftly gathering. One of the men was less than an arm's length from Yacor, and Mara recognized him. He was Arin, Lomel's brother. He was shouting directly into Yacor's face. "We could have had them all! If you had taken the time and weakened them first, it would have been easy. All of them! We could have had all of them over the cliff!"

Yacor was saying nothing. He stood with the other elder hunters on either side of him, facing the young men, eying them coldly.

"Easy, now." It was Graum's voice. He moved into the crowd. "Take it easy. We killed one of the beasts, and no one got hurt. We have all the meat we need. That's what counts."

"But any hunter knows, you weaken the beasts before you attack them." It was Bumar, another of the young men. He was big for his age, slow-witted, and naturally aggressive. Mara had always instinctively avoided him. He looked at Graum, then at the people gathered around. "Everyone knows that."

"One was all we needed," Yacor said. "There was no cause to kill the rest, so there was no need to weaken them." He spoke calmly, but Mara could see the anger in him. His authority was normally never questioned this way.

"It was stupid to let the rest of them get away," said another of the youngsters.

"Show some respect, boy!" one of the elder hunters snapped at him.

"Why?" he snapped back, tossing his head defiantly.

"Ternees!" someone called. "Ternees must settle this!"

The people started turning away from the conflict. Gradually everyone fell silent—for Ternees was nowhere to be seen.

As the rain diminished to drizzle, Mara felt a strange, creeping, hollow sensation. The day was no different from before, yet she had the sudden sense of a dark, cold wind creeping across the plateau, cutting through her sodden clothes and eating into her. It was inexplicable that Ternees shouldn't be here. She would never leave her people at the end of a hunt.

"Maybe she stumbled and fell, back at the valley," someone said.

"No," said another voice. "I saw her down here, pursuing the beasts."

With a strange sense of unreality, Mara walked to the cliff edge. The landscape seemed to shift around her. She looked down to the base of the cliffs and saw the body of the mastodon, still lying where she had seen it before. The rain had almost stopped now, so the body of the beast was clearly visible. And just beyond it, she saw another shape—small and pale, like a strip of deerskin that had been thrown onto the rocks.

Mara felt her stomach churning. She had to reach out and steady herself. It was impossible, she told herself; and yet already, with a penetrating certainty, she saw that it was true.

Another of the villagers looked over the edge and saw what Mara had seen. The woman let out a terrible wail. Others came running—and within moments, all the villagers were crying out in horror, staring down at the broken, bloody body that had been dashed against the rocks and now lay lifeless under the torn gray sky.

Chapter 15

"I was afraid of this," Yacor said. "She was close to the herd. Much too close. I tried to call her back, but she didn't hear me. The animals crowded her over the edge." He pressed the palms of his hands to his face for a moment, then threw his arms wide. "I told everyone to move back," he said, looking around for reassurance. "The young hunters were pushing forward—"

"We did nothing wrong." It was Kormor speaking, cold and defiant.

Yacor turned and gazed at him sadly. "Whatever was done wrong," he said, "I was the leader of the hunt." He took a deep, slow breath. "What has happened here is all my fault."

Shani was close by. She looked pale, and she was crying. "You are not to blame," she said softly, placing her arm around Yacor's shoulders. "It was an accident, Yacor. Please don't punish yourself for this."

At the bottom of the cliffs, the people made a simple wooden frame. Yacor stretched his hunting robe across it, and then, tenderly, he helped to move Ternees's broken body onto the improvised stretcher.

She was carried across the valley on the shoulders of six of the elder hunters. They started chanting a death song, their voices rising and falling on the wind. A long procession of villagers followed them, making their way in silence through the tall grass.

Mara took her place beside Yacor, directly behind the stretcher, with Shani beside her. Mara found herself trying to think of something to say to her sister—something kind, or stoic, or hopeful. But her mind seemed dead, empty of thoughts. It was incomprehensible that her mother was no longer alive. It simply made no sense. And because of that, the world itself suddenly seemed meaningless. She felt the ground through the thin soles of her moccasins, yet she didn't really feel it at all. The wind brushed her face, but that, too, seemed to be happening to someone else.

Mara glanced at Shani. Her face was deeply sad, but she still managed to seem calm. What was she thinking and feeling? Mara couldn't even imagine what was going on inside her sister's head.

She turned to Yacor—and with dismay, she saw that he was crying silently, walking with a heavy tread, staring straight ahead at the stretcher carrying Ternees's body.

"Yacor," she said softly, touching his arm, "my sister spoke truly. No one blames you."

He turned his troubled face toward her. "You know, I actually saw her fall," he said. "The animals pushed her over. I just couldn't believe it. I told myself it hadn't happened."

They were close to the village now, and some of the mothers who had been left behind came running out, shouting their concern. The stretcher bearers called out the news, and there was a new bout of grief-stricken wailing. The sound seemed to close in around Mara, filling her head, and it seemed intolerable. Her own feelings were so mixed up, she needed to clear her head and make sense of them. She couldn't think with all the noise around her.

She turned away from the procession and started running, ignoring people's questioning cries as she headed around the village, toward the lake.

There, finally, she slumped down amid the tall rushes on the shore, completely alone. She gulped air, feeling dizzy and distraught. She closed her eyes, blotting out the world. And now, finally, she discovered her grief. She clutched herself and started crying uncontrollably.

Faintly, from the direction of the village, came the sound of chanting and the slow beat of a drum. Mara was lying on her back, staring at the sky, remembering her mother, thinking of all the things that had never been said or done. They had never understood each other, that was clear enough. Ternees didn't understand why Mara needed to go her own way. Mara couldn't understand why her mother couldn't tolerate her independence. That was the saddest part: The gulf had never been properly bridged. Ternees had failed, and Mara had failed.

She heard footsteps brushing through the grass along the lakeshore, and she saw a figure approaching. It was Kormor, she realized. He was scanning the tall reeds, looking for something. Looking for her?

She sat up, and he saw her. "Mara," he called. He moved closer and squatted down. "People have been wondering about you. I had a feeling I might find you here."

She looked at his face. Surely he wasn't concerned about her? He kept himself so closely guarded these days. "I hear them making preparations in the Meeting Place," Mara said.

"Yes. Ternees has been placed where everyone can see her."

Mara looked out over the sparkling water. "Grief is a private thing, I think," she said. "But I know there'll be a long ceremony." And as she thought about it, she dreaded the prospect. She would have to speak to the people; there was no way around that. Her feelings were so personal, she didn't entirely understand them herself. How could she share them with the whole tribe?

Kormor was watching her carefully. "Are you sad that she's gone?"

"Am I sad?" Her voice rose in pitch as she spoke. "Kormor, she was my mother!"

"Still, you often said you hated her."

Emotions surged up inside Mara, powerful and unexpected. She had to fight a sudden urge to strike out at him. "I cared about her," she said. "I was angry with her because I wanted her to care about me." She shook her head, hiding her face from him. "Perhaps you should just leave me alone."

"All right, I will." He paused. "But tell me one thing.

When you explained the customs of your tribe to me, you never told me exactly what happens when the Chieftain dies. Is Shani our new Chieftain now? Does there have to be another ceremony?"

Why was he bothering her like this? Whatever he had on his mind, it was of no importance to her. "Shani and her clan—my clan—will mourn for a week," she said. "After that, there'll be the ceremony that names her as our Chieftain." She sniffed back her tears.

He paused for a long moment. "Of course, if anything happens to Shani, then you would become the leader."

She gave him a quick, sharp look. "What do you mean? Why do you say that?"

He eyed her steadily. "I like to know how I stand," he said. "Ternees's death was a surprise. It started me thinking about other things that might happen. I'm a cautious man, Mara. I've learned to be." He stood up. "I expect I'll see you later, in the Meeting Place." He turned away, then, without another word.

The mourning ceremony started just before sunset and lasted long into the night. The villagers had disfigured themselves to signify their guilt and grief, ripping their clothes and scratching their arms and legs and shoulders with flint knives, drawing blood. All the people had daubed themselves with mud to signify their shame. Even children and babies had been smeared with gray.

Shani had cut off most of her hair, and she threw one of her finest robes into the fire at the center of the Meeting Place. One by one, the villagers stepped forward, casting something of special value into the flames, begging the spirits to accept these fine gifts and spare the tribe any more misfortune.

Then the speeches began. One person after another stood on the Speaking Stone and praised Ternees, calling on the spirits to forgive the Lake People for any crime that might have brought this terrible punishment upon them.

Mara sat stoically through the laments. She was vaguely conscious of Kormor sitting to her right, Shani to her left, and Ipaw just beyond her. She was aware, too, of the mud that had dried hard on her face and in her scalp, and the night air that touched her skin where she had torn open her robe. It was her wedding robe that she had chosen to sacrifice, though Kormor seemed not to have noticed.

The ceremony itself barely touched her. She was lost in her memories again, trying to understand the feeling of absence that she felt. Her world was incomplete: A piece of it had been taken away.

The stars were bright above. The storm had cleared the air and washed away the oppressive heat. The night was a gentle caress, making Mara wish suddenly that she could escape this endless ritual and run out across the grass, alone in the darkness.

But Yacor was speaking, confessing his guilt again and begging the tribe to forgive him. Like Shani, he had hacked off most of his hair. His face, arms, chest, and legs were crisscrossed with wounds and covered in mud, and he was almost naked, wearing nothing but a loincloth.

"I saw her fall," he said. "I should have prevented it. But I was too far away, and that was my fault. She died because the animals were wild and out of control. It's all my responsibility."

The people made a sound of sadness and commiseration, a sighing noise like wind blowing around outcroppings of mountain rock. Yacor was weeping again. He cast his finest spear into the fire, and then his hunter's necklace of buffalo claws, and a hunting robe embellished with quills and feathers. Then, looking desolate, he sat down and said nothing more.

Mara realized that she and Shani were the only ones who still hadn't spoken. Shani, of course, would speak last, as Ternees's oldest daughter. So it was Mara's turn now. She stood up and looked across at the Speaking Stone; but suddenly she felt too sad and weak to go and climb onto it. She had bad memories of talking to her people from that stone. Surely they could hear her well enough from where she stood.

She looked around at all the faces lit by the firelight. They were turning to her expectantly. They wanted her to tell them of her own grief, she thought to herself, and they wanted to suffer along with her, sighing and crying. But why should that be? Perhaps, by sharing her remorse and crying out their misery and shame, they would feel less guilty for still being alive. Was that the whole point of this ceremony? It couldn't benefit Ternees, because her spirit was gone now. The only people it could help were the villagers themselves.

There was a sense of wrongness about it, Mara decided. She felt guilty for all the times she had fought with her mother, but she felt no guilt about being alive.

Still, she had to say something. "My mother was a strict woman," she said. The words seemed to come of their own accord; she barely thought before speaking them. "We often had fights. I left my Clan House partly because of her."

People stared at her in surprise. This was not the tribute they'd expected. There was a deep, uneasy silence. Mara sensed Shani beside her, glaring at her.

Mara blinked. "I just want to say how things really were," she said. "My life with Ternees was hard. Perhaps that was my fault. I don't know." She felt emotions churning inside her, and she swayed on her feet. She realized she felt faint. She hadn't eaten all day; her stomach was hollow and aching.

She reached out to Kormor's shoulder to steady herself. She grimaced, and the mud cracked painfully on her face. "I feel sad," she said. "I'll miss my mother, even though I don't know how much she cared for me." But this wasn't what she really wanted to say. It was all wrong, and she wished she could pull the words back and start again.

Well, it was too late for that. And she sensed that no matter how much she tried, it would never sound right. Without another word, she sat down.

Once again, the people made their sound of sadness and commiseration, though it was quieter this time.

Shani stood up. She walked to the Speaking Stone, climbed up onto it, and stood in silence for a moment, clasping her hands, looking at each person in turn, showing her love for them all. Then, calmly and gently, she started talking about everything she had learned from her mother: the ways of the tribe, and the customs and taboos that had been handed down. "She taught me always that conciliation is better than victory," Shani said, "for victory causes resentment in the one who is forced to submit, and resentment breeds revenge."

Mara saw many people nodding, looking relieved to hear the sentiments that were so much a part of their lives.

"She taught me that if you care for a person, you can teach that person to care for you in return," Shani went on.

There was a murmur of assent.

So Shani continued, comforting the villagers, bringing them together in their love and respect for the woman who had died. And yet, as Mara looked more closely at the faces around the fire, she saw that not everyone was responding. Many of the young men, in particular, seemed restless. The people who had been born in the village were appreciating Shani's words, but those who had joined The Lake People more recently seemed less enthralled.

Well, Mara thought to herself, that was natural enough. Yet it disturbed her all the same. If the people of the tribe didn't really care for their Chieftain, what did that mean, and what did it portend?

Finally Shani finished her speech. The people cried out their approval and their respect. Then the elder hunters went to the body of Ternees, where it was still resting on its stretcher. They lifted it up onto their shoulders, and everyone stood up, chanting a mourning song, while the bearers carried the body slowly out of the Meeting Place.

The Moon was high in the sky now, clearly lighting the way. With the villagers following behind them, the bearers walked slowly among the round houses to the north side of the village, out across the grassland, to the stretch of land where they buried their dead.

The earth was soft and deep here, and easy to dig using shovels fashioned from the shoulder blades of bison. Men had been out here earlier, scooping out a grave for Ternees. The hole in the ground was a pit of pure black shadow amid the moonlight.

Carefully the elder hunters lowered Ternees into the grave. The members of her clan gathered around, with Mara among them. They cast into the grave objects that Ternees had owned and might need in the realm beyond. A spear, a flint knife, many fine necklaces of shells and stones and wooden beads, several robes, and several fine pairs of moccasins. The things showered down, disappearing into the darkness of the pit.

"Spirit of Mother Moon," Shani called out, turning and raising her arms to the liquid silver crescent, "shine gently on the one of our clan who has left us. Accept her into your realm. Welcome her, we beg you."

There was a murmur of assent.

Mara closed her eyes, thinking of the times in the Spirit House when she had sensed the animal spirits nearby. Could she feel something of that sort out here? For a moment, the skin tightened on the back of her neck, as if something had touched it. But it had just been a breath of wind, nothing more.

She wished Lizel was still in the tribe to conduct this ceremony. Then, perhaps, there would be a true link with the spirit world. And yet, Lizel had left because the spirits no longer spoke to her. Mara suddenly felt as if her tribe had been abandoned. There was no one, now, to protect them.

The people started shoveling earth over the body, and Mara felt herself crying again. Her emotions were no longer her own; she couldn't predict or understand the sudden bursts of sorrow.

She saw Lorm, the old News Teller, sitting on a rock nearby, and she went to join him. "How do you feel, Lorm?" she said softly, looking at his simple face.

"Mara," he said, blinking at her in the darkness, absorbing the fact of her presence. "I feel sad." He gave a melancholy shrug.

That was all. How simple it must be, she thought, to be Lorm. When someone died, he felt sad; and then, as time passed, he would feel happy again.

Mara settled herself beside him on the rock. It was

customary for her clan to stay here in mourning, maintaining their vigil for at least a night and a day. As a child, Mara had seen many of her older relatives die, and she had sat out here every time, staring into the darkness. This time, though, seemed very different. In the past, the ritual had satisfied her and helped her to feel whole again. Tonight, she felt as if nothing could do that.

Chapter 16

As the sky finally lightened, Shani started chanting the Song of Gladness for Life. It was a simple song that Mara had known since she was old enough to speak, praising the Sun for His warmth, the earth for its fertility, the trees for their shade, the animals for their flesh, and the Moon for Her guidance. "Thank you," the people chanted, "thank you to the Sun. Thank you, thank you to the soil of the land. . . ."

Mara joined them in their singing, even though the spirit of it barely stirred her.

By the end of it, her head was aching and nausea was gnawing at her stomach again. It had been more than a day, she realized, since she had eaten.

Mara looked around at the familiar faces. Several of the elder hunters—Yacor among them—had stayed with the clan to show their support. Shani started going to each person around the fresh grave, hugging them and thanking them. Mara was her closest relative, so Shani came to her last. She embraced Mara without hesitation, holding her for a long moment, then thanking her for being there, looking into Mara's eyes with seeming sincerity. Mara felt a fresh rush of confusing emotions: gladness at being briefly close to her sister, and uncertainty as she wondered how much of Shani's warmth was merely a part of the ritual. That was the trouble with rituals: They compelled people to act in a certain way. You could never be sure how people really felt.

"Could I talk to you for a moment?" she said softly, when Shani released her.

"Of course." Shani took a few paces away from the grave. Everyone else was staying close by it, and most of them had pledged to maintin the vigil for the next six days to come.

"I'm not well," Mara said, talking quietly enough so that only Shani could hear. "I know it's customary to fast for the first day, but I'm afraid I may faint." She clutched her stomach, feeling another bout of nausea. "I have to get food. After that, I can return."

"Is this what was troubling you when I saw you two days ago?" Shani's eyes were examining Mara closely.

"I suppose so, yes."

"Did you go to Dira, as we suggested?"

Was Shani scolding her? Mara couldn't tell. "I spoke to her," Mara said, "but we were interrupted." She moved restlessly. "I'm sure if I just eat, I'll be better, and then I can return to you here."

Shani gave a little shrug. "But you don't need to, unless you wish to. I wasn't sure if you'd stay for the night vigil. After all, you're not in our Clan House anymore."

Mara blinked, feeling confused. "If you don't want me," she said, pulling back a little, "I wouldn't force myself—"

"Of course you are welcome here." Shani sounded a little impatient now. "Ternees was your mother as well as mine. Mara, dear—you can do whatever you wish. Isn't that our way?" She gave her a little push. "Go. Go wash the mud from your face and find something to eat. I'm sure that's what you really want."

Mara felt dazed. "How do you know what I want, when I don't know myself?"

Shani sighed. She glanced anxiously at the rest of their relatives, then moved even closer to Mara, till her face was just a hand's breadth away. "Why must you always be so difficult?" Her voice was low, but the words were angry. "I have my own grief, you know."

"And I have mine!" Mara stopped herself. She realized she had raised her voice without really meaning to. People around the grave turned and looked at her in surprise.

"You have your grief?" Shani gave her head a quick little shake. "Your little speech last night was an insult to the memory of our mother."

Mara felt as if her face had been slapped. "Please, Shani, I tried to speak the truth, that was all." Once again, her voice was louder than it should have been. "You don't know how hard it was, all this time, knowing Mother cared for you and not for me."

The little tic was pulling at the side of Shani's cheek again. Her lips were thin and pale. She made an agitated motion with her hand. "Be quiet, Mara."

"But you have everything." Mara couldn't stop herself. The feelings were too strong. "You have what you always wanted. The whole tribe is yours now. You have your people, and your clan—"

"Quiet!" The word was full of anger. "I never wanted the Chieftain's power." Her lips pulled back as she spat the words. "You wanted it; that's why you hated Mother. She had the power, and you didn't." She paused, breathing quickly, and wiped her mouth on the back of her hand. "Go, now. And stay away. I take back what I said. You're not welcome here."

She turned her back. Stiffly, she returned to the people gathered around the grave.

Mara stood, shaking, clutching her stomach, feeling it churn.

"Is she all right?" she heard one of the women say.

"Leave her." It was Shani's voice, calm and authoritative.

Mara stumbled away from her clan, then broke into a weak run.

She went to the lake and washed the mud from her face. Grimly, she thought, if no one was going to believe that she was full of grief, there was no point in abiding by the ritual. She started back toward her tent—then realized there was no food in the cache. And it was probably too early for Hopwa to be out supervising the main store.

Well, she could always get some food at one of the other Clan Houses. There was no shame in that; her tribe believed in sharing everything, and people often borrowed from each other.

Mara walked into the first House she came to. She

paused just inside the door flap, and she looked around. To her surprise, she found that the place was empty.

She paused a moment, trying to understand. Everyone had been up late last night. Many of them should still be sleeping now. If nothing else, there should have been some mothers caring for their babies. She knew the people of this house well. There were several young children.

Mara walked quickly to a stone by the fire where food had been set out. She kneeled there and feasted on some venison, swallowing it half chewed. She remembered when she had fasted for her Ceremony of First Blood, and she had eaten the rabbit meat afterward. She felt even hungrier now than she had then. That made no sense, yet it was so.

She finished all the meat, then sat for a moment, trying to recover some peace of mind. Finally she stood up and walked out of the Clan House. Once again, she wondered where all the people in that clan had gone. Were they out hunting? The day was growing brighter, and the first direct beams of sun were striking through the mountain peaks to the east. But this was a day for grieving, not for hunting.

The whole village seemed oddly quiet. Mara paused and listened. Faintly, she heard voices from the direction of the Meeting Place.

It made no sense that people would have gathered there again. She walked between the Clan Houses, moving more swiftly now. The voices in the Meeting Place sounded louder as Mara approached. And then, as she emerged from among the houses, she found that the whole tribe had gathered—all except for her own clan, with Shani, out at the burial ground.

The villagers had their backs turned to her. They were facing the Speaking Stone. Mara craned her neck, trying to see over their heads. The voice she heard was familiar. And then she realized, with a moment of confusion and surprise, it was Dira's voice.

"... time of such unhappiness," Dira was saying. "I know how sad you must feel about what happened. I feel it myself. It's such a terrible thing to lose someone we all loved."

Mara saw the ugly little woman standing on the Speaking Stone, clasping her hands, smiling sympathetically at the crowd.

Mara blinked, overwhelmed by the wrongness of his spectacle. She tried to understand what could have possibly happened. It had been presumptuous when she, the Chieftain's daughter, had called a meeting. For a newcomer such as Dira, it was unprecedented.

"Ternees was a wise leader," Dira was saying. "Such a kind, dear, wonderful woman. I wish she hadn't put herself at the front of the mastodon hunt. Men are stronger than women, you know, there's no way around that fact. It occurred to me, when I heard the terrible news, that Ternees would still be alive if she had let the men take the risks."

Mara half expected to hear someone make a reply. After all, it was a matter of principle among the Lake People that women should hunt beside men. Yet no one spoke. Some of them were shifting uneasily, glancing at each other, not sure what to make of Dira's speech—but no one was disputing it.

Mara noticed Graum standing near his wife, with his arms clasped behind him. Dira never did anything without Graum's approval, so he must have wanted her to address the crowd. Why wasn't he speaking himself?

Then Mara realized: Dira had served the people as their new healer. That was why she'd been rewarded with the Spirit House. She must have helped many of them, telling them all that she felt a duty to do her best.

"It's always seemed clear to me," Dira went on, "that there are things that men do better than women, and things that women do better than men. Men are stronger, so they make better hunters. But women have a different kind of strength. They are strong in the home. Personally, I think it's unfair to expect a woman to raise her children, and hunt, and lead a tribe, all at the same time."

Now there was some uneasy murmuring, though still less than Mara would have expected. "Why did you call us all out to listen to this?" someone shouted—Mara couldn't see who it was.

"What are you telling us?" someone else asked.

Dira bobbed her head, looking shy and embarrassed. "I'm sorry, I do tend to ramble. I'm very nervous standing here in front of you all. Look, why don't I ask Kormor to explain? I'm sure he can do better than I can."

Mara felt a new twist of surprise. She stood on tiptoe and saw her mate at the front of the crowd, moving toward the Speaking Stone as Dira stepped down. It was eerie, seeing him out there and knowing he must have had dealings with Dira and Graum which she knew nothing about. It was even stranger to realize that the people in the tribe seemed unsurprised by what was happening. What had Mara been missing in all the time she had spent at home alone?

"I agree with Dira," Kormor said, speaking calmly and clearly, turning slowly so that he met each person's eyes. "Women have a difficult task, giving birth and bringing up children. It's unfair to ask them to do more, especially since men are stronger and fiercer with a spear. That's why I feel a man should be leading this tribe—and showing us how to defend it, if that's ever necessary. It's certainly the only way we can feel truly secure."

Mara felt a moment of blank astonishment. Suddenly, then, she felt outrage. Kormor was violating the most sacred tradition of all. Why wasn't the crowd yelling and jeering and pulling him down from the Speaking Stone? There were some uneasy murmurs of dissent—but most people still stood in silence. Were they too surprised to react?

"Not many women come here from across the mountains," Kormor went on. "That's why our tribe has so many men now." He paused. "It seems odd to me that even though we have twice as many men as women, our tribe was still led by a woman."

Finally a man stepped forward. Mara recognized him; he was Ifnir, another of the elder hunters, from Yacor's clan. "It's wrong to say these things, Kormor." Ifnir's voice was clear and strong. "You are young. You haven't been here long. You don't even understand the ways of our people."

Kormor faced him calmly. "With respect, Ifnir, I was trained for a year in the ways of the Lake People. A lot of my training came from Ternees."

Ifnir turned and looked at the crowd. "This is foolishness," he shouted. "We all know that the judgment of women is calmer than the judgment of men. That's how this tribe was founded. That's how it has endured. And that's how it will endure for many more generations to come."

There was a long, uneasy pause.

"I disagree," someone said, barely loud enough to be heard. And then someone else spoke up, and another voice, and another. Mara felt a prickling sensation down the back of her neck. Even though she had rebelled against her mother, she had never imagined how it would feel to see other people doing so, and rejecting not just her commands, but the basic beliefs on which everything was founded. What had happened? Should she speak?

"Well, I say Kormor's wrong," someone shouted out. And suddenly there were other voices being raised, denouncing Kormor. Within moments, there was a whole chorus of cries, some shouting for him, and some against.

Kormor stepped down from the Speaking Stone, and Dira took his place. She waved her arms and started shouting for silence. Bit by bit, the furor diminished.

"People, people," she called out. "You are all gentle, friendly people, I know that from my own dealings with you." She beamed at them all. "I've grown to love many of you over the past months. And you all agree we should be free to make our own choices. So perhaps we should choose freely now. Let's try to see how everyone really feels. Those who think we should have a man as Chieftain of the tribe, step to one side of the Meeting Place. Those who think a woman should lead us, step to the other side. And we'll see which group is larger."

"No!" Ifnir called out. "No, this is a wrong!"

"This is not the way to choose a Chieftain." It was Tiear speaking now. "The legacy of Laena—"

"It has been a long time since Laena lived," Kormor shouted back. "Longer than anyone can count. Times have changed. Things are different. There are many of us from the North Lands who've been impatient for a change."

"Shani is our Chieftain," someone else shouted.

"Not yet," Kormor answered. "Not till the ceremony after her mourning. We have no Chieftain now."

Mara's anger doubled inside her. She saw clearly now why so many people seemed unsurprised by this meeting. Kormor had taken what he needed from her, and he and his young hunters, with Dira and Graum, had gone quickly around the village the previous day, testing the opinions in each house, confiding to the ones they trusted, getting them to pledge themselves. The whole thing had been prearranged. And it had been Dira who had laid the foundations for it over the past months, helping people, ingratiating herself, and getting to know their needs and fears.

Meanwhile, Graum had had an equal length of time to indoctrinate his young hunters and stir their discontent. And the recent immigrants must have been easily persuaded. After all, they had grown up in tribes ruled by men.

People were arguing loudly in the Meeting Place now. "If a man is a Chieftain of our tribe, who should it be?" someone shouted.

"Graum!" one of the young hunters shouted back.

Immediately the big man stepped forward, holding up his arms. "No!" he cried out. "Not me. That wouldn't be right. The Chieftain must be someone who was born in this tribe."

Now there was a new burst of shouting, with some of the men begging him to reconsider and others praising him for his good sense. Once again Dira climbed up onto the Speaking Stone. "Please!" she cried. "Please, let's be gentle and generous, as I know you all are."

She waited for them to calm down.

"Let's just find out," she said, "what everyone wants. Don't concern yourselves about who the Chieftain should be. We can decide that later. Those who think it should be a man, step to this side of the Meeting Place. Those who think it should be a woman, step to this side."

Some people started moving across. Others hesitated,

and there were harsh words between some family members. Mara watched in dismay. If Dira and Graum and Kormor had planned this meeting, they must be feeling confident of the outcome.

She realized what she had to do. Her personal feelings toward Shani were suddenly irrelevant. Shani alone had the power, now, to stop what was happening.

Chapter 17

Mara was gasping for breath by the time she reached the burial ground. The people there looked at her doubtfully as she came running up, but there was no time to concern herself with that. "Shani," Mara gasped. "You must break your vigil. You must come to the Meeting Place. Quickly."

Shani rose to her feet. "What is it now?" She glared at Mara. "I asked you not to come back here."

Mara shook her head. "Listen to me! Graum and Dira are turning people against each other, and against you. They called a meeting. They're demanding that there should be a man as Chieftain. Please, listen to me!"

The other people of her clan were getting to their feet. "Is this really true?" one of the men said.

"Of course it's true!" Mara felt the time slipping away with every moment that they stood here eyeing her and doubting her. "Please, come quickly!"

The people looked at each other. It was unheard of, to interrupt a vigil. Yacor stepped forward. "You actually heard them say that a man should lead our tribe?"

"Yes, Yacor. Listen—Graum and Dira have been spreading their ideas, convincing people privately. It's been going on behind your backs for days, weeks, maybe a month now. I think they have more than half the tribe agreeing with them." She turned back to Shani. "You have to talk to them."

Shani gave her a steady, grim stare. "If I do as you say," she said finally, "and if I find you have deceived us, that will be the end of you, Mara. There will be no place for you in our tribe anymore. Do you understand?"

Mara stared at her sister in shock. "You think I would

deceive you?" Her voice rose incredulously. "Shani, *always* I have spoke the truth. That's why you've been angry with me so often. I speak out!"

Shani gathered her robe around her. "All right," she said, "I'll come with you."

Shani strode into the village with her clan trailing behind. She came to the Meeting Place and saw it filled with people, and she stopped. There were two crowds of villagers, one on the left side of the open space, the other on the right, with Dira standing on the Speaking Stone in the middle.

The Meeting Place was full of noise as the villagers still argued furiously amont themselves. But then some of them saw Shani standing there, and they gradually fell silent. Some looked guilty; others looked defiant. No one spoke.

Shani walked slowly forward, blank-faced, as if she still couldn't believe what she saw.

"Shani!" Dira called out. She stepped down from the Speaking Stone, smiling, holding out her hands as if she was greeting an old friend. "Shani, I'm happyy you're here. We didn't want to disturb your vigil—"

Shani strode past her and climbed onto the stone. "Which of these groups wants to follow the fine traditions of our tribe?" she called out. Her voice was loud, but Mara heard a tremor in it. Nothing like this had ever happened. Nothing could have prepared Shani for this moment.

"Those on the left," Dira said, "are the ones who want things to stay the same. Those on the right—well, they think it may be time for a change."

Shani surveyed the two groups. The one on the left contained a few of the older men, and many of the women. It was half the size of the group on the right. "I see what you have done here, Dira," said Shani. "And by the ways of our people, it is wrong."

Dira shifted uneasily. She turned toward Graum, looking up at him.

Graum was standing in the larger of the two groups. "You and your mother before you," he said, "have al-

ways told people they should be free to follow their
own path."

Shani stared at him. She said nothing. She seemed unable to speak.

"People should be free to choose a leader, like anything else, it seems to me," said Graum. He glanced back
at his group, and they nodded their agreement.

"You mean they should be free to choose *you*?" Shani
eyed him coldly.

"No, no." Graum grinned and shook his head. "I'm
not the one for the job. And I don't even know who is.
We just wanted to make things clear, that's all."

"Shani," Dira put in, "you said yourself just last night,
conciliation is better than victory, because—"

"I know what I said!" Shani turned on the ugly little
woman in a sudden burst of fury. "Be quiet!"

Mara experienced a sinking feeling as she watched her
sister up on the Speaking Stone. Shani was losing her
poise, losing her calm authority. She was sounding spite-
ful and shrill now, where she should have been com-
manding. Mara suddenly remembered what Lizel had
said: Shani had never had to face a real challenge.

Shani wiped her hand across her forehead, then grimaced as she realized that her face was still smeared with
mud. Almost all the people in the square had cleaned
themselves; she and her clan were the only ones still in
full mourning. "Listen to me," she said, sounding plaintive, as if she was afraid that her people might not pay
attention. "You see the fine houses of this tribe, which
have stood here for so many generations. My ancestors
planned and built this village, and all of them were
women. You can see for yourselves, all around you, how
well they served us." She paused, breathing deeply.
"Now, think clearly. Do you still want to ignore all the
lessons of our history?"

Mara groaned inwardly. This, surely, was not the
way—for Shani to ask her people to choose. They had
already chosen, and they had chosen wrongly.

Shani waited. Some of the women in the group on the
right looked uneasily at their mates, as if they wanted to
move across to the other side. But all the men stood firm.

Somewhere a baby cried, and its mother shushed it. A man coughed nervously. People shuffled their feet in the dirt. But no one moved from the one group to the other.

Shani's shoulders slumped a little. "I will add my own clan to those here in the Meeting Place," she said, in a quieter voice. She turned and gestured for them to join the villagers.

Mara couldn't bear it any longer. "No!" she cried out as the people of her clan walked across and joined the small group on the left. "This is not our way! Anyone who rejects the traditions of the Lake People should leave us. They have no business being here." She turned and faced the large group, with Graum and Kormor and the other young hunters among them. "Those who stand against our traditions should be cast out," she cried.

Now there were murmurs of protest—from both sides of the Meeting Place.

"We do not cast people out," Shani said, raising her voice. "Not just because of things they believe."

Mara stared back at her, feeling overwhelmed by the injustice of what was happening. Why didn't Shani lead her people, instead of allowing herself to be led by them?

Clearly, it was hopeless. In despair, Mara strode across the Meeting Place. She joined the rest of her clan in the group that stood on the left.

Shani looked again at the people before her. Even with her own clan added to it, the group on the left was still smaller than the group on the right. People were glancing to and fro, assessing the difference. It was clear for everyone to see.

Shani looked dazed. "I must bow to the will of my people," she said simply. "That was the way of my mother, and her ancestors before her. So you have chosen." She stepped down from the Speaking Stone. "I hope," she said, "you have chosen wisely."

Mara stared in disbelief. Everyone around her started shouting. The group on the right, meanwhile, looked smug in their victory.

She was lying on her bed, cuddling Claws, when Kormor came in. The bobcat hissed at him, jumped down, and hid under the bed. Mara just lay there and waited, watching him, saying nothing.

"I hope," he said quietly, "you've finally learned your lesson."

Somehow, it wasn't what she'd expected from him. She'd thought he might be angry with her for siding against him in the Meeting Place, or for running and fetching Shani. But he showed no sign of that. He seemed very calm.

"What lesson is that?" she said dully.

He sat on the corner of the bed, looking at her. "You are no longer the Chieftain's daughter," he said. "You are not even the new Chieftain's sister." He shook his head slowly. "You will never rule this tribe now, Mara."

It took a long moment for his words to sink in. He was right, of course. She was nothing, now. He and his friends had stolen it all away. She felt as if she had been picked up by a huge gust of wind and thrown down, knocking the breath out of her. "Was that why you wanted this?" Her voice was little more than a whisper. "Just ... to rob me of my privilege?"

He looked scornful. "Of course not. I wanted things to change for the reasons I said out there in the Meeting Place." He paused, still eyeing her. "But I must say, I'm glad that you'll never be the Chieftain of this tribe. It may make you a little less arrogant in future."

"Oh, of course!" she cried, feeling her spirit rising as she understood his crude, simple interest. "You want me to be broken and humble. You want me to do whatever you say."

"I want you to show respect for me," he corrected her, with a little twist of his lip. "As we originally agreed."

She turned away from him. "I've heard this all before, Kormor. But as more and more time passes, I see less and less in you that deserves my respect."

He stood up and strode quickly over to her. He could move so fast when he wanted to. It always scared her. Before she could even raise her hands to defend herself, he seized her by the hair. He jerked her head around, forcing her to face him. His grip tightened, and she cried out in pain.

"You've heard it before," he said, with his face almost touching hers. "But now I'm going to make you pay better attention to what I say. With a man running the tribe, things will change. When women don't show respect, they'll be taught a lesson." He threw her down onto the bed.

She lay on her back looking up at him, and he was so large, he seemed to fill the whole space above her.

He put his hands on his hips. "You're going to learn to obey me," he said. "And if you don't learn, I'll punish you. I'll punish you till that stupid rebellious spirit of yours is broken, once and for all."

She felt as if she was falling into a hollow place where she was worthless, helpless, unable to think or feed herself or breathe. Everything she had trusted and believed in had been taken away.

She suddenly lunged forward, trying to get past him to the door flap. But he seized hold of her easily, grabbed her by the hair, and threw her back into the bed. He slapped her face, hard. "You'll stay here till I've finished with you," he said.

"No!" she screamed at him.

He slapped her again, so hard that her ears rang from the blow. "Turn over," he said, "and do what I say."

Feeling sick and hopeless, she obeyed him. There was no one to help her, she realized. Her mother was dead. Her sister hated her, and had been stripped of her power. The elders of the village had been publicly humiliated. If she screamed for help, what would happen? Would anyone believe her? Would anyone try to defend her? Would anyone even care? The Lake People had seen how close Kormor was to Graum. They'd seen him speak in the Meeting Place, and they'd seen him get his way. At this point, they might even admire him.

"I'll leave you," she cried, pressing her bruised cheek against the bed.

"You have nowhere to go." She heard him stripping off his clothes, and she felt him getting onto the bed behind her. "Your Clan House won't take you back. Your people can see that you're nothing but a troublemaker. If you break our bond, they'll shun you." She felt the heat of his body behind hers, and then he was forcing himself into her, grunting with satisfaction. His hand moved to the back of her neck, holding her down as he always did. He thrust quickly, more brutally than usual, as if it gave him pleasure to have her like this completely at his disposal. He came almost at once, and then he rolled off her and lay beside her, breathing quietly.

"You'd better remember," he said after a moment "you no longer have any place in this tribe without me I can be kind to you, Mara, and perhaps I will be, if you learn to behave yourself. Things may even be pleasant as they used to be when we were courting, if you would just learn how to be a dutiful wife. But if you don't, I will make your life miserable." He turned away, as if she was of no further interest. "The choice is yours."

Chapter 18

Someone was calling to her. For a moment she thought it was her mother, waking her to do chores. She rolled over, making little complaining noises in her sleep—but then she opened her eyes and saw her little home cluttered with possessions, with the dark gray mammoth hide stretched across the yellow ribs above her head.

She felt a wave of relief that it hadn't been her mother, after all, nagging and criticizing her. But then she remembered her mother's death and everything else that had happened, and as the knowledge flooded into her, she slumped back with a despairing sigh.

The voice was still calling. "Mara?" It was someone just outside the door flap. "Mara, are you there?"

It was a female voice, but this time it wasn't Shani.

Mara sat up. "Just a moment," she said. She reached for her robe, noticing that Kormor had already gone out. "Come in," she called.

The door flap was pulled open. Lomel appeared, peering in shyly. "Am I disturbing you?"

"No." Mara squinted into the bright daylight and realized that the sun was already high. "I slept longer than I meant to."

Lomel lowered herself through the entrance. "This is very snug," she said, looking around. She smiled at Mara, and Mara felt again the same simple warmth that she'd sensed when they'd been out on the hillside.

"What brings you here?" Mara asked.

Lomel perched on the tree stump—the same spot where Shani had sat just a few days ago. "Some of the women were talking this morning," she said. "About everything that's happened. Especially in the meeting yesterday."

"And they're discontent?" Mara asked.

"Yes." Lomel hesitated. She fidgeted and glanced around, obviously feeling out of place here, talking to Mara. "They ... I mean, we—we feel as if we were tricked, somehow. And Shani did nothing to stop it."

Mara lay back. She should be feeling hopeful that Lomel was here, telling her these things. Yet she felt weary. Why was she so tired, all the time? "Graum and Dira took advantage of my—my mother's death," she said. It was hard for her to speak of it. The words sounded strange in her ears. "They were very quick, and very clever, and I don't see what anyone can do now." She studied the girl. "Is there something you wanted to suggest to me?"

"Well ..." Lomel hesitated, and Mara realized that the girl was unaccustomed to speaking out or asking favors. "The other women aren't sure what to make of you, Mara. It seems as if sometimes you cause trouble and you make enemies—but I don't know, I have a good feeling about you. So I said I'd speak to you, and maybe you can help us, or you could speak to your sister Shani—" She trailed off.

Mara looked at the girl's touchingly earnest face. "How many of you are there?" Mara asked gently.

"Twelve."

"All women?"

Lomel nodded.

"The tribe made its choice," Mara said. "A man will be our Chieftain. So it seems as if I'm not important anymore, and nor is Shani. I have no special influence. I abandoned my own Clan House. Really, Lomel, I'm as helpless as you are, now."

"You mean, there's really nothing we can do?" Lomel seemed unable to believe it.

"That's right," said Mara.

Lomel brooded for a moment. "The men are going to choose the one who'll lead us," she said. "Out at Grassy Hollow. This afternoon, it'll be done." She hesitated.

fingering the hem of her robe. "I think they'll choose Graum," she added.

Mara frowned. "But he said he wouldn't—"

Lomel looked up at her again. "Yes, but they begged him to! He said the job was too difficult and he didn't want it, but they wouldn't let him refuse."

Now Mara felt some of her lethargy lifting from her, dispelled by her anger. She saw it clearly now: Graum was following the same path as Dira, who had claimed that she hadn't wanted her place in the Spirit House. But obviously power was what both of them really wanted. "Tell me, now," Mara said. "How are they going to choose this Chieftain?"

"Graum said he'd only serve if it was a fair contest. I don't know any more than that."

"It won't be fair," Mara muttered, half to herself.

Lomel moved forward. She knelt on the floor beside the bed, and she laid her hand on Mara's arm. "I'm worried," she said. "My brother Arin is going to be out there. My father told him not to go, but Arin defied him. And my father hit him." She looked down at her hands. "I don't understand what's happening."

"Well, I'm not sure, either," said Mara. "But I've been thinking there's an animal part in men that can lie quietly like a bear in a cave, biding its time, sleeping through a long season. But when it's woken, it can have frightening strength. So long as Ternees governed our tribe, Lomel, there was a balance. But now that balance is gone. There's nothing to restrain that animal spirit, and I can't say what's going to happen."

Lomel looked up at her with anxious eyes. "Maybe if you called a meeting, you know, like you did that time before? You could speak to people, Mara. They might listen to you this time, now that they've seen what's really happening."

Mara squeezed the girl's shoulder. She was glad to hear some friendly words, but Lomel was so young, so naive, it was really no help. "People wouldn't listen," she said gently, "any more than they listened to me the last time." Mara hesitated for a moment, looking at Lomel's face. It was such a sweet face, it made Mara feel protective of the girl. She imagined kissing the cheeks, trying to comfort her—perhaps receiving comfort in return. That was a rare feeling, the kind of feeling she'd imagined, sometimes, she might share with Shani, if only the two of them had been different.

Mara sighed. "We should go outside," she said.

"Go where? What are you going to do?"

"To watch the men play their games," said Mara. "And see who wins."

Almost everyone from the tribe had gathered around the edge of Grassy Hollow. It was a wide, shallow depression in the land, about a hundred paces across. People were sitting in groups up on the rim. Mara's clanfolk were bunched together, some of them looking resentful, others resigned. Shani was among them, wearing one of her finest white robes, with her arms folded, her back straight, and her face proud. Well, Mara thought to herself, that pride meant nothing now.

The elder hunters were sitting in another group. They were wearing the finest trophies they had won over the years: necklaces of bison teeth and lion claws, leggings of buffalo hide embroidered with porcupine quills, and capes stitched from bearskin or lion hide. Yacor was the only one who wasn't in his finery; he was still barechested, smeared with mud, publicly mourning Ternees.

Mara and Lomel sat with the women of the tribe, many of them holding young children, while boys and girls played in the tall grass behind them. And down in the hollow, where Graum stood, the men had gathered.

There were more than fifty of them altogether. Some were young—far too young to be Chieftain, but determined to compete anyway. Others were twenty or thirty years old, and most of these were men who had grown up in the North Lands and had come to the Lake People within the past decade. These were the ones who had resented being ruled by Ternees. For them, it was a time to redress an injustice.

It was a bright, breezy day, with scraps of white cloud moving swiftly from the west. As the wind whispered around Mara, it seemed to tell her of the places it had

come from—where the earth was frozen hard, smothered
in snow, and mountains were sheathed in ice. The wind
brought her a first hint of the long gray days that lay
ahead, when the sun would barely creep above the horizon. Mara shivered. She hated the winter, and she had
a feeling that this one would be especially hard.

"People of the Great Lake," said Graum. "We're here
to find out who's really the best man to lead and defend
his tribe." He paused, looking up at the people sitting
around the rim. He eyed the elder hunters. "I see a lot
of you up there who look strong and brave. There's still
room down here for any who want to change their minds
and compete."

There was a long pause. The elders sat cross-legged,
looking down at Graum enigmatically, saying nothing.

"Well, that's too bad," said the big man, turning away.
"Still, there's some fine men down here, too." He turned
to his companions. "All right, we've discussed how this
should be done. The way it seems to us, there are three
things a chieftain needs. Hunting skill, courage, and
strength."

"And wisdom?" said a voice. It was Yacor, rising
slowly to his feet, standing proud despite his shorn hair
and his ragged dress. "Shouldn't a Chieftain be wise?"

Graum turned and squinted up at him. "Well, of
course, Yacor," he said. "But we have you and the other
elders to give us their wise advice and experience, no
matter who's the Chieftain."

Yacor stood with his arms folded, staring at Graum
through half-closed eyes. Mara had seen Yacor look that
way at small fish and animals which children brought to
him when they were trying to show their worth as hunters. Yacor would say nothing; he'd simply stare at the
sad little trophies, and the youngsters would sense his
disapproval and back away, their pride turning to
embarrassment.

But if Graum understood the meaning of that scornful
stare, he showed no sign of it. "Skill, cunning, and
strength," he said again. "Strength most of all, to defend
the tribe. With so many fine houses, and so much food
stored here—we should have plans to defend this place.

Why, warlike people from the North Lands could come
and take it all."

"When people come here after making the great jour
ney from the north," said Yacor, "they're weakened by
the journey. They beg us for food, they thank us for our
kindness, and then they make their homes with us." He
pointed to the men gathered near Graum. "All of you
know this is true. You should be grateful for it, instead
of turning against our ways."

Graum nodded slowly, smiling at Yacor as if he was
trying to humor him. "Of course we appreciate what the
tribe has done," he said. "I'm just saying we should take
precautions. There's a tribe to the south—"

"They're our friends," Yacor spoke. "How can they
be our enemies, when they need our trade as much as
we need theirs?"

Graum spread his arms. "Yacor, I used to hear people
in the North Lands saying the same sort of thing. But
then the northern tribes began turning against each
other. And the ones who survived were the strong ones
Isn't that right?" He turned to the men gathered
around him.

There were loud murmurs of agreement.

"Another thing," Graum went on. "It seems to me
there's so many people in this tribe, we can't keep wel
coming outsiders. There won't be enough for everyone to
share. We need to be strong enough to keep people out."

"No!" Yacor shouted. "Always we welcome all travel
ers—just as we welcomed you, Graum."

Graum grunted and shook his head. "Yacor, we've
talked it over, and the old traditions have to change. We
have to run things better in the future. We can't risk any
more disasters—I mean, the kind of thing that happened
to Ternees. I'm sure you have to agree with me about
that."

The expression on Yacor's face changed subtly as he
stared at Graum. He was no longer merely scornful. He
seemed sick with disgust. "I will not play this game of
yours, Graum," he said softly. "You sound friendly, but
you turn friends against each other, and you create suspi
cion and fear." He spat on the ground. "Go ahead

choose your Chieftain from these young rebels. I will still follow the customs of my people, and anyone with good sense will follow them, too. And until you understand your mistake, we will have nothing to say to you." He turned his back. Slowly, proudly, he walked away toward the village.

The elder hunters glanced at each other. There was a long, uneasy pause. Then, in a group, they rose to their feet and followed Yacor, with their fine robes and feathers flapping in the wind.

Mara wanted to feel encouraged by their defiance, but the elders had done the same thing on Graum's first night in the village, when he had played the game with the hot stones. It had changed nothing then, and it would change nothing now. Disapproval was a powerful weapon, but only when the whole tribe used it against a few.

"They aren't going to help us," Lomel murmured, staring after the elders.

"They think they're doing what's best and what's right," Mara said.

"I'm sorry to see the elders leave," Graum was saying. He turned to the other villagers who were watching. "Still, I dare say we can manage without them. All right, now. There'll be two contests: the first to test hunting skill, the second to test courage and strength. If one man here wins both contests—well, then, he's proved himself. But if one man wins the first contest and another wins the second, well, we'll have a test of strength between them at the end, to decide the matter." He clapped his hands. "Let's begin!"

Chapter 19

The men lined up with the youngest at the front, the oldest at the rear. Young Lumo stepped out into the center of Grassy Hollow, looking awkward and self-conscious in front of so many people. At first Mara wondered if he might actually try to compete in the contests, but then she saw what he was carrying, and she realized her error. In his hand was a willow bough that had been bent into a circle slightly more than a hand's breadth across, bound with thongs.

Lumo stood alone for a moment, with his long hair stirring in the breeze. Then the first two hunters stepped forward, each carrying a spear. Morro was one of them, and Mara found herself remembering when he had helped to seat her and raise her above the heads of the villagers, just before her wedding. The other man was big, slow-witted Bumar.

Lumo stood facing them for a moment. He looked from one to the other, checking that they were ready. Then he threw the willow circle high into the air.

Morro braced himself, took aim, and cast his spear while the circle was still rising to the top of its arc. The spear chased the circle—and for a moment it seemed that the two would meet. But the spear flew wide, and the circle paused, untouched, beginning its descent.

Now Bumar made his throw. The shaft of his spear seemed too low at first—but the circle was falling faster, and there was a faint sound of wood on wood as the shaft flew up and into the circle, bringing it down to the ground.

There was a cheer from the hunters waiting and watching. Bumar grinned as he walked out to retrieve his

pear, and Morro shrugged philosophically, moving away
o one side. Lumo picked up the willow circle, another
unter stepped forward, and Bumar turned to face him,
o defend the victory that he'd just won.

Mara had played this game, and she knew how difficult
t was. Sometimes, out on the grassland, she'd struggled
o pass her spear through the circle till her arm was
veak, her shoulders were a knotted mass of pain, and
he was half blinded by squinting up against the bright
ky. She'd finally reached the point where she could
ierce the circle one time in two, and that was considered
fine record.

Of course, there were others who could do better.
Bumar, for instance, had long since proved himself, and
he hadn't been surprised to see him win against Morro
own in Grassy Hollow.

But the hunter who truly shone at this game was
Kormor. He had an almost eerie skill. And as Mara sat
eside Lomel on the edge of the hollow, she felt a new,
wful premonition. Kormor, she was sure, could win this
ame. And that meant there was a chance—perhaps a
ood chance—that he could be the new Chieftain of
he tribe.

Mara shivered. The thought scared her. She tried to
magine how he would be and what he would do. He
vas already so proud and so fierce. He already treated
er as if her only duty was to obey. If he acquired real
ower . . .

She closed her eyes. She didn't want to think about it.
Graum wouldn't allow it to happen, she told herself. The
ig man must have planned ahead; he must have found
way to arrange these contests to favor himself.

But would it be any better to have Graum leading the
ribe instead of Kormor? Once again, Mara shivered. The
hoice here was unbearable. She found herself scanning
he faces of the other men waiting to compete. Surely
mong them there was one who would be decent and
air. Yes, she recognized several that she felt she could
rust. But would they have a chance of winning these
ames?

Bumar was defending himself now against the next

challenger: a young man named Gownor. Once again
Lumo threw the willow circle high. Once again, the
spears flew up to meet it. This time, Bumar threw first.
His spear flew true, seized the circle, and pulled it ou
of the sky, leaving Gownor's spear searching for a targe
that had already been stolen away.

So it went on. Bumar faced five more men, and he
beat them all, though sometimes it took more than one
throw. Then Graum stepped out.

The big northerner flexed his shoulders, grinning a
the hunters who had already tried and lost. He seemed
to relish the chance to prove that he could do bette
than they had.

He stood beside Bumar and nodded to him, still grin
ning. He looked like a carnivore, Mara though to herself.
A big hungry beast looking at its prey.

Bumar moved a little to one side. He was sweating
from his previous efforts with his spear, and he looked
intimidated by the big man beside him. Still, he set his
jaw and raised his spear.

"Throw!" Graum shouted out.

Lumo hurled the willow circle into the air. Graum
didn't even look at it, at first. He was still staring a
Bumar. Bumar was staring up at the circle, but still he
must have been aware of the huge northerner crowding
close to him, staring at his face. Bumar cast his spear—
but it was a poor throw, and it went far from its target.

Graum's grin widened. He looked up just as the willow
circle started its descent. Quickly he threw his spear. The
shaft pierced the circle; Bumar had lost.

The hunters cheered Graum, but Bumar didn't join
them. He looked grim as he walked to retrieve his spear,
then joined the other men who had lost.

Now it was Graum who had to defend his victory. In
quick succession, men came out to face him, and one by
one, he defeated them. He was quick and accurate with
his spear, Mara could see that. He was able to hit the
willow circle almost every time. But more importantly,
the men who faced him were cowed by him. He knew
it, and he used it to his advantage. He seemed to make

them feel that they'd lost the game even before the willow circle was thrown.

But then, finally, Kormor came forward.

The two men looked at each other. Kormor stood proud; he returned Graum's stare without flinching. Slowly he smiled.

Something changed subtly in Graum's face. His grin faded, and his eyes narrowed. Abruptly he turned away from Kormor. "Throw!" he shouted.

The willow circle was tossed up before Kormor was ready for it. Graum made a deep growling sound as he threw his spear, and the shaft pierced the circle before it was even halfway to the top of its arc. The big man let out a shout of triumph and turned to Kormor, eyeing him with satisfaction. But Kormor ignored him. As the circle plunged down with Graum's spear embedded in it, Kormor threw his own spear. The hunters gasped in surprise as Kormor's spear flew true and joined Graum's, so that both shafts were threaded through the circle when it hit the ground.

Graum's grin vanished. His face was unreadable as he stared at Kormor. Kormor glanced at him, then quickly looked away, avoiding Graum's eyes.

"We will try again," Graum said.

The spears were retrieved. Once more, Lumo tossed the willow circle up.

This time the circle rose all the way to the top of its arc without either man casting his spear. The circle seemed to hover for a moment, presenting itself as a tempting target. But it was too high. Mara knew that Kormor usually waited till the circle was halfway down its descent—and sure enough, that was when he cast his spear.

Graum cast his own spear almost at the same moment. The two shafts rose side by side. People shaded their eyes, squinting at the sky, trying to tell the two shafts apart. There was total silence among all the onlookers— then a gasp, as only one of the spears found the target.

But whose spear was it? No one seemed to know. Neither Graum nor Kormor spoke. The hunters were turning to each other, shaking their heads.

Lumo ran out to the willow bough. Carefully, he raised it up with the shaft still in it. "Kormor's spear!" he cried in his high, thin voice. "Kormor wins!"

A few people cheered; the rest were oddly silent. Graum stood with his arms hanging loosely by his sides, and he stared at Kormor enigmatically. Without warning, he slapped Kormor on the shoulder. It seemed like a friendly gesture—and yet the blow was a heavy one. Kormor had to step back to keep his balance.

Slowly, grimly, Graum walked to join the group of losers. Mara watched him, and she found herself clenching her fists, digging her nails into her palms. She sensed the anger in the big man, and she didn't like to think what it might portend.

And meanwhile, Kormor was standing holding his spear, waiting to defend his new victory. She had no doubt that he'd do well. He had prevailed against Graum; the other men should be far easier. He seemed calm, relaxed, eyeing his opponents without any trace of concern.

The first of them came up, eager for the challenge. "Throw!" Kormor shouted. He cast his spear almost immediately, and it threaded itself neatly through the circle, pulling it down out of the sky. The other man stared at it, then shook his head and turned away without even trying to throw his own spear.

The rest of the men followed now in quick succession, and Kormor did exactly as Graum had done, moving impatiently, staring his challengers down. In every case, he judged the other man well. And in each case, he won.

Finally there was only one challenger left. He was Ulmei, the thin, sharp-faced youngster who had been the first to stand up and pledge himself to Graum on the night when the men had held the hot stones from the fire. Ulmei looked nervous, facing Kormor. He was weak and scrawny by comparison, and he obviously knew it.

Slowly Kormor smiled. "You can throw first," he called out to Ulmei.

Ulmei glanced around self-consciously. He nodded. "All right," he said, planting his feet wide apart and shifting his grip on his spear.

The willow circle was thrown. Ulmei squinted up at it—yet half his attention still seemed to be on Kormor. The circle rose up, up to the top of its journey. Still Ulmei didn't cast his spear. He hesitated, he waited—and then, when the circle was plummeting down, he made his move.

His spear flew hopelessly wide.

Kormor moved so quickly, it hardly seemed as if he had moved at all. But his spear was flying out on a shallow path. The circle was falling, racing down toward the grass. The spear shot out—and the two met, less than the height of a man above the ground. The spear flew true, and the willow circle was pierced.

The hunters ran forward, shouting. Kormor turned to face them and raised both his arms, victorious. They clustered around him, cheering. Graum pushed among them, seized Kormor by the shoulders, gave him a little shake, then ruffled his hair. The big man had had time to hide his anger. He was grinning again, as if he'd actually wanted Kormor to beat him.

He turned toward the people sitting around the rim of the hollow. "Kormor wins the first contest!" he shouted.

None of the spectators cheered. They glanced at each other uneasily, and some of them looked at Mara.

Mara didn't return their stares. She sat there in the grass, staring down at Kormor as he stood proud, once more holding his spear. She watched him, and she waited. The test was not yet over; there was still the second game to come.

Chapter 20

"This contest," Graum announced, "tests courage and strength." He held out his hand, and one of the hunters gave him a heavy stick. Graum walked to the center of the hollow, held the stick upright, then used a large stone to pound it into the ground. He pulled on it to test it, then nodded to himself. "Bring the animal," he said.

Two of the hunters ran up the side of the hollow and disappeared over the rim. There was a long pause; then they reappeared, dragging something. It was a wolf, Mara realized. A heavy thong had been tied around its jaws, holding them tightly closed. Two long, braided leather ropes had been tied around its neck, and one man was holding the end of each rope, standing on opposite sides of the wolf, dragging it between them. It struggled and reared up, making smothered growling, howling sounds.

The villagers stirred uneasily. No one had expected anything like this.

"Where I come from," Graum said, "we used to have a saying. It takes a brave man to grab a wolf's tail." Quickly he walked over to the animal, straddled it, and pinned its shoulders between his knees. It started struggling wildly, but the ropes around its neck still restrained it.

"We'll see, now," Graum said, "just how brave our hunters are." He used a flint knife to cut the thong binding the wolf's jaws.

The wolf's mouth sprang open. It lifted its head and let out a scream. Then it twisted its head and tried to seize hold of Graum's leg. He backed off quickly. He took the end of one of the braided ropes from the man who had been holding it, and he tied it securely to the stake that he'd hammered in the ground. Then he moved farther away. All the other men were already standing in a wide circle. "Let go!" Graum shouted to the man still holding the other rope.

The wolf was only tethered to the stake by a single rope now. It started running around wildly, jerking at its leash, growling and snapping. "Two by two!" Graum shouted. "Touch the tail! Carry a spear, just in case. But if you harm the wolf, you lose."

The first pair of hunters ventured cautiously forward, holding their spears ready. They circled around from opposite directions. The wolf saw one of them and went for him. The other leaped forward, ran behind, and managed to touch the wolf's tail with his outstretched hand.

The wolf whirled around. It saw the second man, snarled, and jumped at him.

The hunter quickly brought up the shaft of his spear, holding it between both hands to fend off the animal. Even so, the wolf's front claws raked the man's arm. He yelled and tried to kick the animal away from him. Then he turned and ran. The wolf chased after him and would have seized his ankle, but the leash jerked tight at the last moment.

While the wounded hunter licked blood off his arm, two more men ventured into the circle—more cautiously, now. Mara saw Graum grinning as he watched them, and she remembered seeing the same prurient look on his face when he'd persuaded the young hunters to grab hot stones out of the fire. But this time, he wasn't just a spectator. He, too, would have to risk himself with the wolf—and if he wanted any chance of being Chieftain of the tribe, he would have to win.

Another pair of hunters braved the wolf, and then another. Several men were clawed, but no one was seriously hurt. The ones who managed to touch the wolf's tail were grinning, laughing as they gathered at one side of the hollow.

Finally it was Kormor's turn. He and his opponent circled the animal. It had hunkered down in the grass and was panting. Kormor saw that the other man was tensing, getting ready to dart forward. Kormor's eyes widened. He had to act now or risk being eliminated. He jumped toward the wolf, moving impulsively, without any preparation. For a moment Mara thought he would succeed. But the animal saw him and sprang up, turning toward him as he came. Without warning, the wolf leaped forward. It opened its jaws and seized hold of Kormor's left foot.

The other man took advantage of the moment. He dove in, touched the wolf's tail, and ran back. But Kormor was still struggling. He shouted in pain and tried to beat the wolf back with the blunt end of his spear. The animal made a terrible growling sound and shifted, tightening its grip. "The rope!" Kormor shouted. "Grab the rope!"

Graum strode forward. He seized the rope that was trailing in the grass. He hauled savagely on it, and the wolf opened its jaws and yowled as it was dragged backward.

"I have to see," said Mara, jumping to her feet. It seemed foolish for her to be concerned, after everything that had happened between her and Kormor; yet she couldn't stop herself. She ran down the grassy slope as two men took hold of Kormor under the armpits, lifted him, and dragged him to safety.

Mara pushed among the crowd that was gathering. Kormor's moccasin had been torn off, and there were puncture wounds in his lower leg, bleeding profusely. Someone started wrapping a strip of rawhide around it, but suddenly Dira was there, slapping the man's hands out of the way. "Let me," she said.

"No!" Mara cried out.

Kormor was wincing in pain. He looked up, first at Dira, then at Mara.

"I have something to stop the bleeding," Dira said. She opened a pouch containing some green paste.

"What is it?" Mara demanded.

"Let her put it on!" Kormor shouted.

"Shepherd's purse," Dira said. She glared at Mara, daring her to interfere. Quickly, then, she dabbed the paste into the wounds.

Mara watched, feeling confused. She shouldn't be so

concerned, she told herself. The wound obviously wasn't serious; she could see the blood flowing less freely as the skin tightened. She'd acted impulsively, as she always did, running down into the hollow without thinking. She bowed her head, feeling angry with herself. Slowly she climbed back to the place where she'd been sitting. She tried not to notice that everyone was staring at her.

Lomel was looking at her questioningly, but Mara said nothing as she sat back down in the grass. She clutched her knees to her chest, and she waited.

Down in the hollow, Dira moved away from Kormor. A couple of the men lifted him up, and he tested his injured ankle. He winced but nodded, bracing himself on his spear. He limped to one side—and joined the group of men who had been eliminated from this contest.

"All right, careful, now!" Graum shouted as two more men prepared to face the wolf, and the game resumed.

There were no further injuries during the next few rounds. And then, finally, it was Graum's turn.

The wolf was getting tired and was slower to attack its tormentors. To make things still easier, Graum's opponent in this round was Maer. He was a tall, gangly man, good-natured, always smiling, and the best storyteller in the tribe. As a hunter, though, he lacked coordination and skill. Mara was surprised that he'd even bothered to enter the contest.

The two of them danced around the wolf. They made an odd pair, Maer so tall, Graum so heavy. Maer had an opportunity, as the wolf turned away from him and made a rush for Graum. But Maer hesitated—and then the chance was gone.

The wolf ran to the end of its leash and was pulled up short. It snarled, turned back toward Maer—and Graum seized the moment. He threw himself forward, flat on the ground, reaching for the tail.

Mara drew in her breath. Stretched out like that, Graum was defenseless. He'd have a hard time scrambling to safety if the wolf went for him.

But the big man had foreseen the danger. He reached for the wolf's tail, seized it in both hands, and swung his arms up, hurling the animal away from him. It flew a

dozen paces, hit the ground, and rolled over. It was un-
hurt, but by the time it got back onto its feet, Graum
was already retreating to safety, grinning broadly.

He had an advantage in this game, Mara realized. He
had played it before, in the North Lands.

The hunters who had managed to touch the wolf's tail
now started pairing off for the second round. Kormor sat
on the sidelines with the other men who'd been eliminated. He watched expressionlessly as the game continued. It was getting easier and easier as the wolf grew
tired.

Finally, once again, it was Graum's turn. And once
again, he was paired against an easy opponent—a boy
who hadn't even come of age. The boy looked nervous,
despite having made it through the first round of the
game. Under Graum's hostile eyes, he made a half-
hearted run across the circle. The wolf chased after
him—and Graum merely had to reach out and touch the
animal's tail as it passed him.

Could it have been arranged beforehand? Mara looked
at the other people watching, and she saw the same suspicion in their eyes.

So it went on, with Graum easily making his way
through into the final round. His opponent, now, was a
young man named Urngar, small but quick on his feet.
Urngar had won his previous rounds by being faster than
his opponents. But now, faced with Graum, he suddenly
seemed to lose his energy. He made a run behind the
wolf, and it seemed as if he could have easily touched
it, with just a small burst of speed. But when he reached
out, he was still an arm's length away.

Graum grinned. He moved around, reached down, and
took hold of the leather leash. He braced himself, then
hauled hard on the leash, pulling the wolf off its feet.
The animal had exhausted itself. It was tired and slow,
and it yelped as it found itself thrown down on its side.
It made feeble attempts to get back up, but Graum was
already striding forward. With a triumphant shout, he
stamped on the wolf's tail. He stepped back, then, and
the second half of the contest was his.

There was a great cheer from the hunters, and they

all clustered around. He threw his head back and gave an ugly, guttural cry, a raw howling sound, and suddenly they were all doing it, imitating him. It was so primitive, Mara felt herself shivering. There the men were, and there was the animal they had just tormented; and as she looked to and fro, it was hard for her to see the difference.

Finally the howling stopped. Graum seized a spear and walked over to the wolf, which had hunkered down in the grass, watching the men with weariness and fear in its eyes. It started up onto its feet as he approached, but the big man flung his spear in a fast, fluent motion. The spear skewered the wolf and embedded itself in the ground, pinning the animal. It started screaming, trying futilely to bite the shaft that had penetrated it.

Graum held out a flint knife to Kormor. Kormor took it from him and moved forward, limping. The wolf stared at him balefully as he approached. It let out a last despairing bark before Kormor swiftly slashed its throat, taking revenge for the injury to his ankle. A few moments later, making coughing, bubbling sounds, the wolf died in its own blood.

"All right," said Graum, turning away. "There's two of us who are winners. Me and Kormor. Well, we agreed before we started that if we had to break a tie, each man would take a spear and see who throws the farthest." He looked at Kormor. "You go first," he said.

For a moment the two men faced each other. They looked into each other's eyes, and it almost seemed as if something passed between them.

"No," Kormor said carefully. "Cast your spear, Graum. Give me something to aim for."

The big man took a moment longer, still looking at Kormor. Finally he gave a curt nod. He strode up to the rim and stood for a moment, silhouetted against the sky. He was so huge, there seemed no possible doubt that he would do better than any of the other men. Yet Kormor, too, was exceptionally strong.

Graum hefted his spear. He turned sideways, planted his feet securely, and cast the wooden shaft, letting out a great shout as he did so.

It was a good throw, but not the greatest that Mara had ever seen. And if that was clear to her, it must have been clear to all the men, too. They said nothing, but she saw the hunters glancing at each other.

Graum stepped aside. Kormor hefted his spear and followed him up to the rim, limping slightly. His left leg was the one that had been bitten, which was fortunate, since his right leg would take most of the strain when he made his throw.

He stood with his long black hair stirring in the wind and his muscular torso outlined against the sky. Once again Mara saw why she had chosen him as her mate, for he looked so bold, so brave, with the spear in his hand. He turned sideways and she saw his profile: his high forehead, his straight nose, and his strong jaw. She found herself suddenly overcome with nostalgia and sadness. How fine their pairing could have been, she thought, if he had made himself her ally instead of her adversary. He could have drawn upon her strength; but instead, he had felt a need to overcome it.

Kormor paused for a while longer, eyeing the spear in the distance, with Lumo standing out there beside it. Mara swallowed hard, feeling her stomach tighten. If Kormor became Chieftain, she feared for herself. If Graum won, she feared for her tribe. It seemed such an awful choice; but as she watched and waited, she reached her own private realization. He was arrogant, and he had treated her brutishly; yet Kormor was still an honest man. Mara felt suddenly certain that the tribe would be safer in his hands than if Graum led it. Even though she dreaded the consequences for herself, she found herself wishing, deeply and passionately, for Kormor to win.

He brought his arm back and cast the spear quickly, almost before anyone was ready for it. The villagers jumped up onto their feet, everyone staring at the tiny black line that raced across the sky. It plummeted down—and it landed almost beside the spear that Graum had thrown.

Lumo had backed away as the spear came down, but now he ran forward to the two shafts. "Graum!" he shouted to the waiting crowd. "Graum's spear went farther!"

A great shout rang out from the hunters gathered in the hollow. They surged around Graum. They seized hold of him, grappled with him, and finally managed to lift him up onto their shoulders.

Mara was probably the only person who was still watching Kormor. He was already halfway down the slope to the bottom of the hollow. He hadn't even waited to see where his spear would land. He was ignoring everything around him, looking somber, lost in his own thoughts.

He knew, she realized with sudden certainly. *He didn't need to stand there and watch where his spear would land. He knew, before he even threw it.* And that could only mean that he had chosen to throw short.

The hunters were still cheering, marching around the hollow, holding Graum high. He was laughing and waving, though none of the spectators waved back. There was a steadfast silence up on the rim of the hollow as everyone stared at the spectacle below, trying to grasp the full implications.

"Mara," said a voice.

Mara looked up quickly and found Shani standing there. Lomel had gone, she realized. She had run down into the hollow to be with her brother. Other women—wives and daughters—were likewise seeking out their menfolk. Some people were getting up, turning their backs, walking away toward the village.

Awkwardly, Mara stood up. She looked at Shani, feeling reluctant to talk to her. Mara felt deeply distressed by the contests and their outcome. She wasn't sure, even now, exactly what had happened and exactly what it might mean. She couldn't stand the prospect of another confrontation with her sister.

Shani seemed to guess her thoughts. "I don't wish to squabble with you anymore, sister." Her voice sounded weary. There was no spirit in it.

Mara hesitated. "I'm glad," she said.

There were sad lines in Mara's face. She looked older,

wearier than Mara had ever seen her look before. "Sister," Shani said, "I came to apologize to you."

For a moment, Mara wasn't sure she had understood. "Apologize?" she echoed.

"I spoke harshly to you yesterday," Shani said. "I was still too full of grief over Mother's death." She paused, squinting into the distance. "You tried to help me, in your way, when you saw what was happening in the Meeting Place. I doubted you at first. But now I see that you meant well."

The words seemed well-intentioned, yet they aggravated Mara all the same. "I wanted you to save us," she said. Perhaps she shouldn't speak out, but even now, she couldn't stop herself. "They still respected you, Shani. You might have been able to persuade them."

Shani reached out and held Mara's arm. She was shaking her head sadly. "Sister," she said, "a wise leader doesn't force her people to obey her. A wise leader serves them and respects their wishes."

"But their wishes were wrong!" Mara checked herself with difficulty. "I'm sorry, but surely you see that it's so. Graum roused something in our men. They can't be trusted to make wise decisions anymore."

Once again, Shani sighed. "Mara, you were right when you denounced Graum in front of our people. Does that make you feel better, to hear me say that?"

Their eyes met. Mara had never seen Shani like this; she wasn't sure what to make of it. Reluctantly, she nodded. "Thank you," she said.

Shani inclined her head, gracefully accepting the words. "But our people may not be as foolish as you think. They'll find out soon enough if they've made a mistake. We should still trust their wisdom, Mara."

"Their wisdom." Mara clutched her stomach. Once again, she felt a sudden wave of nausea. It was awful to be weak like this and not know what was happening to her or how to fight it. She found herself kneeling down, doubling forward, retching feebly.

Shani touched her shoulder. "You still didn't get a remedy from Dira."

Mara shook her head.

Shani paused, looking at her for a long moment. "Well, I suppose it will pass of its own accord. It always does."

Mara raised her head and stared at her. "What?"

"The morning sickness." Shani raised her eyebrows as she saw Mara's blank expression. "Sister, isn't that what you're suffering from?"

Mara slumped back. She lay in the grass, resting on her side. She closed her eyes a moment, remembering everything that had happened in the past weeks. "I didn't know," she whispered. And then, she thought: Maybe she had known, really. It had just been too difficult, too frightening to contemplate.

"If you tell Kormor that you're pregnant, it should encourage him to treat you more gently," Shani suggested.

Mara looked up at her. "Why are you being so kind to me?" she asked.

It was Shani's turn to be silent for a while. "Perhaps because I don't fear you anymore. After all, I have nothing to lose now."

Mara pulled herself up. The nausea was diminishing again. She shook her head in confusion. "But I was never a threat to you. How could I have been?"

"Because you were always so aggressive. You always wanted things your own way. You always wanted what—what I had." Shani tilted her jaw up a little. "You can't deny that's true."

Mara laughed without humor. "Yes, I was envious of you. Of course I was. You had all the things I lacked. But there never seemed the slightest chance I would have any of them." She sighed. "Look, it doesn't matter anymore. Mother's gone, the tribe is no longer yours to lead—we both have nothing, now."

Shani glanced to one side. "Well, I have Ipaw." Wistfully, she smiled to herself.

Mara saw Ipaw standing a little way away. He was staring off to one side, but obviously he was waiting for Shani.

"Anyway," Shani went on, sounding more purposeful, now. "This is the main thing I came to say: Yesterday,

I told you that you weren't welcome at our house. But some of our clan scolded me for that." She looked into Mara's eyes. "It's probably best if you don't visit often, because ... well, we have never had an easy time with each other, you and I. But after your baby is born, at the very least, we should perform the naming ritual." She nodded slowly. "I think Mother would have wanted that."

Mara looked at her. "The naming ritual," she repeated. It sounded as if Shani must be talking about someone else. She couldn't even begin to imagine herself with a child.

"Just think," said Shani, "by then, I'll be paired. Why, I may even be pregnant, as you are now." She smiled and her lines of sadness softened. "Take care of yourself, sister," she said. "I should go now." She carefully brushed pieces of dead grass off her robe. "And thank you again for trying to help." She turned and wandered across the grassland. Ipaw quickly went to her, and he fell into step beside her.

Mara watched them go. The wind blew again, and she shivered. She found herself remembering something else that Lizel had said, about the wisdom of letting each person choose her own path. If that path was wrong, and if people were too misguided to realize it—what then?

Lizel had asked that question; but she hadn't answered it.

Meanwhile, down in the hollow, the men had set Graum back on his feet. He chuckled and aimed some fake punches at some of them, ducking and feinting. Then he threw his head back, and once again, all the young hunters let out a guttural, howling cry.

PART THREE

▼ ▲ ▼

Winter

Chapter 21

She was alone. Her snowshoes made a rhythmic *shush, shush* as she toiled across the flat, white expanse. There was no other sound.

The sky was heavy gray, and the light was dim. Mara was glad of the ominous weather, for it meant that she would be harder to see if anyone looked out from the village. It was strange, to be thinking like that—to hide from the watchful eyes of Graum, Kormor, and the other men, and to feel like a fugitive from her own tribe. But during the past months, it had become necessary.

She paused for a moment. Her pulse was beating fast from the effort of walking in the snowshoes, and her breath rose in white plumes. She was near the center of the lake, standing alone on the dusting of snow that covered the thick layer of ice. From here, the village was barely visible as a cluster of tiny mounded black shapes on the eastern shore, with thin columns of gray smoke rising to meet the gray clouds above. The only signs of life were some specks near the shore—women at the edge of the lake, fishing with thongs through holes in the ice. Last winter, they would have been using spears; but not anymore. No woman, now, was allowed to touch a spear.

Mara felt a familiar little twist of anger—and just as quickly, she felt an equally familiar feeling of resignation. The edicts that Graum and Dira had handed down were like walls that had been built around her and the other women, and she was not strong enough, on her own, to overcome them. Nor did it seem that anyone else was willing to do so. Many of the women were too scared. Many of the men privately said they had mixed feelings—yet none of them actually spoke out against the new regime, and Mara suspected that they found it more to their liking than they were willing to admit.

She turned her back on the village and pressed on across the ice. Along the western side of the lake were steep slopes thickly covered with pines. Few of her people ever came here. During the winter, there was little game to be found on the wooded slopes, and during the summer, it was too much trouble to walk all the way around the long, long lake to reach its western shore. The hunting was better in the valley and in the hills that lay farther to the east, so why bother with the land that lay in the opposite direction?

Mara felt comfortably, safely alone as she stepped off the ice. Her snowshoes were fashioned from willow branches laced with leather thongs, and they took her easily up across deep drifts, into the shelter of the forest where the underbrush had been shielded from the weather and was only lightly coated with white. Mara paused for a moment, enjoying the silence of the woodland. Here, at least, there were no rules to limit her life.

But then she heard a sound. A twig cracking.

She held her breath and stood listening. She glanced around with new caution, wishing she had her spear. Bears would be hibernating now, and big cats weren't usually out at this time of day. But there could still be wolves.

She heard another small snapping sound, and some faint rustlings, closer than before. She looked for a place to hide. Quickly she pushed into some thorn bushes and huddled down among them. She was wearing a white sheepskin coat, which blended well with her surroundings, but even so, she was very vulnerable.

She waited, straining her ears and peering anxiously through a gap in the bushes. Within just a few moments she saw a movement.

It was a person, not an animal. Someone wearing a sheepskin coat like hers, with a close-fitting hood. Mara heard the footsteps clearly now, and she saw white breath drifting in the frigid air. The figure came closer unaware that there was anyone nearby. And then Mara saw the face inside the hood.

"Hey!" Mara shouted. She plunged out of her hiding place, lurching clumsily on her snowshoes. "Lomel!"

The figured stopped and stared. "Mara?" The girl smiled. She hurried forward and threw herself against Mara, hugging her, laughing. "You scared me!"

Mara looked at her face, the flushed cheeks dusted with frost crystals, the eyes friendly and full of life. Impulsively, Mara kissed one cheek, then the other. "What are you doing here?" she said. "I thought I was the only one who comes out here across the ice."

Lomel shook her head. "I thought the same thing." She slid the mitten off her left hand, reached out, and wiped snow from Mara's face. "It's so good to see you. We've been like strangers the past few weeks."

Mara released the girl and stepped back, feeling embarrassed. "It's my fault," she said. "Kormor doesn't like me to go out much. He's always afraid I'll do something that'll be bad for the baby." She placed her hand across her abdomen. "In any case, I've never really done what most of the women do in the winter months. Weaving baskets, stitching clothes, telling stories—I get too restless."

"I know what you mean," said Lomel. "I'd rather be out here, on my own." She gave Mara a shy look. "Perhaps we're alike, you and me."

Mara doubted that. Lomel seemed so shy and self-effacing. Yet, at the same time, Mara felt genuine pleasure at finding her out here. At the very least, she was a friendly face.

"Were you just wandering?" Mara asked.

"Yes. You know, the men were all in the Spirit House for the ceremony, so it seemed to be a good time to get away for a while." She paused, and some of her cheerfulness died. "I hope Arin will be all right."

"Of course he will. It's only a coming-of-age ceremony."

"But he was scared, all the same," said Lomel. "Graum is not a kind man." She shrugged, shaking off the somber mood. She turned back toward Mara. "Can you keep a secret?"

"Yes."

"Follow me." Lomel moved a little way down the slope, out from the shelter of the pines. She started north, around the edge of the lake.

"Are we going far?" Mara asked. She felt anxious about staying out too long. Kormor was at the ceremony with all the other young hunters, but if it ended early and Kormor returned home and found her missing, there would be another ugly scene, and she didn't want to face that.

"It's close by," said Lomel. She checked the terrain, then plunged up into the forest again. "Look."

At first Mara saw nothing. Then she noticed an object dangling from a sapling. It was a rabbit, she realized, with a thong looped around its foot.

Lomel went over, pulled on the sapling, and bent it down till she could grab the rabbit. It was frozen rigid. She used her teeth to loosen the noose from the rabbit's leg. "Catch!" she said, and threw the game to Mara.

Mara caught it and studied it for a moment. The eyes were closed, and the fur was whitened with snow. It looked as if it had fallen asleep in a drift. Quickly she thrust it into the shoulder pack that she carried.

Lomel started resetting the snare. She widened the noose and hauled on the sapling, curving it over till the tip of it almost touched the ground. A small twig had been knotted into the thong; this twig she wedged delicately at the base of the small branch in a bramble bush nearby. That was enough to take the tension in the thong, though the slightest movement would dislodge it. Moving cautiously now, she raised the noose and draped it over two bramble branches, so that it hung across a narrow path where animal tracks showed in the snow.

"We used to do this in the North Lands," she said, stepping back. "My father taught me how." She grinned at Mara. "The men haven't stopped us from setting snares yet, have they?"

"No," said Mara. "Though I imagine they might, if they decided it allowed us too much pleasure." She gave her an appraising look. "I didn't realize that you knew how to trap."

Lomel glanced cautiously at Mara, as if wondering whether to confide her. "There's more," she said shyly, "if you want to see."

Mara nodded. "All right."

"This way." Lomel started farther up the slope, and together they climbed higher among the trees. Soon they were walking through brush where the snow was so thin, it was quicker to take off their snowshoes. They made better progess now—until, unexpectedly, they emerged in a small clearing.

Lomel walked over to some pine logs that had been piled against an outcropping of rock. She started hauling the wood away, revealing a small cave. "I put the logs here to keep bears out," she said. "Come inside."

Mara climbed over the logs, into the cave. It was shallow, and the roof was low. Still, it felt comfortable and safe around her, walling out the world.

Lomel shifted a stone away from a cache in the floor. There were two more rabbits there, some firesticks, and some dry tinder.

"Are you planning to live out here?" Mara asked, looking at her in surprise.

Lomel smiled as she put her mittens aside, took out the firesticks, fitted one into the other, and started spinning it between her palms. "I just wanted a place to come to sometimes," she said. "I've never been very happy at home. You know, my father's a stern man, and my mother never stands up against him." She paused for a moment, looking unhappy. But then she shrugged, and once again it seemed as if she was able to push her troubles aside. "I've learned to be on my own," she said.

"You seem cheerful, though," said Mara. "Things don't weigh you down."

"That's because I don't let myself think about them." She made it sound very matter-of-fact. She blew on the first few sparks and nudged tinder into the little flickering flame.

"I wish it was so simple for me," Mara said. "If there's something that seems wrong, I can never forget it."

"Then that's the difference between us," said Lomel. She fed the flames, and the wood started crackling. She gestured to Mara's bag. "Shall we skin the rabbit?"

Mara moved uneasily. "I'm afraid that if I don't get back—"

"The ceremony will last all afternoon," said Lomel. "Arin told me so. Anyway, you can always tell Kormor that you went out fishing." She looked at Mara, and she shyly smiled. "I came out here to be alone, but really, I'd prefer to be with you."

While the rabbit sizzled over the fire, they stretched out together, soaking up the warmth from the flames. Lomel was silent for a little while, looking deep in thought. "You know," she said, "Arin's not the only one who's come of age."

"You?" Mara examined the girl's face. Lomel still looked the same—and yet there was just a hint of new confidence and adult composure.

Lomel nodded, looking pleased. "I bled for the first time last month. I'm not just a little girl anymore."

Mara remembered her own ceremony and how proud she had felt. That gave her a pang, thinking back to the hopes she'd cherished.

"I think it's wrong," Lomel went on, "that we shouldn't celebrate a woman's first blood anymore."

Angrily, Mara threw a piece of wood onto the fire, stirring up a flurry of sparks. "Of course it's wrong."

"But perhaps you'll take me a little more seriously, now," Lome went on.

Mara hesitated. "I don't think I ever—"

"Oh, you talked to me like a child. But that's all right. Everyone did." Lomel turned toward her, and this time she stared at her frankly. "You know, I've seen you in the past, walking out onto the lake alone. And I guessed you'd take a walk today, while the men are having their ceremony. That's why I came out here myself. So I could meet up with you." Boldly, she took hold of Mara's hand.

The physical contact gave Mara a strange feeling. It was far more intimate than it should have been, and so delicate, so gentle. Kormor, she thought, had never really touched her that way. Mara looked at Lomel, wondering what was happening. "Why did you want to see me?" she said.

"Because I like you. I think you're a good person, Mara."

Mara felt something stirring in her. Her desires had faded during the past few months, as life with Kormor had become a routine of submitting wordlessly to his demands. Mara had ended up feeling empty, cut off from the vivid feelings that had once surged so strongly. But now Lomel's face seemed strangely enticing. Tentatively, she reached out and stroked her hair. It seemed even thicker than she remembered it, yet it was silky under her touch. "It used to hang below your shoulders," she said.

"Yours, too," said Lomel. "Before they made us cut it short." She was still staring into Mara's face. Her brown eyes were soft, compassionate, and very beautiful.

Lomel reached out. Mara realized the girl wasn't quite as bold as she was trying to seem. There was a tremor in her fingers. But she touched Mara's cheek, then the side of her neck. She hesitated. "Do you mind?" she whispered, as she pulled Mara toward her.

Mara didn't resist. She found herself nuzzling Lomel's hair. She felt Lomel kissing her cheek.

They were so totally alone, here in the little cave beside the crackling fire, it seemed as if time was stretching out around them and the rest of the world no longer existed. Mara's pulse was fast and light, and her skin was tingling, so that the tiniest touch seemed magnified. This was taboo, she told herself; but in a way, that made it more exciting. There had been so little pleasure in the last few months, and so much coldness and anger, didn't she really deserve something like this, which felt so good?

Lomel slowly closed her eyes. She parted her lips. Mara stared at her, feeling her awareness contract until she saw nothing but Lomel's face. Clearly, she was waiting for her. Mara found herself growing tense, scared by her own feelings. And then, before she could stop herself, she leaned forward and pressed her mouth against Lomel's.

She felt a great wave of emotion, so intense it made her shiver. This, she realized, was what she'd always wanted with Kormor. Tenderness, kindness, softness— and in another way, wasn't this what she'd always wanted with Shani, too? Not physically, but mentally: a deep feeling of sisterhood and love.

The emotions were almost painfully strong. Suddenly Mara pulled away, feeling overwhelmed. Without knowing why, she realized that her eyes were moist. She fell back against the side of the cave and lay there for a long moment, taking deep breaths, trying to calm herself.

Lomel reached out. She touched Mara's wet cheek. "Did it feel so wrong?"

"No." Mara sniffed and shook her head. "No, it's just—I've been so unhappy, with Kormor, and with my sister, and my mother before she died, and my whole clan, too. And you're so nice to me . . ." She gradually got herself back under control. "Perhaps I've been avoiding you, Lomel. I think I sensed that this could happen, and I was afraid of it."

Lomel sat cross-legged on the cave floor, watching Mara earnestly. "I've wanted this for some time," she said. "Ever since the mastodon hunt."

Mara forced a smile. "You make it sound simple."

Lomel shrugged. "For me, it is. I've never been excited by boys."

"But this is taboo."

"Well, that's what some people say. But I thought you were a rebel, Mara. Isn't that what you told me once?" Lomel gave her a sly smile. "I thought I might have a chance with you when I heard that."

Mara laughed. Suddenly she felt free. She had crossed the line; it was foolish to think of going back. She reached for Lomel, pulled her close, and this time she kissed her without shame and without regret.

Chapter 22

When they finally started back toward the village, the landscape was shrouded in shadow. They'd felt so snug and comfortable, eating the freshly roasted rabbit meat and dozing together beside the fire, neither of them had had the willpower to get up and leave.

Now, though, Mara felt a deep, cold foreboding as she hurried with Lomel across the icebound lake. They moved together in silence, both of them trying to cling to the warm feelings that they'd shared, but both of them knowing that the warmth was gradually seeping away.

"We should split up now," Mara murmured when they could see the shapes of the Clan Houses through the gloom.

Quickly Lomel hugged her. "We'll have more afternoons like this," she said. "We will, won't we, Mara?"

Mara looked at Lomel's upturned face, so earnest and hopeful. "Of course we will," she said—although she feared for the future. "But now we must hurry." She kissed Lomel's forehead. "Quickly! You go first!"

She stood and watched as Lomel headed away across the flat, white lake. Then Mara took a slightly different path, toward the southern end of the village.

It was almost completely dark when she reached her home. She passed no one along the way, and she wondered if there might even be a chance that the men were still in the Spirit House conducting their coming-of-age ritual. But then, as her little tent of mammoth hide came into view, she saw a figure standing outside it in the gathering dusk.

"Kormor," she said, trying to make her voice sound casual. "Why are you out here?"

"Where have you been?" He glared at her, and she saw the whites of his eyes flash in the waning light.

She stopped in front of him. "I was out fishing," she told him. "Is there anything wrong with that?"

He paused, eyeing her face. Then, quickly, he slapped her. "I've warned you not to lie to me."

She stepped back, holding her cheek. He hardly ever struck her if she was outside their home. She knew, now, this wasn't going to be a trivial matter. "But I was fishing!" she cried out.

"No one saw you in the place where the women fish. And no one could find you when they went looking. Get inside!"

This was intolerable, she thought, to feel so good and peaceful and happy with another person, and then to be treated like this. She clenched her fists, wishing somehow she could enforce justice on Kormor—force him to see how cruel he was and how wrong he was.

She tried to hold her emotions in check. She ducked her head, keeping her distance from him in case he decided to slap her again. She pushed through the door flap, into their home.

He didn't follow her. She sat in the cold, empty little place, and she clutched herself, shivering. Was he still outside? What was he doing?

Well, if nothing else, she needed warmth. Her fingers were nervous and clumsy as she used her firesticks, and it took her far longer than usual. Then she heard old Lorm, the News Teller, moving among the homes of the people, shouting something. She paused and listened. "All men and women to the Meeting Place," he announced. "A special meeting. Graum calls all men and women ..."

Mara closed her eyes. It seemed almost every other night, Graum called the Lake People to meet at sunset. And always it was an unhappy affair. New laws would be announced, or new punishments for breaking the old laws. Someone would be made to stand in front of the tribe and confess to a crime. Usually it would be a woman, and one of the young hunters would accuse her of spreading gossip, or disobeying her husband, or stealing food—for food was rationed now, even though the caches had been full to bursting at the start of the winter.

And of course, all of this was for the good of the people. Graum said that the Lake People had to learn discipline and leave behind their idle habits. They had to be strong, they had to be prepared in case outsiders came to steal from them. Really, this was the only way the tribe could be sure to survive. Anyone who had lived in the North Lands should surely understand that it was true.

Privately, some of the people from the North Lands had started saying that Graum was going too far. Mara had heard complaints from the women and whispers among the elders, in particular. But no one dared to speak out, because Graum and his men were so strict and cruel with troublemakers.

Mara felt a sudden leap of anxiety as she realized that she herself might be called before the tribe tonight. She had disobeyed her husband—and with Lomel, she had broken a strict taboo. Could anyone have followed them or spied on them? Surely not. Mara told herself not to be foolish, thinking such things. Yet she couldn't push the anxiety away.

Abruptly the door flap was dragged aside. "Come with me now." It was Kormor's voice.

"What if I choose not to?" She looked up at him with as much defiance as she could manage.

He reached in, grabbed her by the hair, and dragged her roughly toward the door flap. She tripped and found herself falling, half inside, half out in the snow. "Careful!" she cried. "The baby!"

He made an angry, frustrated sound, and she saw him flexing his fingers, wanting to seize hold of her again, but prevented now by his own concerns. This was her only power over him, the child that was growing inside her. It was precious to him—more precious, apparently, than she was herself.

"Get up," he said.

Slowly, taking her time, she stood and dusted the snow off herself. "What is it to be?" she asked him. "Am I supposed to stand in front of the tribe and confess that I defied you?"

"Yes," he said.

As Mara walked into the Meeting Place, the first thing she noticed was a heavy wooden stake that had been driven into the ground directly in front of the Speaking Stone. It was a pine log, taller than a man and almost as thick as Graum's fat neck. The bark and branches had been stripped off it, all except for one short, stubby branch at the back, near the top. Mara looked at the stake, and instinctively she feared it.

Graum himself was standing close beside it, wrapped in the black bearskin that he always wore now. The bear's head rested on top of his head, its jaw gaping, its teeth gleaming in the flickering firelight.

The Honor Guard stood either side of him. There were two score of them, each man with a snarling bear's face tattooed on his forehead. Tattooing had been a skill unknown to the Lake People, but Graum knew how it was done, though he refused to reveal the secret. Kormor had been the first to submit to it, and afterward, when he returned home with the bear on his brow, he wouldn't talk about it. All he would say was that it had been painful, and the results could never be erased.

"Wait here," Kormor told her, pushing her toward the villagers who were huddling close to each other and to the big fire burning in the center of the Meeting Place. He didn't wait for her to reply. He walked over to Graum and took his place beside the big man.

Mara looked at the young hunters—and she realized that there was one more of them than before. Arin was among them now. His face was deathly pale. A fresh bear-head tattoo was oozing blood on his forehead, and he had a glazed look in his eyes. He was leaning heavily on his spear as if he barely had the strength to stand.

Mara glanced quickly around. She saw Lomel close beside her father, Tiear, and her mother, Rika. Tiear's face was stern and composed, but Lomel and her mother were both looking at Arin with an expression of distress.

Mara scanned the rest of the faces around the fire, and

she saw Shani, surrounded by her clan. Shani looked older these days, and pained by the changes she had seen during the past months. Beside her stood Ipaw, looking ill-at-ease. The two of them had been paired just a few weeks ago, in a simple ceremony inside the Clan House. Mara had attended it, and they had been friendly and polite to her, but she hadn't felt truly welcome. This time, though, there had been no reason to take it personally. Shani had distanced herself from everyone in the tribe since her status had been nullified.

The elder hunters were standing close to her. They looked grim and weary, and there was one fewer of them now than there had been before. Yacor had sickened and died. He had never recovered his spirit after the death of Ternees, which he always felt as his personal burden. After Graum became Chieftain, as the winter closed in, Yacor was claimed by a coughing sickness that had taken all his strength. He lay close to Ternees, now, in the burial ground.

Mara looked at the rest of the villagers. None of them was happy. There was a righteousness in the faces of many of the men, who still seemed to believe it was good for a man to lead the tribe, and good to see more discipline. Graum had stirred up their fears, and he'd made them feel that they should be ashamed if they weren't hard and fierce. But most of the women were sad-eyed and drab, and even the children seemed oddly subdued.

"People!" Graum climbed up onto the Speaking Stone. His eyes glittered as he surveyed them all. He had gained weight, Mara thought to herself Evidently he wasn't bound by the meat ration that he imposed on the rest of the tribe.

"We have some serious matter tonight," he said. "And that's why I've summoned you all." He turned to one of his guards. "Get Hopwa."

There were sounds of surprise from the people around Mara. What business could Graum have with the old keeper of the food caches?

Mara watched in dismay as Hopwa was hustled forward. He blinked in the firelight and turned his face from side to side, only dimly aware of what was happening.

"Feeno, tell us what you saw today," Graum said.

Feeno was the one holding Hopwa's arm. He was a dour-faced, scrawny man, mean-spirited and mean-eyed. "I was on guard duty at the food cache," said Feeno. "My back was turned for a moment, and when I turned around, Hopwa was trying to open one up."

Graum nodded slowly. He wasn't angry, just regretful at having to cope with this unfortunate situation. "Hopwa served the tribe well in the past," he said. "I'm sure that's true." He grunted. "Still, he has to understand that when he steals food, he steals from everyone."

"But there's food to spare," Hopwa said. He was squinting up at Graum, tilting his head, trying to focus on the big man. "It's my job, managing the food. I know what's in there."

"It's not your job anymore," Graum said. "It's been Feeno's job for the past three months. Maybe this will help you to remember that." He gestured to a couple of his guards. "Strip him," he said.

The villagers started murmuring in concern—and disapproval.

"He has to learn!" Graum told them, spreading his arms. "Anyway, this won't hurt. It's a harmless lesson."

Two of his guards moved forward. They grabbed Hopwa's coat and dragged it off him. Then, while the old man struggled feebly, they stripped away his undergarments of caribou skin.

"Stop this!" Hopwa shouted, as his bare skin was exposed to the cold air. "You have no right!"

"Go, then," said Graum. "Run back to your Clan House, old man. And remember not to steal our food, in future."

His guards started laughing as Hopwa clutched his scrawny body with his bony arms and looked around in confusion, searching for help. Some of the guards jeered at him, and one of them gave him a kick. Hopwa stumbled away, crying out in pain and fear as his bare feet plunged into the snow.

A woman in the crowd stripped off her own robe and stepped forward. But before she could offer it to Hopwa, a guard strode over and raised his spear, blocking her path.

"All right," said Graum, as Hopwa hobbled out of sight between the Clan Houses. He rubbed one of his knuckles across the side of his jaw, and seriousness returned to his plump face. "Now we have something more unpleasant to deal with. Bumar, tell us your story."

Slow-witted, bad-tempered Bumar had been paired just a couple of months previously. He stood in front of the villagers and paused, looking uneasy, as if he wasn't sure what he should say.

"Tell them," Graum said, making his voice sound almost kind. "Tell them what happened with your new mate."

Bumar glanced at Graum, then back at the crowd. "Found her with another man," he said. He grimaced and spat onto the snow. "In his Clan House." He eyed the crowd uneasily, as if he was afraid that people might laugh at him.

"All right, Bumar," said Graum. "That's all."

Bumar nodded. He stepped back.

"Bumar's mate is Weena," said Graum. There was an apprehensive silence in the people facing him. "Weena, I see you there. Step forward."

People glanced quickly around. Weena was a drab, sad-faced woman in ragged, unkempt furs. She gazed balefully at Graum, and she didn't move.

"Bring her out," Graum said, gesturing at two of his guards.

They stepped forward and pushed their way into the crowd. Quickly they seized Weena by her upper arms and dragged her forward.

"This post," said Graum, pointing to the pine log, "is what I call the Justice Post. It's going to be used whenever there's a need here to set things straight." He gave the villagers a long, hard look. "Seems to me there's a need for that right now."

"He forced me to!" Weena shouted suddenly. "Him!" She pointed at another of Graum's guards—a man named Oro, who had no mate of his own. "He dragged me off to his Clan House, and he forced me to!"

Graum was shaking his head. "That doesn't make sense. He dragged you through the village, and no one noticed? Don't lie. That'll just make things worse."

Without warning, she burst into tears. "It was just as much his fault as mine," she cried out. "Punish him, if you're going to punish me!"

"We've already disciplined Oro," said Graum. "He did something wrong, I grant you that, and we made sure he understands it. But now we've got you to deal with." He jerked his head. "Tie her to the post so she faces the crowd."

The men holding Weena hustled her to the heavy pine log. Quickly they dragged her arms behind her, around the log, and tied her wrists.

Mara glanced at the people around her. The men looked uneasy; the women looked shocked. Infidelity had always been a taboo, of course, and there was a good reason for that: The tribe needed to know who a child's parents were, so it would be properly cared for. But in the past the only penalty had been the tribe's disapproval. A man or woman who cheated on a mate would be ignored by everyone for months; that was considered punishment enough.

"Bumar, take this." Graum held out a flint knife.

The big man moved forward and took it in his fist.

"Remember what I told you earlier?" said Graum.

Bumar hesitated, then nodded. He started toward Weena. She saw the knife in his hand, and she screamed. The sound was piercing, and it made Mara feel weak inside. Never before had she heard one of her people scream like that here in the Meeting Place.

Weena started struggling—but she was securely tied to the stake, and the two guards on either side of her grabbed her by the hair, hauling her head back against the post so she was forced to face her husband.

"Her cheeks and her forehead," said Graum. "We're going to make sure, here, no one's going to want to cheat with her again."

Bumar struck out with the flint. Two lines blossomed on his wife's left cheek—a red X mark. She screamed again. "Stop him!" she shouted. "Somebody stop him!"

Instinctively, the villagers started moving forward.

Graum's guards responded. They placed themselves as a human barrier between the villagers and the Justice Post, and they leveled their spears.

Everyone stopped. There was a disbelieving silence. Never had one group of the Lake People turned weapons against another. Mara felt tears starting, and she knuckled them away angrily. *Shani*, she thought. *Shani, now do you see?*

"There's going to be justice done, here," Graum said. His voice was loud now. "You men, you should be thankful. Think about it. Have you ever wondered about your women? Have you wondered if they've been thinking about doing things they shouldn't?" He surveyed the crowd. He lowered his voice. "Some women cheat. They do; it's a fact. But they'll think twice about it now they see what the penalties are."

Weena was still sobbing and pleading. Bumar was still standing facing her with the flint in his hand. He wasn't moving. He seemed to have lost his stomach for what he had to do.

"Finish the job," Graum told him. "Go on!"

Bumar took a deep breath, made another X on his wife's right cheek, and then a third, on her forehead.

"Good," said Graum. "Take her home and rub sand in the wounds, so they scar."

Weena was released from the post. She clapped her hands to her cheeks, then looked at the blood on her palms. She stared at Bumar in disbelief. "Why?" she cried.

He grabbed her arm and hustled her away.

Mara saw some of Graum's guards exchanging glances. At first she thought they must feel ashamed. But no; there was something else in their eyes, and it chilled her. She saw a prurient look. Kormor had it, just like the others standing on either side of him. They'd done something evil, and they knew it—but they didn't have to take the blame, because Graum had told them it was right and proper. And the evilness, the wrongness had actually excited something in them. Worse still, she sensed that, having tasted it, they might want more.

"All right, now," said Graum. "There's one last thing we have to settle here." He pointed to Lomel. "You." Then he turned and pointed to Mara, and his lips pulled back from his ruined teeth. "You, too. Both of you. Up here. Right now."

Chapter 23

Mara's legs felt weak as she looked at Graum glowering down at her, as big as the bear whose skin he wore, with the guards on either side of him watching her with their avid eyes.

She moved forward, knowing that if she didn't do so of her own free will, she'd be forced to. She was vaguely aware of the villagers around her, and she saw that they were eyeing her with concern. No matter what they thought of her, none of them wanted to see her hurt as Weena had been. Still, no one moved or spoke in her defense. They seemed paralyzed by what they had seen.

She emerged at the front of the crowd. Now that she stood there on her own, she felt a strange new determination. Where did it come from, this eerie strength which she hadn't even known lay inside her? Maybe it was because she had always depended on herself more than on anyone else. She had faith in herself. And when she was challenged—somehow, it firmed her resolve.

She found Lomel stepping forward beside her. Lomel looked terrified. She glanced at Mara with wide eyes, desperate for reassurance. "Courage," Mara whispered to her. "They will not kill us, Lomel."

"Now, then," said Graum. "You two went missing today, is that right?"

"I went for a walk," Lomel said. She tried to make it sound defiant, but her voice shook.

Graum shook his head with seeming regret. "After all I've told you. You know it isn't safe for women to go wandering outside the village. You know you have a duty to your menfolk, here. You know that, don't you?"

Lomel's lip quivered. She said nothing.

Graum grunted. "You went with Mara, eh?"

"No," Mara said calmly. "She went alone."

Graum glared at her. "You keep out of this. I'm not talking to you. Not yet, anyway."

"But I am talking to you," said Mara. She looked at his fat face, and she felt a wave of unreasoning anger and disgust lifting her up, forcing her on, no matter what the cost would be. "Aren't I allowed to speak to you? Is there a rule against that now?"

She saw the guards glaring at her—Kormor, most of all. She heard the villagers shifting uneasily behind her. And she saw Graum's jaw clench. She should be scared, she thought to herself. She should be terrified. And maybe, in a way, she was. But her anger was stronger, and it stopped her from feeling her fear.

Graum climbed down from the Speaking Stone. He came lumbering toward her. She stared up at him, never blinking, never looking away from his face. "You're a troublemaker," he said. "Always have been, always will be. Seems to me you need a real lesson."

Mara felt herself trembling, but even now she wouldn't look away, and she wouldn't back down. She hated him too much for that. She felt like a bird, lifted by a draft of warm air. "It's true I've caused you trouble," she said. "I embarrassed you by telling the truth about you. You're a liar. I proved it then. And you're an evil man. You've proved that yourself."

He lashed out. She saw his fist at the last possible instant and tried to duck the blow. It caught her on the side of her forehead and she found herself flying backward, thumping down on her back in the hard-packed snow.

For a moment she was dazed. She saw him moving forward, bending over her—

Kormor appeared. He put his hand on the Chieftain's shoulder. "She's carrying my child," Kormor said quietly.

Graum paused, breathing heavily. He stayed where he was for a long moment, glowering at Mara. Then, with a growl, he pulled back. He turned toward Kormor. "She has to be punished!"

"I know," Kormor said calmly. "Trust me to do it privately."

Graum stared at him for a moment. Then, unexpectedly, he turned to Lomel. "You! We'll do to you what we can't do to her!"

"No!" Mara screamed. She lunged up off the ground and threw herself forward. She reached up, seized Graum's long hair, and tugged on it as hard as she could. She didn't even know what she was doing anymore. "No!" she screamed again.

He let out a shout of anger and pain and cuffed her across the face, knocking her away. But as she fell back, she saw that he wasn't angry anymore. He was grinning, because he saw that he'd roused something in her, and he had power over her now.

"Hold her," Graum said, and two of his men seized Mara's arms. He put his hands on his hips. "We punish your friend, and that punishes you, eh?"

Mara saw now that her anger wouldn't serve her anymore. The more she screamed, the more it would satisfy Graum. She stood, gasping for breath, trembling with rage, forcing herself to stay silent.

Graum gestured at Lomel. "Tie her facing the Justice Post," he said. He turned back to watch Mara's face, and he saw how hard it was for her to restrain herself. His grin grew wider.

Two other guards nudged Lomel forward. She gave Mara a helpless look, then went and stood passively, facing the post, while they lifted her wrists and tied them at the opposite side to the stub of the branch that protruded near the top.

Graum reached under his bearskin robe and pulled out something that had been wrapped around his waist. It was a length of braided leather rope.

"Slit the back seam of her coat," Graum said.

A guard looked at him doubtfully, then looked at Lomel's coat, reluctant to damage such a fine skin.

"Go on!" Graum's voice was suddenly a roar.

The guard jumped to obey. He dragged the tip of his spear down through the leather thongs joining the two panels and pulled them open.

"Now cut her undergarment off."

Once again there was a murmur of concern and disapproval from the crowd. But the guard did as he was told. Suddenly the bare skin of Lomel's back was revealed to Graum, to Mara, and to all the villagers staring in dismay.

Graum flexed his shoulders, then raised the braided rope and swung his arm. The leather hissed through the air and smacked against Lomel's back. The girl jerked reflexively and screamed.

Graum looked at Mara. "See that? See how it hurts her?" He nodded slowly. "Any more trouble from you, and we'll take your friend here and do it to her some more. Like this, understand?" Quickly, he swung the rope again. Already there was a bright red mark where the first blow had landed.

For a moment Mara had the eerie sense that somehow Graum knew what she'd done with Lomel. No, she told herself; it wasn't possible. Graum simply saw her response, and he was using it like any tool, to get what he wanted.

Inside herself, Mara felt sick—with rage at the thug in front of her, and with guilt that her friend was being hurt. But if she wanted to help Lomel, the only way was to remain silent and show nothing. Mara blanked her face as well as she could. She looked away from Lomel, over the roofs of the Clan Houses. She pretended that whatever happened to Lomel, she didn't care.

Graum whipped the girl twice more, making her cry out and sob. He swung the rope so hard, it actually broke her skin. Finally he grunted to himself. "Arin!" he shouted.

Lomel's brouther had been watching with a sick expression. He had looked weak before; he looked worse now.

"Come here, Arin." Graum sounded calm, and his voice was friendly. He turned to the crowd. "This young fellow became a man today. It took a while, and he complained a bit, but he came through in the end." Graum grinned. He turned back to Arin and ruffled his long hair. "Isn't that right?"

Arin nodded. He straightened his back, trying to look strong. "Yes, Graum."

The big man slapped Arin across the shoulders. Arin winced and gasped, and Mara realized there must be fresh wounds under his robe.

"Now," said Graum, "you take this." He handed the rope to Arin. "And if you want to show us you're a man, you give your sister a couple of strokes, just to teach her a lesson, eh?"

Arin looked down at the braided leather. He swayed slightly and braced himself against his spear. "She ... just walked outside the village. That's all." His voice was so low, Mara could barely hear it.

"Yes, Arin. She didn't commit a big crime. But you saw her friend here attack me. It's Mara we're punishing, understand?" He paused a moment. "Anyway, Arin, if I tell you to do something, you do it."

Once again Arin tried to stand straight and proud. "Yes, Graum," he said.

"Let me hear that again."

"Yes, Graum!" His voice rang out in the cold night air.

"Two lashes," said Graum. He nodded toward Lomel.

Arin turned to face his sister's naked back. He closed his eyes for a moment. And then, with a little cry, he swung the rope, smacking it across Lomel's shoulders.

"Harder!" Graum commanded.

Arin screwed his face up. He brought the rope back, then swung it with all his strength—and Lomel screamed.

"Good," said Graum. "Good boy, Arin." Once again, he put his arm around Arin's shoulders. "All right, cut her down from the post." He turned to the villagers, and his grin disappeared. His face contorted into a snarl. "You people, you better remember: Follow the rules, and there'll be no trouble. Break the rules, and that's waiting for you." He pointed to the Justice Post. "This can be a fine tribe. A great tribe. We can rule these lands without challenge, without fear. But only if you people learn some discipline."

Mara looked over her shoulder, and she saw the faces of the crowd. Many people looked unhappy and upset. But in the eyes of some of the men, Mara saw the same

thing she had witnessed in Graum's Honor Guard. They
were shocked, and they were shaken—but it had stirred
something inside them. Graum had said that some people
needed to be punished, and now those people had been
punished, and somehow the onlookers felt safer now
than before.

Still, there were many people who were disturbed by
what they'd seen. Some were even weeping. Mara wondered why they had just stood there instead of throwing
themselves forward, rebelling against Graum's cruelty.
Even though they carried no spears, they could have
overwhelmed Graum and his guards with sheer force of
numbers.

But the Lake People had never been faced with such
a situation. Their lives had been calm and quiet, with no
threats to their survival and no enemies to fight. They
were brave when they hunted game, but the idea of conflict among themselves was almost unthinkable.

"Go back to your Clan Houses," Graum told them.
He paused a moment. "By the way, while you were out
here, my wife, Dira, went around and visited each house,
and she gathered up the spears and knives that she
found. We'll keep all of them in the Spirit House in
future, with my men." He nodded toward his guards.
"When you're as strong and loyal and well disciplined
as they are, then you'll deserve to be trusted with
weapons."

The villagers looked at each other as if they were hoping for someone to tell them what to do. But each person's face was as empty as the next, and no one spoke.
The only voice of authority, now, was that of Graum.

Chapter 24

Kormor didn't punish her that night. She eyed him warily as he walked in, but he just told her to get into bed and leave him alone. He had something to do, he said, and he didn't want to hear the sound of her voice.

So Mara stretched out on the bed, petting Claws, feeling the warmth of his fur beside her, and trying not to think about everything that had happened. Kormor sat in the corner which he normally used for working on his flints, and he lit a lump of elk fat. He sat with his back turned to her, doing something that she couldn't see.

In the end, she managed to fall asleep.

When she woke the next morning, she felt his hands on her leg, pulling her foot out from under the skins that covered the bed. She blinked, trying to make sense of what was happening. She tried to sit up. And then, as sleep fell away from her mind, she felt a sharp pain. "Ow!" she cried. She jerked her leg, but he wouldn't let it go. "What are you doing?"

He held her ankle firmly. His hand was frighteningly strong. "Lie still," he snapped at her. "Otherwise you'll get hurt."

He was pushing a moccasin onto her foot, she realized. But there was something inside it. Something rough. Once again she yelped in pain.

"Quiet!" he told her. "It's only some small stones." He started quickly tying thongs around her ankle, holding the moccasin in place.

"Stones?" She wriggled her foot tentatively. It was true, she realized. There was sharp gravel inside the moccasin.

"They're stuck to the inside of the shoe with bison-hoof glue." He tugged on the thongs, making them cruelly tight. "You won't be walking far now."

"Have you gone mad?" She finally managed to wrench her leg out of his hand. "You're crazy!"

He turned to her. "No, you're the one who's crazy. Even now you shame me. Even now, with Graum leading this tribe! How do you think I felt last night when you screamed at him in the Meeting Place?"

He was furious, she realized. She should have expected it. But he hadn't shown his feelings last night. He'd bottled them up. And now she understood why. He'd channeled all his rage into this new way of punishing her—this torture device that she was going to be compelled to wear.

She noticed a fire flickering, and a dish-shaped stone standing above it on a triangle of branches. There was a wet puddle in the center of the stone, and as Mara breathed in, she caught a whiff of hot hoof glue.

Kormor seized her leg again. He picked up a piece of sheepskin and dabbed it into the glue. Then he brought the skin around toward her ankle.

"No!" she cried out. "Don't burn me!"

"I'm just securing the knots," he said. "Lie still."

She watched with numb disbelief as he dabbed the glue over the knots in the thongs. He blew on them till the glue set. Finally he released her.

"Why don't you just tie me to the bed?" she shouted at him. "You could keep me facedown, so you could take me whenever you want. Why don't you do that?"

He stood and moved forward, looming over her. "Because I want you to behave like a normal wife," he told her. "And I'm going to train you till you obey me." He paused, eyeing her. "Each time you step on that foot, you'll be reminded to do as I say."

She swung her leg over the side of the bed, and she rested her foot experimentally on the floor. The grit was sharp enough to be uncomfortable, but not sharp enough to cut her. Still, she thought, it would abrade her skin painfully if she tried to walk far.

She glanced around, wondering what she could do. She

could cut the thongs, of course—except that Dira had gathered all the knives and spears. But then she saw Kormor's spear standing beside the door flap. Of course, he would still have his weapon; he was in the Honor Guard.

Kormor saw what she was looking at. "If you touch my spear," he said, "I won't protect you from Graum the way I did last night. I'll turn you over to him and let him deal with you. And maybe he'll punish you, or maybe he'll punish your friend instead."

So there it was, the one threat that she was powerless to cope with. Mara felt a sudden wave of hopelessness. Kormor had found a way to cripple her, and Graum had found a way to punish her so unbearably, she could never dare to provoke him. She had lost her freedom because she had dared to care about another person.

Mara slumped back on the bed. Maybe, she told herself, when the springtime came and there was enough game out on the grassland, she would simply run away. She'd steal a spear—somehow—and go south, and maybe she'd gather enough food to last her till she reached the Silver River People, and maybe they'd accept her, and maybe Kormor would not come after her and try to get her back.

It all seemed hard to believe. And in the meantime, with the land smothered in snow, it was impossible. "Very well," she said, looking dully at him. "What do you want me to do?"

He studied her face for a moment. He saw the resignation there, and the defeat. Slowly he nodded. "I want you to take better care of our home," he said, gesturing at the mess littering the floor. "I want you to feed yourself better, since you are eating for our child now as well as yourself. You often miss meals—"

There was a faint noise from behind him. He turned and saw Claws slinking in, following a path that kept him as far from Kormor as possible.

"And that's another thing," Kormor said, compressing his lips in disapproval. "I'm tired of seeing that cat in here. It must stay outside in future, and you'll stop giving it our food."

Mara blinked. She'd thought there was nothing left now that he could take away from her. But she realized she had been wrong. She reached for Claws and pulled him over to her. He struggled at first, then reluctantly let her hold him. "This is my cat," Mara said. "He's as precious to me as your spear is to you. You mustn't try to take him from me."

Kormor looked at her and slowly shook his head. "Mara, you're talking like a fool. A wild animal has no place in our home. It certainly can't be here when the baby's born. So we may as well get rid of it now."

Mara told herself to be calm. It surely wouldn't help if she started screaming at him. She had to make him see reason. "Claws may die if you put him out in the snow," she said. "If he had to live outside, then let's wait till the spring weather."

"No," said Kormor.

She stared at him. She didn't want to believe that this was happening. "Don't do this," she said. Her voice sounded plaintive.

"Give the cat to me." He held out his hand.

Mara clutched Claws more tightly. "You can't have him." Her anger was rising, despite all her efforts to control it. "Kormor, I warn you—"

"Give it to me!" He reached down.

"No!" Mara's voice was a scream. She glanced down and glimpsed the bobcat's golden eyes growing wide, startled by her voice and by her arms pressing in on him.

"Mara, you'll do as I say." Kormor grabbed her wrist. He wrenched it, twisted it, forcing her arm away. She started struggling. Claws yowled. Kormor reached out and grabbed the bobcat by its scruff.

"No!" Mara screamed again. Suddenly she felt as if he was threatening not only the cat's life, but hers. If she lost this last thing she cared for, she would die. She scythed her arm and raked Kormor's face with her nails.

He grunted in surprise and reared back from her. Then his surprise turned to rage. Still holding the cat in one hand, he hauled Mara up off the bed and then hurled her bodily aside.

She found herself flying, falling, landing painfully across the tree stump that stood near the end of the bed.

For a moment she couldn't breathe. She felt paralyzed, and panic leaped inside her. She heard Claws yowling and Kormor cursing as he turned toward the door flap.

Mara squirmed around. She glimpsed a struggling bundle of fur in Kormor's outstretched hand. "Let him go!" she said, though she could still barely breathe and her voice was little more than a whisper.

Kormor pulled the door flap aside with his free hand, and the bundle of fur struggled more fiercely. Claws squirmed and lashed out, hissing and yowling. As Kormor lifted him, the cat managed to rake the side of Kormor's neck.

Kormor grunted with pain. Instinctively, he dropped the bobcat. Claws landed on his feet and backed away, crouching down, flattening his ears, baring his fangs. All his muscles bunched up under his fur.

Kormor swore, wiping blood from his neck. Then, with a mean look in his eyes, he stooped and reached out to grab the cat again.

Claws sprang. He leaped at Kormor's face and clung there, screeching.

Kormor's voice was suddenly added to the din. He yelled in pain and horror. Mara saw him stumbling around like a blind man, with the cat still clinging to his face, raking him with his claws.

Finally Kormor got a grip on the cat's short, stubby tail. He pulled with all his strength, and the screeching reached a new, piercing pitch as the cat was dragged free.

Suddenly there was blood everywhere, running down Kormor's face, spraying from his wounds as he whirled around and smashed the cat down on the floor.

Mara yelled in horror. But Kormor was already raising his foot, stamping his heel down onto the cat's neck, snapping it.

The screeching stopped. Kormor groped for his spear. Mara started to struggle up, but she was too late. She saw the spear stab once, twice.

Kormor stood there for a moment, gasping for breath. Strips of skin had been torn off his face. Blood was running freely down his cheeks and onto his robe. His whole left eye was a bloody mess. He dropped the spear and sat down hard on the side of the bed. With a shaking hand, he touched his cheek, then edged his finger toward his injured eye. "I can't see!" he shouted.

Trembling with shock, Mara lifted herself up and edged toward him. The eye, she saw, was ruined. Kormor's entire face would never be the same again. Mara felt a deep, sucking coldness.

"Help me!" Kormor cried, turning toward her.

"Lie on the bed," she said. It sounded to her as if someone else was speaking. "Lie on the bed!" she told him again, louder. "I'll get Dira. I'll get help for you."

"Please." He was trying to stay calm, but she could see the fear in him. And strangely, that made her strong. She glanced down and saw poor Claws, dead on the earth floor, and she felt like bursting into tears. But no, she wouldn't allow that. There was not time now.

"Hurry!" Kormor told her.

"I have to get this moccasin off." She bent down, picked up his spear, and slid its point inside the thong that he had glued around her ankle. With a grunt of satisfaction, she sliced through it and kicked the shoe away.

Quickly she grabbed her sheepskin boots, then her snowshoes, her coat, and her bag. She bent over the cache in the corner, keeping her back turned so Kormor couldn't see. The cache was almost empty, but there was some pemmican and a few dried berries. She stuffed the food quickly into her bag.

She glanced quickly around. What else? Firesticks. She grabed two pairs.

"Mara, what are you doing?" He sounded pitiful.

"I'm going to get help for you." She grabbed the spear. "Wait here. Do you understand?" She gave him a hard look, then lunged out of the door flap.

Chapter 25

It had started snowing. Yesterday's heavy gray clouds had moved lower, and now they were shedding their burden. Mara flinched as a flurry of tiny ice crystals was blown into her face by a harsh gust of wind. She tugged her wolverine hood tighter around her face and braced herself against the storm.

"Mara!" A shadowy figure was coming toward her, slipping and stumbling along the path beside the lake. "Mara, what's happening? We heard a scream."

It was Ewna, she realized, her neighbor, whom she'd known most of her life. "Kormor's badly hurt," Mara shouted to the woman. "He needs help right away. Get Dira."

Ewna paused. "He's hurt?"

"My cat scratched out his eye. And his face is bleeding. Hurry, Ewna! I'll stay here and do what I can."

"All right, Mara." Ewna didn't sound happy about it, but she started backing away. "I'll see if I can find Dira."

Mara waited till the woman had disappeared into the curtain of falling snow. Then she glanced quickly around, strode down the sloping bank, and hurried away across the lake.

When she finally reached the opposite shore, she guessed that it must be almost noon. But the clouds were so heavy and the snow was falling so fast, she was trapped in perpetual twilight.

She took shelter from the storm under the pines, grabbed her pack, dug down into it, and pulled out a handful of powdery pemmican. She stuffed it eagerly into her mouth. She was shivering, but at the same time she was sweating under her furs, which was a dangerous combination. She didn't want to die of cold out here in the wilderness.

After she had fed herself, she trekked back down to the lake, found a small frozen puddle near the edge, smashed the ice, and put a lump in her mouth. Then she started trying to retrace the steps that she and Lomel had followed the previous day.

It was a difficult business. There were few distinguishing features on the shore, and it was hard to see much in the swirling snow. Mara walked north for a while, then finally decided she had gone too far, and turned back. She had been following Lomel yesterday instead of guiding herself; that was the trouble. She hadn't even been trying to remember the path they took.

She started to feel desperate. She couldn't survive indefinitely out here in the storm. She would have to make a choice soon—either shelter again under the trees or head back to the village. The idea of going back there was almost intolerable, and it filled her with fear. But she was beginning to think there might be no other way.

Then she saw a thin black line in the forest—a thong dangling from a sapling. She gave a little cry of excitement, and she hurried toward it. Yes, this was the same snare that Lomel had set just yesterday; and it carried a new prize. A fox was dangling at the end of the thong. Surely, Mara thought, this had to be a good omen.

The fox had already died from exposure, but it hadn't been dead for long. Eagerly, Mara started tugging at the knot in the thong, trying to loosen the noose around the animal's back leg. But her hands were shaking with the cold, and she was too impatient. She seized the thong in her teeth—and it snapped.

Well, she thought, she could try to repair the snare later. She thrust the fox into her pack and started up the hillside, feeling certain now that she knew where she was going.

She found the clearing with the logs stacked against the outcropping of rock. She heaved them out of the way. The cave was cold and bare, but still it looked welcoming. She shook as much snow off herself as she could, then ducked in and squatted down. There was still some dry wood left. Mara thanked Lomel for her providence as she pulled out a set of firesticks. She shook off her mittens, clapped her hands hard to revive her circulation, then started working the sticks with quiet desperation.

A while later, she was lying by the fire, watching the fox roast over the flames. She had piled some of the logs back in the mouth of the cave to keep out the howling wind and the gusts of snow. She was warm enough now to open her furs, and for the first time since she left the village, she was calm enough to think.

She thought of Kormor clutching his ruined face, and the memory made her shudder. It had horrified her to see him injured like that. And yet, she thought, there was justice in it. He had tried to take away the very last thing that mattered to her. Until that moment, deep inside her, there must have been a little part of her that was still loyal to him. But now, when she thought of him, she found a strange emptiness. She no longer cared, she realized, that he had been injured. He had brought it upon himself when he had tried to take Claws away from her, and he had erased the last of her sympathy for him.

So she felt free, now, from her feelings for Kormor. And that meant she was totally alone. For some reason, the thought didn't frighten her, and it didn't even make her feel sad. She felt strong, just as she had when Graum called her out to be disciplined in front of the villagers. She had always survived on her own in the past, and she had no doubt she could continue to do so.

Of course, she was still carrying Kormor's child. That was something she didn't want to think about.

She pulled the roasted fox off the fire and laid it on the stone floor of the cave, waiting impatiently for it to cool a little. Her hunger was like a living thing inside her, demanding to be satisfied. Finally she could wait no longer, and she started ripping into the meat with her bare hands, gorging herself, eating with a vigor that she hadn't known in months.

*   *   *

She fell asleep by the fire, and she dreamed. She was running through a dark forest. The snow had disappeared, but it was still bitterly cold, and when she stared up through the tree branches, the sky was black and empty, and she realized she was running to find the Moon.

"Be strong, Mara!" a voice told her, and she realized it was Lizel's voice. She wanted to cry out to Lizel and ask her where the Moon had gone, but she had no breath left, and she could only run and run—until, suddenly, she was falling into a vast, dark pit. Her body shook with sudden pain. She was impaled, she realized, on stakes that had been placed at the bottom of the pit. But no: When she looked down, she saw that a young bear was there, eating her alive. At first it was too horrifying for her to accept, but she looked again, and it was true. The bear was tearing at her, gnawing her stomach, consuming her flesh. Terrible pain danced through her, and she screamed.

"Be strong, Mara!" the voice said again. Mara hardly heard it; she was crazy with the pain. She seized the bear's head between her hands and tried to pull it away from her, but the pain wouldn't stop—

—and she woke, with her fingers digging down into her sheepskin coat, clutching herself. The pain was real, she realized. Terrible cramps were gripping her abdomen. She rolled over, trying to understand what was happening. She was still in the cave, the fire had burned down to a heap of embers, and the sky was dark outside.

Mara cried out as the cramps seized her still more tightly. Surely the fox meat couldn't have poisoned her; it had been fresh. She doubled over, and then she realized what was happening.

She felt a wave of conflicting emotions—grief, and gladness. She pulled her coat tight around herself, pulled her hood close around her face, and shouldered the logs away from the mouth of the cave. She stumbled out into the snow, and she waded through it, clumsily seeking a spot under the trees. There was barely time for her to loosen her leggings and squat down. She felt a tearing sensation, and the hot trickle of blood, and something leaving her—something that had been a part of her, but was hers no more.

It took a long time for the cramps to die down. By the end of it she was shivering, weeping silently, still not sure whether her tears were from gladness or sorrow. She cleaned herself with snow as well as she could, and then she hunted around for some dead brambles and dry wood. She clutched them against her chest and struggled back to the cave.

She huddled over the fire, gently feeding it with the fresh fuel that it needed. For a moment she thought of Kormor, and she wondered what he would do when he eventually found out that she had lost his child. She didn't care, she realized. He had thrown her aside; it was his fault that she had landed on her stomach across the tree stump. And he had forfeited her feelings for him when he had tried to take Claws from her and cast him out.

The fire was burning brightly now, and she settled herself beside it. She didn't know how long she could last here, out in the woods on her own, but she had the frozen game in Lomel's food cache, and she had Kormor's spear. It was as good a place as any to sit quietly and recover her strength.

Five days later, she was down by the lake, dangling a thong through a hole in the ice. Tied to the end of the thong was a piece of twig from a bramble bush, bearing a long, curving thorn. Impaled on the thorn was a fragment of gristle, and just above the twig she had tied a pebble to the thong to sink it.

She was feeling perpetually hungry now, and the unbroken solitude was beginning to trouble her. There were few living things in the forest, and even though she had reset Lomel's snare, it had only caught one more rabbit. She had been out here fishing for the whole morning; but she had still caught only one small fish, and her feet and legs were numb from squatting on the ice.

The storm had long since moved on, and the day was bright. Far in the distance, she could see the tiny black shapes of the Clan Houses, and she spent a lot of time trying to imagine what was happening there and what they were saying about her. Did they blame her for the damage that the bobcat had done? Were they calling for her to be brought to justice? Did Graum want her to be cast out, or even killed? She didn't dare to go back there. But even if she managed to find larger game out in the wilderness—a wolf, perhaps—she might go crazy from the solitude and the total silence.

She stared at the dark water in the hole in the ice, wishing she could reach down and somehow grab a fish in her bare hands. She had never enjoyed fishing; it required far too much patience. Also, the sunlight on the snow was beginning to give her a headache. She had tied a fringe of grasses across her forehead so they dangled in front of her eyes, but even so, the glare constantly nagged at her.

She looked up for a moment to adjust the improvised sun shade. That was when she saw the figure on the ice, in the far distance, coming toward her.

Mara huddled behind some bushes, waiting with her spear ready. She had dusted her tracks as well as she could, but as she peered down at the lake, she saw the intruder inspecting the snow, then squinting up at the forested hillside.

The person on the ice moved forward, walking purposefully toward the lakeshore. She started up into the trees. "Mara?" she called.

The sound of a human voice was startling after the days of solitude. It toook a moment for Mara to realize how familiar the voice was. Slowly, cautiously, she stood up. "Lomel?" Her own voice felt stiff in her throat, and she coughed to clear it. "Lomel, is that you?"

"Of course. Who else would have known you were here?" She came up the slope, and Mara saw her. Yes— it was truly her.

Mara took a hesitant step forward. Then she felt her anxiety ebb in a great wave, releasing her. She ran out, seized Lomel, and hugged her. The human contact was like breaking a fast. It was a delicious, heady feeling to be holding her friend alone here under the trees.

"Does anyone know you're here?" Mara asked. "Did you slip away? Can we be alone for a little while?"

Lomel's smile faded, and a profound sadness took its place. "I wish that were true," she said.

Mara felt the warmth ebb out of her. She eyed Lomel apprehensively. "Tell me," she said.

"Very well." Lomel was silent for a moment. She looked as if she was gathering her courage to make a confession. "Kormor is very weak," she said. "His face is an awful sight, all swollen and leaking pus, and he lost his left eye. The wounds that your cat made seemed to go bad, and they poisoned him. He has a terrible fever. He may not even live."

Mara blinked, trying to adapt herself to this news. But she saw from Lomel's face there was more.

"He started calling for you," she went on, "and no one knew where you were, except me, of course. And . . . I didn't know what to do. I knew you'd had terrible fights with him, but even so, I thought you might want to see him. So I decided to sneak out on my own to find you, just to let you know."

Listening to Lomel's tone of regret, Mara felt a premonition. "Were Graum's men watching you?"

Lomel looked away. The corners of her mouth turned down. Her lip trembled. "I hope you can forgive me." Her voice was so low, Mara could hardly hear it. "I tried to be careful, but Graum guessed that I might know where to find you. He had his men keep watch on me, and two of them grabbed me as soon as I snuck out onto the lake. They took me back to him, and he demanded that I should tell him where you are."

Mara looked at her in dismay. "What did you do?"

Lomel looked up, and some of her pride returned. "I refused, of course. But then Graum said, if I didn't lead them to you, he'd take revenge on my family. He said he would seize my mother—" Lomel broke off.

Mara realized the implication. For several days she had felt free, untouched by the grimness that she had known in the tribe. And now that freedom was gone. "So you told them?" she asked softly.

"No! No, I said I would come here alone, and it would be your choice whether to hide or return."

Mara squeezed Lomel's shoulder. "You did your best," she said, trying to conceal her emotions and make her voice gentle. "But if your mother is in danger, that gives me no choice. I don't see how I can stay out here."

"I'm sorry, Mara." Lomel's pride faltered. "I failed you."

Mara gave her a little shake. "Please. Don't think like that. It doesn't matter now how it happened. What worries me is what lies ahead. Why do you think it matters to Graum to have me back? He should be glad to have me out of the way."

Lomel shook her head. "He's been telling people that you're dangerous. He says you used your cat to kill your husband, and you may come sneaking back into the village and kill other people, too." She sighed. "Mara, he says you have to be brought to justice. He wants you to pay for what you've done." She was crying now; tears were creeping down her cheeks. "Mara, I'm so sorry."

Mara hugged her. She felt no anger or regret—just weary resignation. "Listen," she said, "I'm not sure I could have lasted out here on my own for much longer. I think I would have had to go back to the tribe sooner or later. So it might as well be now."

Chapter 26

With a dull sense of dread, she walked beside Lomel across the frozen lake. "When I first heard you were missing," Lomel said, "I was very worried. I thought you might have gone out to lose yourself in the snow." She gave Mara a shy, plaintive look. "I was afraid you might never come back."

For a few moments, the only sound was of their snow-shoes as they made their way through the crisp, cold air under the empty blue bowl of the sky.

"I wanted to get away from everything," Mara said. "But I missed you, Lomel. I thought of you."

Lomel smiled shyly. "I'm glad of that."

Mara wondered for a moment whether she should mention that she had lost her child during her first day of solitude. No, she decided; she wasn't ready yet to talk about it. And if Kormor was really dying, she wasn't sure if she wanted him to know.

"Tell me," she said, "anything else that happened while I've been away."

"I think Graum has a little less respect now than before," Lomel said. "I've been talking to people, Mara. They trust me, because they know me as someone who speaks the truth. Many of them are beginning to understand now that it was a mistake to trust Graum. My brother, especially, has changed his mind."

Mara looked at her in surprise. "But Arin is one of Graum's men. And he hurt you in the Meeting Place. He did it in front of everyone. That was so terrible—"

"Please!" Lomel placed her hand on Mara's shoulder, stopping her. She faced Mara and looked directly into her eyes. "Don't be concerned about that, Mara. I still bear the marks, but you know, in a way, it was a good thing. It made people see how cruel Graum is. And Arin can never forget it was Graum who made him do that."

"Really?" Mara wondered if she could trust Lomel's judgment. The girl was so trusting and kind, it would be hard for her to believe that her brother had turned against her.

"Arin suffered himself, in the initiation they put him through," Lomel said. "They pierced his flesh with sharp sticks of hardwood, and they tied leather ropes to the sticks, and they lifted him up, and they beat him." As the words tumbled out, Lomel's face changed. The soft kindness had gone, and in its place was something darker. "Arin wants revenge against Graum now," she went on more quietly. Once again, she started moving across the lake.

"But Graum took away all the spears," Mara said.

Lomel smiled; but it wasn't a friendly smile. "Two evenings ago, when Graum called everyone to the Meeting Place, Arin slipped away and stole some spears from the store in the Spirit House. He's hidden them near our home, in the snow."

"Really?" That was more than Mara would have hoped for. And yet, she realized, it wasn't nearly enough.

"Most of Graum's guards are still loyal," Lomel was saying, "but—" She stopped abruptly. She looked ahead, narrowing her eyes. "Here are some of them now."

Four young hunters were coming out across the ice.

"One last hug," said Mara.

The two of them embraced quickly, tightly.

"Maybe you're right, and people will rise up against Graum one day," Mara murmured in Lomel's ear. "But he's a shrewd man, and he protects himself well. You and Arin must be patient, Lomel. Be very careful."

Lomel shrugged. "I don't worry about my own safety, Mara. It's you that I worry about." She touched Mara's cheek. "I hope you can forgive me for leading them to you. I didn't mean to. I really didn't."

Two of the guards took Lomel away to her family's house. The other two took Kormor's spear out of Mara's hands, and they said they would escort her back to her home. One of the men was Bumar, who had marked his mate's face in the Meeting Place. The other was Ulmei, a youngster who had come of age just before Arin. Mara could still remember Ulmei jumping up, eager to hunt with Graum, on the first night that the big man had been in the tribe. Well, Ulmei finally had his wish. His forehead was marked, now, with the bear-head tattoo.

"What will happen to me?" Mara asked them, as they walked her along the path at the edge of the lake. The village seemed strangely quiet, she noticed, as if the people had been ordered to stay in their homes.

"You're going to see your husband," said Ulmei. "See what you did to him." He glared at Mara with righteous disapproval.

"See what the cat did to him, you mean," she said.

"Yes, the cat." It was Bumar talking. "Your cat." He sounded indifferent, as if he didn't much care what happened to Mara, or why.

"And after that?"

"After that—" Ulmei began.

"We're going to keep you there," Bumar interrupted him. "That's all. Till we see whether Kormor lives or dies."

"And if he dies?" Mara asked.

Bumar shrugged. "Then you'll pay the price."

"You should hope that he'll live," said Ulmei. His high-pitched voice had a scolding tone. "I certainly wouldn't want to be you if he doesn't."

The familiar little mammoth-skin tent come into view then, and Mara felt a familiar sense of dread.

"We'll stay outside," said Bumar. He peeled open the door flap and motioned for Mara to go in.

"So I'm to be a prisoner in my own home," she said.

"Yes, till we see whether Kormor lives," said Ulmei. "Bumar already told you that."

Mara faced the boy. He was a year younger than she was, and he had a pinched, callow face. She looked at him with distaste. "I hope your mother won't worry that you're out so late," she said.

Ulmei's knuckles whitened where he gripped his spear. "You should be careful—"

Bumar grunted with irritation. "Just get inside the tent," he told Mara.

She eyed each of the men in turn. She had grown up with them here in the village; she had wrestled with them and run with them across the grasslands. Yet they saw nothing strange now in trusting Graum and carrying out his commands, even if it meant punishing one of their own people. If Graum said that something must be done, they automatically obeyed.

Wearily, Mara stepped down into her home.

She found Kormor stretched out on the bed, lying on his back with a green poultice concealing most of his face. His bad eye was covered; his good eye was closed. He was taking quick, shallow, rasping breaths through parted lips. His whole face was bright red and badly swollen, and Lomel had been right: The wounds that Claws had inflicted had gone bad. They had festered and poisoned him.

Dira was sitting beside the bed, chanting softly, rattling a medicine bag over Kormor's prostrate form. She stopped and turned when she heard Mara come in, and she gave her a startled look. Then she hunched her shoulders defensively, like an animal cornered in its lair.

The two women stared at each other, and Mara felt a moment of anger that Dira should be in here. Then, just as quickly, the emotion died. It really didn't matter, she realized, what Dira did or where she chose to be. She no longer recognized Kormor as her mate, and she no longer thought of this tent as her home.

Mara nodded toward Kormor. "How is he?"

Dira eyed her a moment longer. "He's in a coma," she said, "and I don't think he will live." She gave Mara a nasty look, then stooped and gathered her herbs and salves with quick, angry movements. She stood up, pushed past Mara, and hurried out through the door flap.

Mara wondered if Dira really cared at all what happened to Kormor. She might have even tried to worsen his condition, knowing that if he died, Mara would suffer.

Mara sighed. She set down her pack and loosened her coat.

She noticed dark spots on the floor, and she realized that they must be Kormor's blood. Then she noticed a bigger patch near the bed, and she felt an awful qualm as she saw that it was where Claws had lain. She squatted down for a moment and touched the earth. It was dry now, and the smell of the bobcat had gone.

She thought for a moment of his spirit, which had seemed so close to hers for so many months. Claws had never harmed her, and he had never demanded anything, though he had been grateful for her gifts of food. He had trusted her, and he had repaid her kindness in the only way he could, by lying with her, sometimes licking her hand, staring at her with simple pleasure.

Really, he had been her friend. But he had gone, now. Could his spirit have followed the same path as his mother's, and merged with hers? She liked to think that it might have happened.

She stood up, thinking that she might as well confront what Claws had done. She kneeled on the bed and bent over Kormor. He was panting, and his skin was frighteningly hot when she touched it. When she scraped away a little of the green poultices, she saw that his wounds were terribly inflamed and leaking large quantities of thick, yellow pus.

Mara looked at him for a long while. He no longer seemed the same man who had hurt her and humiliated her and tried to break her spirit. As things had worked out, his was the spirit that had been broken. He was like a wounded animal now, and she felt vague compassion, the same as she would feel for any living thing that she saw in such a terrible state. But the feeling was impersonal and detached.

There was a leather bucket of water beside the bed, but it wasn't very cold. She went to the door flap, reached out, and grabbed two handfuls of snow, ignoring Ulmei, who stared down at her suspiciously. She went back to Kormor, spread most of the snow on his forehead, and edged the rest of it through his parted lips.

He stirred slightly. He swallowed convulsively, and his body shook. He opened his good eye, and he saw her.

For a long moment, he was silent. He muttered her name. His eye regarded her sadly. Then it slowly closed, and once again he slept.

She spent the evening doing all the things she had put off doing for the past months: gathering the litter of oddments from the floor, putting things away, making the little home look neat and clean. Several times, Ulmei or Bumar looked in, saying that Graum wanted to know if Kormor's condition had changed. Each time, she simply showed them his sleeping body, and she let them judge for themselves. Did they, too, want Kormor to die, so that they could see her punished?

Mara thought wistfully of Lizel. If the old woman had still been in the tribe, she would have been sitting a day-and-night vigil, calling on the spirits to heal Kormor, and trying a dozen different remedies. She would have refused to leave till he showed some sign of improvement, or until he was beyond help. But Lizel was gone, and Mara lacked the skills of a healer. As far as she could see, the only thing she could do was wait.

A rich variety of meats and delicacies had been laid out, in case Kormor felt any interest in food. Since he hadn't touched anything, Mara ate it all herself. At last she satisfied the hunger which had grown inside her during her time of solitude.

Then she made herself as comfortable as she could on the bed beside him, and she slept.

She woke suddenly. It was completely dark in the tent, and the only sound was of Kormor's restless breathing. What had disturbed her? She strained her senses.

"No."

It was him, she realized. His voice sounded urgent, as if he needed something from her at once. She sat up quickly. "What is it?"

"Wrong. That was wrong."

Slowly it became clear to her: He wasn't conscious. He was having a fever dream. She groped her way to the door flap and scooped up more snow, noticing that Ulmei had gone, but Bumar was still out there, draped in thick furs, standing guard in the moonlight.

She took the snow back to Kormor and pressed it to his forehead. He was muttering something now in a voice that was so low, she couldn't hear the words.

Without warning, he rolled onto his side. She had left the tent flap open, and a slice of moonlight illuminated his good eye. It was wide and staring—yet when she leaned over him, he didn't seem to see her.

"Ternees," he said. The word was quite distinct. "Not Ternees. Don't."

His voice sounded hoarse and strange, as if something possessed him. Mara shivered, feeling a tingling sensation that started at the back of her scalp and spread slowly across her shoulders. Was some night spirit possessing him? Now she really wished Lizel was here. "What are you saying?" she whispered, gently shaking his shoulder. "What is it, Kormor?"

"Don't, Graum!" The last words were loud.

Mara sat absolutely still, trying to make sense of what she was hearing. "What?" she whispered.

"Don't! Not Ternees!" He tried to sit up. His eye was still blindly staring. His breath started making a rattling sound in his throat.

"Kormor!" She shook him harder.

He slumped back onto the bed, and he went limp. "Too late," he muttered, sounding deeply distressed.

Mara felt a sudden terrible suspicion. The idea of it was so huge, it seemed impossible; but the possibility that it might be true was like a dark hand, closing slowly around her. "Kormor, listen to me," she whispered urgently. "Listen! What did Graum do to my mother?" She clenched her fists. "Tell me!"

"The cliff," he muttered.

Mara seized the sheepskin cover and dragged it up to her chin, clutching it so tightly, her fingers hurt. She shuddered and gave a little cry of distress. She should have known, she told herself. It was her fault; she should have guessed right away.

But then she remembered that Yacor had said he saw

the mastodon herd push Ternees over the cliff. Why would he have said that if Graum was really to blame?

Yacor was dead, now. He was gone, and she suddenly feared there would be no way ever to learn the truth. "Kormor!" She shook him, trying to waken him. "Kormor, can you hear me?"

He didn't respond, and there seemed to be no way to rouse him.

When dawn light showed at the edges of the door flap, she heard him call her name. This time, when she looked at him, he seemed to see her.

Quickly she felt his forehead. It was drenched with sweat. The fever had broken.

"Need water," he gasped, in a voice that was so hoarse, she could barely understand him.

Quickly she seized the leather bucket. She lifted it up, tilted his head, and poured some of the water between his lips.

He drank greedily, gulping it down. Then he slumped back, exhausted. But he wasn't panting anymore. He was breathing normally.

For a long moment, the two of them stared at each other. "You came back," he whispered.

She thought of all the things she could say: that he had betrayed her, and she had wanted never to see him again, and she no longer carried his child, and she felt nothing for him when he looked at her. But none of those things was important compared with the thing she needed to know.

"I dreamed," he said. His voice was a little stronger. He licked his lips. "I saw the spirits of my mother and father. They spoke to me, Mara."

She wondered if that had been a true dream. Some dreams were sent from the spirits, others were just the person's mind talking to itself, and even a priestess could have trouble telling the two apart. "What did your parents say?" Mara asked.

"They said . . . I have been wrong." His mouth turned down, and his eye seemed to grow moist. He was crying, Mara realized with disbelief. It seemed impossible, and she felt a sudden impulse to touch the tears to make sure that they were real. In all the time she had spent with Kormor, she had never seen him show a sign of weakness.

"They told me I shouldn't have hurt you," he said. "They said I was wrong."

But it had been his own voice, in the night, saying he was wrong. Most likely his conscience, not his parents, had been speaking to him. But Mara said nothing; if he wished to believe that the words had come from his parents, she saw no reason to interfere.

"Mara, listen!" He reached for her feebly. "They told me my spirit will be ... will be set free, soon. But it may roam. Because of what I've done." He was trembling, now. "Mara, the cat, it punished me. I'm afraid. For my spirit to roam—"

He broke off, and his face was full of fear. He had changed so much, she hardly recognized him. She couldn't imagine what could have broken his will, until she remembered his belief that some spirits were not worthy to move to the land beyond and were forced to dwell in night creatures. So that was it! He feared that he would die and would find himself forever roaming through the darkness as an owl or a bat. His superstition had a power over him that was far greater than anything in the material world.

She moved closer to him. "You were very feverish," she said. "You were talking in your sleep."

He paused, giving her a wondering look. "I spoke?"

"Yes. And I think you had another dream."

He hesitated. "I don't remember—"

She steeled herself. This had to be done in such a way that she seemed to show no doubt. "You were talking," she said, "about Graum, and how he killed my mother."

There was a long, long moment of silence. He stared at her. He shivered, and she saw his eye grow moist again.

It was true, she realized. It was true! She felt incredulous, then overwhelmed with fury. He wasn't denying it, so it *had* to be true. She jumped up onto her feet. "Why did you never tell me?" Her voice wasn't loud, for fear of the guards hearing her. But if she'd had the choice, she would have screamed at him. "You never told me! And you still served that disgusting man!"

His cheek was wet with tears. "I was wrong," he said weakly.

She fought to bring herself under control. She hugged herself, trembling, wild with anger, but thinking ahead now, realizing what this could mean. She had to be gentle with him. She couldn't afford to lose him now.

She forced herself to be calm. It was a struggle, but bit by bit she succeeded. She sat down beside him again. She made herself pat his shoulder. "It's all right, Kormor," she said, though the words sickened her. "It's all right, just explain to me, now. Then everything will be all right."

He looked up at her. "You forgive me?"

"Of course." She had to pause and close her eyes for a moment. "Of course I can forgive you. But first I need to know . . . how it happened."

He swallowed, trying to gather some strength. "Please don't make me—"

"If it was wrong, and you want to be forgiven, you must tell me!"

Gradually he accepted what she said. He drew a shuddering breath. "It happened very fast," he whispered. "The animals were crowding everyone. Ternees was between him and the cliff—and he pushed her."

"You're absolutely sure?"

"Yes. Of course." He sounded certain. And she knew that he was a careful, reliable observer.

"Did he plan it somehow?"

"No." Kormor coughed weakly and winced. "I think it happened by chance, and he took advantage of it."

Mara though for a moment. "I remember just before the hunt, when everyone was berry picking, Graum had been so agreeable, telling everyone to respect Ternees—"

"He knew people in the tribe would fear him otherwise," said Kormor. "He had to seem respectful while he was gaining power. But I'm sure, sooner or later, he planned to get rid of her."

Mara felt another burst of anger as she thought of that

hateful man smiling amiably, biding his time, waiting for a chance to kill her mother. "When it happened, did no one else see?"

"No. Everyone was looking at the herd."

"But Yacor said—"

"Yacor didn't see. He was ashamed. He couldn't admit he hadn't been paying attention."

"Ah." So that was why Yacor had said he saw Ternees fall. He had been trying to convince himself, to save his pride. "Thank you for telling me, Kormor," she said, still keeping her voice soft and her emotions repressed. "But now I need to know why you went on serving Graum."

He grimaced. "I hated your ... your mother. I hated the way she ruled the tribe. And ..." He drew an awful shuddering breath. "I thought we needed a strong man like Graum. To keep us safe."

"But he killed my mother!" She couldn't keep the anguish out of her voice.

"I know." He closed his good eye for a moment. "I was afraid of him." His voice was a whisper.

She suddenly remembered the contest to see who would become chieftain. "When you cast your spear that day, in grassy hollow," she said, "you threw it short. You did it deliberately."

Weakly, he nodded. "I was afraid. If I became Chieftain, Graum would kill me, too." He tried to reach out to Mara. Feebly, he touched her hand. "I thought I could do more if I served him. I could keep watch on him and stop him from ... from anything else, like that. But I was wrong, Mara. Please forgive me. If you don't forgive me, I'm afraid ... my spirit ..."

She looked at him and felt she was finally seeing the essence of him, the small boy that had always been inside him, behind all the pride and the posturing. He was afraid—not just of the spirit world, but of everything. He had lost his parents along with his whole tribe, on their trek from the North Lands, and he was always convinced that it was his fault for not being strong enough to save them. So he always needed to be in control, and he was obsessed with being strong. She had seen that, but she had never guessed that still, beneath it all, he was afraid.

Then she saw another thing. He had even been afraid of her. Each time she spoke out, he must have feared that it would undercut his pride and his status. Each time she defied him, **he'd been** afraid that she might be stronger than he **was, on** the inside, where it really mattered.

She looked at him and felt disgusted. She felt like seizing him and slapping him and shaking him, treating him like the child he was. But once again, she reined in her emotions. "Listen to me," she said, leaning closer, speaking in a tense, fierce monotone. "I can forgive you for the way you treated me. But if you want me to forgive you for keeping Graum's secret and serving him, you will have to do something more. Do you understand?"

He watched her uneasily. "What?" he whispered.

She stared at him, letting him see her determination. "If you want my forgiveness," she said, "you'll have to go in front of the tribe and tell them what you told me."

Chapter 27

He said that he was too weak, and he begged her not to make him do it. Finally he asked her just to let him sleep for a little while and think about what she asked. But she refused. She still insisted that if he wanted his spirit to be free, he must share his secret with her people.

In the end, he had no strength left to fight her, and he was too scared to refuse. Weakly, he gave his consent. And then, looking deathly pale, he passed out.

Mara went to the door flap and peeked outside. It was a clear, bright day, with sunlight gleaming on the snow. Bumar was gone, but Ulmei was back there, standing guard with another man named Ponuro. The two of them were chatting idly. They glanced at her without much interest. She felt confident now that they hadn't overheard her conversation with Kormor.

Mara eyed them, deciding what to do. Ulmei was suspicious and difficult, always trying to prove his superiority and put other people in their places. Ponuro, on the other hand, was more easygoing.

"Ponuro," she called, "Kormor needs your help."

The two men turned and looked at her. "My help?" Ponuro sounded doubtful.

"I think he's losing the last of his strength," Mara said. She lowered her voice. "I think it may not be long now."

"He's dying?" Ulmei asked. There was no concern in his voice. It sounded more like a challenge than an inquiry.

"Yes," Mara said, giving him a hard stare. "I think he may be dying."

"So what is this help—" Ponuro began.

"He wants to speak to Arin, and he asked if you'd fetch him here."

Ponuro glanced at Ulmei, and the two of them exchanged a doubtful look. "Why Arin?" Ulmei said.

Mara felt herself losing her patience. "I don't know! I don't question the requests of a dying man. Do you?"

Ulmei looked uncomfortable. "I just want to know—"

Mara turned to Ponuro. "Please, do as he asks. Fetch Arin. It seems important to Kormor."

Ponuro grunted. "Seems it can do no harm," he said, with another quick glance at Ulmei.

"Thank you," said Mara. She waited, watching him.

Ponuro nodded. "I'll bring him here," he said. He turned, then, and started away.

Mara ducked back inside. She felt impatient now and full of new determination. Before, she had been powerless, and that had sapped her will. But Kormor's weakness had changed everything. It had made her strong.

Of course, there was still danger, and if she forced a confrontation, there could be bloodshed. The thought of that made her shiver—not out of fear for her own safety, but because she would carry the burden if anyone was injured or killed.

Still, she thought, it had to be done. And no one else was in a position to try. Probably no one else even had the strength to do so.

So it was up to her, and her alone. There was a feeling of pride in that, as well as fear.

Arin arrived a little while later. Mara looked at his face and saw the same clear-eyed, simple good looks that she knew so well from Lomel. The tattoo of the bear's face on his forehead was ugly and out of place compared with his clean features.

Arin looked at Kormor and saw him sleeping. Then he looked back at Mara, and his eyes were full of questions. He opened his mouth to speak.

Mara put her finger to her lips and gave him a warning look. She beckoned him closer. "Arin." Her voice was a whisper, and she kept her lips close to his ear. "I don't want Kormor to know you're here."

"Wasn't he the one who sent for me?" He looked at her suspiciously.

She shook her head. "I was the one who called you. Listen, Arin ..." She hesitated. There was no way to find out, except by asking; but it was so dangerous, it gave her a feeling of deep anxiety. She steeled herself. The words had to be said. "Is it true, Arin, that you're no longer loyal to Graum?"

He gave her a slow, wary look. "Who told you that?"

She shook her head. "No one told me." She wasn't going to implicate Lomel. "I saw your face, in the Meeting Place," she said, "when Graum told you to hit your sister. I saw the shame you felt, and the anger. I could tell how deeply it troubled you."

He seemed to think about that. He looked down, avoiding her eyes.

She pulled him close. "Isn't it true?" she whispered.

He shook his head. "I don't want to talk about it."

Mara felt a stab of concern. What if Lomel had been wrong? "Why won't you say?" she hissed at him.

He eyed her cautiously. "I don't know if you can be trusted, Mara."

She searched his face, looking to see if he might be playing some game with her. But no—he seemed genuinely unsure. So she would have to convince him, and really there was only one way. "Sit with me, Arin," she told him. She gestured to the tree stump—the same stump that had struck her so painfully and so fatally across her stomach, when Kormor had thrown her aside.

When he had seated himself, she kneeled beside him. "Let me tell you," she said, "what I've learned." And softly, insistently, she described everything that Kormor had said.

By the end of it, Arin was leaning forward, pressing his fingers to his temples, looking pale and shaken. "There could still be some mistake," he said. "Perhaps it was the fever speaking in Kormor. Perhaps—"

"He wasn't feverish this morning when he admitted the truth of it," she said calmly. "Nor would he lie to me at a time like this. He's convinced that he will die soon and his spirit will be punished if he doesn't confess.

He's terrified, Arin. And the fear has made him speak truly."

"I would never have guessed," Arin said. He looked at the sleeping figure on the bed. "He always seemed as if nothing really touched him."

"We all have our secrets," said Mara.

He nodded slowly. "All right, why did you call me here?"

She hesitated. "Before I tell you," she said, "I must be sure of you, Arin. It's just as hard for me to trust you as it was for you to trust me."

He thought about that for a moment. "That's true," he said.

"So tell me," she said, "why you were loyal to Graum, and why you changed."

He stared down at the floor, looking as if he was thinking back to a time that was months, rather than days, in the past. "At first I just wanted to learn from him," he murmured. "I wanted to be accepted. I wanted to be one of his men, so I would have respect—and power. I wanted that, very much." He paused, still frowning. "But to earn that respect, it was ... very hard. There were many tests."

"Like holding the hot stone, on that first night beside the fire?"

"Yes. A lot of things like that, all of them painful. But finally I was accepted, and then—then I was one of the chosen ones. I had authority. But even so, it still wasn't easy. There was strict discipline—so many rules, and punishments. Sometimes I was punished. Other times, when someone broke the rules, we all took turns punishing him." He grimaced. "After a while I felt I wasn't really thinking anymore. We were like wolves, a little afraid all the time, and snapping each other. That was the only pleasure, really, finding someone weaker, or someone who Graum said should be punished, and ... hurting them. And wanting more power, so we could feel safe."

"And all the hurting and the pain—it flowed down from Graum. He was the source."

He looked up at her. "Yes," he said, with a strange, distant look. "It all flowed from him. But you know, many of the men took pleasure in it. Being in his Honor Guard became their whole life, especially the ones who had no women." He spread his hands helplessly. "I'm still confused about it, Mara. I don't entirely understand what happened to me. I feel as if I'm recovering from a sickness. And it wasn't till—till Lomel was punished, in the Meeting Place, that I really understood what I had become."

Mara took his hand and squeezed it. "Thank you, Arin," she said. "You should feel thankful, now, that you have a chance to undo all the wrong that has been done, here."

"What chance is that?" he asked.

She wondered how best to phrase what she wanted to say. "Do you have any weapons?"

He met her eyes. He hesitated for a long moment. "Some spears," he said, finally. "But I think you know that. I have a feeling Lomel confided in you, Mara."

"Perhaps so." She confronted Arin, staring at him as commandingly as she knew how. "Tonight, you must move your spears into the Meeting Place. Hide them in snow drifts near the Clan Houses. Make sure you can find them again, instantly, when you need them. But be very careful that no one will come across them by accident."

His face was deeply earnest, and for a moment his seriousness reminded her of Lomel. That helped her to trust him a little more. "What are you planning to do?" he whispered.

"This afternoon, you must talk with Lomel," Mara told him. "Decide who else you can trust with Kormor's secret. Talk to women, not men. The women have more reason to be angry. Tell each of them the position of one spear. Make very sure that there's no confusion. Tomorrow morning, I'll force Kormor to go before the tribe and tell everyone what he has told me. That will be the time to act, when Graum and his men are caught by surprise. You and your people must seize your spears and force him to surrender."

Now Arin looked unhappy. "The men who serve

Graum—they're our kin, Mara. They're my friends. They were foolish to follow him, but ... I was foolish, too."

She wondered how fierce he would be when the time came. How much could she really count on him? "Listen," she said, staring at him hard again, trying to infect him with her own determination. "We must be brave and strong. If we fail tomorrow morning, it will be over. Do you understand? Graum will make an example of me, and of you, and of Lomel, for defying him. He will certainly hurt us, he will probably torture us, and he may kill us. Do you understand?"

Arin blinked. He looked disconcerted by Mara's intensity, and still doubtful about what she said. "You think our people would let him do such a thing? Surely, when everyone understands that he killed Ternees—"

"Graum wants to rule this tribe. He'll do anything to hold on to his power. And the only way he'll be able to do that is by frightening people. You've served him yourself, Arin. You must know this is true."

Reluctantly, he nodded. "You're probably right." He brooded for a moment. "All the same, I wish there could be another way."

"Well, there isn't. There's no point in wishing. Arin, you must help me. For the sake of us all."

He shifted uneasily. "More people are beginning to speak out against Graum in private. Maybe if we wait till the spring—"

"No!" She glared at him. "If we wait till people speak more openly, Graum will find a way to deal with them. He'll cast them out, or—there's no way of knowing what he'll do. He killed my mother, remember that. And he keeps gathering more loyal young men around him. He's an evil man, Arin. Each time we've put off trying to deal with him, things have grown worse. We can't afford to wait any longer."

He brooded for a long moment more. Finally he sighed. "So, I'll do as you say." His voice was low, but he sounded decisive, as if he truly meant what he said.

She wanted to believe in him. She squeezed his shoulder. "Swear you will keep your word."

He nodded again. "I swear it."

That made her feel a little better.

Slowly Arin stood up. "I'll tell Lomel what you've told me," he said. "We'll only confide in people we're absolutely certain we can trust."

"Good. But be very careful."

He turned, then, and left the tent.

For the rest of that day, she sat with Kormor, biding her time, watching him while he slept. It had been necessary for her to seem strong and confident while she talked with Arin. But really, she wasn't confident at all. She felt afraid and alone in the little tent, and she desperately wished there was someone else she could confide in. Most of all, she wished she could talk to Lomel. But even if Graum's men allowed Lomel to come to her, it would surely make them suspicious.

Several times, guards came to check on Kormor. Twice he woke and stared up at them balefully with his good eye. They grinned at him and joked that he would soon be out again in the valley, hunting alongside them when the snow melted and the game was theirs for the taking. But behind their smiles, Mara could see that they didn't expect him to live, and she guessed that Kormor saw it, too. He barely answered them, and when they pressed him to eat the gifts of food that they brought for him, he barely touched it.

And so for most of the day she sat alone with him, watching him sleep, and waiting.

When darkness had fallen outside, he woke again. This time he seemed a little stronger. He tried to sit up, but he couldn't quite manage it, and he slumped back, looking at her as if he hoped, somehow, she could make him whole again. "Mara," he whispered. "I dreamed some more."

That made her nervous. "What did you see?"

"My parents. Calling to me again." He moved restlessly. "I fear it will be soon, Mara."

Her nervousness receded. She'd been afraid that he might dream of them telling him that he had nothing to be concerned about after all. As for him being on the edge of death—she didn't believe that. He was weak, but he no longer had a fever. If he would start eating, he should recover.

She was tempted to say something to reassure him. But she held the words back, because she couldn't risk having him feel more secure. She felt a little disturbed by her own callousness, but there was no avoiding the fact: She still needed him to believe that he was dying, and she still needed him to feel deeply afraid.

"If it will be soon," she said, "there's all the more reason for you to cleanse your spirit by confessing to our people."

"Yes," he said. "You're right." He gave her an imploring look. "And then, you promise to forgive me?"

Inside herself, she knew she could never forgive him. But she was more than willing to conceal that. "Of course I'll forgive you," she said, resting her hand on his shoulder. She forced herself to smile at him.

"Maybe it should be done now," he said, trying to sit up again. "Call the people together, Mara, and I'll speak to them."

She felt a great leap of fear. "Not tonight!" she told him sharply. Arin wouldn't possibly have time to do what he had to do before tomorrow morning. She paused a moment, forcing herself to be calm. "It's late, and there's a storm outside," she improvised. "People are all in their homes."

"But what if—" He broke off, trying to hold on to the shreds of his courage. "What if I die before morning? Then what will happen to me?"

She shook her head. "I won't let you die. I'll watch over you all night."

That was meaningless, of course; yet somehow it seemed to reassure him. He looked at her with gratitude.

Once again she forced herself to smile at him. He tried to smile back, and winced as the muscles of his face pulled at the lacerations which the cat had inflicted. Even now the wounds were horribly inflamed and still thick with pus.

"Some water?" he asked.

She raised the bucket and trickled water between his lips. Strange, she thought, that she had once tantalized herself with fantasies of these cracked lips pressing against hers, kissing her body, caressing her. She felt a little spasm of anger at the way he had betrayed her. He had been so generous and gentle with her through all their courtship, yet all the time he must have known that once he was paired with her, he would take quite a different role. Still, she told herself, her anger was of no use to her. There were more important things than her pairing with Kormor. Her own life, and the lives of her people, were at stake.

"Rest," she told him. She patted his shoulder. "Tomorrow morning, you'll go before the tribe. Then you will be forgiven. Just a few more hours, Kormor, that's all."

He nodded weakly. "Thank you," he said.

Chapter 28

Mara hardly slept that night. Her thoughts were a constant chatter in her head. Again and again, she saw herself with Kormor in the Meeting Place, denouncing Graum, accusing him of his crime. She imagined Arin and Lomel and their trusted friends rising up, seizing their spears, confronting Graum's men. And then, in a dozen different ways, she saw the uprising turn into a terrible catastrophe, a bloodbath that ended with the rebels prostrate on the ground, screaming and dying, their blood soaking into the dirt.

Mara tried to banish the terrible pictures from her mind. She told herself that she needed to rest, to be alert and strong. But she was too tense to sleep, and her imagination gave her no peace.

Finally she saw morning light filtering around the door flap. It was almost a relief, now, to know that there was no more waiting and the event itself was at hand.

She ate some meat, feeling sick with apprehension but forcing herself to consume the food so that she would have something to sustain her.

Then she turned to Kormor. He was sleeping, lying on his back with his lips slightly parted, his arms by his sides. His skin looked very pale in the faint morning light.

"Kormor?" Gently she shook his shoulder.

He didn't respond.

"Kormor." She shook him more sternly. Then, with a terrible sense of foreboding, she leaned closer. She held her hand in front of his parted lips. She couldn't feel him breathing, and his skin seemed cold under her hands.

"Kormor!" She shouted his name, feeling a spasm of

panic. "Kormor!" she cried. She seized both his shoulders. "Kormor, wake up!"

He opened his good eye. For a moment he didn't seem to see her. He muttered something, swallowed, and winced.

Mara sat back on the bed, breathing in little gasps. She tried to calm herself. She closed her eyes a moment. Then she looked at him again, and she found him staring back at her, looking confused. "Kormor," she said, more gently. "Can you see me? are you listening to me?"

He nodded weakly.

"It's morning. Are you ready?"

He coughed. It was a terrible, guttural sound. Had the sickness spread to his chest?

Finally the spasms subsided. "Water," he said.

She felt so anxious and impatient, it was all she could do to hold the leather bucket steady and trickle the water into his mouth.

"Are you strong enough to do as you promised?" she asked, putting the bucket aside.

"I have to," he said. And now, finally, his voice sounded normal again.

Mara felt some of her confidence return. She went to the door and peered out. Ulmei was on duty—alone, this time—looking miserable out in the snow. The sky was glowing bright above the peaks to the east, but the sun wasn't up yet, and the air was bitingly cold. Mara looked around and saw the full Moon still visible in the sky toward the south. She paused a moment and said a little prayer, begging for guidance and protection.

Then she turned to Ulmei. "Kormor believes he is dying," she said, speaking the words with clear deliberation. "He wants to speak to the tribe."

Ulmei blinked at her uneasily. "Are you sure?"

"Of course I'm sure." She returned his stare. "I'm going to help him to the Meeting Place. He has something very important to say."

Ulmei shifted uneasily. "But Graum said you're not to leave your home."

"I realize that. But this is what Kormor wants. Ulmei,

I asked you once before, would you deny a man's dying wish?"

He flexed his hand in his thick mitten, shifting his grip on his spear. "I think I should speak to Kormor."

"All right." Mara stepped back from the tent flap.

Ulmei pushed inside. His bulky furs made it difficult for him to get through the small door. "Kormor," he said. "Tell me, is Mara telling the truth?"

Kormor closed his eye for a moment. Mara glared at him, willing him to say the words that needed to be said.

Finally Kormor looked up at Ulmei. "I have something to tell everyone."

Ulmei frowned. "What is it you have to say?"

"He wants everyone to hear his words at the same time," Mara put in quickly.

Ulmei flashed her an annoyed look while wearily Kormor nodded.

"All right." Ulmei hesitated. "Both of you stay here. Wait till I send some men with a travois to carry Kormor."

Mara thought about that. Yes, she decided, that would be best.

Quickly Ulmei left the tent.

Mara's impatience was almost too much for her to bear now. She paced quickly to and fro. Distantly, she heard shouts. Then there was a lull, and then more shouts. This time she heard old Lorm, the News Teller, calling people out of their homes.

But no one came to the tent. Why not? She told herself to be patient; not enough time had passed. But still, she began to wonder. What if Graum knew that Kormor had seen him kill Ternees? What if Graum had guessed somehow that Kormor was going to reveal his knowledge? That seemed unlikely—impossible—yet she was so nervous, she couldn't stop the thought from nagging her.

She turned to Kormor. His eye was closed again, and he seemed to have fallen back to sleep. "Wake up!" she told him.

He blinked at her. "Are they here?"

"Not yet. But I want to get you up. Can you sit?"

With her help, he finally managed to sit up. She guided

his legs over the side of the bed. She threw an extra fur around him. Then she maneuvered her shoulder under his armpit. She would get him to the Meeting Place herself, if she had to.

There were footsteps outside. A heavy tread. The door flap was jerked aside; and then, suddenly, Graum was there.

Mara froze, staring at him as he pushed inside the tent. He was so tall, his head brushed the peak of the roof. He stood there in his bearskin robe, looming over her. He glared at her with narrowed eyes. Then he turned to Kormor. "What's happening?" he asked, without preliminaries.

Mara felt Kormor's strength leave him. He rested heavily on her shoulder. He truly was afraid of the big man, she realized. "Something I have to say," Kormor muttered.

"So, speak," said Graum. "I'll listen."

Kormor shivered. "No," he said. "It must be to everyone." Mara felt him straightening his back, gathering up the remnants of his strength. "I'm dying, Graum!" He finally managed to look up at the Chieftain. "You must let me speak. Otherwise ..." he hesitated, "I fear for my spirit."

"Why?" Graum's face was full of suspicion. "What is it you have to say?"

"He just wants to say good-bye to everyone," Mara said.

"Yes," said Kormor, sounding grateful to her for prompting him. "That's all, Graum. Just a farewell."

Graum seemed to relax his guard a little. He patted Kormor on the shoulder. "All right, friend. We'll do as you want." Unexpectedly, he turned on Mara. "And afterward, we'll deal with you."

A freshly built fire was crackling in the center of the meeting place, and its smoke mingled with the white exhalations of the people clustered around it. Mara saw Shani, and her husband Ipaw, and the other people of their clan. She saw Ifnir and Tiear and the elder hunters huddled in a group as they had on the night when Lomel had been stripped bare and beaten.

But these faces were not the ones she was searching for. Where was Arin? She looked around with mounting anxiety as Kormor was carried in on a stretcher made from antelope hide tied across a frame of wooden poles. Then she saw the face she was searching for. He was standing far to one side, close to a deep drift that had flowed up against one of the Clan Houses. For an instant, her eyes made contact with his. Then he looked away.

Surely, if he had failed her or changed his mind, he would have given her some sign. *Trust him,* Mara told herself. He had given his word. He surely wouldn't let her down.

And now, as she glanced quickly around, she saw a scattering of women standing around the edges of the Meeting Place. All of them were clutching themselves against the fierce chill in the air, but they made no move toward the fire that burned in the center. They held their positions, trying not to meet anyone's eyes. And Lomel was among them.

Mara found herself feeling surprised, then elated. A part of her hadn't quite believed, till now, that her plan would become a reality. But clearly, Arin had listened to her and obeyed. There was something exciting about that—but at the same time, it terrified her.

The men carrying Kormor's stretcher were tilting it up, resting the top end of it against the Justice Post. There was a gasp and then a murmur of concern as the villagers saw Kormor's one good eye and his ruined face still smeared with pus and green salve. People edged forward, and instinctively, Graum's guards took up their customary position, facing the villagers as if they were the enemy. Well, Mara thought, that was closer to the truth than they realized.

Mara moved forward, and Bumar blocked her path.

"Let me past," she said, speaking with far more strength than she felt. "My place is beside my mate."

Bumar gave her a slow, suspicious look. He glanced at Graum, and the big man nodded. Reluctantly, Bumar waved Mara past.

"People," Graum said, climbing onto the Speaking Stone. "You know what a fine, brave warrior Kormor is. And you know how he's been suffering."

Mara edged closer to Kormor. He turned to her, and his face wore a pleading look.

"You know what did this to him," Graum went on. "And we'll see justice here, you can be sure of that." He gave Mara a speculative look. Then he turned back to the villagers. "But we'll get to that in a moment. What matters now," he went on, "is this: Kormor wants to say something to you all." Graum paused. He frowned and lowered his voice. "These may be the last words you hear from this young man. That's why he wanted to see you all. To say good-bye."

Once again, there was a murmuring of concern among the people in the Meeting Place.

Kormor looked at the villagers, and then he turned to Mara. "You promise," he whispered, "that after I do as you say—"

"I'll forgive you." She tightened her grip on his arm.

He shifted uneasily on the stretcher. "This will cause so much trouble, Mara." He looked at her plaintively. "Graum will deny it. There could be bloodshed."

"But it has to be done. The people deserve to know." She stared at him sternly. "It's the only way."

He sighed deeply, then suddenly went into another coughing fit. She watched him anxiously. She remembered how she'd felt when she'd called the people to the Meeting Place to denounce Graum, all those months ago. This, now, was far worse, beyond anxiety, beyond fear. She felt in a dreamlike state, light-headed and wild.

Finally Kormor's coughing died down. "People," he said. "Hear me, now." But his voice was hoarse and faint.

"They can't hear you, friend," said Graum. He turned and saw his wife nearby. "Dira, you better go over there. Listen to him, then tell everyone what he says."

Dira nodded and started forward.

"No," Mara said, trying not to show the desperation that she suddenly felt. "No, I think it would be right . . .

if Lorm conveys what Kormor has to say. He's the News Teller. He always has been."

Dira stopped a couple of paces away. Her eyes narrowed as she stared at Mara.

Mara quickly turned to Kormor. "Shall we summon Lorm? Is that your wish?" She gave him a hard look.

Weakly, he nodded.

"Come forward, Lorm!" Mara shouted out.

Awkwardly, the old man made his way through the crowd. He nodded respectfully to Mara, eyed Dira uneasily, then took his place beside Kormor. He looked self-conscious, but proud. For him, this was a rare honor.

"Now," Mara said. Once again, she turned to Kormor. "Now." And she watched him steadily.

For a moment, he closed his eyes. The villagers stared at him, craning forward, eager to hear what it was he had to say. The only sound was the crackling of the fire. The sky was slowly brightening, turning from deep gray to blue. The first rays of the sun were striking between the Clan Houses, laying lines of gold across the white snow. And toward the south, the disc of the Moon still showed ghostly pale, looking down on her people.

Kormor licked his cracked lips. "I've been wrong, and I ask my tribe to forgive me," he said.

Lorm gave Mara a questioning glance. She nodded impatiently. "Tell the people each thing he says."

"He says he did something wrong, and he wants us to forgive him," Lorm called out.

Kormor shivered in his furs. He gave Mara a last imploring glance.

She clenched her fists inside her mittens. She glared at him.

He saw the determination in her face. He sighed. "There is a secret I have to tell." His voice was barely a murmur.

But Lorm seemed able to hear it well enough. "He has a secret," the News Teller called out.

"I kept this secret," Kormor went on. His voice was a little stronger, now that he had finally started on the path that would lead to his revelation. "I was wrong. I kept the secret to keep the peace. But it was wrong." He paused between each phrase for Lorm to relay it to the crowd.

Graum was beginning to look suspicious. "What secret?" he demanded.

Weakly, Kormor turned toward him. For a long moment he said nothing. Mara saw fear in his eyes; but then resignation took its place. *That's right,* Mara thought to herself. *You will die either way. Or so you believe.*

"The secret is your secret, Graum," Kormor said.

"Graum's secret," Lorm relayed to the crowd.

Something changed subtly in the big man's face. Mara saw him grow tense, like an animal getting ready to spring.

"You killed our Chieftain," Kormor said. "You pushed her from the cliff. When we hunted the mastodon."

Mara felt exultant. The emotion lifted her like a huge wave. "Tell them!" she shouted to Lorm.

The old man looked horrified. He stared at her, speechless.

"He's sick!" Dira shouted out. "He's feverish. He doesn't know what he's saying."

"Tell them!" Mara screamed at Lorm.

He nodded dumbly. "Graum killed Ternees," the News Teller called out in a trembling voice. "Pushed her from the cliff."

Graum was stepping down from the Speaking Stone. Mara glimpsed his face. It was fearsome.

"It's true!" Kormor was trying to rise up from his stretcher. Now that he had made his confession, it seemed to have given him new strength. "You killed her, Graum!" His voice was louder. "I saw you. I saw you kill her."

"Liar!" Dira screamed out the word. "Filthy, filthy liar!" And she started toward Kormor with a murderous look in her eyes.

"A dying man tells no lies," Mara shouted at her.

"Wait. Wait a minute, here." Graum was glancing from Kormor to the villagers. There was a rising tide of sound in the Meeting Place, like the growl of a great beast. People were pushing forward. Graum's guards were raising their spears, glancing at each other in confusion. From the corner of her eye, Mara saw Arin watching her, wide-eyed, waiting for her signal.

She started to raise her arm—yet something held her back. Somehow she sensed it still wasn't the time.

"I saw you kill her." Kormor looked up at Graum defiantly.

"Kormor saw Graum kill her!" Lorm shouted out.

"Liar!" Dira screamed again. Without warning, she pulled something out from under her furs. Mara looked and saw, with amazement, that it was a flint knife. The little woman's eyes were glassy. Her face was contorted.

"But you know it's true," Kormor told her. "He must have told you."

Maybe, Mara thought, that wasn't so. She remembered how the little woman had assaulted her here in the Meeting Place. Dira was fanatically loyal. If she truly thought that Kormor was lying about her mate—

Mara took a quick pace forward to block Dira's path, but Dira was already running at Kormor. Mara reached for her, seized her furs—and the woman half fell, knocking the stretcher sideways. It toppled and crashed down on the ground with Dira on top of it. She let out a cry of wild rage, and her arm rose and fell. Kormor screamed.

"Arin!" Mara shouted. Graum's guards had turned away from the crowd. They were staring in horror as Dira stabbed Kormor, and stabbed him again. Graum was striding forward, seizing her, pulling her back.

"Arin!" Mara cried out again. "Lomel!"

Already they were delving into the snowdrifts, seizing their hidden spears.

Meanwhile, the villagers were all running forward. Everything was happening at once. People were shouting in horror, in outrage. Mara glimpsed Graum lifting his wife bodily into the air. She screamed and writhed like an infant. Her bloody knife scattered droplets onto the guards who were millling around.

"Get back!" Graum bellowed. "Make room!"

The villagers paid no attention. They threw themselves forward in a wave. They overran Graum's startled guards and seized hold of him. They pushed him up against one of the Clan Houses.

Then Arin and Lomel and their rebel allies were racing into the mob of bodies, holding their spears high. Three of them converged on Graum, aiming the points of their weapons at his throat.

Arin quickly disarmed one of the guards and kicked him in the stomach, sending him sprawling into the snow. Arin grabbed the fallen man's spear and looked quickly around.

"Here!" Mara shouted.

He saw her and hurled it to her, over the heads of the milling crowd.

The shaft almost slipped out of Mara's grasp, but she managed to hold on to it and spin it around as Bumar came at her. His eyes widened as he saw her weapon. He hesitated, and she swung the spear shaft, smacking it across the side of his head. He yelled and went down with a comical look of surprise.

Mara turned and found Dira suddenly in front of her, lunging for her, still holding her bloodied knife.

"Stop!" Mara shouted. She lowered the point of her spear.

Dira paid no attention. Her face was a mask of rage. She came running at Mara with her knife held high.

Mara hesitated. She stepped back. She had hunted game for most of her life, but she had never even leveled her spear at a person before. "Dira, stop!" she screamed again.

Dira didn't stop. Mara took another step back—and found herself tripping over someone, falling backward.

Dira yelled inarticulately and leaped forward.

Mara brought her spear up to defend herself. It was a matter of instinct, nothing more. The point rose toward Dira at the same time she flew toward Mara—impaling herself.

The spear jerked in Mara's grip, almost pulling free from her hands. She watched in horror as the flint point plunged through Dira's furs, deep into her chest. The woman's mouth opened wide. She made a hoarse, gasping sound and lurched to one side, dropping her knife and clutching the shaft that was now embedded in her. Then she fell into the snow and started screaming.

Mara scrambled up out of the drift where she had fallen. She saw Dira writhing, tugging at the spear shaft, with blood starting to bubble between her lips.

Mara turned and looked quickly around. All Graum's men had been disarmed. They were being held at spearpoint. A couple had been wounded.

Graum had heard his wife scream. He was forcing his way through the crowd while people clung to him, trying to hold him back. "Dira!" he cried out.

"She tried to kill me," Mara shouted.

Graum raised his head. He stared at her in slow understanding, and his face changed. She saw pure hate—so fierce, so evil, it made her feel liquid inside.

Graum let out a terrible growl of rage.

"Stop him!" Mara cried. She tugged at the spear that was now embedded in Dira's chest, but she couldn't pull it free. "This is the man who killed my mother! Stop him!"

Suddenly Lomel was beside her, pressing a spear into her hands. And then another woman was there, and another. Together they faced the huge man, while the other villagers clung to his arms and his furs. He struggled, writhing his shoulders, trying to throw off his tormentors. But even his great strength was not enough.

"We should kill him now," Lomel said.

Mara glimpsed her face. Lomel had changed. The shy, sweet girl had vanished. She looked wild and eager for Graum's blood.

"Kill him!" someone else echoed her.

"Kill him!" It sounded around the Meeting Place, a terrible chant, galvanizing the villagers, waking them from their stupor of fear and indecision.

"No!" The word was a scream.

The chant went on—but it began to falter. People turned to look. Shani was standing on the Speaking Stone.

"No!" Shani screamed the word again.

Mara stared at her sister in blank confusion. In all her

visions of what might happen here in the Meeting Place, this was something she had never imagined.

"I am your rightful leader," Shani cried out, as the villagers turned toward her. "And I say there has been too much killing."

Gradually the chant died away. The people kept their grip on Graum, but their attention was on Shani now. Graum ceased struggling, and even he turned his attention toward the young woman on the Speaking Stone. He stood panting, his breath rising in clouds.

"Listen to me!" Shani shouted. And the people fell silent. "We will hold Graum as our prisoner," Shani told them. "We'll hold his guards, as well. Then we'll decide what to do."

Suddenly it seemed as if Graum's cruel reign had never been. Shani stood in front of her tribe like her mother before her. Mara saw the faces of the villagers. Instinctively, they were accepting her, honoring her.

Mara felt a sudden wave of anger. She started pushing through the crowd. "I'm the one who should decide," she called out. "You have no business, Shani—"

"I'm your rightful leader," Shani shouted again, looking down at Mara.

"You threw away that right!" Mara's voice was shaking—not just with anger, but with anguish. "You stood aside and let that man run our lives. You did nothing! I was the one who warned everyone, and I was the one who saved us today. With Arin, and Lomel—I saved this tribe!"

"We're thankful, Mara." Shani inclined her head. "You were brave and you were bold."

There was a loud shout of agreement.

"But the time for violence is past, now," Shani went on. "For too long we've turned away from the ways of our people. The good ways, the peaceful ways. As your rightful leader, I say it's time to return."

This time, the shout was louder.

"Take Graum to my Clan House," Shani said. "Put his followers with him. There are no weapons there, so it's a safe place to hold them. But put ten hunters on guard at the door."

The villagers who were holding Graum started pushing and dragging him toward the house.

"Is anyone wounded?" Shani called out. "We must help them. It's time to heal all our wounds."

Mara felt faint and dazed as she saw people moving to obey. She looked at Lomel, and at Arin—and they, too, seemed stunned. For a few short moments, they had had more power than they'd ever imagined possible. They had been able to change their world and their destiny. And now, as swiftly as it had come to them, that power had been taken away.

Chapter 29

The snow was red where Kormor lay. Mara squatted beside his body while some of the villagers stood close by, watching her, maintaining a respectful silence.

Dira had stabbed him three times—once in his chest, once in his shoulder, and once in his neck. The neck wound had been the fatal one. It had cut an artery, and he had bled to death.

Mara shook off one of her mittens, reached out, and touched his face. Already his skin was cold. In this cruel weather, the body's heat was soon gone.

His good eye was closed. The wounded side of his face was half covered with snow. His lips were parted, as if there had still been something more that he wanted to say.

"You feared that your life was almost over," Mara murmured, "and you were right." She reached inside her furs, took hold of the thong that she still wore, and lifted it over her head. With a sadness that she couldn't quite name, she laid her Bonding Stone upon Kormor's lifeless form.

"Mara." The voice was soft yet intrusive. It was Ewna, Mara realized—her neighbor. "Mara, do you still carry his child?"

Slowly Mara stood up. There was no point now in denying it. "I lost his child," she said, "while I was away across the lake."

There was a cry of dismay from the people around her. She looked at their faces and saw that they genuinely grieved for her. That made her feel awkward, because she still wasn't quite sure, inside herself, how she felt about it. Kormor had already lost all his other relatives, and now his family line had truly ended. That was a terrible thing—yet at the same time, Mara couldn't guess how it would have been, raising a child of his. If it had turned out to be a boy, and if it had reminded her of him . . .

Kormor had been a terrible error in her life—a source of hurt and unhappiness. In some ways, she had to admit, she was relieved that fate had lifted the burden from her shoulders. But how could she possibly explain all that to the people around her? They wouldn't understand, and they'd disapprove of her. They knew that Kormor had mistreated her, but even so, they would expect her to grieve for him without reservation.

She stood up and turned away. A smaller knot of people had gathered around Dira's body where she lay on the ground a few paces distant.

Mara walked across the Meeting Place and looked down at the little woman. She was lying on her back with one leg twisted under her. Her stiff hands still gripped the spear in her chest. Her eyes were staring, her mouth was open in a silent scream, and her face was a mask of pain. She had not died an easy death.

"Build a bigger fire," Mara said to the people around her. "We will have a Winter Burial this evening for the two of them." Without waiting for a response, she started out of the Meeting Place.

A Winter Burial was actually not a burial at all. The ground was frozen so hard at this time of the year, no one could dig a grave. And so, in the winter months, the Lake People were forced to burn the bodies of their dead. After the ashes from the fire had cooled, relatives could salvage the bones of their loved ones and keep them for proper burial in the spring.

Mara felt a hand on her arm. She turned and found herself face-to-face with Lomel.

"Are you all right?" Lomel was looking at her strangely.

"Yes." Mara's tone was flat. Too much had happened; she wasn't ready yet to let herself feel the meaning of it all.

"We owe everything to you, Mara." Lomel drew her

close and hugged her. "It was all your doing. Thank you for being so bold, and confident, and strong."

For a moment Mara felt her composure slipping. It would be so easy to let herself weaken. She should be feeling shock at the fact that she had killed a woman; anger at her sister for stealing her moment of triumph; regret that her tribe had blindly accepted Shani as their Chieftain, even while they knew that she had abandoned them to Graum just a few months ago.

But she didn't have the strength to think of such things. It would take time to come to terms with it all, and solitary contemplation. "You're kind, Lomel," she said. "But it's you I have to thank. You and Arin." She saw him standing close by, proud of his part in the uprising. He had wiped mud across the bear-head tattoo on his forehead, to obliterate it. "I trusted you, Arin," she said. "And you were true to me. I could never ask more of someone than that."

He seemed pleased by her praise. "I did my best," he said.

She looked from Arin to Lomel, and back again. They were both watching her, waiting for something more from her. Gradually she realized that they expected her to tell them what should be done. They respected her judgment now. They looked up to her.

That was a strange feeling. She felt flattered, but uncomfortable—because she didn't see what she could do.

"I think it's wrong," Arin said haltingly, "that Shani should have—"

"Our people are happier this way," Mara cut him off. "They want everything to be the same as before. They're afraid of change, don't you see? And they're ashamed that they let themselves be led by Graum. They don't want to be reminded of it."

Arin and Lomel exchanged glances. Lomel reached for Mara's arm. "Come with us. We should eat together. There'll be food to spare now. You should talk to my parents. I'm sure my father will respect you for what you did, and he might have some advice for us."

For a moment Mara almost weakened. It would be so easy to accept the kind invitation. But she was afraid that if she did, her emotions would break free and overwhelm her.

"Thank you," she said, "but I need to be on my own for a while." She hesitated. "You see, the situation is still not resolved."

"We did succeed," said Arin. "We did rise up against Graum and overthrow him."

"Yes," said Mara. "But he still lives."

She went to her old Clan House and checked that it was securely guarded. Some of the elder hunters had clustered around the entrance together with the women who had disarmed Graum's guards. Everyone was carrying at least one spear.

The women thanked Mara, and they, too, looked at her with new respect. The elders, though, were more cautious. She could see that they still saw her as an impulsive, reckless spirit. She had saved them; but that didn't mean they trusted her now to lead them in a time of peace and reconciliation.

Well, there was nothing she could do about that. She saw that they were all alert and well armed, and then she walked away to her home by the lake.

She spent the rest of the morning and most of the afternoon gathering Kormor's possessions and wrapping them in deerskin. Here were the spearheads that he had fashioned so painstakingly; here were some blue and green stones he had collected up on the cliffs; here were the hunting robes, the moccasins, the winter hoods that he had worn. Some of these things she could cast into the flames with his body. The rest she would keep until the weather was warmer and she could bury them with his remains.

Many times she broke off, sitting and thinking, remembering Kormor, and trying to come to understand that he was gone. When she'd spent her days of solitude in the cave across the lake, she'd thought she had moved beyond any feelings of loss for him. And certainly she wasn't grieving as most women would. Yet there was something bad about his absence, all the same. It seemed wrong that a person should vanish out of the world as if he had never lived.

She sat for a while, looking out of the tent across the frozen lake. But the weather was turning bad again, and heavy clouds were gathering. Soon, she sensed, there would be more snow.

She closed the flap, lit a fire, and huddled beside it, dozing intermittently, thinking of everything that had happened—and the things that still needed to be done.

When the light began to fade, she decided it was time. Soon the people would be gathering for the Winter Burial ceremony. There would be wailing and grieving, and people would speak for the dead. If Mara was going to act, it should be before then.

She ventured out of her tent and found that dense, shifting curtains of snow were swirling down from the leaden sky. She had thought that without Graum, her problems would be solved. But once again, it seemed, she had to be strong.

She walked among the Clan Houses, nodding and smiling to the few people who were out in the storm. Finally she came to the Spirit House.

Inside, she found a festive scene. It seemed as if half the tribe had gathered there, feasting on the food that Graum had hoarded, telling stories and laughing and singing together, celebrating the return of their old ways. Most of them were women, and the faces that Mara saw were flushed and childlike, smiling, erasing all memory of the things they had witnessed in the Meeting Place.

Mara saw Shani at the opposite side of the house, surrounded by several elders of the tribe. Slowly Mara started picking her way among the happy villagers. Many of them greeted her warmly. Word had evidently spread among them that she was the one who had planned the uprising, but she doubted they understood the details. Dira had died, Graum and his people were disarmed, and now everything was back the way it had been before. That was all they wanted to know.

Finally Mara reached her sister. Shani was sitting in the ceremonial chair—the same chair where Mara had sat during her Ceremony of First Blood. Mara paused for a minute, watching Shani talking with the elders. They all stood straight and proud now. The beaten look had vanished from the men's faces.

Finally someone noticed Mara. The conversation died. "Mara!" shouted Ifnir. "We were wondering where you were. Join us here, Mara."

"Thank you," she said, moving a little closer.

"Is it true," Ifnir went on, "that it was all your doing this morning? Kormor's confession, and the spears hidden in the snow—"

"Yes," Mara said. "It was my doing."

"A brave plan, for such a young woman," said Clewna, one of the elder women. She gave Mara a measuring look.

"Mara has always been the bold one," said Shani. "Bold and daring." She nodded to Mara, but she seemed cautious and reserved.

Mara met her sister's eyes. "Sometimes being bold and daring is the right path to take," Mara said. "It may even be the only path."

"It may be," Shani said carefully. "Of course, there may also be other, safer paths."

Mara felt herself getting impatient. She hated this kind of sparring. "Tell me what you're trying to say, sister."

Ifnir stepped forward, sensing the mistrust between the two women. "Shani sees what a catastrophe it could have been if your plan had gone wrong," he said. "That's all she's saying, Mara. But she's also thanked you publicly for your courage. Remember that." He spread his arms. "So eat with us now, Mara. Sit a minute."

Mara looked up into his face and saw that he meant well. She felt an instinctive need to respond; but that wasn't why she was here now.

"Thank you, Ifnir," she said. "But first I must ask you all a question."

"Well, of course," Ifnir said, still sounding amiable. "What's on your mind, young Mara?"

Mara looked from him to Shani, then to the rest of the elders. None of them seemed to feel entirely comfortable, having her here. None of them quite knew what her status was now, or how to deal with her, or what to expect from her. "I would like to know," Mara said, "what will happen now to Graum and his followers." She raised her voice above the talking and laughter of the villagers in the other half of the Spirit House, but she took care not to speak so loudly that people behind her would overhear.

Shani leaned forward. "We'll wait and see what the tribe decides to do," she said.

Mara paused a moment, then shook her head. "Sister, in a little while we gather for the Winter Burial of Dira and Kormor. All the people of the tribe will be there. Surely you'll have something ready to suggest to them. And when they hear your plan, they'll probably go along with it."

Shani moved restlessly in her chair. "Sister, we're grateful to you, as Ifnir said. But your part, now, is done. It is our task now—"

"If you please, Shani." Ifnir raised his hand. "Let me speak on this matter."

Shani gave him an annoyed look. Then she shrugged.

Ifnir glanced at the other elders, then back at Mara. He beckoned her closer. "Mara, it seems to me things will be easier for us all if you understand our point of view. We certainly don't want you speaking out at the Winter Burial. This should be a time of healing, now. There mustn't be any more conflict."

Was he warning her, or asking her? It was hard for her to tell. Ifnir was the eldest hunter, now that Yacor was gone, and he seemed to want to follow Yacor's example, serving as a friend to everyone. Mara suspected, though, that Ifnir wasn't as open-minded as Yacor had been. He was a conservative man. He was being friendly, but only because he wanted to get her to do as he wished.

"We've decided, " Ifnir went on, "that it would be wrong to harm Graum. It's not the way of our people, as you well know."

Mara stared at him. "You mean you're going to let him go?" She couldn't keep the astonishment out of her voice.

"No, no, of course not. We can keep him prisoner, at least till the spring. Then we can cast him out."

Mara looked at all their kind, well-meaning faces. "Graum is a powerful man," Mara said, trying hard to stay calm and reasonable. "He won the loyalty of two score of our young hunters. He turned them against all our traditions. He made them into beasts who found pleasure in hunting other people."

"Of course," Shani said. She seemed impatient now. "We're not fools, Mara."

"All right, then. Please tell me what you expect Graum to do after you cast him out. And tell me what his followers will do." Mara looked from her sister to the elders.

At first they didn't react. But then she saw uncertainty in their faces. They hadn't really thought about it, she realized. They imagined that if they cast him out, Graum would be gone, and that would be the end of the problem.

"His followers, as you call them, are our kin," Shani said reprovingly. "Young Arin already seems to have come around. With time enough, I expect the others—"

"Graum will want revenge!" Mara's voice was rising. She couldn't repress her anger any longer. "Don't you understand? His wife was killed today. By me, a young woman who has defied him in the past. He's been humiliated. He'll want revenge against me—and you, and anyone else who stood against him. And those young men who follow him—some of them worship him. *He's* their kin, now! Don't you see?" She looked from one face to the next. "If you cast him out, we'll never be safe from him. He'll come back and kill us in our sleep!"

There was a long silence. "Well," said Ifnir, "I'm not entirely sure—"

Shani gestured, cutting him off. "Sister, you're attracting attention." She nodded toward the people in the other half of the house. "This is really not the time—"

"I think perhaps there's some truth in what Mara says." It was Clewna speaking. She sounded tentative, almost apologetic. "My own son followed Graum. He became a stranger to me. The man does have a powerful influence. And he killed your own mother, Shani. There's no telling what he might do."

Shani turned her chair. "We only have Kormor's word for that."

Clewna looked defensive. "He seemed to speak truly."

"All right, suppose he did." Shani was starting to sound shrill. She wasn't confident of her authority, Mara realized. She was afraid of being challenged. "What do you want us to do, Clewna, kill the man?"

"Well, as Ifnir says, that would not be our way. But—"

"Killing him is the only answer," Mara said flatly.

Shani turned back to face her. She looked at Mara with disdain. "He is the killer, not us. If we kill him, then we're no better than he is."

"So what's the alternative?" Mara stared at her sister.

Shani slowly stood up. She glared at Mara. "We will keep him captive, as we originally decided. There's been enough recklessness and bloodshed. We can take our time—"

"You mean you don't know what to do, so you're going to put off making a decision," said Mara.

"Please." Ifnir stepped forward again. "Please, Mara, be polite. Shani is your sister, but she's also your Chieftain. Some respect—"

"Let me speak to our people at the Winter Burial ceremony," Mara interrupted him. "Let them decide."

"No," Shani snapped. "I will not permit it."

Mara felt a hot burst of anger. "Are you afraid they might turn against you, sister? Are you so afraid of losing your new power?"

"Leadership is a duty," Shani snapped. Her voice had grown even louder than Mara's. "I've told you that before. But you'll never understand it." She gathered her fine robe around her, and she glared at Mara. "You still think power is a pleasure, and you're angry that you don't have it yourself. That's why you paired with Kormor, because he had that ugly physical power, and you wanted some of it." Shani paused, breathing deeply. "Power is a weapon," she went on, a little more calmly. "It should be used sparingly, if it's used at all. And the person who wields it should be thoughtful, slow to act, and swift to forgive."

"You mean, like you," Mara said.

Shani tossed her hair back. She tilted her jaw up. "Perhaps, yes, like me. But definitely not someone as impulsive and dangerous as you."

Mara noticed that the elders had moved a little closer together while Shani spoke, grouping themselves behind her. Very well, Mara thought, they had made themselves clear enough. She turned without a word and started walking away, back across the Spirit House, between the villagers.

"Where are you going?" Shani called sharply.

"To my home," Mara said over her shoulder.

There were a dozen spears leaning against the wall beside the door flap. Mara picked one up as she passed.

The snow was still falling heavily, and the sky was a dim, deep gray. Mara paused, trying once again to find the courage that she needed. She realized that she was as guilty as anyone of not having looked far enough ahead. She, after all, had imagined that if she led an uprising against Graum, the danger that he posed would be over.

She started out into the snow, back toward the Meeting Place. The fire was burning high, defying the storm. No matter how bad the weather became, the Winter Burial would take place. It was a ceremony that the tribe never postponed.

Slowly, purposefully, Mara walked toward her old Clan House. A dozen men and women were still huddled together at the door, guarding it. As Mara came closer, she recognized Lomel and Arin among them.

"Greetings," she said.

They saw her, and they smiled. "Mara!" Lomel took her arm. "Where have you been?"

Now that Mara had decided what to do, she felt time as a burden. There was certainly no time for small talk. She knew she must act immediately; otherwise, she would lose the stomach for it. "I have to see Graum," she said.

Lomel and Arin exchanged surprised glances. "What for?" Arin asked. "Surely you have nothing to say—"

"I was just speaking with Shani and the elders in the Spirit House," Mara said. "There was . . . a disagreement. The only way I can settle it now is by seeing Graum." She nodded toward the door that they were guarding. "We can call him out. There are many of us, and all of us are armed. It will be safe enough."

"But I still don't understand," Lomel objected. "What is it you want to settle with him?"

Mara looked at her kind, trusting face. She knew she couldn't confide in her about this. Arin, likewise, couldn't be trusted to share Mara's belief about what must be done. This was something she would have to do on her own.

But could she do it? When she had killed Dira, it had been in self-defense. And even then, Mara had hesitated. It had been a terrible thing to see her weapon take another person's life.

Even if she did have the nerve to kill Graum—what would happen then? Would she, too, be imprisoned, for breaking the most fundamental taboo? Would the tribe turn against her, as it had so often in the past?

She had to take that risk. She felt utter certainty that so long as Graum lived, the village would not be safe. Even now she saw again her vision of the Clan Houses in flames.

"Lomel," she said, "you must trust me. Arin, I asked you once before to follow my plan. I'm asking you now again. We must call Graum out here. Just for a few moments."

They looked at each other. Then they looked at the other people guarding the House. Some of them shifted uneasily, but no one spoke out.

Arin turned toward the door of the House. He gestured for the others to back him up. They circled around him, leveling their spears. Arin pulled the door flap aside. "Graum!" he called through the gap. "Come out here, Graum!"

Mara took a pace back. She was directly facing the doorway. There were a couple of people in front of her, but Graum was so tall, she had no doubt she could cast her spear over their heads. And then, if the wound wasn't fatal, she still had a flint knife in her belt.

She glanced quickly behind her. There were two people throwing wood onto the great fire, but otherwise the Meeting Place was empty. Curtains of snow were still swirling down.

"Graum!" Arin called again.

Mara shifted her grip on her spear. The tension was growing in her. Her mouth was dry and her throat felt tight. There was a hollow feeling in her belly. She stared at the door flap, anxiously waiting. At any moment she would see Graum's face—

Arin turned away from the door flap. He had been peering through a narrow gap. "I see no one inside," he said.

It took a moment for Mara to understand what he was saying. She blinked. "No one?"

"It looks empty." There was a quaver in Arin's voice. He sounded as if he couldn't believe his own words.

Everyone started pushing forward.

"Careful!" Mara shouted, from behind them. "They could be hiding in there."

But even as she spoke, she doubted it was possible. There were no hiding places in the big, round House. Not for two score of men.

She saw the people in front of her moving ahead. The door flap was pulled quickly aside. Arin and Lomel were striding into the house. The others were following, with Mara behind.

The familiar sight and smell of the Clan House was suddenly around her. A fire was burning brightly, and some dim light from the cloudy sky filtered down through the smoke hole in the center of the roof. Mara looked quickly around. She looked around again. She could see the house clearly, in every detail. It was utterly, completely empty.

Concern was yielding to panic. Arin and Lomel and the others were fanning out across the circular dirt floor, still not wanting to believe what they saw. Graum and his men couldn't have disappeared. It was impossible.

Mara felt a cold wind, and she saw where it was coming from. In the opposite wall, a hole had been burned in the close-spaced willow branches that lined the inside of the house. The mud behind them had been chipped away. The stout poles beneath that had been reduced to charred stumps. Snowflakes were drifting in, carried on the wind.

Graum and his men had fled.

Chapter 30

A little later, the Clan House was filled with people. No meeting had been called, but word had spread quickly enough, and the villagers had gathered of their own accord. The happy faces that Mara had seen in the Spirit House were now full of worry and fear. In the Meeting Place, the fire still burned high; but for the time being, the Winter Burial had been forgotten.

Mara stood to one side, with Lomel and Arin and the women who had taken up spears against Graum's men. Together they watched, saying nothing, as Shani climbed onto one of the tree stumps near the center of the house.

"My people!" Shani shouted out, raising her hands for silence.

"Her people," Arin muttered.

Mara heard the bitterness in his voice, and it momentarily disconcerted her. In the past, she had always been the only rebel. It was strange, now, to think that there were others who shared her outlook. She looked at Arin, and at Lomel, and at the faces of the women near her. Many of them were young—even younger than she was. Most, she knew, were not yet paired. They all seemed discontent, and when a couple of them met her eyes, she sensed that they were hoping that she, somehow, would be able to help them as she had before.

"My people!" Shani cried again. Gradually the villagers quieted down. So many had crowded together in the Clan House, there was no room for anyone to sit. The people were packed together, and the air was quickly growing hot.

"Graum and his men have gone," Shani said. "They burned a hole through the wall of this house, and they fled through the storm." Her voice was loud, but it sounded brittle as she turned, surveying the crowd around her. "Alas, we should have guarded Graum more carefully."

Beside Mara, Arin grunted with irritation. He started pushing forward, shouldering his way between the people in front of him. "Listen here!" he shouted out. Faces turned toward him in surprise. "I was one of the guards," he shouted. "We did what we were told. The fault wasn't ours."

The villagers murmured uneasily to one another. They weren't accustomed to this kind of dissent.

"Who speaks there?" Shani said, peering over the heads of the people.

Angrily, Arin forced his way through to the center of the House. He climbed up on another of the tree stumps near the fire pit. "My name is Arin." His voice was higher pitched than normal, and Mara saw his confidence waver as he looked around and saw so many people staring up at him. But then he raised his head, and she saw he was determined now to finish what he'd begun. "You all know me," he told them. "I was the one who stole the spears from Graum's store and hid them in the Meeting Place. I was the one who helped carry out Mara's plan." He paused as if he wasn't sure what more to add. "We did what you told us to do," he said again, turning back to Shani.

"All right, Arin. Thank you." She nodded to him, acknowledging him but at the same time dismissing him. It was exactly the way her mother would have done it, yet somehow it wasn't effective. Shani lacked the confidence to bring it off. "You're right, of course," she went on. "You and the others who guarded Graum were not at fault." She looked at Arin, waiting for him to step down.

"Then who's to blame?" Arin said.

Shani hesitated. "This is not a time to cast blame."

Mara felt her own anger stirring. "You were the one who spared his life!" she shouted out. "People were ready to kill him in the Meeting Place. You were the one who stopped them."

Faces turned toward her, looking shocked.

"That's enough!" Shani shouted. She paused a moment, trying to regain her composure. "People, please let's remember the rules that we honor. We never turn our spears against each other."

There was a murmur of assent from most of the elders, but the younger people in the crowd said nothing.

"Graum has left us," Shani went on, "and perhaps it's for the best. You've seen the storm outside. He can't hope to survive in it. He and his men have no weapons—"

"They emptied the food caches in the house here," someone else shouted.

"But there was only food enough for a day," Shani answered. "Without a doubt, the men who ran out into the storm will die in it."

"I don't believe that." It was Arin speaking again, and his voice was stronger than before.

Shani glared at him. "Arin, you know the customs of our people. You're not one of the elders here. You should ask permission to speak."

He faced her. He didn't step down. "All right, I ask for permission to speak."

Shani was beginning to look flustered. "Now is not the time—"

"Let him speak!" someone shouted.

"Let's hear him," said somone else.

"Let Arin speak!" The voices came from around Mara.

Shani's face was growing red—whether with anger or embarrassment, Mara couldn't tell. All she knew was that she had never imagined she would see her people behaving like this, shouting out, rebelling against their Chieftain. It was unnerving. A taboo was being broken.

"Very well," Shani said in a tight, clipped voice, "you may speak."

Arin turned and looked out over the crowd. "You all know," he said, "I followed Graum—for a while. I am ashamed of that now. But anyway—sometimes we would question him. One time we asked what he would do if the Lake People turned against him or cast him out. And he laughed. He said he had made plans, and he would have no trouble surviving." Arin paused to let that sink in. "I think he has food caches in the hills somewhere," he went on. "You remember how much game we brought in, in the summer. It seemed to me not all of it has been accounted for. Some of it is missing."

There was an ominous silence now. People heard the calm certainty in Arin's voice, and they believed him.

"Another thing," Arin went on. "In all the times I saw him, Graum never took a risk. He never did anything unless he felt sure of himself. He wouldn't have led his men out into the storm unless he knew exactly what he was doing." He paused. "I think that he'll return. I think he'll want revenge." He hesitated. "That's all I have to say." Abruptly he stepped down.

Shani seemed shaken. There was no easy way to deny what Arin had said. Among all the villagers gathered here, he alone had actually known Graum.

A slow murmur of concern began, and it didn't ebb away. It rose, bit by bit, till it filled Mara's ears. Suddenly everyone in the Clan House seemed to be talking.

Shani looked at them all, and clearly she didn't know what to do. The elders had ranged themselves protectively around her; she stooped to confer with them, while the tide of talk rose still higher.

"Mara." It was Lomel's voice, close to Mara's ear. "It's up to us to do something."

Mara turned to her. "Do what? Follow Graum into the storm?"

Lomel shook her head. "I just mean that the village must be protected."

"Yes," Mara said. "You're right. We should be placing guards at this very moment."

Lomel gave her an anxious, searching look. "Then why don't you speak out—"

Mara gestured angrily. "Shani is still the Chieftain. She won't hear advice from me. And I've tried speaking out, Lomel. I speak too loudly, or I say things that people don't want to hear. You've seen what happens when I speak out."

For a moment, the two of them looked at each other.

"All right," Lomel said finally. And without another

word, she started pushing through the tightly packed crowd.

"People!" It was Shani, calling again for silence. "People, hear me!"

It took much longer this time for the noise to die down.

"People," Shani went on, "our elder hunters will keep watch tonight so that we'll be safe."

"No!" It was Lomel's voice, Mara realized. And there she was, now, at the center of the house, standing up where her brother had stood. "Let me speak!" she cried out.

"I think there's no need for more speeches," Shani said. "I have decided—"

"Our elders didn't defend us before," Lomel cried. "Why should we trust them to defend us now? When Graum challenged them, they just walked away."

There was a roar from the crowd—half the people shouting at Lomel for her lack of respect, the other half cheering her.

"Quiet!" Shani cried, looking distraught. Her mother had never had to manage a meeting like this. There had never been such a meeting.

"I have a suggestion," Lomel said.

"We don't need—" Shani began.

"Hear her!" Mara called out.

Other people picked up her cry. "Hear her! Hear her!"

Shani wiped her forehead. Her hand was shaking. Wordlessly, she gestured to Lomel to speak.

Lomel turned to face the crowd. She looked small and very, very young, and Mara felt a moment's guilt, as if it was her fault that Lomel was standing there. Yet Mara knew how it would be if she had been the one to stand up opposite Shani. Shani would taunt her, or she'd tell the crowd that Mara was too unstable, too wild to be trusted. Mara would get angry, and she'd show her anger. She wouldn't be calm and clear, like Arin. She'd be impatient, and she'd be emotional, ruled by her own passion. Shani would see this, and it would make her more

confident in return. The situation would slip away from
Mara. . . .

But now Lomel was standing in front of the crowd,
and she was shy and unsure of herself. That alone made
her seem more sympathetic and trustworthy.

"Today," Lomel said, "my brother and I led a dozen
rebels against Graum and his thugs. And we conquered
them. We wouldn't have been able to do it, except that
Mara persuaded Kormor to tell his terrible secret—about
Graum, and how he killed Ternees."

Simply, quietly, Lomel had forced everyone to face,
once more, the most disturbing fact of all. The Clan
House was suddenly silent.

"It was Mara who made Kormor speak, and convinced
us to rebel against that evil man. It wasn't Shani, nor
our elders. And another thing: When Graum first came
to our tribe, it was Mara who told us that he was evil
and a liar. I'm sure you all remember that."

"Thank you, Lomel," said Shani. "It's good that you
remind us of the part that my sister played. But we're
not thinking of the past now. We're making plans for
the present."

"I haven't finished!" Lomel's voice was no longer gentle. The words were angry and cutting.

Shani blinked. She hesitated.

"Graum has good reason to take revenge on us,"
Lomel went on. "He has two score strong hunters, all of
them trained by him, completely loyal. My brother can
tell you that. So here's what must be done. Our elder
hunters are fine, brave men, but they aren't enough to
protect us. All able-bodied people should help to defend
our tribe. And Mara should be the one who decides how
it should be done."

Once again the crowd made noise, though Mara
couldn't tell how many were supporting Lomel and how
many were shouting her down.

"I am the rightful Chieftain of this tribe!" Shani
shouted out.

"Yes." Lomel turned to her. "And no one is asking
you to step down." She paused, and the noise slowly
diminished. "All I say is that Mara understands Graum.

She saw through him before anyone else. She planned an attack on him, and she succeeded. So give her the task of planning our defense. Let her organize her own band of guards, women and men, to keep the village safe."

Mara had the strange feeling that Lomel must be talking about someone else. To be standing here among her people, in her old Clan House, being praised by this young woman in front of the whole tribe—she had never imagined such a thing. And she saw, clearly, that it couldn't possibly work.

"Mara!" Lomel cried, raising her clenched fist. "Let Mara protect us!"

An instant later, all around Mara, the rebels who had risen up against Graum raised their fists in response. "Mara!" they cried—and it became a chant. People nearby took it up, without seeming to understand why. Perhaps they just felt happy that someone was suggesting something to make them feel safe at night. Perhaps they saw also that there was a big advantage in keeping Shani as their Chieftain, while delegating the warlike task to Mara. It made sense to pit their troublemaker, their rebel, against the man who had terrorized them. After all, she'd killed Graum's wife, hadn't she? At the same time, if Shani kept her position of authority, everyone could feel that they were holding on to the old ways of the tribe. This way they could have the best of both worlds.

"Mara! Let Mara defend the tribe!"

Lomel looked around at the people, and she almost lost her balance. Their enthusiasm seemed to surprise her almost as much as it surprised Mara. She turned back to face Shani, and she spread her arms, waiting for an answer.

It took a long time for the noise to die down. Shani stood rigid, with her arms by her sides. Finally, when the crowd was quiet, Shani inclined her head. "My people want my sister to decide how to defend us." Her voice was subdued. "Very well, a leader must follow the will of her people." She took a slow breath, obviously not wanting to go on, but knowing that she no longer had any choice. "Mara shall arrange for the safety of our tribe," she said.

The rebels around Mara started cheering. But Shani held up her hands. "I have more to say!" she cried. She waited for the noise to abate. "It is wrong," she went on, "for people to turn their spears against each other. Never forget that!" She turned slowly, eyeing everyone in the Clan House. "Any plans that Mara makes, they must be approved by me and by our elders." She drew herself up. "Remember this: I am still your rightful Chieftain. I am true to the laws and customs that my mother laid down, and her mother before her. Mara may defend us in this time of need. But I will never let her turn my people into a warlike tribe."

PART FOUR

▼▲▼

Adversaries

Chapter 31

Spring had come. The snow had drained away, the skies were tranquil and clear, and the land was alive again. Lying on her stomach in the tall grass, with Lomel close beside her, Mara gazed down at a stream that tumbled busily through a narrow cleft in the land. She said nothing, for nothing needed to be said. The sun warmed her back. A gentle breeze touched her cheeks.

Mara closed her eyes. It would be easy to doze out here under the sun, with the insects humming and the water making chuckling noises as it leaped over the stones in the stream. There was nothing for her to worry about, and no one to tell her what needed to be done. Her thoughts drifted—

Lomel gave her a quick little shake.

Mara opened her eyes. She found Lomel staring straight ahead, wide-eyed and intent.

Mara had learned to recognize that expression. "Blacktail," Lomel whispered.

Mara looked at a gentle slope that led down to an area of pale mud beside a bend in the stream. It was a favorite watering place for animals, shielded from view by the tall grass and the steep sides of the cleft. The mud here was sulfurous and had a salty taste. Deer and bison liked to lick it as they drank.

A blacktail deer was venturing cautiously down to the water, pausing to raise its head and sniff the air. Mara watched the animal as it finally decided there was no danger, then spread its front legs and dipped its mouth toward the stream. It was no more than a hundred paces away.

"Yours," Mara whispered.

Lomel shook her head.

Mara pushed Lomel's elbow. "You saw it first."

Lomel turned and looked at her. "I give it to you. Go on, Mara. You're always letting me take the game."

That was true, and there was a reason for it. Over the past months, Mara had discovered that kind, gentle Lomel became uncompromisingly fierce when she stalked game, just as she had been a fierce fighter when they had risen up against Graum in the Meeting Place and she had called on people to kill him. She pursued her prey like a cat, with fearsome intensity.

"All right," Mara said. She reached into the grass beside her and grasped her spear. She consciously clenched her muscles, gathering her energy, preparing to spring. She paused, and for a moment she heard the lapping of the deer's tongue above the chuckling of the stream.

The moment stretched out. Mara wondered if the deer would turn around when it finished drinking. There might be a moment, then, when its head would face away from her. That would be the instant to strike. She waited, feeling impatient now. The deer drank, and it paused, and it drank some more—and then, almost too quickly, it raised its head and turned to walk back the way it had come.

Mara jumped up, ran forward, raised her spear, and cast it. The spear flew straight and true—but the deer had heard her, and it was bounding away, taking great graceful leaps, with its black tail held high.

The spear fell short. The prey was gone.

The flurry of sudden motion roused birds in the forest close by. Sparrows twittered, a chickadee gave a shrill cry, and a jay vented its rasping call. Mara thought that the birds sounded as if they were mocking her as she walked down to the water and irritably retrieved her spear.

"You know, there really are some things that a man can do better than a woman," Mara said as she returned to Lomel and dropped her spear. "If I'd had a man's strength, I could have taken that deer."

Lomel wrinkled her nose. "You're being foolish."

"But it's true." She thought back to the times when

she'd been hunting with Kormor. No doubt about it; he would have taken the prize, though it annoyed her to have to admit it. "It's not just that men are stronger," he said. "They have longer arms. I think that gives them an advantage in itself." She sat down in the tall grass, then flopped onto her back.

"Your arms are long enough," Lomel said, giving Mara a playful look. "They're just not strong enough."

"I'm stronger than you are," Mara said sharply.

"Oh?" Lomel sat up. With one quick motion, she rolled across, seized Mara's wrists, and pinned them to the soft earth. "Stronger than I am?" Lomel grinned. "You're just older than I am, that's all."

Mara struggled. Lomel dipped her head and nipped the side of Mara's neck. Together, the two of them wrestled for a moment, till they both started laughing. And then Lomel was kissing Mara's neck instead of nipping at it, and Mara felt the soft, warm pressure of the young woman's body sinking down onto hers, and Lomel's hair falling around her face.

For a moment Mara let herself yield to the good feelings that rose up inside her. She embraced Lomel, and the kisses became more serious, touched with passion.

But then Mara pushed her away. "We're not safe here," she whispered.

Lomel frowned in annoyance. "Why do you always have to say that?"

"I don't. Not always. But often it's true." Mara struggled free. She sat up quickly and glanced around. The land seemed peaceful, and there was no sign of human life; but she could never be sure. And this was a place where the Lake People often came to lie in wait for game. "You know, Lomel, the tribe might cast us out—"

"So let's go somewhere that is safe," said Lomel. Her full lips parted just a little, and her dark eyes looked at Mara with frank desire. She wasn't shy anymore; she was bolder than Mara herself.

"But we came here to hunt," Mara said.

Lomel grunted dismissively. "When I saw that blacktail, you had your eyes closed. Some hunter you are."

She paused a moment. "Anyway, there's not enough game to make it worthwhile."

That part was true enough. The spring migrations had come and gone, and the land seemed strangely empty.

"Still," said Mara, "we should wait here a little longer. Just in case." She gave Lomel a sidelong glance. "Later we can go into the forest."

Lomel smiled. "All right." She settled back down in the grass and was silent for a while, staring down at the river. "I still think Graum killed too much last year."

Mara considered that. "There are probably more people south of us, now," she said. "The Silver River People must have grown in number, just like us. And what if there are some new tribes, as well? When the caribou come north in the spring, people south of here could be picking off all the best game."

"Maybe so. But if it's true, what should we do?"

Mara shrugged. "Eat more fish, or more fruits. We're not like Graum, too proud to eat anything but meat."

Lomel wrinkled her nose. "That's twice you've mentioned him, and twice is two times too many."

Mara sighed, staring up at the sky. "I don't like talking about him. But I still think of him. I still think he's out there somewhere with the men who followed him."

"And I say that when the rest of the snow melts on the mountain slopes, we'll find his bones." Lomel pointed at the white ribs and skull of a bison in the tall grass upstream. "He'll look just like that. Picked clean by the eagles."

"I wish it could be so," Mara said, half to herself. The specter of Graum had haunted the tribe through the second half of the winter and on into the spring. She had worked hard, gathering together young people who were strong enough and fierce enough to defend them all. She had tried to infect them with her own fear and hatred of Graum, and she had put Arin before them many times, describing the cruelties he had seen while he was one of Graum's men. But through it all, Mara only wished that she could be proved wrong, and Graum could be found dead. If that ever happened, she could finally forget her vision of the burning village.

She wasn't alone in wanting to put Graum out of her mind. She could see how the people of her tribe were starting to tell themselves, now, there was no longer cause for concern. The difference was that, unlike them, she wasn't willing to be guided by wishful thinking. So long as there was no proof, she had to act as if the threat was as great as ever. She still insisted on maintaining a vigil every night, and she forced her band of followers to refine their spear throwing and knife fighting.

"You know," Lomel said, "in a way, I almost wish Graum was still alive."

"So you could kill him?" Mara asked.

Lomel looked annoyed that Mara had seen into her so easily. "Yes," she said. "For what he did to me in the square. And for what he did to my brother."

"And for the crime of being a man," Mara said, with a faint smile.

Lomel looked more irritated now. "There's nothing wrong with men. Provided they know their place."

Mara looked into Lomel's eyes, wondering how much she really meant what she said. In the past few months, as Lomel had gained confidence, her fierceness had shown itself more and more. She was always eager to show that she was more than the equal of any man. The simple, gentle side of her nature was still there, but it seemed now as if it had just been camouflaging the wilder spirit beneath.

Mara put her arm across Lomel's shoulders. "I remember when I was the angry one, and you were the one who seemed serene."

Lomel was silent for a moment. "I wanted you to like me," she said in a subdued voice. "I thought if you saw that I was angry inside, you might be shocked, or frightened of me, or—I don't know." She shrugged. "You know how it is in my home. Tiear's a strict man, and my mother runs around doing whatever he says, and Arin and I are supposed to just ... do whatever we're told."

"I know." Mara hugged her and stroked her hair. It hadn't grown back to its full length yet, but already it was thick again, the way it had been before. "I wasn't being critical, Lomel." Even now she was a child in some ways, looking up to Mara, wanting approval.

Lomel gave her a shy smile. "Tell me how much I please you. More than Kormor?"

Mara laughed loudly. "Kormor never pleased me. Not really."

"Then what about other men? Do you still think of them?" She eyed Mara doubtfully. "I've seen some of them looking at you, now that it's springtime. Have you noticed?"

Mara looked into Lomel's eyes. She was deeply happy with her; yet she still remembered, vividly, her courtship with Kormor, and the feelings she had known then. In truth, Lomel didn't rouse that kind of wild, unreasoning desire. But maybe that was for the best. Mara feared that if she ever felt like that again, she would lose all her ability to think clearly. Certainly that was what had happened the first time.

"There's no man that interests me," Mara said. And that much was true—for now, at least. She kissed Lomel on the forehead.

There was a sudden, faint rustling sound.

Lomel squirmed in Mara's arms. In an instant she was on all fours, crouching like a cat, looking quickly around.

Mara's skin prickled. "What is it?" she whispered.

Lomel fumbled in the grass, grabbed a fist-sized stone, then jumped up and hurled it.

Mara saw Lomel's arm curve around, saw the stone fly across the pale sky—and saw it tumble down into the grass just behind the bushy tail of a squirrel. The squirrel bounded away and leaped up into the nearest tree.

"A squirrel," Mara said, with a rueful laugh. She stood up and brushed dried ends of grass off her deerskin robe.

"I almost hit him." Lomel flexed the fingers of her hand.

"You see, it's true, you need a longer arm," Mara said.

Lomel turned to make a response—then shrugged. "Well, maybe you're right."

Mara scrambled up out of the grass. She was getting restless, as she always did if she stayed in one place too long. It wasn't in her nature to lie patiently, waiting to pounce. In any case, she didn't believe there'd be any more game by the stream. The sun was high now, and most animals would have retreated into the shade of the forest.

She stooped and picked up her spear. She felt the weight of it, and she imagined herself casting it. Then she remembered, in her imagination, how Lomel's arm had looked as it cast the stone. Mara made a throwing motion, first with just her forearm, then with the whole length of her arm.

Lomel looked up at her. "What are you doing?"

"I have an idea." She walked across the grassland to the bones of the bison. She bent down among them, rummaged around, and picked one out that had been part of a foreleg. The joint at the end of the bone had a hollow socket in it, just the way she'd imagined it. She carefully matched it to the end of her spear shaft. It was a good fit.

"Mara?" Lomel was walking over to her. "What are you *doing*?"

Mara took hold of the small end of the bone and lined it up so that it lay alongside the spear shaft, still with the end of the spear fitted into the joint. Now that she was holding the ungainly combination, it seemed foolish to think that it would really do her any good. Lomel was going to laugh at her, and she would have to admit that the whole idea had been ridiculous. But ... she had to be sure.

She gripped the bone so that it extended out from her hand, in line with her arm. She stretched her arm back as she normally would before casting her spear. Then she swung her arm around, using the length of the bone to add force to the spear.

The shaft flew away—not cleanly, as it normally did, but wobbling as it flew. Lomel did laugh—but Mara wasn't paying attention. She was watching the spear, seeing how far it went. When it finally hit the ground, it was farther away than any spear she had ever thrown before.

Lomel's laughter died as she, too, realized the power that Mara had just won for herself. "Hey," said Lomel. "Hey, you were serious!" She stared at the bone that Mara was still holding in her hand. "Let me try that."

Chapter 32

They spent the rest of that afternoon practicing with their spears. When the sun finally crept down toward the peaks of the western mountains, both women had mastered the use of the bison bones to multiply their throwing power, and Mara was almost as accurate as she had been using her hand.

Together, the two of them walked down from the hills into the wide, shallow valley. Mara always felt a little sad when one of her stolen days with Lomel was over and they had to rejoin the tribe. But then, in the distance, she saw a scattering of figures, and felt better as she realized that they were her own people—the guardians of the tribe.

Lomel shouted out to them, and they turned and waved, waiting for the women to catch up.

Privately, Mara wished they wouldn't call themselves guardians. It reminded her too much of Graum's "Honor Guard." Yet, they had chosen the name for themselves, and it had stuck.

"I hope they killed more game than we did," said Lomel. "Look, that's Arin. He's carrying something." She sounded mildly annoyed.

Arin was standing with a half dozen rabbits dangling from thongs tied across his shoulders. He grinned as the women approached.

"He's getting to be a fine hunter," Mara said quietly.

Lomel grunted. "Rabbits! He must have spent the whole day waiting by a burrow."

"Well, that takes its own kind of skill. And I'm sure you remember, two days ago, he came back with that young wolf he'd killed."

"He does quite well," Lomel said grudgingly, "but I don't think he has a true hunter's spirit. His experience with Graum—it crushed the fierceness in him somehow."

That wasn't such a bad thing, Mara thought to herself. It certainly made her trust Arin more than other men. He never felt a need to prove himself now. He was subdued and diffident, and always cautious. Strange that he had turned out that way, while Lomel, who had seemed so shy, was now so fierce.

"Empty-handed?" Arin called out as they reached him.

"Not quite," said Lomel. She showed him her bison bone.

He peered at it in puzzlement. "A *bone*?"

"In our hands, it's much more than that," said Lomel. "It makes a spear fly farther than it's ever flown before."

Arin took the bone and turned it over. Then he looked blankly from one of them to the other.

"Maybe we'll show you later," said Lomel, taking the bone back. "If you're worthy."

"Worthy?" He laughed. "I'm the one who came back with six rabbits."

Lomel peered at them, then wrinkled her nose. "I hate the taste of rabbit," she said.

Mara remembered the rabbit that Lomel had snared in the woods on the other side of the lake, and she remembered sharing it with Lomel, who had eaten it with relish. Still, she wasn't going to interfere between brother and sister. She turned away and greeted the rest of the guardians.

There were a score of them altogether. Ewna was among them—a far better hunter than Mara had ever thought she could be. And there was Weena, who had been Bumar's mate and still bore the scars that he had cut on her face in the Meeting Place. She, too, was strong and fierce, now.

Mara looked at the others. Was it her imagination, or did they seem more subdued than usual this afternoon? Perhaps they, like her, were worried about the lack of game.

She saw Maer, the tall, gangling man who was a better

storyteller than he was a hunter, but was valuable to her because his good humor helped to keep everyone happy. There were more young women, but very few men, because Graum had taken most of the young ones with him. The only other male guardian was Lumo, the young wanderer who had called everyone out to the herd of mastodon. Lumo was shy, and he didn't like to fight. But he had spent so much time wandering, he knew the land better than anyone.

Mara turned back to Arin. She thought that it was too bad his friendly, open face was still disfigured by the bear-head tattoo on his forehead. He had tried to get rid of it in every way he could, even scraping away the skin with the side of a flint ax. But that had merely added scars, and the design still showed through. He, too, seemed subdued this afternoon, and she wondered what was troubling him. She patted the sleek fur of the rabbits. "You did well," she said.

He frowned. "Mara, there's something important that I have to tell you."

So it had not been her imagination. There really was something on his mind.

"We met a traveler today," he went on. "While we were in the foothills. He was a strange man—thin and ragged and sore, with all his possessions in a bag on his shoulder. He told us that he'd come from the far south, and he'd passed by the Silver River People on his way. I questioned him, and I couldn't find any fault in his story. He was a wanderer, there's no doubt of that."

"Where is he now?"

Arin gestured toward the village. "We sent him to see Shani." He gave her a long, brooding look. "Mara, this wanderer brought us bad news. He says there is a new Chieftain in the Silver River People. A large man, with gaps in his teeth. He has a scrawny son named Joh, and he calls himself Graum."

When Mara walked into her old Clan House, she found it filled with people. For a moment she remembered that amazing meeting in which Lomel and Arin had stood up and spoken for her, changing everything.

It had been easier for her since then. Even Shani was easier to deal with, for she saw now there was no denying the influence and the following that Mara had, and it made her more cautious about speaking out against her sister.

The Clan House wasn't crammed full, this time, as it had been then. But still, there was barely room for people to sit. Mara picked her way through the crowd, looking over their heads at the hunched, skinny figure sitting beside the fire pit with Shani and the elders ranged around him. He was wearing a ragged old elk skin, and his feet were bare. His face was deep brown, weathered by the seasons. But the strangest thing was on his head: a leather hat holding dozens of eagle feathers. Mara had never even heard of such a thing, and she couldn't imagine the skill that must have been needed to spear the great birds and steal their tails.

As Mara walked forward, talk in the Clan House ceased. The stranger turned and looked at her. Slowly, then, he got to his feet. He grinned, showing toothless gums, and he bowed. "Greetings," he said. His accent was strange, reminding her of the way the Silver River People spoke.

"This is Ulfor, a wanderer," Shani said. "He has been telling us many stories. Ulfor, this is my sister Mara, who leads the volunteers who keep our village safe."

Mara nodded to Ulfor, and he sat down. She squatted opposite him. There was a hush, now, in the Clan House. Mara felt very conscious of the people all gathered around, watching and waiting. Once again, she realized, her perceptions of Graum had been proven right, and people must be aware of that. They would be waiting, now, for her to voice some judgment. She felt concerned about that, but more, she felt sad to think that it would be a long time before she felt safe, again, to stray from the village with Lomel and lie out in the grassland with her eyes closed, enjoying the peace of a springtime day.

"Tell me," she said to Ulfor, "how it is among the Silver River People."

"They're in fear of this man," said Ulfor. "He forced himself on them, and now he rules them. Some of them hate him, though they don't dare to say so." He drew a wheezing breath, then coughed, hugging his arms across his sunken chest. "Excuse me," he said. "It's the cold and the damp. I've been sleeping out, these past weeks."

"If the River People are so unhappy, they could leave their tribe," Shani said.

"No, no." Ulfor shook his head. Wisps of white hair protruded from under the rim of his hat, and they gleamed in the firelight. "Most people are scared to leave, because they fear he'd send out his men and hunt them down. It's only old people like me who are allowed to go. Graum had me cast out as soon as the snow began to melt. He could see I was in weak health." He wheezed and coughed again.

"How long did you live with the Silver River People?" Mara asked him.

"A year, just about. Before that I was with the Brown Grass Tribe. That's where I learned the custom of this hat. All the hunters wear it there. And before that—"

Mara held up her hand. She knew, from talking to other wanderers, it could be difficult to interrupt their tales. "All I want to know," she said, "is what you think Graum intends to do. Did he talk about our tribe, the Lake People? Did you hear anyone speak of traveling here?"

Ulfor rubbed a bony hand across his forehead. "Well, no, I don't think so. But then, he didn't talk much to anybody, except his own men. He turned up with two score of them, you know, in that snowstorm—"

"Thirty," said Mara. "They were from our village. Didn't he mention that?"

Ulfor looked at her in surprise. "No, never said." He coughed again and took a piece of meat from the square of birch bark that had been laid out beside him. He ate it as well as he could with his toothless gums. Then he spread his hands. "I'm sorry. I don't know that there's much more I can tell you."

Mara turned to Shani and looked at her across the fire pit. Her husband, Ipaw, was sitting to one side and behind her, saying nothing. He seemed just as devoted to Shani now as he had been during their courtship, and she seemed to accept it as her natural right. Evidently they were happy together.

"What do you think?" Mara asked Shani. She had learned to be diplomatic and ask Shani's opinion before expressing her own. And now that Mara had some authority, she actually found it easier to be conciliatory.

"Maybe he'll be content with the new village that he's taken," said Shani. "After all, when he was here, he never talked about attacking other tribes. He only seemed concerned with defending himself from outsiders."

Mara nodded to show that she took her sister's opinion seriously. "Remember, though, he was humiliated here. His wife was killed."

Shani paused, hesitating to contradict Mara. "Our village is well defended," she said. "You've seen to that, sister, haven't you?"

Mara glanced at the crowd of villagers. She noticed her guardians standing at the back, with their arms folded around their spears. "I'm proud of the people who protect us," she said. "But what if Graum has more men than before?" She turned to Ulfor. "Has he recruited young men among the Silver River People?"

Ulfor nodded. "Oh, yes, there's more all the time, with the tattoos on 'em. Can't say exactly how many, but there's more, I know that."

"So what do you suggest we do?" Shani said, looking at Mara. The implication was clear: It was Mara's responsibility to suggest a plan, and Shani's right to accept or reject it.

"It's possible that Graum will leave us alone," said Mara. "But we certainly can't be sure of that. Personally, I believe he'll come here. That's why he's gathered more hunters around him." She paused, making sure everyone understood the implications. "Unfortunately," she went on, "we don't know exactly how many men Graum has serving him, now. So I think I should take my ... guardians ... down the Silver River and hide ourselves, and watch their comings and goings to see what we can learn. If we can find someone from the tribe and question him, so much the better."

Shani pondered for a moment. "All right. A dozen of your people should be enough."

"A dozen?" Mara frowned. "But we have more than thirty now."

"Of course, I'm aware of that." Shani paused, taking her time. "This is a dangerous journey, sister. We should risk as few of you as we can. Also"—she smiled faintly— "if you go there with all your hunters, I think you might be tempted to do something rash. You might even try to go into the village and kill Graum. And you might succeed—or you might not. Even though you and I have had our differences in the past, I would hate to see you lose your life." She turned to the people all around. "So that is my decision. Does anyone here disagree?" She waited just one beat, then nodded decisively. "Very well. You shall take a dozen people down the Silver River to see for yourselves what's happening. I have spoken, and it shall be so."

Most of the villagers had left the Clan House. Shani was sitting close by the fire with Mara, Lomel, and Arin, while old Ulfor lay slumped forward, snoring, his head cushioned on his arms. In the shadows, Ipaw had retreated to his sleeping nook and was carving a design onto a piece of birch bark. Probably, Mara thought, it would be a gift for his wife.

"There's another reason why I want only twelve of you to go down the Silver River," Shani said, speaking softly, looking at each person in turn. "It seems to me there's a danger that in defending us from Graum, you are liable to end up imitating him. Already I see the first signs."

"I served Graum," Arin said, sounding annoyed. "I can tell you, this is completely different."

Shani regarded him placidly. "Perhaps so. But already, in a way, you've become a clan of your own. You're loyal to Mara, and some people in the village may fear your fierceness just a little bit." She narrowed her eyes. "Is it true you even have initiation ceremonies now?"

"We test a person's hunting skills, that's all," said

Mara. "There's no point in having people who can't use a spear properly."

"And their courage?" Shani asked. "Do you test that, too? And what about their strength?" She paused. "Hunting skill, courage, and strength—those were the tests that Graum used, out in Grassy Hollow, to choose a new Chieftain for our tribe."

"Clearly, this is different," Arin said again, with an expression of wounded pride. "Graum ruled us, and hurt us. We're serving our people."

Shani smiled condescendingly. "Of course, Arin. That's how it is now. But how will it be in the future? When one person threatens another, and the other makes himself strong enough to fight back . . . who can be sure of the difference between them? Power can work both ways: for good or for evil. As our Chieftain, it's my task to see that warlike power must always be kept closely controlled." She calmly folded her hands in her lap.

"Well, I see things differently," said Lomel. She looked at Shani defiantly, with little respect. Ever since she had confronted Shani on the day Graum and his people escaped from the house, there had been a coldness between the two of them. "I don't see why you have any more right to control this power of ours than we have ourselves."

"Because I am your Chieftain," Shani said simply.

Mara sensed Lomel getting ready to phrase an angry response. She put her hand on Lomel's arm. "There's something you should all know," Mara said, "which I have never mentioned before—only to Lizel, before she left the tribe." She turned to Shani. "Sister, you were at my Ceremony of First Blood. You were already a woman, then. Perhaps you remember my life vision."

Shani looked at her carefully. The change of subject had made her cautious. "You saw a bear, I recall."

Mara nodded. "Yes. A bear. But there was more. I saw the bear drenched in blood, and our village in flames." She paused, looking from one face to the next, trying to convey to them the seriousness that she felt. "The very next day, there was a bear in our Meeting

Place, brought there by Graum, drenched in blood, just as I had foreseen it. I've lived in fear, since then, that the second part of my vision might come true."

There was a long silence. The fire hissed; old Ulfor snored quietly. Shani's face seemed frozen. Her eyes regarded Mara steadily. And then, suddenly, she laughed. It was a brittle sound. There was no humor in it, and there was no joy in her eyes. "What do you want—that I should decide the fate of our people based on a dream that you had a year ago?"

"When Laena, the mother of us all, came across the mountains from the north, she was guided by a vision," Mara said quietly. "Perhaps I should take more of our people down the Silver River. Not only my guardians, but the elder hunters, and anyone else who can throw a spear. Perhaps a hundred souls, all told. We'd have the advantage of surprise. We might overrun Graum and destroy him. Then, I think, our village would be truly safe."

Shani quickly shook her head. For a moment Mara's words seemed to have touched her, but now she was herself again, calm and dismissive. "Your name is not Laena," she said. "And I doubt that it's your destiny to guide us—to a new land, or to a battle." She stood up. "It's getting late." She gestured to the old man snoring close by. "Perhaps you can find somewhere for Ulfor, here, to stay."

Once again, Mara sensed that Lomel wanted to speak out, and she saw anger, too, in Arin's face. Mara glanced at them, telling them with her eyes that this was not the time to argue. She had more influence over the Lake People than she used to, but without Shani's support, there would be no chance of convincing the tribe to do what she thought should be done. When she and her scouting party came back from the Silver River and told everyone exactly how powerful Graum had become—then, perhaps, Shani would be more willing to accept her advice.

Chapter 33

The house was square, built from pine logs caulked with mud, with a low, sloping roof of reeds and willow branches. A fire burned in one corner. The rabbits that Arin had hunted were roasting over the flames on spits of hardwood.

Six people made themselves comfortable on elk hides that had been spread across the dirt floor. Lomel and Arin sat together near one wall. Their mother, Rika, squatted by the fire, turning the spits. Mara sat cross-legged, sipping from a leather cup of bear-root tea that had been dipped from a bigger bowl sitting out on hot stones beside the fire. Tiear, Rika's husband, sat close by, idly reflaking a spear head, while old Ulfor warmed his bony hands at the flames.

Mara had spent many evenings like this with Lomel, Arin, and their parents during the past few months. She had found a sense of peace here which she had never known in her own House. Tiear was a grim-faced man who seldom spoke, but Rika was a kind woman, always offering food and finding a place for Mara to sit. Mara felt accepted here. No one eyed her suspiciously, or spoke against her.

Rika was chatting to their new visitor, doing whatever she could to make him feel at ease. "Tell us," she said, "the story of your hat. You must have speared half a dozen eagles to gather so many fine feathers."

Ulfor chuckled. "No," he said, "that's not how it's done." He glanced around at the faces lit by the flames. "But I'll share the secret if you want. Seeing you're kind enough to take me in and give me food."

Rika saw him staring at the rabbits, and she took the

hint, pulling one of them off the fire and sliding it from its spit onto a hot, flat stone. She used a flint knife to divide the sizzling meat, and she placed the first portion on a piece of bark in front of Ulfor. "So, tell us," she said.

"Ah, thank you, yes." He plucked at the meat with his gnarled fingers and grunted with appreciation. "Well, it's like this. You take a wolf skin, and you stuff it with grasses and stitch it up so it looks like the animal itself, lying on its side. You peg it to the ground out near the foothills, where the eagles soar." He gummed some meat from a bone, then set the bone aside, smacking his lips. "You tie some raw meat to the back of the wolf skin. Raw liver, maybe. And you make a shelter close by, to hide in. Rocks piled up, or a skin on poles covered with grasses. And then you wait."

"But you don't know that an eagle will be the one to take your bait," said Arin.

"Well, of course you don't." Ulfor grinned. "There's little birds come pecking, and ravens especially, they're persistent. You have to keep a long stick and poke them away. But sooner or later, an eagle will come down. He'll stand there, turning his head one way, then the other." Ulfor made birdlike movements with his own head, and he held up his hands like claws.

Mara found herself smiling. The old man was a good storyteller, and storytelling was an art that the Lake People always valued highly.

"Bit by bit, the big fellow comes over to the bait," Ulfor went on. "He has to climb up there on the wolf skin to get at the raw meat. And then ..." he paused, with his eyes gleaming, "then ... you grab him!" He lunged forward and seized Arin's ankle with his clawhands. "You jump out of your hiding place and grab him by the legs!"

Arin smiled uneasily.

"And how do you kill it?" Lomel asked. She was leaning forward intently.

Ulfor let go of Arin. He swung his arms around. "You throw him down, and you keep hold of his legs in your hands, and you crush him. Push your knee straight down on his chest. Quickly, before he has a chance to peck your face!" Ulfor chuckled and shook his head.

"That sounds dangerous," said Arin.

"Well, I didn't say it was easy. It's been many years, I tell you, since I did it myself."

"This is truly how it's done?" It was Tiear speaking, from the shadows. His voice was slow and deep, and it was edged with doubt.

"That's how I learned it," said Ulfor. "And that's the way I did it." He accepted another portion of rabbit meat and started into it eagerly. "You know, it's the same with people. I've never been a fighter myself. Makes no sense. But if a man insists on it—well, then, I'll find something he wants, and I'll lure him out, so I can pounce!" He chuckled.

"Perhaps we could learn from you," Mara said, "now that we have our own enemies."

"Perhaps so. You're thinking of that man Graum, eh? Maybe you can tempt him out of his village." He licked his fingers. "But first you need to learn the lay of the land. And that's what you're setting out to do, isn't it?"

Mara nodded slowly. There was so much that she didn't know—so much that none of them knew. She had grown up among people who had always been at peace. Even the elder men of the tribe, who were proud hunters, were not necessarily as fierce and brave as they liked to seem. After all, many had been driven out of their homes in the North Lands by more warlike tribes.

Mara turned to Tiear. "Do you have advice for us?" she asked him.

Tiear set his spear aside, laying it against the wall with careful precision. "I've seen more fighting than I ever wanted to see," he said. "The way I look at it, I'd rather see us defend ourselves than go out and attack Graum. We should fortify the village and have more guardians here, protecting us."

"I've done my best—" Mara began.

"You've done well. And I've done my part, helping out in your night vigils. But I'd like to see every able-bodied man helping out."

"And every able-bodied woman, too?" It was Lomel speaking out.

Tiear ignored her. He said nothing more.

There was an uneasy silence. "Well, that's all easy to say," said Ulfor. "But you still need to know who you're up against. And I still say I'd rather trap a man than pick a fight with him."

"I agree with you," said Arin. He glanced cautiously at his father. He never liked to disagree openly with Tiear.

"Well," said Rika, taking another rabbit off its spit, "I'll say this for Shani. She has people smiling and working together now. The men are hunting beside the women, and everyone's friendly again." She looked at her husband. "Almost everyone," she said, with a cheerful laugh. "Here, eat now. Me, I'm just as happy we're not going out and starting a war. You two"—she eyed Lomel and Arin—"you'll keep well clear of that Silver River village, and you won't do anything foolish."

"Don't worry, Mother," said Lomel, while Arin ignored her.

"Tiear," said Mara, "would you come with us on our expedition? Most of the elder hunters are loyal to the old, peaceful ways, and they're too proud to listen to young people."

He shook his head. "Like I say, I'd rather stay here and build a strong defense. Anyway, I'm not as fast as I was. You'd be best on your own, I think."

Mara wondered about that. Why did Tiear really not want to get involved? Wasn't it really that he was comfortable here, with a fire to sit beside and his wife cooking for him? It seemed a lot of the men in the tribe were like Tiear, hoping that someone else would deal with any trouble, so they could lead their lives in peace. True, Tiear had done his part on the night vigils, but it had only been a few times, and he hadn't done it willingly.

Mara turned to Ulfor. "I've traveled to the Silver River People myself, three times, with my mother and my sister in years gone by. But even so, I'm not certain that I'll recognize the terrain. Perhaps you could guide us—"

He raised both hands and shook his head, chuckling. "No, girl. I'm a loner, always have been. I make sure not to get mixed up in other people's problems."

Well, Mara thought, at least he was honest about it.

"Perhaps you'll stay with our tribe?" Rika asked him. "You can lodge with us for a few days, till you get settled into a place of your own."

Ulfor chuckled again. "No, no. Summer's almost here, and I feel the old wanderlust. At dawn tomorrow, I'll say good-bye to you all. Only time I stay with tribes is in the winter." He turned to Mara. "But I wish you well, young woman." He plucked one of the eagle feathers from his hat, and he handed it to her. "Take this, for good luck. And you know, if I were you, I'd add a few people to the dozen your sister allowed you. Take your best fighters, just in case. How's she going to stop you, eh, if you leave before first light?"

She nodded slowly. "Maybe I'll do that."

Rika urged Mara to stay in their home, as she always did. She fussed over Mara and wrapped some food for her, and she told her that she shouldn't be living alone in the tent by the lake. She told Mara not to think so much about fighting all the time, and find herself a new mate. This thing about Graum would probably not come to anything. Men were all talk, most of the time. Look at her husband, sitting there talking about defending the tribe. When their own people had been attacked, up in the North Lands, Tiear hadn't had the stomach for warring. He'd taken his family and fled. And that's why they were alive today. They'd had the sense to run for their lives.

Mara had heard this little speech from Rika a dozen times. And really, it was hard to know what to think. Everyone had advice, and there was always something in the advice that sounded reasonable. But how could she decide which to follow?

Mara called good night to Lomel and Arin. She hugged Rika, and then she walked out into the darkness.

It was late, but she still felt restless, and her little home didn't seem inviting. She'd promised herself, during the

winter, that when the warmer weather came, she'd build
herself a new place to live—somewhere farther away
from her neighbors, so that Lomel could stay with her
safely sometimes. But there were always other things to
do, and Lomel still hadn't even planned what her new
home should look like, or how big it should be.

She hefted her spear in her hand and stared up at the
sky, looking at the rich tapestry of stars and smelling the
sweet tang of wood smoke drifting from the tribe's fires.
She needed help, but she didn't know where to find it.
Lizel would have been the one to turn to, but Lizel had
never returned.

Mara started out of the village, walking alone across
the grassland. Once again, she stared up at the sky; but
on this night, Mother Moon wasn't there to help her.

Eventually, she came to the Rock that Moves. She
climbed onto it and lay there, staring up at the blackness,
remembering when she had been here a year ago. She
had found her spirit creature, and ultimately it had given
her strength. Its kitten-child had even saved her from
Kormor, when all else had failed.

But now the questions in her life seemed to loom far
larger. Should she try to do more than just observe the
Silver River People? Should she even think of trying to
lure and trap and kill Graum, as old Ulfor suggested?
Or should she try to rouse her people enough so that she
could lead a war party, as she really wanted? It seemed
impossible, yet it had seemed impossible the first time
she had led people against Graum, and she had won.
Was it right even to consider such a thing? There would
be so much bloodshed, so much suffering. Surely there
had to be a better way.

She remembered what Shani had said months ago: that
Mara wanted power and had tried to find it through
Kormor. Those words had haunted Mara many times
since then, because there was truth in them, even though
she hated to admit it. It was Kormor's power that had
fascinated her at the start, no doubt about that. And yes,
she had found a delicious thrill in holding herself out of
reach during their courtship. And then she had found it

intolerable when he had seized control of her after they were paired.

So—did that mean she was no better than Graum, wanting to rule other people? She couldn't accept that. She thought she was a good person. Injustice was intolerable to her, and she always wanted to do what was right. Yet still she wanted other people to agree with her and believe in her vision. She had to admit, it pleased her when her guardians respected her courage and her judgment.

There were too many questions, and no clear answers. Mara lay staring into the void, listening to the tiny sounds of the night—the rustling of small creatures, the whisper of the wind. She felt weariness claiming her, and she slipped into sleep.

Before her, she saw something strange. It was a place where the land was red instead of green; where the soil was sandy and there were no trees. A hot, barren place. And directly in front of her was the strangest sight of all: a fat pillar of rock whose sides were banded with red and brown. "There is a sanctuary here," a voice told her—and with a shock, Mara realized that it sounded like her mother. Many times she had dreamed of Ternees, but always her mother had been far away, and she had never spoken. Now it sounded as if her lips were beside Mara's ear.

Mara turned and looked—and found an eagle standing on a dry, dead tree branch beside her. The eagle preened itself, and a feather fluttered down. It launched itself into the air then and flew away toward the pillar of rock. It settled up on the pillar. And then the scene darkened, as if storm clouds were covering the sun.

Mara woke with a start. She gave a little cry.

There was a flurry of wings beside her. She flinched and brought up her arms. But it was not an eagle that had been sitting beside her on the rock; it was an owl. The owl screeched and flew up and away—and it turned toward the south.

Mara felt her pulse racing. "Mother?" she called, tentatively. But her voice sounded foolish in the reality of the cool, dark night.

She took the eagle feather that old Ulfor had given

her, and she placed it on the rock as a small sacrifice, a token of thanks for the vision that she had been given. Then she climbed down from the rock, and she started back toward the village.

Even now she could still see the red landscape inside her mind. But where could such a thing exist? Even wanderers like Ulfor had never spoken of such a thing.

The owl had flown south. And when she remembered her dream of the pillar of rock, the sun had been in front of her, high in the sky. That, too, was where the eagle had flown: to the south.

Chapter 34

She did as Ulfor had suggested: She took more than the dozen guardians that Shani had permitted. There were a score of them, all told, slipping out of the village when the air was still cold and the only light came from a murky band of gray outlining the mountains to the east.

Most of the people in her party were women. Most of them were young, and all of them felt a mixture of anticipation and fear. None of them had ever set out on such a journey, into the territory of a man who probably wished them dead.

There were no elders among them. A few had volunteered to come along, but Mara had put them off with various embarrassed excuses. She sensed they weren't truly interested in helping her; they wanted to watch over her, and if necessary, they were ready to restrain her. She saw the doubt in their eyes when she told them that this journey might be the first step toward fighting Graum and killing him. It was already difficult for her, sometimes, having some guardians in her group who were a few years older than she was. There was no point in making things impossible by bringing elders who were twice her age and liable to contradict her judgment.

They walked in single file along the shore of the lake, watching the day grow gradually brighter. Flocks of waterfowl had flown in from the south, and the lake was busy with ducks and wild swans.

Each person carried a couple of flint knives and a spear, with several extra spears tied to their packs. They also carried bison bones, for Mara had shared her secret the previous day, and there had been some time spent practicing out in the valley. Only a few of her guardians had really mastered the technique of using a bone to add extra force behind the spear shaft, and no one really felt comfortable with it yet. But everyone could see how much farther the spears flew, and Mara imagined that if she was unlucky enough to encounter her enemies in the open country that lay to the south, she might be able to scare them off by displaying her newfound power, even though the spears couldn't be cast accurately.

The weather was clear, and the going was easy. By noon they reached the southern tip of the lake, and they stopped briefly to eat some of their provisions. Mara sat with Lomel, wishing she could touch her to express some affection, as she did when they were alone. They exchanged a few secret smiles and glances, but most of the time they simply watched everyone else. There was a lot of joke-telling and laughter, but Mara sensed something behind the good spirits—anxiety that no one really wanted to admit.

"Should I talk to them?" she murmured to Lomel. "Should I address their fears and try to reassure them?"

"You can't," Lomel said. "You have no idea what the risks are. And they know that."

Arin came over to them. "I have a question," he said to Mara. "The Silver River flows from the end of the lake down into Snake Valley. We follow that valley all the way to the Silver River People. Isn't that so?"

"Yes," said Mara.

Arin brooded for a moment, looking unhappy. "That valley is very narrow. The sides are steep, and thick with trees. There could be people hiding in the trees. If we walk down beside the river, we'll be very easy to see."

"That's right, we'll be very vulnerable," said Mara.

He gave a curt nod.

"It would be better if we could follow a different path," Mara said. "But even Lumo doesn't know the country well enough here to be sure of finding that path. And the undergrowth in the forest is so dense, we'd soon be exhausted from the journey. It would take us more than a week, and we'd have to hunt and trap game to survive. Worst of all, we might find no water."

Arin shifted uneasily. "Then what should we do?"

"One of us will walk well ahead," Mara said. "She'll look for any sign of danger."

Arin grunted. "You?"

Mara nodded. "It will be me."

"No." Lomel said it flatly and firmly. "You can't take that risk. Without you, Mara, this expedition will fail. The people need you to lead them. I'll be the one who walks ahead."

Mara looked at Lomel. Her mouth was set, and there was a determined look in her eyes.

Mara didn't know what to say. She hated the thought of Lomel endangering herself. But she was reluctant to sound too protective, for fear of betraying her true feelings in front of Arin.

"Lomel's right," Arin was saying. "But I should share the risk and take her place on the second day of our journey."

"We could ask one of the other people—" Mara began.

"Arin and I are second only to you," said Lomel. "We should set an example, not ask others to sacrifice themselves for us."

Mara shrugged. "If you insist." She looked from Lomel to Arin, and saw both of them wearing the same uncompromising expression. They had inherited their stubbornness from Tiear, she realized.

"All right," she agreed, "Lomel will walk ahead. The rest of us will split into two groups, with a gap between us. That way, if our enemies lie in wait, it will be harder for them to attack us all."

"But there's no reason," Arin said, "why they should be lying in wait."

"No reason at all," Mara agreed. "But we'd be foolish ever to underestimate Graum."

So they moved on into the narrow part of the valley where the hillsides loomed closer and the river became a swift torrent. There were no more grasslands here. The only clear path lay beside the rushing water, where the ground was too rocky for trees to grow.

While Lomel walked ahead, Mara led the first group of her people, moving cautiously now and constantly scanning the forested walls of the valley. The rushing of the river made it impossible to hear any faint sounds that a person might make in the undergrowth, and Mara found herself squinting in the glare reflected by the water. There was no more talking and joking in her followers. Everyone was grimly watchful.

Still, the day passed peacefully. The only incident occurred when a young woman named Iora slipped on a wet rock and fell into the stream. Even then, there was no laughter. People were cautious, watching the forest for the slightest sign of life, while they pulled her out and helped her to dry herself.

At dusk, Mara chose a campsite in deep underbrush amid the trees. They were well hidden here, huddled together among bushes and brambles while they ate their rations of pemmican and dried berries. Everyone was weary from the whole day's trek, because the rocks beside the stream were uneven, constantly liable to shift underfoot.

It would have been nice to light a fire, but that was a risk that no one wanted to take. As darkness closed in, the people lay together, nestling close to share their warmth. Weena volunteered to stay awake for the first part of the night, watching for danger, and Arin joined her. They sat back to back, one of them looking up the valley, the other looking the way they'd come. But it was another moonless night, and the valley was almost completely shrouded in darkness.

Mara found herself lying close to Lomel. She could barely see her face in the starlight that filtered down through the trees, but she picked up Lomel's familiar smell, and she heard the rhythm of her breathing. Feeling a little scared by her own boldness, she reached up and followed the contours of Lomel's face with her fingertips. She kissed her fleetingly on the cheek. And then, amid the press of bodies, Mara slept.

This time, her sleep was dreamless. She did wake once in the night, though, when she thought she heard a branch snap. Suddenly she was sitting up with all her senses alert, straining her eyes in the darkness.

She saw two women sitting watch now—black silhouettes against the starlight. Judging from their posture, they, too, had heard something. But there was no further sounds—till an owl suddenly fluttered out of the trees close by and wheeled away with a screech that echoed between the walls of the valley. Mara tensed, wondering if it could possibly be the same bird that she had seen two nights ago. Was it guiding her southward?

Then a new, dark thought occurred to her. Perhaps Kormor had been right in his superstition. Perhaps his soul had been captured in the night creature, and now *he* was the one who was leading them south. Could he be taking revenge on her, leading them to disaster?

She told herself she was being foolish. She forced herself to lie down again beside Lomel, and her familiar warmth helped to calm Mara's nerves. It was wrong, Mara told herself, to be ruled by superstition. That was the error that Kormor had made, and in a way, it had led to his death.

The morning was gray, and the valley was filled with mist. Some of the people were complaining, rubbing their stiff backs and shoulders and hugging themselves as they stood and stamped their feet. It had been a cold, damp night for them, hiding in the brush.

Mara shared their feelings, but she forced herself up, and she forced herself to be cheerful. She went from one person to the next, thinking of something friendly to say to each. She made simple jokes, and she told them that next time, they'd build a raft and float downstream to the Silver River tribe. Either that or they'd bring mattresses stuffed with pine needles. No more cold nights. She'd prayed to the Moon—which had finally risen now and was a pale shape lurking low in the lightening sky—and the Moon Spirit had promised warmer weather.

No one laughed, but they smiled, and she could tell they appreciated her. More than that, they trusted her. They all remembered that she had defeated Graum once before, and as far as they were concerned, it gave her an air of infallibility. She was just a young woman, yet they believed, in a way, that she was much more.

Their faith made her uneasy, even though, at the same time, it was a fulfilment of her childhood fantasies. Hadn't she always dreamed of being queen of the water kingdom, with the fish serving her? She had much more than that, now.

Together they ate more of their unappetizing rations. Mara forced them to eat generously, knowing they would need the fuel to take them through the rest of their journey. Walking down the Silver River normally took three days, but she was determined that they would do it in two. The less time they took, the less time they'd be vulnerable out here in Snake Valley.

Gradually the sun burned the mist away. The day became bright, and the trek took on its own steady rhythm. Mara found her thoughts wandering, and she kept forcing her attention back to the present time. Each footstep had to be judged carefully on the slippery, sliding shale. People were stumbling more often, she realized, and growing careless. One of the men fell and narrowly missed hitting his head on a boulder.

When they stopped for lunch, she gave them a short, sharp lecture. If someone sprained an ankle here, it would put them in a terrible dilemma. They wouldn't want to abandon the person, but they wouldn't want to endanger themselves, either, bringing along someone who needed help. Everyone had a duty to be cautious. They were getting close now to the place where Graum had gone. This was a time to take more care, not less.

Her people listened. And as they walked on through the afternoon, there were no more little accidents.

Finally Mara recognized that they were close to the place where the Silver River tribe made their home. She ran ahead to Arin, who was still walking out in front, and she brought everyone together under the trees.

"Many of you have never been here before," she told them softly. "I myself have only made this journey three times, when my clan came to trade. The tribe lives on a piece of the hillside which is too steep and rocky for trees to grow. It sticks out over the river, so they can see in all directions, upstream and down."

She looked at each person, making sure they were paying close attention.

"We'll have to move up into the forest now," she said. "I believe I can find the way. On one of our visits here, we spent some days with the Silver River People hunting and trapping around here. If we follow the ridge,"—she gestured to the top of the steep eastern side of the valley—"it should lead us around above their camp. Then we can see if there's anything to be seen, and we can hide ourselves when dawn comes."

She paused, looking again at the faces around her—pale ovals in the gathering dusk. What else should she say? They seemed to be expecting something from her. Should she tell them to have confidence, because everything would work out right? No; her conscience wouldn't let her say such a thing. "You must have courage," she told them quietly. "We had courage in the winter, when we rose up against Graum. Our courage won us our victory then. If we'd had the courage to kill him at that time, we wouldn't need to be here now."

No one argued with that.

"Our courage may see us through again," she went on. "But be very cautious. Tread silently. Move slowly. Pause often. And if we find a stranger—silence him, but don't kill him. We'll learn nothing from a dead man."

She sensed their mood changing. They seemed to feel more sense of purpose now. Maybe they'd just needed to hear her sounding decisive.

"All right. Follow me." She started up the hillside, under the trees. The slope was very steep, and there was barely enough light to see by. They had to shift their spears off their backs, so as not to snag the overhanging branches. Mara found herself groping forward, probing with one of her spears, feeling her way across boulders, around thickets of brambles. By the time they finally reached the top of the slope, the last light had faded from the sky and the darkness was complete. Well, Mara thought, that could be an advantage as well as a disadvantage. With no Moon in the sky, the night would hide them more safely.

She led the way along a stony ridge, and with a great sense of relief, she recognized some of the landmarks. Still, the going was very slow and difficult. Bare rock showed through the thin soil, and there were only a few stunted, scrawny trees up here. In many places she and her people had to drop forward onto their hands and knees, feeling their way over the uneven terrain.

Finally she stopped. She waited till everyone had gathered around her, and she pointed into the forest, back toward the river. "Down there," she whispered.

She led them down the slope. She felt fearful, now, to be exposing herself like this to any enemy who might have posted lookouts far out into the woods. And yet there was no reason why Graum's men should be lying in wait. He had underestimated her before. He wouldn't expect her to come snooping on him.

With infinite care, she felt her way between the trees. The thought crossed her mind that people were not necessarily the only danger here, and big cats probably lived among these pines. Mountain lions and cougars would be roaming in the darkness. Still, with so many people in her party, just the smell of humanity should keep the predators away.

She gently pushed some ivy aside—and she saw a point of light.

She edged forward. The forest ended just ahead, and the village of the Silver River People lay in front of her, a hundred paces farther down the hillside, on its promontory overlooking the river. There was a cooking fire in their Meeting Place, glowing like a spark in the darkness.

Mara felt a strange kind of euphoria growing out of her anxiety. She remembered that that was the way it had been in the Meeting Place, just before her people rose up against Graum. She was beyond fear now.

The Silver People had long since felled most of the trees around their village. That was why the hillside was bare, with just a sprinkling of grass among the old tree stumps. Mara shifted back and hunkered down at the edge of the forest. She heard stealthy rustlings as her people gathered around her, and she sensed the warmth of their bodies.

"Look there." It was Arin's voice. Mara saw him stretching out his arm.

Near the outbuildings of the village, she saw a small silhouette against the point of firelight—a man standing and peering into the night.

"There were never guards here in the past," Mara said, half to herself.

"Graum probably scared the people about outsiders, just as he did our tribe," said Arin.

Mara sat in silence for a while, watching and waiting. The village was very quiet—almost unnaturally quiet. She watched the guard, and then, as if he was growing bored with his duty, he turned and started to move on around the village.

Quickly, almost without thinking, Mara seized a piece of deadwood. She held her hands high and snapped it.

The cracking sound was very loud in the stillness of the night. Mara saw the people near her looking at her in shock. Farther down the hillside, the guard stopped and turned.

Mara picked up a small rock. She took aim, then lobbed in halfway down the slope. It made a hollow thump as it hit the ground.

Now the guard started walking quickly out from the village, toward the sound that the rock had made. He came halfway to where Mara and her people were hidden. Then he stopped and glanced back as if wondering whether he should proceed any farther.

"We need him," Mara muttered.

"I'll do it." It was Lomel's voice, close by.

"But we must silence him instantly," Mara whispered. "He mustn't call for help."

"I'll do it," she said again, sounding confident—perhaps too confident.

Mara peered at her in the darkness. "Are you sure?"

"Yes."

Mara wondered if it was wise to trust her—but then it was too late to wonder, because Lomel bolted out from where she'd been hiding. She was a shadow-shape, moving fast, leaping headlong down the hillside. The guard turned toward her, instinctively bringing up his hands. But he had no time to defend himself. Lomel flung herself at him, butting him in the stomach. The two figures went flying, and there was a thump as they landed on the ground.

"Arin! Han! Opir! Mart!" Mara whispered the names urgently, picking the four strongest men. "Quickly, drag him back up here."

They ran down the hillside, hunching low, making no sound. Mara waited impatiently while they seized the guard by his arms and legs and brought him laboriously back up the slope.

"I told you," Lomel said, as they dumped the man in the tall grass at the edge of the forest. "I told you I'd do it."

"You did well," Mara said, grabbing her arm and squeezing it. She bent over the guard and heard him gasping for air. Mara's blow to his stomach had been so powerful, he was only just beginning to get his breath back.

Then Mara saw the man's face, and she froze. "Bumar," she whispered. Quickly she looked up at Weena and saw her leaning forward, glaring down at this man who had disfigured her.

If Bumar was surprised to see her, he didn't show it. He grunted and tried to sit up.

Mara drew her knife and pressed it to the side of his throat—and that was a wild, heady feeling, having this enemy lying here under her and knowing it was in her power, now, to decide whether he should live. "We want to talk to you, Bumar," she hissed at him. "But if you shout, you'll die."

She saw him peering at her in the starlight, and she sensed his hulking, lowering hostility. Still, he said nothing.

"I didn't realize it was him at first," Lomel whispered.

"I did," Weena said. "I knew right away." There was an awful coldness in her voice.

"Bastard," Lomel said. Without warning, she suddenly kicked him in the side as hard as she could.

"Stop that!" Mara hissed at her.

Lomel was breathing heavily. "He deserves it," she said. "He deserves more."

"I said stop!"

Lomel turned her face toward Mara. There was a long, uncertain pause. "I say we should do to him what he did to Weena," Lomel said, pulling out her knife.

"That won't help me now," Weena said. "All that matters to me is that he shouldn't hurt any more people in our tribe."

"Listen to what she says," Mara hissed at Lomel. She stared steadily at her till finally Lomel shrugged and put her knife away.

Mara turned back to Bumar and rested her weight on his chest, still keeping her own knife against his throat. In truth, she wasn't sure she would be cold-blooded enough to kill him if he defied her. But she felt the sudden certainty that if she gave the command to Lomel, this man would be dead within moments. And that was a dark, frightening idea.

"All right," said Mara. "Tell us, Bumar. Where's Graum?"

He took a long time to answer. His mind had never been sharp, and she sensed the thoughts running through it slowly, slowly. "He's down in the village there," he told her. "Asleep."

She felt a moment of elation—and then, just as quickly, deep caution. "It's early for him to sleep, isn't it?"

"Long hunt, last few days," Bumar whispered back. "Everyone went to sleep early."

Arin leaned forward. "Everyone except you, eh?"

Bumar shrugged. Mara saw his eyes move, looking up at the faces crowding around. "I'm on guard."

Mara eyed him skeptically. "Where's your spear?"

There was another long pause. "Dropped it back on the hillside," he muttered.

Mara turned to Lomel. "Was he carrying a spear?"

"No." Lomel's voice sounded sullen.

"You're sure?"

"Of course I'm sure. I saw right away that he had no spear. That's why I ran at him like that."

Mara felt under Bumar's robe, first on his left side, then his right. "And no knife," she said.

"Well, my job's just to sound the alarm," Bumar said.

"So why don't you?" Mara felt a sudden, intuitive certainty. She took the knife away from the man's neck. "Go on, shout for help." She watched him.

"Mara, what are you doing?" Arin sounded nervous.

"He's been lying to us." Mara put her knife away. "Graum would never put men out on guard duty without weapons. There's something wrong down there." She nodded toward the village.

"What do you mean?" he asked.

She gestured to Bumar. "Pick him up. Stand him on his feet."

Several people struggled with the man and did as Mara said.

She looked closely at Bumar's face. He was scared, she saw. There was no doubt about it. "You and I will walk down to the village now," she said to Bumar. "Just the two of us, with no weapons. What do you say to that?"

He flinched. "No," he muttered.

"Why not, Bumar?" She grabbed his arm and shook him.

"Because . . . you'll get killed," he said.

"Oh, you care so much for me, all of a sudden." Her mind was truly made up now. "Come on." She took his arm.

"Mara, no." It was Arin's voice again. "You said yourself you don't know what's happened down there."

She turned to him. "Don't worry." She glanced quickly at her people. "Wait here. You understand? Don't think of attacking the village. Wait here till I call for you."

Chapter 35

As she walked slowly down the hill, with Bumar stepping reluctantly beside her, she kept reminding herself that he had made it sound as if Graum was there for the taking. He'd wanted her to launch an attack, and he'd wanted the people in the village to be caught by surprise. That was why he hadn't shouted for help when he'd had the chance.

Even so, she felt a rising trepidation as the dark silhouettes of wooden huts loomed up ahead of her. The village looked strangely empty, and it was strangely silent. At least there should have been the sounds of people talking, or perhaps a child crying.

Bumar balked as they reached the first of the huts. He stood there, breathing heavily, reluctant to move any farther.

All right, Mara thought to herself, *maybe that is just as well.* "People of the Silver River," she shouted out. "I am Mara of the Lake People. I come peacefully. I mean no one any harm."

She waited—and she waited. Finally she heard some faint noises. Murmured words, then footsteps. A silhouette came into view atop one of the huts, peering over the roof. And then another. These men were holding spears.

Bumar muttered something. He sounded angry and disgusted.

"I bring this man alive and well, to show I mean no harm," Mara shouted out.

Now a figure appeared between the huts. "Mara," he called out. "Are you alone?"

The voice sounded familiar. She recognized it, she real-

ized, from when she had last been here. She felt a wave
of relief. The tension drained out of her so suddenly, her
knees literally felt weak. "Chieftain Fridor," she called
to him. "I'm alone down here. My people are up at the
forest. But we mean no harm. Not to you."

"Come forward, then," said the Chieftain.

"But where's the man we're looking for?" she called
to him, as she took a hesitant step forward. "Graum. Is
he no longer here?"

The chief grunted and waved his arm. "Graum has
gone."

One by one, the people emerged from the huts where
they had been hiding. They looked hungry and fearful.
They showed little interest in Bumar, barely acknowledging his existence. But they stared at Mara as if she were
an apparition. Even young children clung to their mothers and peered apprehensively at her.

And then, as the people gathered around her in their
Meeting Place, Mara saw something that she had never
expected to see. A young boy with a solemn face, saying
nothing, making his way toward her, pushing through the
crowd. "Trifen!" she cried. "Trifen, is it truly you?"

He smiled and nodded, and then he ran up to her, and
she hugged him impulsively, while all the Silver River
People stared in wonder.

"Then Lizel is here, too?" She looked eagerly at his
face. "Or . . . is she—"

He tugged at her robe and pointed to one of the huts.
Mara turned quickly to the Chieftain. "This woman—
Lizel—she was very important to me. Is she here?"

He nodded slowly. "Yes, Mara. It was she who told
us that you could be trusted. She's a wise woman. We
should both pay our respects to her."

The hut smelled eerily familiar, and Mara suddenly
realized why. The odor of herbs and scented wood smoke
was the same as she remembered from the Spirit House,
back in the days when Lizel had lived there, before
Graum had ever come to the tribe.

"Lizel," she cried, seeing an old, hunched figure reclining on a patchwork of wolfskins in one corner. It was hard to see clearly in the hut. The only light came from a lump of fat burning and sputtering on a stone dish. "Lizel, is that you? Are you all right?"

The old woman raised a hand. It looked skeletal in the feeble light. "Mara. Mara, dear. Yes, it's me."

Mara ran forward and knelt on the ground. She reached out—then hesitated. The old woman looked so gaunt, Mara was afraid to touch her. "What happened?" she whispered.

Lizel coughed. It was a deep, guttural sound, and it made her hunch forward, clutching her chest. Slowly, then, she subsided, taking difficult, rasping breaths. "I haven't been well," she whispered. She gestured at the skins draped across her knees. "My legs. I can't walk anymore."

Mara felt emotion welling up inside her—distress, and outrage. "What happened? How did it happen?" She reached out and clutched Lizel's hand.

"She came to our tribe from yours," said Chief Fridor, standing behind Lizel, while Trifen stood beside him and the rest of the Silver River People clustered outside the hut, trying to peer in through the doorway. "She asked to stay here for the winter, and we welcomed her. She's a wise healer."

"Yes," said Mara, "I know."

"But then Graum came," the chief went on. "He told us he had been persecuted. He said there was a dangerous woman in the Lake People—an evil, enchanted woman who used dark forces against her enemies and killed without remorse."

Mara looked up at him. "Me?"

The Chieftain nodded. "Graum told us you had killed his wife, and he said you would have killed him, too, had he not escaped with his followers. We didn't know what to believe. Lizel defended you and I had met you myself, Mara, when you were younger. It seemed strange—and yet, all the men with him told the same story."

"I spoke against them," said Lizel. Her voice was dry and faint.

"But many people believed Graum," said the Chieftain. "He scared them. And he impressed them—because he came here in the winter, leading men through the snow and ice. No one had ever made that winter journey before. And no man would choose to do such a thing unless he had been forced to. So the people believed him, and they feared that what had happened to him might happen to them. He gathered more warriors around himself, and bit by bit, my tribe became his." The Chieftain made a sound of disgust. "I was a fool to let it happen. By the time I really understood him, it was too late. He was an evil man, and he ruled us cruelly."

Mara nodded slowly. "I understand," she said. She turned back to Lizel. "But are your legs—"

"I was out on the hillside setting traps," Lizel said. She reached for a cup of water, raised it shakily, and took a sip. "We were using deadfalls. Boulders on logs. One of them fell on my legs. Crushed them, below the knee." She shifted, and winced. "I almost bled to death. It was an accident, Graum said." She grimaced. "He didn't want to kill me, you see, because he knew I was a healer. He just wanted to keep me here and scare me so I wouldn't speak against him."

Mara felt sick inside. She could think of nothing to say.

"Lizel is a brave woman," the Chieftain said quietly. "She still whispered behind Graum's back. She encouraged us. And now we have our tribe back again. After Graum left us, only six of his people remained. We rose up against them and took their spears away."

"Bumar," Mara muttered. "When I saw him without his spear, I knew that Graum wasn't in power here anymore. He'd never allow one of his men out unarmed." She looked up at the Chieftain. "So where is he? Where did he go?"

The Chieftain glanced at Lizel, and the two of them exchanged a look that Mara didn't understand. "You should bring your people down out of the forest," said the Chieftain. "They must hear what we have to say."

"We set Bumar outside the village to warn us if anyone came near," Fridor said, as he stood with Mara waiting for her people to make their way down the hillside.

"We thought if we took his spear away, he'd be sure to shout for help if there were strangers close by. And then we'd decide for ourselves if the strangers meant us any harm. We didn't imagine that Bumar would deliberately try to set you against us."

Lomel was the first down the slope. She came forward cautiously, followed by Arin, and Weena, and all the others. There were dozens of questions, all being asked at once, and Mara saw her people looking doubtfully at the Chieftain, still not convinced that the Silver People could be trusted.

"Come," said Fridor. "Sit in our Meeting Place. I wish we could offer you food; but Graum and his people took almost everything we had."

The Silver River People eyed Mara's people as warily as they'd eyed her. They stayed at the edges of the Meeting Place, huddling together, as the Lake People came in. Most of them, Mara realized, were elders. Elders and women. The young men of the tribe had gone; they had followed Graum.

"Lake People," Chief Fridor called out, spreading his arms wide. "We welcome you. We've always traded with each other and trusted each other. We're friends. We've exchanged food, and gifts, and even brides." He paused. "I'm sad about what I have to tell you." He paused, looking down at his hands. "Graum warned us that you were coming here," the Chieftain went on. "He said that you would attack us tonight or tomorrow night."

Now there was complete silence. None of Mara's people even looked at each other. They were staring at Fridor, trying to make sense of what he said.

"Ulfor," Mara whispered. Instinctively her hand tightened on her spear. She saw the old man in her mind's eye, and she saw his strange headress, and now she knew that underneath it, he had had a bear's head tattooed on his forehead. "Ulfor!" she shouted out.

Chief Fridor nodded wearily. "Yes, he was here, this winter. A wanderer. But he became an ally of Graum. He left us five days ago, and we didn't know where he had gone. Then he returned just last night. He said you'd be on your way. When Graum heard that, he led his men out of here, promising to find you on the river trail and kill you all. But he warned us to be on guard in case he failed."

Mara remembered waking the previous night, hearing a sound. She'd been convinced then that someone had been nearby. That must have been when Graum passed them.

Mara stepped forward. "Graum lied," she spoke out. "He could have confronted us if he'd chosen to. But he snuck past us in the darkness."

Chief Fridor nodded slowly. "I think you're right. He hoped that we, here, would fight his battle for him, and kill you ourselves. Probably he hoped you would kill some of us, too. After all, we were of no further use to him. In the meantime—he left six of his warriors here with us, when he set out last night. Bumar was one of them. They were all from your tribe. And Lizel tells me that all of them have relatives in your tribe."

"What are you saying?" Mara couldn't allow herself to draw the obvious conclusion. It was too frightening, too awful.

"Graum has gone to destroy your village," the old Chieftain said. Shadowed by the firelight, his face was deeply lined with an expression of pain. "He made sure your tribe would be undefended, by sending Ulfor to draw you away, bringing your best warriors with you."

Mara suddenly remembered the old man sitting on the floor by the fireside, eating rabbit meat in his fingers, and telling them that he'd rather lure and trap an enemy than fight him. "Bastard," Mara muttered, feeling frustration welling up inside her.

"Graum left only a few of his men here," Fridor went on. "They were Lake People who have close relatives back at your tribe." The Chieftain slowly shook his head. "By now, I have no doubt, he has killed everyone by the Great Lake and laid waste to your homes."

"No." It was Lomel stepping forward, raising her voice. "This can't be true."

And then, one by one, all the people started speaking up. Soon they were shouting, begging the Chieftain to tell them that it wasn't so.

Mara said nothing. To her, it was obvious. The Chieftain was correct. A trap had been baited. And Mara had done what Graum had wanted her to do.

She turned and ran out of the Meeting Place. She pushed between the silent ranks of the Silver River people. With her thoughts in turmoil, she ran to the house where Lizel lay.

The old woman was still lying on the wolfskins. Trifen was sitting beside her, feeding her some scraps of meat. "Lizel!" Mara cried. "Lizel, what should I do?"

Slowly, Lizel turned her face. She had been crying, Mara realized. "I'm sorry," Lizel whispered to her. "I had no way to warn you. When I realized what was happening, Graum was already on his way north."

Mara sank down on her knees. She grasped Lizel's thin, bony hand. "It's not your fault. It's my fault. My vision, Lizel! My vision of the burning village! I fear it's true now. And it's all my fault."

Lizel winced as she struggled to sit up. "No." Her old voice had an edge to it. She almost sounded angry. "No, Mara! It's Graum you must blame."

Mara hardly heard. "I had another vision," she whispered. "I dreamed my mother was talking to me, telling me to go south. She said it would be safe. And she showed me a place I'd never seen before, all red and orange rock."

Lizel grunted and grimaced. "Visions, Mara. I warned you once, some are true, some are false."

Mara felt herself crying, now. "So what should I do?" she said again. "Tell me, Lizel. How can I set things right?"

"You must kill Graum." The old woman said it as if it was self-evident. "Surely you see that."

"Yes." Mara nodded weakly. "Yes. I would have killed him before, if I'd had the chance. Shani stopped me—"

Lizel made an angry, irritable sound. "Pursue him," she said. "He fears you, Mara. Do you understand? If he thought he could kill you easily, he would have tackled you by the river instead of sneaking past and hoping that the Silver River People would do the job for him.

Graum doesn't take chances, understand? He gets other people to fight his wars for him. Young men with no sense, and tribes who fear they're going to be overrun."

"But do you think he'll come back here?" She stared at the old woman, hoping for something, though she didn't know what it was. She was hoping for hope, she thought bitterly.

"I doubt he'll come back here," Lizel said, narrowing her eyes and staring into the dark shadows at the far side of the little cabin. "He took what he wanted from the Silver River People. Food, shelter, and men who should have known better. No, I don't think he'll come back here."

"Then," said Mara, "perhaps he'll move on after he takes his revenge on my tribe—"

"But it's you he really wants!" Once again the old woman struggled to sit up. "Listen to me, Mara, and listen well, because you may never hear my voice again."

"No." Mara quickly hugged Lizel. The old woman's shoulders were frighteningly thin. "Please don't say that."

"I say what I know. Now listen. Is it true you killed his wife?"

Mara nodded wordlessly.

"Well, I'm sure you had good reason. But listen: A man like Graum will want his vengeance. He'll think about it night and day. It'll be like a friend to him. But don't expect that he'll try it right away. Likely as not, he'll take his time. He'll be hoping you'll relax your guard. And then, when you aren't expecting it, he'll try to lure and trap you—just as he did this time. That's why you must chase him down, Mara. Follow him, wherever he takes his men. And kill him." Her old eyes stared up into Mara's face. "Kill him, do you understand? Otherwise you will never be safe."

Chapter 36

Mara pressed Chieftain Fridor to tell her a way north that would strike across the hills and avoid the valley where the Silver River ran. But the Chieftain shook his head and said that it was impossible. "The forest covers all the land south of your valley," he said. "The underbrush is thick, which makes travel very slow. And if there's a day when the clouds are heavy, or if you travel at night, you're sure to get lost." Once again he shook his head. "Even our trappers think twice before striking out far into the forest. You'll have to follow the river, Mara, if you want to reach your tribe quickly. It's the only way."

So they set out in the darkness, weary and full of sadness, but desperate to make the journey as fast as possible.

They walked all through the night, picking their way upstream, barely speaking to each other. Mara was the most silent of all, stricken by the burden of her own guilt. Again and again she imagined her village in flames, her people fleeing, spears flying, bodies bleeding. And all because she had taken her guardians south, following the lure that Graum had laid.

At dawn they rested, Mara moved away from the rest of her people and ate some of her rations on her own, sitting on a rock at the edge of the stream. She heard them talking quietly among themselves, and she knew they were agonizing over the fate of their kinfolk. She felt guilty for not being able to say something to them which would give them hope; but privately, she had lost all hope.

After a little while, Lomel came over to her. Mara looked up. Lomel seemed deeply unhappy, and she hesitated before she sat down beside Mara. "May I speak to you?" she asked.

Mara shrugged. "Of course."

"Are you angry?" Lomel's voice was so timid, Mara could barely hear it above the rushing of the river.

She looked at Lomel blankly. "With myself, you mean? With Graum?"

"No." Lomel quickly shook her head. "With me."

Mara stared at her in surprise. "Why should I be angry with you?"

Lomel picked up a pebble and threw it into the water. She threw another, and another, hurling each one harder than the one before. "You were angry at me last night," she said. Her face changed. One moment there was anger and resentment; the next moment, she was crying. "After I kicked Bumar, you scolded me in front of everyone."

"All I care about, Lomel," Mara said patiently, "is our tribe. My family. Your family. I don't care whether you kicked Bumar. It means nothing to me now."

"So you're not angry?" Lomel eyed her balefully.

"No, Lomel." She took the girl's hand and squeezed it.

Lomel didn't seem reassured. "You shouldn't have criticized me in front of everyone." Her voice was low and edged with resentment.

Mara sighed. "I had to get you to stop. I was afraid you'd hurt Bumar so much that he wouldn't be able to talk."

Lomel sniffed. "I hope you realize," she said, "I do all I can to please you, Mara. You mean more to me than anyone." She gave Mara a shy, sidelong glance. "When you criticize me, it hurts so deeply, I feel as if you've speared me." She pressed her hand against her chest.

Slowly, reluctantly, Mara realized that she could no longer count on Lomel. The girl's loyalty was so extreme, she was incapable of hearing criticism. "I'm sorry, Lomel." There. Was that what she wanted to hear? "I'll try not to do it again."

Abruptly Lomel hugged her. For a moment the girl's

young body pressed close, and her arms seized Mara
fiercely. Then she pulled away and stood up, looking
embarrassed. She picked her way back to the rest of
the people.

Mara glanced quickly at her followers and noted, with
relief, that no one seemed to have taken any interest.
But then she saw Arin sitting on a boulder a little way
away from the others. He was frowning at Mara, giving
her a strange, thoughtful look. And when her eyes met
his, his frown deepened.

They forced themselves on, through the morning. Mara
grew anxious as the day brightened, in case Graum and
his people were coming back down the valley. She agreed
with Lizel's judgment that Graum had probably abandoned the Silver River People, and if he had avoided a
confrontation with her before, he would probably do the
same again. Still, she didn't dare to trust her judgment
anymore. At each new bend in the river, she looked
anxiously ahead, half expecting to see Graum's men coming toward them with their spears ready.

Finally, around noon, they reached the place in the
woods where they had spent the night on the way south.
It had served them well then; maybe it would serve them
again. People were so tired now, they were leaning on
each other, stumbling as they struggled along.

"We'll sleep here," said Mara. "And then we'll eat,
and then we'll walk again. And we won't stop till we
reach our tribe." She looked at each person, waiting to
see if anyone would disagree or complain. No one said
a word.

Mara hadn't expected to be able to sleep. But she
found herself opening her eyes, and she saw that the sun
had moved. So she had slept, after all: suddenly,
dreamlessly.

All around her, she saw her people stretched out on
the ground. No one had kept watch. Everyone looked
exhausted. What good would they be, she wondered,
when they reached their tribe?

Still, she couldn't bear the thought of staying here any

longer than she had to. As kindly as she could, she started waking them. Then she forced them on upriver.

They walked on through the night. Sometime during the darkest hour, they finally emerged from the narrow valley. The Moon was peeking above the mountains, and in its welcome light, Mara saw the lake ahead, stretching far into the distance.

The sight seemed to give her people new energy. They forced themselves on with no further encouragement from her. This was their land: wide and welcoming, a vast swath of tall grass bordered by gentle foothills where the pine trees grew.

They trekked on, following the edge of the lake, still watching for any sign of Graum, but feeling more and more confident now that he had chosen to continue on elsewhere. It was a good feeling to be back here in this familiar territory, and Mara found herself almost daring to hope that Lizel and Chieftain Fridor had guessed wrongly about Graum's intentions. She found herself having a delicious fantasy that the village by the lake would still be there, looking exactly the same as it did in her memories. All the people were the same as before, and the worst she had to face was Shani, scolding her for taking so many more of her guardians than she had been supposed to.

But then the first light of dawn brightened the sky, and Mara saw the village lying ahead, and her fantasy was swept aside.

Fragments of black debris lay where the village had once stood. Blackened stumps stood smoldering amid a great circle of scorched earth. Smoke was still rising from the Clan Houses—or what was left of them. The domed roofs were gone. The huts and tents at the edge of the village were gone. The village had been burned to the ground, and all that was left now were the ashes.

At first Mara couldn't allow herself to believe what she saw. The village was still in the distance, and the sun wasn't yet up. It was hard for her to see clearly what had happened. She told herself, with growing desperation, that it could still be a trick of the light. Or, at the very least, there were probably some buildings still intact.

But she found herself breaking into a run, and she noticed, vaguely, that the people around her were running, too. And as she came closer, as the day grew brighter, she saw that her very worst fears were fulfilled. The village where she had spent her entire life was gone. The buildings that had stood through so many seasons, for so many generations, had been burned to the ground.

She found herself running desperately, with tears on her face and a terrible, clutching pain in her chest. Her people were shouting their grief and horror. Their voices were a rising wail.

Finally she reached the smoldering wreckage. She ran among the blackened logs which had once been the proud, strong Clan Houses. She saw rings of stones—the fire pits where safe, welcoming flames had once burned. She saw huge heaps of blackened clay which had fallen when the domed roofs collapsed. And then she found herself in an open area, and she realized she was in the Meeting Place.

She stood, gasping for breath, turning slowly, staring, still not able to accept the truth of what she saw. Here, she had been paired. Here, she had challenged Graum. Here, she had led her followers against Graum.

She saw the Speaking Stone, blackened but still recognizable. She climbed onto it and gazed with despair at the devastation. She breathed the tang of burned wood and the thick stench of scorched leather. Everywhere was sooty wreckage and gray ash.

She started out of the Meeting Place then and ran to the lake. A little way to the south, she found mammoth ribs standing naked with fragments of charred hide still clinging to them. Here it was, the home that Kormor had made for her. She found herself tumbling down into it, digging through the warm ashes. She dragged out a leather cup, blackened but still usable. She dug deeper and pulled out a fragment of a robe.

"My parents are gone."

The voice came from behind Mara. She turned, blinking, feeling confused. She looked up and saw Arin standing silhouetted against the brightening sky.

"I went to our hut," Arin went on. "I mean, I went where it used to be. I dug through the ashes, the same as you're doing now. There were things there, but—but no bodies."

Gradually Mara managed to get a grip on her emotions. She hugged her arms around herself for a minute, shivering, feeling a coldness that struck through to the core of her.

"There are hardly any bodies anywhere," Arin went on. "A lot of people must have escaped. Maybe most of them."

"Yes?" Mara struggled up out of the remains of her home. She faced Arin for a moment. He seemed much more calm and self-possessed than she was, and she wondered if that meant he was stronger. But then she remembered that he had come here from the North Lands. This was not the first time his home had been destroyed.

"The wind was from the south last night," Arin said. "Probably Graum would have set his fires on the south side of the village, so the wind would spread the flames."

"Our people would have run toward the north," said Mara. She clutched Arin's arm. "Do you really think so?" She was afraid now to hope for anything.

He shrugged. "There's hardly anyone here." He gave Mara a worried look. "Are you all right?"

How good it was, she thought, to hear someone ask kindly about her.

"Yes, I'm all right." She turned away from him, knelt by the lake, and splashed water into her face. She stood up, blinking, feeling dizzy but trying hard to regain her composure. "This is where I grew up, Arin. More than that: My family was here for generations. Laena, the mother of us all, built this village. And now—it's my fault that this happened." Tears welled up as she spoke. "It's all my fault, Arin." She covered her face with her hands.

Vaguely, she felt him touching her. She felt his arm around her shoulders, then both his arms holding her, trying to give her comfort. "Graum did this, Mara. And if Shani hadn't stood in your way, it would never have happened."

Slowly she managed to calm herself. She felt better, in a way, for having cried, even though she despised her own weakness. She looked at his face, full of understanding. "Thank you, Arin," she said. And then she turned away, feeling embarrassed.

She found herself facing several of her people, Lomel among them. They had gathered close by, and they were staring at her. There was anger in Lomel's eyes, and jealousy. That was more than Mara could cope with now. "We must search the land to the north," Mara told them. She brushed her hair away from her wet cheeks. "I'm sorry, I—I lost myself, just now. My family made this village. For generations, we—" She broke off. "You all know this. Come, let's get everyone together and see if our families and our loved ones are still alive."

Chapter 37

Mara and her followers spread out across the grassland, walking to the north. At first they held on to some hope. But then, very soon, they came to the bodies.

The people were lying where they had fallen in the tall grass. Many of them were elders who hadn't been able to escape their pursuers. Some were young children. Most were wearing nightclothes—caribou skins and light, simple furs. Most had been speared in the back. Wabin, who had been too old to hunt but loved to fish, was lying here. So was Hopwa, who had watched over the communal stores for so many years; and Ifnir, the elder hunter; and Vola, whose mother-milk had nurtured Mara's bobcat; and Clewna, Elmay, Jorno, Tamra, Peigor—they were all broken and bloody, lying in the tall grass out here where the massacre had taken place. She would never hear any of them speak again.

"First he set the fires," Arin said, looking around at the carnage. His voice was still quiet, but his face showed his anguish. "Probably they threw flaming spears wrapped with dry grass soaked in oil or fat." He grimaced. "Graum told us about that once. He said we should be on guard against an enemy doing that to our village."

"The fire drove the people from their homes, and they ran here," said Mara. "They didn't think to take their spears to defend themselves. And the rest of Graum's men were waiting."

"The flames would have shed some light," said Arin. "And that would have made it easy to see everyone and kill them." He broke off as he came to another body hidden in the tall grass. He stood there and stared, and he fell silent.

Instinctively, Mara knew what he had found. She went to him. Lying on the ground was his mother. She was sprawled facedown with her arms stretched out as if she had been reaching, trying to hold on to something.

"Rika," Arin muttered. And then, more loudly: "Rika!"

Mara squatted down. Gently she pulled the woman's hair back from her face. There was no doubt: It was her. Her eyes were wide and staring. Her mouth was open in a silent scream.

Mara heard footsteps hurrying through the grass. She looked up and found Lomel standing over her. Lomel's face was pale. She clenched her fists and let out a strange cry—half grief, half rage. "I'll kill him!" she cried.

Slowly, Mara stood up.

"We must find him," Lomel said, as if it could be done immediately, if they only wanted it enough.

"Yes, Lomel," Mara said wearily. "We will find him, and we will take our revenge."

Lomel wasn't listening. She seized her spear and stabbed it savagely into the ground. She pulled it out and stabbed it down again, and again. "I will *kill him*," she cried.

Mara glanced at Arin. He shook his head and motioned her not to interfere.

Mara went over to Arin. "So, perhaps it's my turn to help you now," she said. She rested her hand on his shoulder.

He shrugged. "I expected this. I served Graum. I know how he thinks and how he acts. When we were with the Silver River Tribe, and they told us he had left them and traveled north—I realized then that I would never see my parents again."

"But your father could still be alive," Mara said.

"I think not." He pointed to another shape in the grass, barely visible, a dozen paces away. "That's his robe. He always wore it to bed."

Mara looked at Arin's face. "I don't understand how you can seem so calm."

"I'm not calm, Mara. I feel the grief." He shrugged. "But I went through so much, when I served Graum. So much pain—" He gestured helplessly. "I feel as if nothing can touch me now."

Mara looked out over the grassland. Her followers were scattered here and there, and there were more cries of distress as relatives and loved ones were found among the dead. "I can't understand," Mara said, "how he could do this thing. And why his people, who had once been our people, would help him do it. It's so terrible, so evil—"

"But it's simple, Mara," Arin said. "If someone crossed Graum—if someone even made a joke about him—he always moved against them. I saw that many times. He couldn't stand anyone insulting his pride or defying his authority. And you did much more than that; you killed his wife, and you took away his power as Chieftain." He slowly shook his head. "I'm sure that Graum won't be happy unless he kills the rest of us, as well. And as for the ones who serve him—remember, he had to leave six of them behind with the River People, because he didn't trust them to do this deed. The rest, who did come here with him—they're driven by fear, Mara. Fear of Graum, fear of strangers, fear of their own weakness. They probably believed him when he told them that you and your tribe were dangerous and evil. So they came here, and they proved they were stronger than you."

Lomel had been squatting on the ground beside her mother, staring at her, touching her, as if she thought she could somehow bring her back to life. "Why are you standing there?" Lomel said suddenly, looking up at Mara and Arin. "How can you just stand there and talk?"

"What would you have us do?" Arin asked gently.

"Find him! Find him, and kill him!"

"Lomel." Mara went to her. "Be calm, Lomel." She reached out to the girl.

"No." Lomel shook Mara's hand away. She jumped up, took a step backward, seized her spear, and wrenched it out of the ground. "Don't try to reason with me,

Mara." She turned and started away through the tall grass with her spear held high, as if she expected to find Graum and kill him when he leaped out of the cover like a startled deer.

"Have you ever seen Lomel like this before?" Mara asked Arin.

He shook his head. "Never." He brooded for a moment. "She was always the quiet, shy one, smiling and cheerful, just like her mother. But I always knew there was something about it that wasn't quite real. She took so much abuse from my father—you know, he was really a cruel man." He paused, looking confused. "It's so strange." His voice wavered. "To talk about them like this. As if . . . they're not here anymore."

Mara went to him then and put her arm around his shoulders.

"There! Look there!"

It was Lomel's voice, from somewhere up ahead, almost lost in the wind. "Look! Up on the cliffs!"

Mara shaded her eyes and peered at the cliffs that stood at the top of the valley, where the mastodon had fallen, and where Ternees had died. For a moment she saw nothing, and she wondered what was wrong with Lomel now. But then, straining her eyes, she saw tiny black figures standing against the sky.

It took patience and persistence to convince Lomel that the people on the cliffs weren't Graum and his men. "They wouldn't show themselves like that," Mara said, taking hold of Lomel by her upper arms and giving her a little shake. "Listen to me! Graum hasn't risked himself face-to-face with us. If he was up there, he wouldn't show himself and let us see him."

"But our tribe is all dead." Lomel's voice was so shaky, Mara could hardly make sense of the words. Lomel turned and looked around. She stumbled and leaned her weight on her spear. "Everyone's dead."

Perhaps it was just the lack of sleep, Mara thought, on top of the shock of seeing the village destroyed. Many of her people were showing the strain. A lot of them had been weeping and shouting out curses and vows of revenge. "Your parents are dead," she said patiently. "But not all the people of our tribe are lying out here in the grass, Lomel. My own sister isn't here, so far as I can see. There must be some survivors who managed to run from Graum and his men. It's likely they took refuge up on the cliffs. Up there, they could defend themselves even though they had no weapons. They could throw down rocks at anyone who tried to pursue them."

Lomel stared dully at Mara. "You think so?"

"Yes," Mara said, feeling suddenly so weary, she wondered how she could still stand and speak. "So we'll find out now who's still left alive."

The climb up the cliff path had never felt so steep and hard. When Mara finally reached the top, her legs were shaking and she had to sit and rest for a moment. Most of her people were equally weary, but some of them stumbled forward with cries of gladness as they saw their kin alive and unharmed, here on the rocky plateau. For a moment it was a happy scene, as people held and hugged one another.

Mara looked at Shani and felt a strange pang. She was glad, she realized, that Shani was still alive. Nothing so strange in that; Shani was her closest relative. But there had been so few times in her life when Mara had felt happy in her sister's company, it was strange to feel warm feelings welling up inside her now.

She took Shani's hands in hers. She squeezed them for a moment, and it seemed as if Shani must feel the same way. "Welcome, Mara," Shani said simply. "We were afraid Graum had killed you all in the Snake Valley."

"No." Mara shook her head. "He chose to avoid us."

"Well." Shani looked down at her hands and Mara's, clasped together. "It seems ... you were right about him," she said.

Mara looked at her sister's face. There was a hollow, empty look in her eyes, and she seemed physically weakened by the horror of everything that had happened. She no longer seemed like a leader. She seemed like a shaken, lonely young woman.

As Mara saw the change in her sister, it made her feel

more generous toward her. And her generosity made her feel able to admit her own fault. "It was my mistake," she said, "to take so many guardians away from the village." It was hard for her, even now, to say these words. She was so accustomed to guarding herself, never exposing a weakness that Shani could use against her. But the words needed to be said. "It was a mistake for me to believe the word of that old man Ulfor."

"He was sent to us by Graum?"

Mara nodded, feeling the guilt and the responsibility heavy inside her. "He lured us south at a time when there would be moonless nights, so that Graum could attack the tribe without fear of it being defended."

Shani nodded slowly. "When the attack came, I guessed we had been wrong to trust Ulfor." She rubbed a shaky hand across her forehead. "They killed my husband, Mara. Did you see him down there among the dead?"

Mara stared at her sister. She blinked, feeling shaken by the sudden revelation and trying to think of something meaningful to say. "I didn't realize," she muttered.

"Yes." Shani clasped her hands. "He was a good man, and we were paired for less than three months."

Mara stood for a moment, remembering Ipaw. He had seemed a figure of fun, to her, but he had made Shani happy, all the same. That was more than Kormor had done for Mara.

Shani breathed deeply and straightened her back, raising her face to the wind. "Well, this is no time to dwell on our sorrow," she said. "We must decide what to do." She swept her arm out, taking in the valley below and the blackened, ruined village. "There it is, sister. What do you suggest?"

Mara noticed that the other villagers on the plateau had come clustering around as the two sisters talked. Were they expecting a plan? Were they looking for hope? If so, Mara thought, it would be hard to give them what they wanted. There was no hope, as far as she could see. The tribe was decimated, and the survivors were helpless.

Still, there was one thing that Mara knew must be

done. "I found Lizel among the Silver River People," she said.

"Lizel?" Shani frowned as if the word was a distraction. "What of Lizel?"

"She's a wise woman, Shani, as you well know."

Shani nodded.

"Lizel and Graum were both in the Silver River Tribe through the winter," Mara went on. "Lizel watched and listened, and she learned about him. She told me, sister, that Graum will not be satisfied with just destroying our village. He won't rest till he kills the rest of us—and me in particular, to avenge the death of his wife. I've talked to Arin, who says the same thing."

There was a murmur of dismay from the people around her.

Shani stared at Mara. "He hasn't already done enough?"

Mara shook her head. "We'll never be safe," she said, "till we kill him."

Slowly, Shani sank down onto the ground. She sat there on the rocky plateau, and she covered her face with her hands.

Mara shifted uneasily. This kind of behavior from her sister was outside her experience, and she had no idea what to do. She hesitated, then stepped forward and touched Shani's shoulder. "Sister? If you are still our Chieftain, you must give us advice. Or if you have none, then you should tell us so."

Shani looked up. Her eyes were bleary and her cheeks were wet. "I've been wrong about Graum before," she said, "while you have been right. Do you agree with Lizel and Arin? Will Graum return?"

Mara nodded. "One day, he'll return."

Shani still sat there on the ground, looking hopeless and beaten. "So, can you do it?" she asked Mara. "Can you . . . get rid of him?"

Mara glanced quickly at her guardians standing among the rest of the villagers. Lomel was no longer trustworthy; her face looked haunted. None of them looked strong. They were all exhausted, in need of food and rest.

Even so, none of them avoided her eyes, and none of them seemed ready to admit defeat. "I think," Mara said, "if my people have food and rest ... maybe ..." She trailed off.

Shani was silent for a long time, still sitting on the ground, staring bleakly out across the valley. "All right," she said. "I've decided. We should follow your lead in this, Mara."

Mara stared at her sister. "What exactly do you mean?"

"I mean you should lead us now." Shani looked up at her. "After Graum is dead, then we will dwell here peacefully again." Her voice grew stronger as she spoke, as if the words could somehow make it all come true. "We will rebuild our village. We will honor the memory of Laena, the First Mother of our tribe. In the meantime, those who want to help you should do so. Those who have no stomach for it can stay here and see what can be salvaged from the ruins."

"But what of you?" Mara asked. "What will you do?"

"I'll help you against Graum," Shani said. "It's my duty now, because I've come to the conclusion that you're right—this is the only way to make our tribe safe again." Once again she started quietly crying as she stared out over the landscape. "I have reason to want revenge myself, now, against that man. Revenge is not my way, and it's not the way of my people. But in this case ... I feel it might be justified." She took a slow, shuddering breath. "While we're hunting for Graum, you will be in charge. I've failed in our dealings with him. We'll see if you can succeed." She turned suddenly to face everyone who had gathered around. "Does anyone here object? Do you trust Mara, now, to kill our enemy?"

The villagers looked uneasily at each other.

"Mara will prevail." It was Lomel speaking. She was lifting her spear, holding it high, as if she could see Graum and was ready to strike him down.

Mara knew that the words were empty—that Lomel was shocked, irrational, barely aware of her surroundings. But the girl's words rang out, and they had an air of conviction.

Mara saw the effect. People began standing a little

straighter, and their faces showed some new resolve. One by one, they started pledging themselves. Their voices were a growing murmur of support, and Mara could see that they were finally willing, now, to face the task they had shied away from before.

Shani watched them all, then turned back to Mara with a strange, twisted smile. "So, it seems you have what you always wanted," she said softly. "The tribe is yours to lead—at least till Graum is dead." She inclined her head toward Mara. "May you use your power wisely."

Chapter 38

They climbed down the cliffs to the valley floor. There were sixty-one people altogether, most of them young and strong. Mara told them all to spread out across the village, probing the ashes and the scorched timbers and bringing out all the food, clothing, and weapons they could find. Everything had to be gathered together in the old Meeting Place.

She established herself there with the packs, the spears, the bison bones, and the remaining food that her party had carried on their journey south. She felt strange, giving instructions to everyone. It was especially strange that Shani was among them. Mara half expected her sister to reverse herself and take back the authority that she had surrendered. But no; she honored her decision. It seemed that the destruction of the village had shaken her confidence to the point where she had lost faith in herself as a leader.

Within a short time, people were bringing many useful things to the Meeting Place. The fire had been fierce, but there were some homes that had only been touched lightly, and almost all the food caches held their supplies unharmed. Mara began to feel a little more confident as she moved to and fro in the Meeting Place, examining spears, taking the points from those that were too badly burned, then gathering together all the clothing and choosing the best, warmest, lightest robes.

Around noon, she called everyone together to eat. She watched the people as they feasted on dried meats and berries and pine nuts, and she saw that their hopelessness and grief were beginning to lift. They had needed someone to tell them what needed to be done. Because she had given instructions and sounded confident, they'd believed in her more than they believed in themselves.

That seemed strange, because she herself had always been so ferociously independent. It puzzled her that people would trust someone else's judgment more than their own. Yet that was the way they seemed to feel. The villagers had been demoralized and desperate, with no idea of what to do, till she started giving instructions.

After the food was eaten, she divided everyone into six groups, each under the command of one of her guardians.

The first group, containing the strongest men, was told to dig a wide, shallow grave in the burial ground, so that all the people that Graum's men had killed could be laid to rest. In a sense, this was a luxury they couldn't afford, since it wouldn't contribute directly to the survival of the tribe. At the same time, though, Mara couldn't bear the thought of her kin being left out under the open sky as carrion for predators. And if she felt that way, she knew that her people would feel it, too. Already, crows and hawks were starting to circle over the scene of the massacre. Burial was the only answer.

She chose the best hunters for the second and third groups, and told them to go out and bring back as much game as they could find.

The fourth group, mainly of older women, was sent to the lake with fishing spears that had been recovered from one of the weapons caches.

The fifth group was told to make simple shelters from scraps of wood and hide that had survived the fire, so that everyone would have somewhere to sleep that night.

And the sixth group was put to work assembling packs containing spare clothing, firesticks, flint tools, bone needles, dried food, and a dozen other essentials for a long trek. Mara wanted to set off in search of Graum the very next day. She had no real confidence that she could succeed against Graum's tough, loyal band of men, yet she saw no alternative. The only thing that encouraged her was that the numbers, now, were on her side, assuming all sixty-one survivors of her tribe joined her on her quest. Graum, she guessed, had no more than forty men.

She made sure that everyone was working hard at the

tasks she'd assigned, and she saw to it that the weakest people, who had been deeply shaken by the disaster, were paired with others who were strong. She was concerned about Lomel, in particular, and put her with Arin in the fishing team. It was a shame to squander Arin's hunting skills, but Lomel needed him to watch over her—and perhaps, Mara thought, it might help Lomel to release some of her hostility if she could plunge a double-pronged fishing spear repeatedly into the clear waters of the lake.

Finally, when everything seemed properly organized, Mara went to her sister.

Shani was working with the team that was making up the travel packs. Mara quietly drew her aside. "If I'm going to lead our people," she said, "I must have your advice."

Shani looked at her cautiously and said nothing for a moment as she searched Mara's face for some sign that she might not really mean what she had said. But Mara was sincere, and it showed. "I'll be glad to tell you whatever I can," Shani said.

Together they walked away into the grassland. The day was growing warm, and the valley had never looked more peaceful and welcoming. If Mara avoided looking toward the lake, she could almost imagine that nothing had happened. The grass waved in the wind, the breeze whispered around her, and the birds and the insects were busy going about their own affairs. It was of no importance to them if some buildings burned down and some human beings had lost their lives. The land and its other living things endured.

"What is it that you need to know?" Shani asked when they were out of earshot of all the villagers. She gave Mara a curious look. And then, showing just a trace of her old spirit, she smiled faintly. "You always seemed to act as if you knew everything already, sister."

"And you always seemed to act as if I knew nothing," Mara countered. "But this is no time to bicker, is it?"

Shani inclined her head. "You're right," she agreed.

Mara sat down in the grass, and Shani joined her. "I want you to tell me," she said, "about each and every person who's still alive. You understand, I've not been as intimate with them as you, over the years. I know everyone by name, of course, and I sometimes heard gossip—but there were a lot of people I never got to know very well. If I'm going to lead them and rely on them, I have to understand all their strengths and weaknesses. "

Shani looked at Mara with appreciation—with respect, even. One by one, she started describing the Lake People who had survived.

At the end of it, Mara was silent. Shani had been helpful, in her way. She had warned Mara which women tended to squabble, and which men were difficult and argumentative with their wives. She'd told Mara who was reliable, who was forgetful, who was fair-minded, and who was mean. She was clever and resourceful, describing the ways to preserve harmony in the tribe, with everyone working toward a common goal.

But when it came to the things that Mara really wanted to know, Shani seemed to know nothing at all. She had no idea who was best at tracking, or finding berries, or setting traps. She wasn't sure who was strongest, and who would be calm in an emergency.

"Thank you for your help," Mara said, not knowing what else to say.

"Be sure to ask me if there's anything else you need," Shani said graciously.

"I will," said Mara. In her own mind, though, she decided that she would simply have to trust her own instincts and the score of people she had trained herself. Shani had her mother's talent for persuading everyone to compromise and live peacefully together. But those days were over—for the time being, at least.

A little before sunset, the hunters returned carrying three deer between them. That was good fortune, and it seemed like a good omen. Mara congratulated them on their skill, and she watched them smile as she gave them her praise. They had hunted the game for themselves and for the whole tribe, yet at the same time, she saw, they had done it for her—because she had assigned them the task. She saw it in their eyes: They respected her, and they wanted to believe in her.

But how would they feel a week or a month from now, if she failed them? Would they feel betrayed? Would they still serve her so eagerly then?

One of the hunters—a young man named Torno, who had just come of age—was especially excited. "I used a bison bone the way you showed us," he said, "to cast my spear. I would never have felled that deer otherwise. You're a great woman, Mara, and a great leader. Laena herself would be proud of you."

Mara paid little attention to that, but at the same time, she wondered where the truth really lay. What did it mean to be a great leader? To be loved by your people, and to seem confident, and to make cautious, careful decisions—was that really all it took?

She had always imagined that some sort of mystical quality was involved. After all, people spoke of Laena— or Ternees, for that matter—with reverence in their voices. But now Mara was leading the tribe, and they were starting to show the same kind of faith in her. She felt puzzled. She was no different from the way she'd been a year ago, when these same people had complained that she was a troublemaker and had turned their backs on her. So why were they so respectful of her now? Were they projecting traits onto her which she didn't actually possess?

She told herself that it didn't matter. She had no time for this kind of contemplation. She quickly organized a team to skin and gut the deer and roast the meat over three fires. Then, while the food was cooking, Mara gathered everyone at the burial ground.

The pit was long and wide, and it was completely full of bodies. The villagers stared at the terrible sight, and Mara saw their newfound confidence melt away. Women started wailing, and many of the men shed tears. The ones who had dug the pit stood off to one side, grim and silent, while more than a dozen people climbed down among the dead, touching their loved ones' faces for the last time or to leaving trinkets, knives, or favorite pieces of clothing beside them.

Mara watched with dismay. Once again, she saw she would have to provide some guidance and some hope. "Let's not forget who's to blame for this," she shouted out.

At the sound of her voice, the villagers turned away from the carnage in front of them.

"It was Graum who committed this terrible crime," Mara told them. "Truly, he's our enemy. See there, the people that he and his men slaughtered. They were unarmed, terrified, running for their lives, and they were brutally murdered while their homes burned. Truly, this was a most despicable crime."

There were shouts of agreement.

"We must search him out," Mara cried. "We must kill him, because that's the only way we can be sure that a crime like this will never happen again." She stared hard at the faces turned toward her. Many still looked shaken and weak. Well, she would force them to be strong. "Who is our enemy?" she shouted.

"Graum!" the people cried.

"When we find him, what must we do?"

"Kill him," the villagers answered her.

"Louder!" she commanded.

"Kill him!" they shouted.

In their faces, their grief turned to anger, and their anger hardened into hate. She felt a shiver run through her as she saw the transformation. This was a wild, dangerous feeling, to inspire such potent emotion in so many people.

"Let us cover our dead now," she said, more gently. "But never forget who did this terrible thing." She gestured to the gravediggers, and they quickly started scooping earth back into the pit.

All the villagers quickly joined in. With so many people working together, the job was mercifully brief. Finally, as the sunset colors died in the sky, the dark, rough earth completely covered the dead.

"Look forward, now," Mara said. "Don't look back. We are the living, and we must see to our own needs. Come; there's fresh meat roasting. We'll eat well tonight. And tomorrow we'll set about avenging those we loved."

They shouted their approval. They raised their clenched fists, and some of them waved their spears.

Shani came up alongside Mara as she followed the crowd back to the Meeting Place. "You've turned them into a mob," she murmured.

"I've given them courage," Mara said. "How else are they supposed to fight this man?"

Shani was silent for a moment. "I'm sure you're right," she said. "But even so, it saddens me to see our people behave so unthinkingly."

Mara gave a short, humorless laugh. "If they sat and thought about this, they might decide they don't have the courage for the task, after all." She shook her head. "It has to be done this way, if it's to be done at all."

Chapter 39

At dawn she gathered them around her. She had slept soundly—her first solid night of sleep in four days—and she felt new strength in her mind and body. But when she thought ahead to what might lie in store, her strength was touched by fear, because she knew that Graum was far more powerful, far more vicious, and far more cunning than she could be.

"This journey may last many days," she said as the villagers faced her, huddling together in the cold morning air. "We don't know where our enemy is. We don't know what he'll do. We have no reason to feel confident today."

The people stirred uneasily. This wasn't what they wanted to hear. But Mara had seen some of the young men boasting about their skill and their fighting prowess the previous night. She couldn't allow them to be overconfident.

"There are three things in our favor," she said. "First, there are sixty-one of us, while Graum probably has no more than forty."

She paused, letting them grasp the implications of that fact.

"Second," she said, "I doubt he'll expect us to go out looking for him. He thinks we are timid, cowardly people, and he'll expect that our spirit will have been broken."

She paused again, measuring the effect of her words. Predictably, she saw anger in people's faces. That was necessary, too.

"Third," Mara went on, "and most important, Graum will underestimate us, because he knows that our most experienced hunters are all dead now, and only the young ones remain. He believes, also, that women are gentle and weak." She smiled. "On that score, I will prove him wrong."

They called out their approval to that.

"All right," she said, "I've spoken to everyone who was here when Graum made his attack. They all agree that Graum led his men away to the north, and some people say that in the first light of morning, looking out from the cliffs, they saw men in the far distance on the opposite side of the lake." She pointed across the water to the woodland where she had spent her days of solitude. "So that's the way we'll go. It hasn't rained, so we should be able to track them easily enough. Forty people can't travel without leaving signs of their passing."

The villagers started picking up their belongings. Everyone seemed impatient to begin.

"Wait!" Mara held up her hand and paused till she had their attention again. "Everyone must stay together," she warned them. "No one must run ahead. Listen for my orders, and be patient. Graum's a cautious man, and he won't make it easy for us to confront him." She nodded to them all. "Now, let's begin."

The terrain around the north end of the lake sloped gently, and there were few trees in the thin soil. Despite what Mara had said, the villagers started hurrying across the open land, impatient to close the gap between themselves and their goal.

"This journey may take days," she warned them when they reached the far side of the lake and rested for a short while. "Graum has already proved that he doesn't want a fair fight. He'll bide his time and avoid an open confrontation."

"Then we should chase after him as quickly as possible, and meet him on our own terms." It was Lomel speaking out. She was calmer than she had been the previous day, and the haunted look was gone from her face. Still, she seemed deeply preoccupied inside herself, and Mara almost felt as if she had become a stranger.

"I understand that you're impatient, Lomel," she said.

"But there are limits to our strength. We have to eat, and this is a good place to do so. I'll say when it's time for us to move on."

Lomel's face hardened. Wordlessly, she turned away.

All along the lakeshore, there had been broken grass blades and scuffed earth showing that Graum and his men had passed this way. But when Mara took her people farther south, the signs suddenly ceased.

She sent Torno and Lumo to scout back along the edges of the forest, and within moments Torno called to her. Brambles had been pushed aside, and leaves had been crushed underfoot. Graum had led his men away up the hillside.

"How far have you explored west of here?" Mara asked Lumo.

"There are two long, wide hills," he told her. He was still just a boy, and his voice was high-pitched. He had an odd, halting way of speaking, and he seemed to feel uncomfortable now that everyone was watching him, hanging on his words. "Beyond the second hill," he went on, "there's the Blue River. That's as far as I've ever been. But we could be there by sunset."

"You think that's where Graum has gone?" Mara asked.

Lumo nodded. "Forty men—he'll need water. That's the only water west of here."

It was impossible to move quietly through the forest. The trackers went first, constantly searching for signs. Mara followed them, and the rest of her people trailed behind her in single file. Everyone held spears ready, and when she glanced back, she saw people constantly peering among the trees and bushes. She was glad of their vigilance, even though the forest was an unlikely place for a battle. The close-spaced trees and the underbrush would make it difficult for a party of men to launch an effective spear attack.

They followed the trail almost directly west, down into a valley, up another hillside, and then down a long slope beyond. Finally they came to the Blue River, as Lumo had said they would. That was where they found the clearest evidence that Graum had been there before them.

There was a great tumble of gray rocks on the far side of the river, and a cave was up there, with a broad ledge outside it. A fire had been built on the ledge, and the ashes were still smoldering.

Mara was wary of an ambush. She asked Torno if he was willing to go upriver a little way, wade across, and circle around through the forest on the other side till he could get a clear view of the campsite. Torno agreed without hesitation, eager, as always, to prove himself. But she could see that the task made him nervous.

Privately, she thought that Graum wouldn't stop and wait for her here. The camp up on the rocks looked like a secure refuge, but it wouldn't serve well for launching an attack. There were too many places under the trees where Mara's people could take cover and protect themselves, and ultimately they could lay siege to the retreat. So she sent Torno out, feeling confident that he wouldn't be in danger.

A while later, he appeared on the ridge opposite, overlooking the cave. "No one there!" he shouted down. "It's safe."

The river flowed fast and the stream bed was slippery with moss, so Mara told her people to form a chain, linking hands as they waded across. Once they reached the far side, the villagers swarmed up the rocks. At the top, they found that the fire outside the cave had been a large one. Mara looked closer, and she realized that the fire hadn't been made just for cooking meat or giving warmth. There were fragments of cured skin around the edges of the ashes. There were leather thongs, charred wooden poles, and what seemed to be willow boughs, partially burned.

"This wasn't just a temporary camp," Mara murmured to herself. "It was a refuge. And he burned the things he couldn't take with him, so that we wouldn't be able to use them."

"Look in here!" The voice echoed, coming from inside

the cave. Mara stood up and turned around. She saw people pushing into the cave, eager to inspect it.

She followed them. The rough gray rock sloped low overhead, forcing everyone to stoop as they made their way inside. There was the smell of human beings here, and Mara found herself walking over stray willow branches and clumps of grass that had been used to stuff leather mattresses.

"I'm sure this must have been where he hid his extra supplies," said Arin, moving up alongside Mara. "He must have come here first, when he made his escape and led his men out into the snow."

"Yes," she said. "I think you're right." She noticed crude drawings on a sheer face of rock at one side of the cave, showing men with spears and other men running, bleeding. She saw a blackened circle where many, many fires had been made. "And I think perhaps he was here even before he came to our tribe. You remember he said he came to us from over the mountains, during the winter months, from the North Lands?"

"We respected him for that," Arin said. "No one had ever come from the north during the winter." He frowned, going back into his memories. "I think we wanted to believe he could do anything. It made us feel good to have someone as powerful as that to guide us."

"Well, I think he lied to you," Mara said. "I think if he had truly journeyed from the north during the winter, he would have been far more exhausted and desperate when he arrived. He must have spent the winter here with Dira and his son. He could have survived by fishing and trapping. And before that—maybe he followed a different path from the North Lands, which led him here instead of to our valley."

"Lumo," Arin called to the scout. "Is this the first time you ever saw this place?"

Lumo had been sitting on his own, staring down at the river, lost in his own thoughts. Reluctantly, he stood up and walked over. "I've been up and down Blue River," he said, "but I never saw this cave. Must have been well hidden. Must have had tree branches covering it."

"Do you think someone could have come to this valley directly from the North Lands?"

"Don't know," he said. "More ice melts in the mountains every year. There could be new paths now."

Mara imagined separate streams of wanderers making their way from the high mountains in the north to the separate river valleys in the south. She had always thought of her village as lying on the one true path from the North Lands; but really, there was no reason it should be so. "There may be more people who came directly to this valley from the north," she said. "We may find them south of here." Privately, she wondered if they would be hostile.

"Shall we camp here?" Lumo asked. "Getting dark, outside."

Mara nodded. "This place was secure for Graum, so it should be secure for us. Still, we should post lookouts." She turned to her people. "We'll camp here," she shouted out. "Gather wood before the light is gone. We'll build our own fire."

"Sister." It was Shani's voice. Mara found her standing close by. "Shouldn't we push on farther down the valley? If we're anxious to catch up with Graum and his men—"

"He knows this terrain," Mara said, "because he's been here before. There may be a place south of here where he could ambush us in the darkness. Remember, the Moon won't be up till late in the night. I led my people up Snake Valley at night, but only because we felt we had no choice."

Shani nodded slowly. She wasn't trying to question Mara's authority; she just seemed to be naturally cautious. "And you think it's safe to show our position here with a fire?"

Mara glanced at the villagers and saw that they were gathering around, watching and listening. "I believe we're safe here," she said, loud and clear, "because the only approach to this place is over the rocks that we just climbed. No one can sneak up on us. In any case, I have no doubt that Graum has gone south. This isn't the kind of place where he would want to confront us. Would you try to track and trap a herd of caribou in a forest? No;

there are too many hiding places, and no clear space to cast a spear."

She saw people nodding to themselves, looking satisfied by what she said.

"We'll catch up with him sooner or later," she told them. "It may take time, but it will happen. And remember, we have three people for every two of his."

Once again they nodded to themselves, looking reassured.

"Go, now," Mara said, turning back to the villagers. "Spread out and find wood before darkness falls. We must eat well and sleep well for the days ahead."

Later, when the fire had burned down to embers and the people had finished their meal and were huddling beneath their sheepskins and bison hides, Mara sat out on the ledge overlooking the valley. She had volunteered to be lookout for the first part of the night, and she had asked Lomel to be there with her. It was time, she decided, to see if she could do anything to bridge the gulf that seemed to have opened between them.

For a while, they sat in silence. The river below murmured in the darkness, and somewhere in the pines, a nightingale cried. Meanwhile, in the cave, Mara heard the regular breathing of her people as they slept.

"I'm glad to be sitting here with you," she whispered to Lomel. "I hope you realize I never wanted anything to come between us. I still care for you, just like before."

It was awkward speaking like this, so close to her tribe. But the murmuring of the river helped to mask her words, and she spoke softly, with her lips close to Lomel's ear.

Lomel stared out into the night, and she said nothing for a long while. "Perhaps you didn't mean to hurt my feelings," she said finally. "But you did hurt me, all the same."

Mara frowned. "How so?"

Lomel sat cross-legged on the shelf of rock. She hunched forward, putting her elbow on her knee and resting her cheek in her hand. "There were many times," she said. She didn't sound angry; there was a tone of resignation in her voice. "When I asked you if you would pair with a man again one day, and I saw the uncertainty in your eyes. Or when you criticized me in front of other people. Or today, when you told me sternly not to walk into the forest, and said I had to wait till you decided it was time to move on." She made a little sound of distress. "In front of everyone, you ordered me."

"Hush. Not so loud." Mara squeezed her shoulder. "Lomel, I need my people to respect me as their new leader. The only way is to show them that I'm in command. I have to be the one who makes decisions. Don't you see?"

Lomel looked away. "I just don't like it when you speak to me that way," she said. "For so many years, my father—" She broke off and fell silent.

"Lomel, please." Mara rested her arm across the girl's shoulders. "I'm not your father. I'm your friend."

Irritably, Lomel shook the arm aside. "I don't know if you can be my friend anymore." Her voice was sounding increasingly subdued. "Not if you have to give me orders." She was silent for a moment. Then, unexpectedly, she turned and faced Mara. "He used to beat me, you know," she said. There was a deep sadness in her face. "I could never please him. He was always hitting me. That's why it didn't matter so much when I was beaten in the Meeting Place. I was used to it." She grimaced, and there was anger now, side by side with her sadness. "But in another way, it made it worse. I felt I could never escape. There were always going to be people hitting me, shouting at me."

Mara glanced cautiously behind her, but no one seemed to be listening or watching her. Once again, she circled her arm around Lomel's shoulders. "Lomel, I care for you. I'll never hit you, and I never want to hurt you. Please be calm."

Lomel laced her fingers together. She looked down at her hands. "I've never trusted men," she said in a low voice. "But I thought I could trust you."

Mara was beginning to lose her patience. The things that were hurting Lomel seemed much more on the inside than the outside. "What about your brother?" Mara whispered to her. "Arin seems so gentle. Surely he's been a friend to you."

Angrily, Lomel shrugged Mara's arm away. "Don't you see the way he looks at you? He wants you for himself. He's always wanted anything that I had." She paused, breathing heavily. "And he never tried to protect me. From my father."

Mara stared at the faint shape of Lomel's face in the darkness. How strange, she thought, to have known Lomel so closely, but not to have known these secrets. "You always seemed so calm and content," she whispered. "I thought I was the emotional one, the worried one who was never happy."

Lomel made a dismissive sound. "My mother made me smile all the time. You saw how she was, always giving people food and chatting to them and pretending we were contented. Well, I tried to be like that. I really did. I always held things in. That's why you never knew any of this. I kept it to myself."

"I see." Mara looked down at the river below, barely visible as it reflected the starlight. She thought of all the times when she had felt happy with Lomel, and she experienced a great sense of weariness and loss. "I'm sorry," she said.

"Yes, well, there's nothing to be done about it." She sounded bitter. "I looked up to you too much. I felt as if you were the only good person in the whole world." She reached in her belt, drew her flint knife, and turned it over in her hands, watching the reflection of the fire-light in the polished flint blade. "There's no way you can live up to the way I wanted you to be. So it's better for me to stay on my own."

"I still wish I could help you," Mara whispered.

"Well, you can't." She ran her fingers across the edge of the knife. "The only thing that will help me now is to find Graum, and—" She broke off, breathing deeply. "I dream of spilling his blood. Cutting him open and dragging out his heart and his liver. I want to make him scream."

Mara shivered. The coldness of Lomel's voice sounded alien, as if the spirit of some night creature had found its way inside her. "Lomel, Graum is not your father."

She turned abruptly and faced Mara. "No, my father's dead. So it's too late for me to hurt him now."

Gently, Mara reached out and stroked Lomel's cheek. The skin was warm, and the touch brought back a rush of feelings and memories.

Lomel seemed to feel it, too. Just for a moment, the tension eased out of her shoulders, and she seemed to weaken.

But then she twisted away. "That doesn't mean what I thought it meant," she hissed at Mara. "So please don't do it anymore." She shifted away and turned her back, leaving Mara sitting alone.

Chapter 40

At dawn, they started walking downstream. Once again there were signs that Graum's men had passed this way. It was harder to track him on the rocky soil beside the river, but still there were footprints in patches of mud, and places where gravel had been scuffed and scattered.

"I think he's just one day ahead of us," Lumo said, as he squatted beside a leaf that had been trodden down by a man's moccasin. He peeled the leaf away from the earth beneath, then ran his fingers over the veined green surface. "Just one day." He squinted up at the sky. "Maybe he's hoping it will rain, so he'll be harder to follow."

"The sky looks clear," said Mara. "The wind is from the west, and the air feels dry."

Lumo nodded. "There's no rain coming."

"So we'll continue as we are," she said.

The villagers moved as quickly as they could, following the river. The valley wasn't as steep-sided and narrow as Snake Valley, but still the ground was strewn with small stones and boulders, and there were rocks which slid and tilted underfoot.

At dusk they came to the place where Graum and his men had spent the previous night. Once again, there were ashes from a fire. This time it was on a small island in the center of the river, no more than five paces across. There was just enough room for Mara's little army, and it was a good, secure place to rest.

Some of the hunters had managed to spear fish during their long walk beside the water, and they cooked it to go with their other rations. They sang some songs together—softly, wearily. Mara moved among them, trying to find encouraging things to say. She smiled at them, and they smiled back at her, seeming cheerful despite the hard day's journey. Clearly, they still believed in her.

"How long do you think their good spirits will last?" Mara asked Shani a little later, when everyone was settling down to sleep. "Graum can stay a day ahead of us, if he chooses. So we could be following him for days, or even weeks. What then, sister?"

Shani was kneeling by the stream, cupping water in her hands and bathing her face. She took a bone comb from her pack and started pulling tangles out of her hair. "I think within a week," she said quietly, "some people will want to turn back."

Mara looked at her in the gathering darkness. It still seemed strange—miraculous, even—to be on friendly terms with Shani after so many years. But Mara was wary of their truce. If the situation changed in some way, she was sure they could quickly be at odds with each other again. "What about you?" she murmured. "Will you want to turn around?"

She gave Mara a calm, frank look. "Perhaps." She paused. "I've said before, you seem to understand Graum, so I have to trust your judgment. But if we follow him for a week, we'll be far from our lands. Do you really think if we turn back then, he'll bother to follow us?"

This was what Mara been afraid of, and she knew there'd be others who felt the same way. "You're thinking the way he wants you to think," she said. "That's why he's avoiding us—so we'll give up and go home and forget about him. The fact is, Shani, he'd travel overland for a month if that would make it possible for him to kill us all. I have no doubt of that."

The next day, around noon, they came to a place where six little huts had been built from wood and grass on a shelf of rock halfway up the side of the valley.

Mara called a halt and stood for a moment, watching the huts, waiting for any sound or movement. But the place was still and silent. No smoke rose from a fire.

There were no sounds of work or chores being done. No villagers called to one another.

Cautiously, Mara ducked under the trees and climbed the steep side of the valley till she was high enough to see down into the camp. A breath of wind reached her, blowing from the south, and it brought her a faint, sweet, metallic smell. It was the smell of blood, she realized.

She climbed around to the huts and stepped onto the table of rock. She walked among the primitive buildings and saw that they'd been lashed together with grasses and ivy where heavy leather thongs should have been used. The roofs were sagging, and the walls looked as if a small storm could have blown them away. Only a few people had lived here, subsisting precariously on fish from the river, pine nuts, and perhaps some animals that they trapped in the summer months. And now those people were dead.

Their bodies were everywhere, covered in blood. There were two old women, thin and frail. Both of them had been killed inside their homes. Four other women had tried to run away and had been felled with spears. Two of them had been clutching young children, and the children, too, were dead.

Five men seemed to have tried to defend themselves, but their only weapons had been wooden fishing spears. Mara looked down at their bodies, slumped on the ground among the huts. The men were small and thin, and their faces were gaunt. Life here had not been easy for them, especially during the winter.

Mara called down to tell everyone that the place was safe, and soon her people were with her, looking at the carnage.

"Why?" said Ewna, looking first at Mara, then at Arin. "Why would Graum do this terrible thing? These people did nothing to him. Look, they don't even have stone tools or weapons."

"The way Graum sees things," said Arin, "any stranger is an enemy till he proves himself as a friend. Graum would have distrusted these people. And he wanted their food. And he wanted to be sure they wouldn't help us in any way."

Mara looked farther down the river valley, wishing she could see around the twists and turns that still separated her from her quarry. "Since he took the food," she said, half to herself, "that must mean that he's hungry."

Arin shook his head. "Probably not. He took it so that you wouldn't be able to eat it. He understands now that you're ready to pursue him for many days, and he wants to make it difficult for you."

"He wants us to give up," said Mara.

"Yes," said Arin. "Exactly."

That night, again, they came to a place where Graum and his men had spent the night. This time the Lake People reached it while there was still light in the sky, and Mara was tempted to push on farther. But really, it wouldn't be long till darkness fell. She didn't want to find herself with no safe place for her people to bed down. And she was beginning to wonder, now, how far this narrow valley could take them. Something, surely, must lie at the end of it—perhaps a wider, grassy space like the one where her own village had been. It would be much harder then for Graum to evade her. If she could just bide her time, she told herself, she might find things changing in her favor.

But the valley continued leading them south for the whole of the next day, and when they reached Graum's next camp, the hillsides were as steep and as close as before. For the first time, Mara heard some of her people complaining about the length of the journey. They were footsore, they were tired, and they could see no hope of catching up with the people they were pursuing.

Mara gathered them around her and reminded them of everything Graum had done. She told them that if they ever wanted to feel safe again, they still had no alternative. They must find him and kill him. She reminded them that she'd said it might take days or even weeks.

Her speech seemed to bring most people around, but she wasn't sure how many more times she could manage it. And there was something else worrying her now: their dwindling supplies of food.

The fish that they speared along the way hadn't been nearly sufficient to sustain them, and there was no time to go foraging or hunting in the dense forest on either side of the river. Everyone knew that a forest like that was the worst place in which to hunt. Traps, not spears, were the way to catch the game that ran through the brush beneath the pines. But there was no way they could set a trap, then come back to it a day later.

So they had been forced to eat more of their rations. They were almost halfway through them now—which meant that after the next day or two, they wouldn't have enough food to take them back to their own lands. Would her people be willing to press on anyway, knowing that they would have to hunt fresh game if they were ever going to return? Mara didn't want to think about that.

The next day, yet again, the valley continued without much change, though the river did seem a little broader and a little deeper where they stopped for the night.

But the day after that, everything was different.

Around noon, they found themselves descending a steep gorge where the water frothed and roared over a bed of boulders. The footing here was treacherous, and they had to link hands as they zigzagged down from one wet rock to the next. It was a long, arduous business that taxed everyone's strength and patience, and it took them most of the afternoon.

Finally they reached the bottom, where the water collected in a wide, deep pool. They followed a path around its edge—and suddenly they emerged from the pine-covered valley into a new, different land.

Mara heard people around her crying out in dismay. She looked at their faces and saw they were afraid— because they were confronted with a place so strange and alien to them, it seemed as if they had gone beyond the edge of the world. Even Mara herself felt nervous, staring at the plain in front of her. She had spent her whole life in a landscape of green grass and thickly wooded hillsides. Every day, no matter where she journeyed, she had always seen trees. But the land that stretched ahead of her was covered in prairie grass, so dry and yellow, it look as if it was no longer alive. There were hills, but they were low and rounded, not like the steep slopes that marked the sides of the valley where her village had been. Here and there were things that seemed to be trees, but their trunks were twisted and gnarled, and their foliage was sparse, dark green, as if all the sap had been baked out by the sun.

The river snaked away across this wide, endless space, but it no longer flowed in a valley. It had cut itself a steep-sided trench in the ground, as if the soil was so soft, the water had washed it away.

Mara squatted down and scratched the earth with her fingernails. It was powdery, with little moisture in it. No wonder the grass was so brown. And yet the river did flow on across this wasteland, and in the distance she saw animals grazing. The place was alien, but living things still could dwell here.

She turned to her people. "Hear me!" she shouted.

Her guardians, she saw, seemed calm enough, but some of the other villagers had stepped back as if they wanted to retreat into the gorge that they'd just emerged from.

"This is great good fortune," she said, as firmly as she knew how. "Graum can't hide from us here. He's in the open now. Do you hear me? And see, animals grazing out there." She pointed. "They, too, have nowhere to hide—no forest to run to. With the river to quench our thirst, we'll have no trouble surviving here. Why, it should be an easy place to live."

She turned again to face the prairie. "See, the game is so tame, it grazes in the light of day." She narrowed her eyes. "And there, where the river curves around that hill. See there! I think that could be Graum's men."

It was hard to be sure. The sun was setting, and there was a purplish haze over the land. Away in the haze, there seemed to be tiny black specks close by the river.

People started talking nervously to each other. Many of them were still afraid, Mara realized—not just of the

strange land, but of their enemy. They had been brave
enough as long as Graum was somewhere out of reach,
but their courage failed them now that there was a real
prospect of facing him. "People!" She turned to them
again. "Have you forgotten so soon? Where are your
loved ones and the people of your clans who aren't with
us today? Who killed them as they ran in fear? And who
would kill you, too, if he had the opportunity?"

She looked from face to face. "Lomel." She beckoned
her forward. "Come, Lomel. Speak to the tribe."

Lomel looked at her. At first she seemed surprised.
Then her expression was clouded with caution. She took
a reluctant pace forward. "What would you have me
say?"

"Tell them your greatest ambition now. And tell them
how you would feel if people decided to turn back."

Lomel paused for a long moment.

"Please, Lomel." Mara met her eyes.

Lomel gave a curt nod. She turned to the villagers and
stood for a moment, resting on her spear. "You all know
Graum's men killed my parents. And you all saw what
happened when . . . when he tied me to a stake and had
me publicly beaten." She grimaced as she said the words.
"I want to spill this man's blood," she went on. "I make
no secret of that. And I say that anyone who turns back
now is a traitor to us all, and a fool besides. If we give
up now, we will all die. He will find us and kill us, there's
no doubt of that." She looked at each person in turn.
"So your choice is simple. Risk your lives to kill him. Or
turn away like cowards and be killed."

Mara touched her arm. "Thank you," she said. Lomel's spirit was so strong, other people couldn't help
being touched by it. She saw it, now, in the faces of her
people. "Lomel is right," Mara told them. "So tell me,
now: Does anyone want to turn back?"

She watched and waited. Shani, she saw, was glancing
around, trying to measure the mood of the people
around her. Only a few, now, looked as if they wished
they could run and hide, but they were too ashamed to
confess their fear. So Shani, too, stayed silent.

"Very well," said Mara. "We are united. We are

strong. We will defeat this man, for our safety and for the honor of our tribe and our kin." She turned again and scanned the darkening landscape. "Look there!" she cried. A tiny yellow spark had blossomed in the dusk, close to the place where she thought she had seen the tiny shapes of men. "There's his campfire."

"We should march through the night," Lomel spoke up. "We can get there before dawn, We can overrun him."

Now there was a sudden, rising bedlam of voices, some in favor, some against.

"Quiet!" Mara held up her hands.

Reluctantly, they obeyed her.

"I'm your leader," she reminded them. "And I say, think carefully now. Graum's a cautious man. His camp will be well guarded. He'll know that we've seen the light of his fire. We'll sacrifice ourselves if we go there now and try to overrun him."

"First we should light a fire of our own." It was Arin's voice, speaking calmly. "Show him that we're camping here."

"Yes," said Mara. "And after that, here's what I suggest we do. We can march through the night and circle around his camp. We must find a place where we can lie in wait, safely hidden. At dawn, when he starts out— that's the best time to strike against him. Even then, if the place and time aren't right, we can still remain hidden in the tall grass and bide our time till there's a better chance."

There were murmurs of assent.

"Very well, then," she said. She scanned the faces in front of her. "Sister! Please join me here."

Calmly, Shani stepped forward.

"You told us, up on the cliffs, after our village had been burned down—you agreed that it has to be this way. Isn't that so?"

Shani looked at Mara with a mixture of emotions— weariness, sadness, regret. "Yes," she said quietly. "It has to be this way."

"You will fight with us, then."

"Yes, I will fight." She looked unhappy as she said the words. But, she said them.

Mara took one of her spears. Even though Shani already had spears of her own slung behind her back, Mara pressed the wooden shaft into her sister's hand.

"We're not a warlike people," Mara said. "We think it's wrong for one person to take up a spear against another. But we know, tonight, there is no other way."

There was a ragged cheer.

She eyed their faces and wondered how many of them could really be counted on to serve her and to fight. "Be fierce, my people. Our party is far bigger than his, and we'll be fighting with righteousness on our side. Think of what you are fighting for, and let it give you strength. And show no mercy!" She nodded slowly. "Build a fire, now. And then we'll do what we came here to do."

Chapter 41

They built a fire from deadwood and bundles of dry grass, and soon the flames were leaping high. "There'll be no talking from now on," Mara said. "Avoid making even the smallest sound. You'll all follow me. And you'll wait for my order to attack. Do you understand?" She surveyed the faces lit by the fire. "No one may cast a spear till you hear my command."

Once again, she wondered if they could be trusted. There were several of them—Lomel, especially—who looked eager to fight and kill. She wasn't sure she could restrain them if a time came when they saw Graum's men in front of them.

This was not a proper army, there was no doubt of that. It was a mismatched mixture of male and female, fierce and gentle, weak and strong. They had all hunted game in the grassy valley that they still thought of as their home, and they all knew how to cast a spear. But that was the most she could say for them.

"Come, now!" she called to them. "Be quick, be brave, be silent, be cautious. Follow me!"

She started forward without bothering to look behind her. She strode down the slope toward the level floor of the plain. Tall, dry grass and long-stemmed weeds brushed across her legs. The powdery earth was soft underfoot, a pleasure after so many days of picking a precarious path over loose stones. Here and there she noticed rabbit holes, and there were dark, dense gorse bushes scattered at intervals, but there were no other obstacles, and the plain stretched out flat in front of her.

The Moon was just up, a dim orange crescent almost touching the horizon. She hoped it wasn't bright enough to

reveal the presence of her people. Certainly it seemed
to shed very little light. She glanced behind her, and she
saw only faint shadows in the darkness. Farther back,
she couldn't pick out individual figures at all. She just
heard their breathing and the rustling of their clothes,
and the distant crackling of the fire they had built, standing like a beacon.

Mara set a steady pace, fast enough to carry them to
Graum's camp well before dawn. She felt strangely calm,
now that this moment had come. The succession of events
that had led to this point seemed like a stream that had
been carrying her along, and it was moving so fast, there
was no way for her to swim against the current.

Of course, she felt apprehensive as she struck out
across the alien landscape, heading toward an enemy
who was far more powerful than she could ever be. She
certainly believed that she might die out here and never
see another sunset.

But if she didn't kill Graum, he would hunt her down;
so her life was at stake either way. Surely it was better
to be bold, like this, than running and hiding like some
timid woodland creature.

After a while, the yellow pinpoint of Graum's campfire
faded from yellow to orange. Then it died altogether.
But she knew exactly where it had been, at the top of a
rounded rise in the land which she could see plainly now,
silhouetted against the night sky.

Thin, high streamers of cloud had moved in from the
west, veiling the Moon. Mara liked to think that the
Moon Spirit had chosen to clothe herself this way, to
protect her people. She muttered a little prayer of thanks
for that kindness.

Finally she neared the base of the hill where Graum
had made his camp. Without a doubt, he would have
posted guards. But the night was so dark now, she was
sure her people couldn't be seen on the floor of the plain.
Also, they were concealed now by the rounded bulk of
the hill itself, which stood between her and anyone who
was looking out from the summit.

She thought it was likely that Graum would continue

south in the morning. So she needed a hiding place that would overlook his most likely path. If he set out that way, they could strike him down. If he didn't, they could still hope to follow him and wait for another opportunity.

Mara led her people in a wide, slow circuit around the hill. They moved stealthily, creeping through the grass, making no more noise than the wind. And now she found a gift: a ridge that stretched out southward from the hill. She could lead her people along the line of that ridge, staying just out of sight behind it. Another ridge ran parallel, a little way to the east, leaving a cleft between them. If Graum and his people took that path, that would be the perfect time to strike.

Mara dropped down onto her hands and knees and made her way slowly, painstakingly along the line of the ridge, always staying just below its crest. She glanced back often, and as far as she could see in the darkness, no one was behaving foolishly. All her people were keeping well hidden.

She moved forward a little farther till she reached a point where the ridge started rising higher and the furrow in the land became a narrow little valley. The sides of that valley were too steep to run down, so she stopped short of it. She stretched out in the grass, and everyone followed her example—faint, shadowy figures blending in with the contours of the land. There was nothing to do now but wait.

Someone came up beside her, slinking through the darkness. It was Lomel, Mara realized; she recognized the scent of her.

"May I lie here with you?" Lomel whispered.

"Of course," Mara whispered back. In fact, she was glad of it. She could think of no one she'd rather fight beside, and it would also give her a chance to control Lomel's wild impulses, if that was necessary.

Lomel was silent for a long time, lying there in the darkness. "If you see Graum," she said finally, "and if he's in front of us, where we can spear him—"

"You should cast your spear first," Mara whispered. "Just like the times we hunted deer together, Lomel. I know you. You'll always be a fiercer hunter than I am."

"Thank you." She touched Mara's arm fleetingly. Then she edged away a little, and she settled down to wait.

It took a long time before the first faint light touched the sky. Mara was stiff and cold, and she was starting to feel muzzy-headed despite the anticipation that gripped her. She glanced along the ridge, and now, finally, she could see places where the grass had been disturbed, marking the positions of her people where they lay upon the land. A couple of them were getting impatient, and they were trying to peer through the grass toward the hill where Graum had made his camp.

"Pass the command," Mara whispered to Lomel. "Stay down. Don't look, listen. And wait for my signal. Anyone who shows herself risks all of our lives."

Lomel nodded. She gave the instructions to the man next to her, and the words flowed from one person to another.

Mara waited, straining her ears for any sound from Graum's camp. As the sky brightened, the waiting became a torture. What was happening? Why was there no noise?

Finally she couldn't stand it any longer. She edged forward through the tall, dry grass, crawling on her belly, till she reached the crest of the ridge. From there, when she raised her head a fraction, she could see across to the top of the hill.

The hill was bare.

She stared at it for a long moment, not wanting to believe what she saw. She knew Graum had camped there; she was certain of it. And as the light grew brighter still, she saw that he had been there. There were the remains of the campfire, and patches of flattened grass where men had slept.

It seemed almost impossible that Graum and his men could have roused themselves so silently that Mara and her people would have heard nothing. It seemed even less likely that Graum could have passed by before dawn without making any noise at all. Yet there was no other explanation. Mara looked to her right, along the cleft that lay before her, and as her eyes followed the line of the narrow valley, she saw figures moving.

"There!" said a voice, almost in her ear.

Mara started. Her guts seemed to twist inside her. She jerked back and found that Lomel had crawled after her.

"There they are!" Lomel whispered more urgently.

"Yes, I see them," Mara said, trying to slow her pulse. "Keep down, Lomel!"

"But it's Graum. See?"

Mara squinted at the distant figures. There were only a handful of them—but one of them was a giant, dwarfing the rest.

Lomel started up onto her hands and knees.

"Wait!" Mara hissed at her. She was still trying to understand exactly what had happened. If Graum had been so stealthy, it must mean that he suspected Mara of being close by. And in that case—

Lomel was getting up. Her eyes were wide and staring. Her mouth was a thin, angry line. She was raising her spear.

"Lomel, wait!" Mara called. "Do you hear me?"

But the rest of the villagers had seen her, and now they, too, came out from their hiding places. They saw the abandoned campsite. Then they saw the men at the opposite end of the valley.

The Lake People let out a wild cry. It was a terrible sound, like the shout of a beast that had been taunted and tormented with countless little spear thrusts and was determined now to wreak revenge.

"Wait!" Mara leaped to her feet. "Come back!" Her voice was as loud as she knew how to make it. "Everyone, hear me!"

Her guardians hesitated, staring at her in confusion. The rest of the villagers paid no attention. They went charging down the slope as a wild, undisciplined mob, screaming out their revenge.

"It's too late," Arin called to Mara. "We have to follow them. We can't stay back here."

She agonized over what he said, and saw that he was right. She cursed, feeling furious—not at Graum, but at

Lomel and the villagers, and at herself for having been unable to control them.

She ran down the grassy slope with Arin at her side, and she started along the narrow valley, following the rest of her people. She glanced up apprehensively, fearing that Graum's other men might have hidden themselves on either side of the valley, ready to hurl their spears. But no figures came into view against the sky. She still couldn't be sure what had happened, but she was painfully aware that many of Graum's men were unaccounted for.

Her feet thudded across the earth, the air blew past her face, and the screams of her people were in her ears as she ran after them along this deepening cleft in the land, with Lomel still leading the pack. Mara glanced behind her, full of fear, half expecting to see the rest of Graum's men chasing after her. But there was no one there.

And then, chillingly, she heard cries of surprise from those who were leading the way. Mara tried to see ahead, but it was impossible. Her people seemed to have raised a cloud of dust. There was a gray tint at the bottom of the V-shaped wedge of sky.

The cries of surprise turned more shrill, and Mara felt cold despair eating inside her. Something terrible was happening; she was sure of it. She stopped and turned to the side of the valley, and she dragged herself up from rock to rock till she could peer along it.

That was when she saw the flames.

Now it was clear to her, and she let out a helpless cry of distress. She realized that Graum had guessed that she might lead her people across the plain. He'd seen, too, that she'd deploy her party along the ridge. He'd roused his men before dawn, and a few of them had crept around this cramped little valley. They'd waited, and they'd shown themselves at the end of it. That had been the bait, and this time, poor, foolish Lomel had been the one to be tempted by it.

The flames were leaping higher now. Graum and his men had set fire to the dry grass all across the end of the valley, and the wind was blowing from the south,

wafting the flames toward Mara's people. She saw the
smoke, and she heard the crackling of the blaze. She
saw her people stopping, turning, shouting in surprise
and fear.

"Look there," said Arin. He was pointing back the
way they'd come. There were figures hunkering down
behind the ridge where the Lake People had been. If the
fire forced them back the way they had come, they'd
be slaughtered.

"Stop!" Mara shouted, as she saw her people streaming back toward her, running from the flames. "Hear
me! Stop!"

Some of them heard her, but many more were too
scared to listen or think.

"Go forward through the flames!" she shouted. It was
the only way. The sides of the valley were so steep, they
were almost impossible to climb—and anyone who tried
to do so would be easily picked off by a spear.

Mara jumped down onto the valley floor. "Stop!" she
shouted again, holding up her arms, trying to stand in
the path of the people stampeding toward her. But fully
half of the villagers pushed past her and ran back the
way they'd come.

Mara felt as if something was tearing her apart from
the inside. She couldn't abandon her people. But as she
saw them running back, she saw Graum's men rising up
from behind the ridge.

Suddenly the air was full of flying spears. There were
terrible screams, and Mara saw the villagers clutching
themselves and toppling in the prairie grass.

Quickly she looked around her. Most of her guardians
were still with her. Shani was there, and Lomel. Lomel's
face was full of horror; she clearly saw the consequences
of her mistake. "Kill as many as we can, then back
through the flames," Mara shouted to them. Without
waiting for an answer, she charged forward, grasping her
spear, raising it, and shouting out a war cry.

Perhaps a quarter of the people at the mouth of the
valley had already been slaughtered. The rest were casting their own spears, hurling them up at the men on the

ridge. Mara saw a couple of Graum's men fall; but most were able to duck down and protect themselves.

The battle was disintegrating into a mess of running bodies, people screaming, people falling, people throwing spears with wild desperation and little hope of striking anything.

Mara still hadn't cast her own spear. There was no clear target. Once again she paused and climbed a little way up the opposite side of the valley, even though that made her more vulnerable. She saw one of Graum's men standing up to make his throw, and she seized the moment, hurling her own spear at him. She watched as it followed a clean, smooth trajectory. Right till the last, he didn't see it. He knew nothing until it struck him. Mara saw him lurch and cry out, with the shaft embedded in his chest. He fell forward and started rolling down the slope. Then, as he reached the bottom, one of the Lake People seized him and stabbed him to death.

Mara felt a strange, sick sensation. She had helped to kill a man. She didn't even know who he was. He could have been one of the ones from her own tribe, who had escaped with Graum from her own Clan House.

Something struck a rock close behind her. The impact was a sharp sound that she heard above the noise of the people screaming and shouting. She looked around and saw that a spear had only just missed her. The shaft was toppling toward her now, and she reached out instinctively to stop it from striking her head. She grabbed it and held it, glancing quickly around. She couldn't see who had cast it, but it didn't matter. She took aim at another one of Graum's men and hurled the spear. This time, it went wide of its target.

Graum's men were growing bolder. Some of them started running down into the cleft in the land, closing on the people at the bottom. Meanwhile, the fire was advancing closer along the valley, and the smoke was drifting low. Mara felt it stinging her eyes, and it caught in her throat. Instinctively, she moved away from the flames, toward the fighting.

Bodies of the Lake People were strewn upon the ground, and the powdery earth was thick with their blood. Mara's guardians were mostly still alive, since they were the ones who had heard her and obeyed. They were pressed up against the sides of the valley, trying to find shelter behind small rocks and clumps of grass. Mara saw one of them cast his spear, and it hit one of Graum's men in the thigh as he started down from the ridge. Mara recognized the man—it was Ulmei—staring at the shaft and plucking at it as if he couldn't understand what had happened. He lost his footing, cried out, and fell.

Mara searched the hillside for Graum. Was he still back behind the wall of fire? She squinted into it, holding up her hand to shield her face from the heat. She couldn't see. She glanced at her guardians and saw them looking at her. The flames would reach them if they waited much longer.

Each of them still had three or four spears apiece. There hadn't been enough targets for them to throw at. Meanwhile, the villagers who had panicked and fled were all dead or dying. The bodies lay in heaps like animal carcasses after a hunt. Mara felt tears rising to her eyes. She felt like a traitor, abandoning them; but really, they were the ones who had abandoned her.

"People!" she shouted.

The survivors turned toward her. Wordlessly, she pointed into the fire. She didn't want to shout the command.

The flames were taller than a man. Would everyone have the courage to plunge through them? "Follow!" Mara cried. She seized another of her spears, raised it, and went running toward the wall of fire.

At the last moment, her own courage almost failed her. She felt as if she was leaping into oblivion, incinerating herself and all those who followed her. Then she screamed her defiance and dived into the flickering yellow glare. Her scream turned to a scream of pain as the flames licked her skin. There was a sudden scorching smell, and it was her clothes, her hair, her eyebrows burning up in the heat.

And then, blessedly, she was through and out the other side, where the fire had already consumed the grass and the land was black and bare. Her people were following her, running desperately, yelling and covering their faces with their hands as the fire touched them.

Mara blinked. For a moment she feared she had been blinded, but it was only the smoke stinging her eyes. Her vision cleared and she saw the valley empty ahead—a path to safety. She summoned all her strength and ran madly, her feet pounding across the blackened earth, blessedly cool air rushing into her lungs.

She heard her people coming after her—and then, at the exit from the valley, she saw a half dozen figures standing high up on either side. It was Graum, she realized, with the men she had seen originally. They'd stayed here in case anyone tried to break through.

She didn't hesitate. Clearly, the only way was forward.

She screamed again, this time in rage. She veered from side to side as she ran, trying to make herself a harder target. She glimpsed something falling fast toward her, and at the last moment she threw herself down, just in time to avoid the falling spear.

She looked up and she saw the figure who had cast the spear. He was halfway up the steep side of the valley, where it opened out into gentle, rolling land. He was a big man, silhouetted against the sky. So big, she immediately knew who he was.

Mara scrambled up, reaching for another of her spears. But her pack had shifted, and the weapons were out of place. She tugged at them futilely.

Meanwhile, the figure up on the rocks raised another spear of his own, taking careful aim at her.

From behind Mara, a shaft hissed up and away in a graceful arc. Mara glanced around and saw that Lomel had thrown it. Her face was screwed up in an expression of hate.

Her spear found its target. There was a shout of pain and anger from above. The big man staggered, then hurled his own spear carelessly down into the valley.

Mara cried out in alarm as she saw it falling. "Lomel!" she screamed.

Lomel stepped backward, but she tripped and fell. The falling shaft hurtled toward her. She screamed and raised her hands instinctively, just as the spear struck her in her chest up near her shoulder, plunging deep.

Mara scrambled onto all fours and ran to Lomel where she lay in the grass. Lomel stared up at her blankly, unable to believe what had happened. She seemed to feel no pain—at least not yet.

Mara stared at her and knew with sick certainty what needed to be done. She seized the spear, placed her foot against Lomel's shoulder to brace herself, then wrenched the spear free. The barbed flint made a terrible wet noise as it came out of Lomel. With a cry of anguish, Mara cast it aside.

Lomel clapped her hand over the wound as blood started flowing freely. "Why?" she gasped.

"Come on," Mara shouted at her. She smacked the back of Lomel's hand with her fist, over the wound. "Hit it like that. While you run. It'll help stop the bleeding."

There was no more time. The rest of the guardians were streaming ahead now, dodging a couple more spears that were being cast down by the warriors on the sides of the valley. But Graum himself was no longer visible, and his men seemed to be hesitating, disconcerted by the blow that had been struck against their leader.

Lomel was still lying on the ground, staring up at Mara with an uncomprehending expression. There was no more time for talk. Mara seized the girl by her hair and hauled her onto her feet. Then she grabbed her wrist. "Run!" she screamed.

Together they ran, desperate and incoherent with fear, out of the valley where so many of their comrades had died.

Chapter 42

They ran out into the tall, dry, yellow-brown grassland. Mara glanced back and saw the sky dark with smoke from the fire. She thought she glimpsed a couple of figures still up on the rocks, but she couldn't be sure. All she knew was that no one was coming after them—for now, at least.

She saw the river not too far away, or rather, the deep, winding trench that it had carved in the soft soil. It seemed like the only possible refuge in this wide, empty land.

Once again Mara glanced behind her, and still she saw no one in pursuit. Perhaps Lomel's spear had killed Graum. Even if it had merely wounded him, he might be incapacitated. Or he might want to wait till he had gathered up the rest of his men who were still at the other end of the valley, killing the last of the Lake People who had been left behind.

Mara counted as she ran, and found twenty of her companions still left alive. Graum had probably started the fight with as many as forty on his side, but a few of those had died. He must still have at least thirty men, though. Once he gathered them all together again, he would be the one with an advantage of numbers.

All these thoughts passed through her head as she forced herself on. She realized she was making a kind of sobbing sound as she ran, because everything hurt so much. Her skin had been scorched by the fire, and it was throbbing and burning. Her chest was aching, her vision was blurring, her body was trembling, wet with sweat under her robe.

Finally she reached the miniature canyon where the

river flowed. Her people stopped when they reached the edge, because the sides were tall and steep. Mara glanced behind, and still there seemed to be no one following them across the grassland. She shrugged off her pack and threw it down into the canyon, together with her spears. Then, boldly, before she could allow herself to hesitate, she dropped down onto the ground, covered her face with her arms, and rolled over the edge.

The world spun around her. A dozen sharp, hard stones slammed into her body as she fell. And then blessedly, the slope leveled out and she found herself rolling down to the bottom, coming to a halt in some tall grass, with one of her feet in the shallow water at the edge of the river.

She was alive, she told herself, though she hardly dared to believe it. She was alive, and if she was fortunate, she might still stay alive.

She looked up and saw her people following her example, one after another. They rolled and tumbled, stirring up dust, some of them shouting in fear or pain as they bounced down the slope. But finally all of them were there at the bottom with her, bruised, burned, but otherwise unharmed—except for Lomel.

Mara went to her. The girl's face was terribly pale, and the whole of the front of her robe was saturated with blood. The spear had struck deep. Mara pried Lomel's hand away from the wound, and she found that it was still bleeding fast.

"I had to pull the spear out," Mara said, feeling a terrible burden of guilt. "You wouldn't have been able to run, otherwise. It was the only way."

Lomel nodded weakly. She said nothing. She was slumped on the ground, taking desperate gasps of air. There were red bubbles at the corners of her mouth.

Arin joined Mara. "You did the right thing," he said, placing his hand on her shoulder. "Don't blame yourself for anything, Mara."

"Feel cold," Lomel gasped. She slumped back on the stony ground and started shivering.

Mara stripped off her robe and put it over Lomel.

Then she lay beside her and hugged her close. She realized she was crying. "Be strong!" she said.

"My fault," Lomel gasped. "All my fault. All those people dead."

There was nothing Mara could say to that, because it was true.

"Forgive me?" Lomel whimpered, staring up at Mara.

"Of course." And she did. After all, there had been no malice in what Lomel had done.

"I'm sorry," Lomel gasped. "Hold me." She flung her arms around Mara and hugged her tightly. Then she let out an awful gurgling cry. She arched her back and started coughing up blood.

Mara pulled away instinctively. Lomel curled up, clutching her stomach. She vomited more blood, and she moaned; and then, she shuddered and died.

"Lomel!" Arin cried. He dropped down on his knees beside his sister. He shook her shoulder. "Please, Lomel!"

"Come." Mara felt empty now. She had no room inside her for more grief. All that mattered was that she and her people should survive. The rational part of her mind was still working, still weighing possibilities and trying to guard against dangers, even while the rest of her was trembling with exhaustion and fear. The cold, rational part of her said that it was fortunate that Lomel had died quickly, because now she wouldn't hold the rest of them back. They must move at once, as far and as fast as possible.

"Come," she said again to Arin. "There's no time to bury her."

"We shouldn't have followed you down here."

It was Shani speaking. Mara turned and faced her, feeling momentarily disoriented by the sound of her voice. Shani's eyes were wide and fearful. She looked like a deer that had been hunted in the grassland and now feared that its life was over.

"He'll find us down here, and we can't get out!" Shani cried.

"That may happen," said Mara. "But on the open land, he'd be able to see us. Down here, he won't know which way we go—upstream or downstream. The canyon twists and turns. It's a hiding place. It's our only hiding place."

Shani heard the words, but she didn't seem to grasp their meaning. She looked plaintively at Mara. Her lip trembled. "I'm scared," she said in a small, weak voice.

"So am I," said Mara. "So are we all." She looked around at her people. She counted them again. Nineteen, now, not including herself. Ten women, nine men. Torno was still there, and Mart; but young Lumo, the wanderer, was gone. Han and Opir had died—she stopped herself from thinking about the rest of them.

Mara suddenly felt furious—at Lomel, for leading so many to their deaths, and at Shani, for having let Graum live. But there was no point in dwelling on that. "Come on," Mara said. "This way." And she started toward the south.

"Why?" Torno called to her. "Can't we go north?"

"He'll expect us to go running back home," said Mara.

"But we don't know what lies south of here," Shani complained. "No one knows. Perhaps no one has ever come so far south before."

"Good," said Mara. "In that case, we'll find no enemies." She turned to Arin. "Leave her there." She tried to soften her voice, but it was starting to anger her, trying to cope with people who were so slow to see what had to be done. "She's died, Arin. We've lost her, now. Leave a spear beside her, to help her on the other side." Privately, Mara thought it was unwise to sacrifice even one of their spears. But she sensed that Arin wouldn't let go of Lomel if he couldn't make a sacrifice.

Arin nodded dumbly. He picked up Lomel's last three spears, then placed one gently beside her. He closed her fingers around it, then turned away, slipping the other two spears under the strap of his own pack.

"All right, now," said Mara. "We must hurry. We'll walk as far as we can. When one of us collapses, then we'll rest. But not till then."

Around noon, they reached a point where the river divided. There was a spot here where the water had eaten away at the wedge-shaped section of the wall separating the two streams. A long, narrow cavity lay beneath the overhanging rock. It was a good hiding place, and a good resting place.

Wordlessly, Mara pointed to it. One by one, the people slumped down and crawled into the gap, groaning with exhaustion.

Mara lay flat on her back and closed her eyes. She actually felt secure here, with the slanting shelf of rock less than an arm's length above her and the sandy ground under her back, cool and hard. She felt herself trembling. It had been such a hard, terrible thing, to see her people running to their deaths. It had been so terrifying to be trapped in that narrow valley, with Graum's men laying waste to everyone. Mara reached up and covered her face with her hands—then gave a little cry of pain. The skin on her forehead was raw and blistered. The backs of her hands, too, were burned. Suddenly she felt overwhelmed with self-pity. It wasn't her fault that this had all happened to her. She had warned her people about Graum on the day after he came to the tribe. She'd warned them! They hadn't listened!

She found herself crying. Nearby, she heard other people sobbing, too. Maybe that was natural enough. It was terrible to be weak, Mara thought to herself; but perhaps, now, it was necessary.

Much later, the canyon was full of purple shadows. Mara and her people had slept a little, and they had eaten a little. The water in the river was bitter with mineral salts, but it seemed good to drink, all the same.

She eased herself out from the hiding place, and she looked around. It had been a mistake, she realized, to feel secure here. If Graum was still alive and had followed them down into the canyon, he could track them just as they had tracked him. Probably he would have started looking for them upstream, but sooner or later he would have realized his error and turned back.

"We must move on," Mara said softly.

There were groans of protest. "Sister, Graum may not

even be alive," said Shani. "Wasn't it him that Lomel hit with her spear?"

"Yes," said Mara. "I think it was. But we don't know how badly he was wounded. Do you want to guess, and have your life depend on it?"

Reluctantly, giving little cries of pain as they moved their aching muscles and their burned hands, the people struggled out of their resting place. Mara looked at them, and she felt a brief twinge of compassion. These were the ones, after all, who had listened to her when she screamed at them not to run back out of the valley.

She went from one to the next, looking each of them in the eyes, touching them, hugging them. "We will survive," she said, over and again. "Trust me, people. We will survive."

"But will we ever see our homeland again?" someone asked. It was Ewna. Her parents had been killed, back by the lake, and she looked lost and scared.

Mara went to her. "Ewna, we may never see our homeland," she said quietly. "But I say to you: We will survive." She patted her shoulder. "Be strong, now."

She turned, then, and contemplated the fork in the river. One way branched toward the east. The other continued south. Which should they choose?

She glanced at her people. They were looking at her, waiting for her to decide. So it was to be her responsibility, and if she guessed wrongly, they might find themselves following a stream that petered out and left them without water in this strange, arid wilderness.

Mara remembered her dream of the eagle, and her mother's voice. She had thought that the dream had lied, but perhaps she had simply misunderstood it. She was much farther south than she had traveled to the Silver River People, and she was still alive now, while those who had turned back were dead.

South, then. She started forward. "Walk in the shallow water," she told her followers. "Try not to leave tracks for anyone to see. If Graum comes after us, I don't want it to be easy for him to find us."

*   *   *

They walked through the evening, and they continued as darkness fell. The Moon was brighter tonight, and the canyon was a mysterious place of silver light and deep, black shadow. The river flowed slowly, and its surface was like a mirror reflecting the jagged walls of rock.

They had ceased stepping in the water. It had made the leather of their moccasins heavy, chafing everyone's feet. Now they picked their way along the narrow, gravelly strip of land beside the river, and every little sound seemed loud in the stillness.

There was something almost sacred about this place, Mara thought. She had never seen a landscape so stark and lifeless, and yet it seemed familiar to her, as if her spirit had traveled here. Perhaps, she thought, she could actually learn to enjoy this barren land, even though it was so different from the one she knew.

Around the middle of the night, her people began protesting that they were too tired to go on. Mara thought she could have forced them to continue a little farther, but she didn't want to stretch their loyalty, or their strength, to the breaking point. She thought, too, that Graum was probably a safe distance behind them—assuming he was still alive.

Once again, they found a place where the water had eroded a gully out of the rock. They lay there, eating and resting, not speaking.

As Mara ate her rations, she saw that there were barely enough for two more days. Other people must be noticing the same thing; but no one said anything about it. Perhaps their faith was so strong, they genuinely believed her when she told them they would survive. Or perhaps she had made them feel afraid to complain anymore.

"I think," said Arin, "the walls of the canyon are lower here than when we last stopped."

Mara looked up. He was right, she realized. Was that good or bad? Sooner or later, they would need to find a way to climb out. On the other hand, if the canyon was shallower, that must mean that the river had been less powerful cutting its way through the land. She was still haunted by the idea that they might follow it to a point where it just disappeared into dry earth, baked by the sun.

"We should sleep," she told them. "We'll start again at dawn, and then, my people, if we continue far enough, I'm sure we'll find something to help us, just as we did when we followed the green valley all the way down to the plain."

No one said anything. They were too weary to speak. All they wanted now was to rest.

She shared that feeling—and yet, strangely, her mind was still alert. She found herself thinking ahead, trying to imagine all the challenges and ordeals that might still be in store. And then she found herself missing Lomel. Lomel had become haunted by her own fears and longings, and she had retreated from Mara; yet still she had been the only person Mara had ever completely trusted and cared for.

"Mara?" The voice was a whisper, close beside her.

She started. The voice sounded eerily familiar, and for a moment Mara feared that it was Lomel's spirit calling to her. But then she looked around and felt foolish as she realized that it was Arin speaking her name. His voice sounded a little like his sister when he spoke softly.

"What is it?" she whispered back.

"I want to thank you, Mara," he said.

She saw his face as a black silhouette against the moonlit canyon wall. She smelled his scent, and she felt the warmth of him close to her. Even though it had been hot under the sun in this barren land, she realized it was growing cold now in the depth of the night.

"Why do you want to thank me?" she whispered.

"For being brave. For leading us out of the trap that Graum laid. For saving our lives."

She heard the words, and she felt herself grow weak inside. Perhaps this was all she had ever really wanted, to feel worthy and be appreciated by people who trusted her. Arin's statement was so simple, yet it affected her as if he had reached in and touched the most sensitive part of her. She couldn't think of anything to say.

"Most of all," Arin went on, "I want to thank you for forgiving Lomel. It was a kind thing to do, Mara. You knew it was her fault that our people went down into that narrow valley. But still, you forgave her, and it eased her pain when she was dying."

"I can't blame a person who has no malice toward me," said Mara.

Arin nodded slowly. "You're a good, fair person, Mara," he whispered to her. "I admire you." He hesitated. "But this isn't the time to say more than that."

"Thank you, Arin."

He reached out, fumbled, and found her hand. He squeezed it briefly—and that was eerie, because it was something that Lomel used to do. "Good night," he whispered.

"Good night," she said. She felt confused and uncomfortable, and in a way she wished he hadn't intruded on her, disturbing her contemplation and her peace of mind. But then, as he shifted away, she found herself missing his presence close by. He was a sweet-natured man, a gentle man, never trying to prove himself. Fleetingly, she wondered if she could ever feel drawn to him as she had to Kormor. It hardly seemed likely; he lacked the flamboyance that had always excited her in men.

Well, this was all too difficult for her to think about. Arin had pledged his loyalty, and that was what really counted in this time of constant danger.

Chapter 43

Around noon the next day, it began to seem as if Mara's worst fears were coming true. The canyon had grown narrower, and it was so shallow, she could almost see over the rim. The river, meanwhile, was flowing sluggishly and had an oily, greenish look.

The twists and turns of the canyon made it impossible for her to see very far ahead, but she felt certain that the river wasn't taking them anywhere. And everyone else could surely see what she was seeing.

As the day wore on, her people talked less and less, till finally they became completely silent. *They all know,* she thought to herself. They feared she was leading them into a wasteland where there would be nothing to drink. And they were waiting to see when she would admit it, and what she would do.

Finally she called a halt. She stood for a moment, surveying them all. They were ragged, windblown, scorched by fire, smeared with dirt. They looked desperate and exhausted. "It's time," she said, "to look over the rim and find where we are." She pointed ahead at a piece of the canyon wall that had collapsed on the opposite side of the river, leaving a steep slope strewn with loose earth and stones. "I'll climb out and see what there is to be seen."

"We can't go back." It was Shani speaking. The fear that had haunted her face the previous day was gone, but still she sounded plaintive. "He could be alive, and he could be following us."

"Yes," said Mara. "I know."

Shani glanced at the people around her, then back at Mara. "So what are you going to do?"

"Be patient," Mara said. "Let me look around up on the plain. Then, perhaps, I'll be able to answer you."

She turned away before Shani could voice any more doubts, and she splashed across the shallow river, leaving her people behind. Inside herself, Mara was worried; yet she didn't feel despair. She still had a sense that in some way she had been destined to come here. Surely, she thought, the spirits hadn't lied to her.

It was hard work, climbing out, because the earth and gravel kept sliding underfoot. Finally, though, she reached the plain above, and she cautiously raised her head.

To the north, in the far, far distance, was a hazy, jagged, purple line—the mountains where she and her people had come from. Closer to her, there was a small range of low, mounded hills like the ones where Graum had staged his attack. And all around, the plain seemed to stretch away forever, carpeted with prairie grass.

There were animals grazing close by. In fact, as Mara turned her head, she saw one of them only a dozen paces away. Instinctively, she ducked down, afraid that it might attack her. Then she realized that it was eating the grass and it had hooves, not claws. So it wasn't a predator. It looked like a bison, but it had a thicker, shaggier black coat, and a larger hump between its shoulder blades. It showed no fear of her, and with a feeling of awe, Mara realized it might never have seen a human being before.

Slowly, cautiously, she climbed out and confronted the great beast. It stared back at her, showing little interest. She turned to call to her people—but then she saw the vista that stretched away to the south.

She stopped and stared. There were mountains in the far distance that were completely different from the range that lay to the north. The peaks were as red as raw skin, and the rock was striped with horizontal strata of white and brown, as if one layer had been piled on top of another.

But even this wasn't the real source of her amazement. Not so far from where she stood—just a thousand paces—was a wide, fat pillar of rock, isolated and alone in the prairie.

Mara shaded her eyes and squinted up at it. She felt suddenly dizzy. Without a doubt, she had seen it before in every detail. This was the place the eagle had tried to take her to, and the sanctuary that her mother had told her to seek.

"People!" she cried. "Come here!"

They heard the urgency in her voice. She watched them as they splashed across the river and scrambled up the slope on their hands and knees. Soon they were gathering around her, staring first at the beast close by, then at the mesa a little farther away.

"I've seen this place!" Mara cried out to them. "I know, now, that we'll be safe here." She felt excited, filled with new confidence, and it seemed to her that if she could just explain herself, everyone would understand. "Many days ago," she said, "before I set out to the Silver River People, I went out at night and lay down on the Rock that Moves, and I dreamed of this place. I saw it clearly. I heard my mother's voice, and she called to me, and she told me that here we could find a refuge."

Her people glanced uneasily at each other. They didn't smile, and they didn't seem reassured. They looked deeply uneasy.

She turned from one face to the next. "Don't you believe me?"

"You saw this in a dream?" It was Shani, sounding doubtful. "And you heard our mother speak?"

"Yes!" Mara glanced around. "Look, you see the beasts grazing here? We'll have all the food we can eat. And the river is close by. And when we climb up on top of the mesa, we'll be safe. Don't you see?"

"But this is a strange place to be," said Ewna. She eyed the animal close by. "It's not natural for a beast to have no fear. And it's not right for rocks to be red. Perhaps you did see these things in a vision, Mara. But we did not."

She understood, then. At the backs of their minds, they had still been hoping to return to the land that they loved. Shani, in particular, had been looking forward to the time when the village by the lake could be restored and everyone would follow the old ways once more, serving her as their Chieftain.

But at some point during the past two days, Mara had finally given up hope of ever returning to the village by the lake. More than that, she realized she no longer yearned for it. Her life had never been easy there. It held memories that were filled more with pain than with pleasure.

"People, hear me," she said. "I'm not saying we should stay here forever, only that we have a refuge here. We have food, and we have water, and we have a secure place to stay. Isn't this more than we dared to hope for?"

"We don't know that there's a way to climb up onto that great rock," said Arin, sensible and practical as always.

"I'm certain we can discover a way. Come, let's go and find out." She started walking quickly across the land.

Behind her, she heard her people murmuring uneasily to each other. But she felt so confident, their doubts didn't worry her. Soon enough, they would see that she was right. They had to.

As she approached the mesa, she realized that it was taller than she'd originally thought. It rose up out of the plain like a vast, fantastic tree stump, with sides that were almost vertical. Its flat top was rimmed with sparse, dark green bushes and stunted trees that had somehow found a toehold in the rock.

Mara walked around the base of the mesa, and she stared up at it in wonder. Like the canyon in the moonlight, this place, too, seemed sacred. It felt infinitely old, as if it existed outside of the normal cycle of things. Plants grew, they flowered, and they died; but this great rock looked as if it had endured forever without change.

Halfway around it, she came to a fissure that ran up one side. It was just wider than a person. She saw she could climb it by bracing herself with her back against one side of the gap and her feet against the other. That would be uncomfortable, but it would be possible.

"Here!" she called out to her people. She waited impatiently for them to follow her around the rock. "Here, you see?"

They gathered close to her, as if they were afraid to stand too far apart. "I suppose it could be done," Arin said.

"But how will we get our packs up there? And food, and water?" said Shani.

"We'll place ourselves at intervals along the fissure and pass them up to each other," said Mara. "And maybe there's water at the top. We don't know till we go up there."

Shani shook her head. "Sister, this is all so strange."

Mara felt her patience unraveling. "Isn't it time for you to trust my judgment?" she snapped. She looked at their faces. "Have I misled you, ever? Where's your faith in me? I warned you about Graum. My vision that time spoke truly. I warned you not to run down into the narrow valley where he'd hidden his men. And I warned you, when we overthrew him in our own village, that he had to be killed." She glared for a moment at Shani as she said that. Then she swept her arm in a circle, taking in the endless plain. "Do you see any other place where we can be safe?"

"Mara. Please." Arin stepped forward. He held up his hand. "Be calm. This is a strange new place, and a wild new idea of yours. We need time to consider it."

Mara suddenly remembered when Arin had stood up at that meeting in her Clan House—the crucial meeting where he had told everyone to trust her. He had persuaded them then with his calm, sensible speech. She was always too impatient, and when people were reluctant to follow, she got angry with them, and her anger turned them against her.

She struggled to control herself. "You're right, Arin," she said. "Look, why don't you decide the best way to proceed? Meanwhile, I'll climb to the top of the mesa, so we'll know what there is up there."

"Good," said Arin. He smiled at her. "Very good."

She lay down her pack and her spears, and she went to the fissure. Meanwhile, Arin and the others went back to the river to gather up the possessions that they'd left there.

Mara found that the climb to the top of the mesa was

actually a little easier than she'd expected, bracing her back against one face of rock and pushing herself up with her feet opposite. The rock was pitted and worn, giving her many footholds. In a short time, she was clambering out onto the top of the mesa.

She had imagined it as a flat slab, but what she found was very different. There were rills and gullies and little caves where the soft stone had been eroded by wind and rain. Small trees were growing here and there, offering some shade. And in the center of the mesa was a deep pool of water—rainwater, Mara realized. She ran over to it, stumbling across the fissured rock, and she dropped down on her knees at the edge of the pool. Cautiously, she cupped her hand and lifted a little of the water to her lips. She tested it on her tongue. It was tainted with silt, but there was no hint of an alkaline flavor that might warn her not to drink it. Nor were there any bones nearby of creatures that had drunk from it and been poisoned.

She sat back and found herself smiling. This was a little world of her own here. If they killed and preserved enough meat, her people could be secure for days or even months.

She looked out across the vast plain. The canyon that they had walked along was a zigzag line, disappearing into the haze. There was a special grandeur to this place that excited her even while it soothed her spirit.

She heard shouts from below. For a moment she felt herself tensing, fearing some new calamity. But the shouts were not shouts of alarm. She hurried to the edge of the mesa and peered down. Her people were standing around one of the big, tame beasts that had been grazing on the prairie grass. They had speared it and killed it, and it was lying on its side under the warm sun.

So there would be no more concern about food. In the distance, she could see hundreds—thousands, even—of the big beasts scattered across the prairie. There were far more than her people could consume, even if they devoted the rest of their lives to it. True, Graum might still be out there, searching for her. But for the time being, she felt safe.

*   *   *

By the evening, Arin had coaxed everyone into accepting the pillar of rock as their new home, and they actually seemed happy, sitting around a fire, feasting on fresh meat. The only thing they really lacked was wood. Mara was reluctant to cut any of the small, stunted trees, since they looked as if they had taken many years to grow. Fortunately, though, the plain was littered with dried droppings from the great beasts that grazed there, and the droppings burned slow and hot.

Already, Mara was planning ahead. They needed to make braided leather ropes so they could hoist supplies from the plain below. Then they would need to search the land nearby for a source of flints. The rock here was different from anything she had seen before, so red and sandy it was hardly like rock at all. She was concerned that they might find no easy source of new spearheads and tools.

Her people started singing one of the old songs. Their faces were flushed and happy. They had full stomachs, and they felt secure for the first time in many days. Shani was leading the singing, as she always did, and her spirit was infectious. She made all the separate people feel like one, and they needed that.

Strange, Mara thought: When her people had felt in danger, they had clustered around and turned to her for leadership. But now that they felt safe, she wasn't the one that they wanted. It gave her a pang to see that they only needed her when they felt threatened, but maybe they were right, in a way, to want someone now who made them feel calm and secure, rather than someone who was still full of restless ambition.

At the end of one of the songs, she stood up and excused herself from the circle around the fire. She walked to the northern edge of the mesa, stepping carefully in the darkness. It would be foolish and ironic if she hurt herself now by falling, after all the dangers she had survived.

She squatted down near the edge and stared into the night. In her mind, she thanked the spirit of her mother for guiding her to this special place.

The clouds were a little thicker tonight than they had

been on the previous night. The moonlight was so dim, Mara could barely see the vast sweep of the plain. But as she scanned it, there was one thing that she saw almost immediately. In the distance, perhaps a day's trek from where she sat, there was a tiny, flickering point of light.

The warmth that had grown inside her, holding her like a friend, suddenly drained away. She felt the smile fading on her face. A breath of wind touched her cheeks and rustled the leaves of the twisted tree that stood close by, and she pulled her robe closer around her.

The point of light was a campfire; she had no doubt of that. Of course, there could be another tribe out there on the plain—but she didn't think so. If the beasts had seen people out here, they would have shown more fear.

Mara realized that to some extent she, too, had been seduced by the comfort of the songs and the feasting. She had pretended to herself that she didn't need to think about Graum and his men. But that had been a fantasy. Graum was still alive, and he had tracked them part of the way south. Sometime the next day, he would reach the mesa.

Mara lay on her back, staring up into the sky, searching for an answer. Surely, in this sacred place, she would see or hear some voice to guide her, just as she had on the Rock that Moves. Surely the spirits wouldn't desert her now.

In her mind, she called out to the spirit of her mother, and to Lizel, and even to Laena, the First Mother of her tribe. *I've been strong,* she thought. *I've worked hard to protect my people. I've done everything that I could do. But now I need your help.*

She waited and she listened, but all she heard was the wind sighing around the mesa and the rustling of the trees. Her mind was as empty as a dry stream bed. No words came to her.

At first she felt betrayed. But then, gradually, it came to her that the spirits had already done their part. They had guided her to this place; it was up to her now to find out how to keep what she had won.

She tried to imagine what would happen the next day,

when Graum arrived. He wouldn't be foolish enough to come close enough for them to strike him with their spears. He would make a camp out on the plain, and he would wait there with ample game for his warriors to eat and water for them to drink. He could sit there for days or months, till the Lake People ran out of food and were forced to come down.

Mara and her people might try to sneak down on a moonless night. They could try to creep away in the darkness, but even if they succeeded, the next day Graum could track them and pursue them.

So what could she do?

She could act now, this very night, and deploy her people out beside the canyon to ambush Graum and his men when he arrived. But she didn't know for sure that all his men would be down in the canyon. He might keep at least a couple of scouts up on the plain itself, watching for danger as they made their way south.

She could try to rouse her people for a battle out on the plain, facing Graum's men squarely the next day. But would the Lake People be strong enough or brave enough now for such a confrontation? She could hear them still singing together around the fire. It would be hard to rekindle their fighting spirit, and even if she succeeded, Graum still outnumbered them. The fight could turn into another massacre.

Well, she could lead her people back down to the plain tonight and head farther south, trying to stay one day ahead, just as Graum had stayed one day ahead of her when they were traveling down the green valley. But what if the river disappeared into a trickle of mud? Then they would be stranded.

In any case, Mara couldn't bear the thought of fleeing from her pursuer. Frustration welled up inside her. To find this special place, to feel secure at last, and then to have it taken away—that was intolerable.

Think harder, she told herself. *There has to be a way. Learn from your enemies.*

She thought again of sly old Ulfor. But what could she use as bait to tempt Graum? How could she make sure that he would be the one this time to act foolishly and expose himself to danger?

She considered his weaknesses—his pride, and his overriding need for revenge. And then, suddenly, clearly, she saw a way. It came into her mind as if it had already been there, fully formed.

Mara heard a footstep. She turned and looked up, and she saw Arin squatting beside her. "Won't you come back and join us for the rest of the songs?" he said quietly. "I think people would like to see you around the fire."

She sat up, blinking, returning from the world of her thoughts to the real world around her. "Look there," she said, pointing out across the land at the tiny point of light. And then, after Arin had seen it and understood what it meant, she took his arm. "I need your help, Arin. I've thought long and hard, out here, on my own. When I tell you all the things that I've considered, I think you'll agree that my plan is the only one that has a good chance of saving us. But after I tell you what it is, you must be the one to explain it to our people. You talk to them far more persuasively than I ever can." She squeezed his arm. "If you help me, Arin, I think this place can be truly ours."

Chapter 44

The next day, as the sun climbed high, she stood alone at the base of the mesa, leaning her shoulders against the rough, red rock. She waited, knowing that this, now, was the final test. The beasts of the prairie grazed nearby, ignoring her. The land lay quiet and empty under the warm sun. She stood, and she waited.

For a little while, she closed her eyes, trying to link herself with the spirit that she sensed in the mesa. With the sun hot on her face, she tilted her head up and spread her arms, pressing her palms against the rock, praying for it to help her overcome her enemies. It had stood on this plain for so many seasons, rooted in the land, untouched by time. Surely it could share some of its strength with her.

When she opened her eyes and stared up into the deep blue pool of the sky, she felt no different. Yet she believed that if the land and the mesa possessed a spirit, it was linked with hers. That thought gave her new courage as she looked out over the tall yellow grass swaying in the wind.

Mara carried no spear. She had not even brought her flint knife. She wore a simple loose deerskin robe, and that was all. She could feel the gritty soil directly under the naked soles of her feet. Arin had argued with her, urging her to wear her moccasins; but she had refused.

She thought briefly of her people—and yes, she still thought of them as hers, as long as Graum lived. Arin had spoken to them last night, and he had spoken well, as she'd known he would. At first the people had argued against her decision—Shani, especially—but Arin had been persistent, and in the end he had prevailed. Reluctantly, nervously, everyone had agreed to do as she wanted, though she'd seen in their eyes that they doubted it would work, and many of them feared that she would die out here on the prairie.

Would they support her when the time came? Some of them she could trust. They would be loyal, and they would be brave. Unfortunately, though, she would need the support of every one of them, and there would be no way of knowing if she had that support till it was too late.

Mara breathed deeply, trying to banish the uncertainties from her mind. She turned her face away from the sky and looked across at the plain. As she did so, she saw tiny dark shapes in the distance, climbing up from the river canyon at the same spot where she and her people had emerged the previous day.

So the moment had finally come. There was no point in worrying now about her preparations. It was too late to do anything more.

Mara pressed her palms one last time against the mesa, trying to draw sustenance from the rock. Then she pushed herself out from it and walked forward across the plain, unarmed, barefoot, to face her enemies.

She felt fearful now, as if a fist was closing around her insides, making it hard for her to breathe. All her instincts told her to turn and run.

In the distance she saw the men pausing, and she sensed that they were turning toward her. She drew three quick breaths, then raised her hands and cupped them around her mouth. "Graum!" she screamed.

There was no reply. Had he heard her? Was he with them? She thought she saw some of the men glancing at each other. It was hard to tell, because they were so far away. She could see their spears, though. Where she stood now, she was out of range, but with every step she took, she was making herself more vulnerable.

"Graum!" she called again. "I have no spear. I have no knife." She stretched out her hands, showing her empty arms. "I want to talk, Graum! Leave your men where they are. Come forward. Meet me alone, just you and me, if you have the courage."

Would he do it? He was a proud man, and she was challenging him—again. She was gambling that he was too proud simply to cut her down in the wide-open plain. She was hoping, also, that he would be puzzled by the way she was presenting herself, alone and unarmed. He would suspect a trap, of course. But there was nowhere for anyone to hide out here on the plain. The grass wasn't thick enough to conceal a person, and a few stunted bushes were the only other vegetation nearby.

Graum would suspect that people were hiding up on the mesa, perhaps, or behind it; but as long as he kept his distance, he would feel safe.

She walked on, with the sun high in the sky looking down on her. She reached a patch of land where no grass grew and the sandy soil dipped slightly below the surrounding plain. She stepped around this little bare area, so that she would remain in full view. "Graum, leave your men, leave your spear!" she called. "Come and talk, Graum!"

Now, finally, one man separated himself from the rest. Mara shaded her eyes. Yes, he was taller than the others. And he carried no spear.

The tension inside her clenched so tight, she feared she might not be able to go on. She felt a tingling pain, as if she had just been struck in the chest. She gasped and winced, clutching herself. Her heart was racing, but its beats came erratically. She had to stop for a moment and reach down inside herself, trying to loosen the knot that was crippling her.

She took slow breaths. She told herself to have faith. She had been brought here not by chance, but by a vision. There was a purpose to her being here with her people. She could not possibly fail now.

The tension eased a little, and her heart stopped fluttering—though it was still pounding fast, and her throat was so dry, she couldn't swallow. She forced herself to walk a little farther on.

Graum was clearly visible, taking slow, measured strides, glancing cautiously to either side, while his men remained back by the river canyon. There were as many of them as Mara had feared—at least thirty, she thought. But she drew some satisfaction from seeing a bloody strip of hide lashed around Graum's left arm, which hung uselessly at his side. Lomel's spear was responsible for that, Mara realized. The big man was not invulnerable, after all. He had been wounded, and he might have been killed if the spear had only struck him a little farther in.

That thought gave her a little more confidence as she faced him. She paused, trembling, hoping that he couldn't see or smell her fear. Meanwhile, he continued walking toward her. She could see his face now, and he looked malevolent, hungry, like a carnivorous animal that wanted to knock her down and rip her open.

"Stop there!" she shouted to him when he was just six paces away.

He grinned, baring his ruined teeth at her. "You think I'm going to obey your orders, girl?" He gestured at the prairie with his good arm. "There's no one to stop me from doing whatever I please."

But he paused just the same. His curiosity, after all, had gotten the better of him. His mean little eyes gleamed as they studied her.

Mara drew a deep breath. She clenched her fists. "Why are you here, Graum?"

His grin became a sneer. "I've come to kill you, girl. You and the dregs of your stupid people."

His face was grimy from his days on the trek south, and it had been reddened by the sun. It loomed like an angry god. "Leave us," Mara shouted at him. "You've murdered too many of us already. You're a hateful, evil man. If you leave us now, I'll let you live."

He let loose a derisive laugh. His little eyes narrowed into slits. "You killed my wife, girl. And my son, Joh, died back there." He gestured behind him. "I'm going to make you pay for that."

Mara wondered if Joh had been the one that her spear had struck. She found herself hoping that it might be so.

"I'm going to take your life away," he went on. "You understand that?" He reached under his robe and pulled out a knife. She saw the sun gleam on the flint.

Mara felt herself weaken. He was so huge, so powerful. *Courage,* she told herself. *Courage!*

"And after I finish with you," he went on, "I'll kill your people. If they're up there"—he nodded toward the mesa—"I'll wait till they starve. If they're on the plain, I'll track them to the end. You understand that, girl? They're all going to die. But you'll die first."

"I have no weapons," she cried out. Once again she spread her arms.

His lips pulled back from his teeth. "I see that," he said. And he started forward.

She smelled the bloodlust in him. The sight of her had roused his hunger to the point where it ruled him completely. He wasn't cautious anymore. If she ran, he would follow.

She turned back toward the mesa, and she ran.

She felt as if she had never run so fast—not even when she had run from the narrow valley where her people had been slaughtered. The gritty earth was hot under her feet. The sun glared down at her. All the tension that had clenched tight inside her was suddenly released in a furious, desperate burst of energy. The dry grass lashed her bare legs. The hot air rasped in and out of her lungs. *Don't stumble,* she told herself. *If you stumble, you die!* The world seemed to tremble and shimmer in front of her. *Faster,* she told herself. *Faster!*

But even so, he was gaining on her. She heard his heavy footsteps thudding into the soil. His legs were twice as long as hers. There was no way, ultimately, that she could outrun him, and he must be aware of that.

Of course, it would have been more prudent for him to step back, call to his men, and get them to send a hail of spears down upon her. But he saw no danger out here, and he wanted the satisfaction of killing her with his own hands.

He was getting so close to her, she imagined she could sense the heat of him. She felt a wave of desperation. He had such bulk, she hadn't imagined that he would be able to run quite so fast. She gave a little cry of pure fear as she tried to find just a grain more of strength inside her.

Something touched her shoulder. It was his hand. She screamed—and he heard the scream, and he let out an exultant cry. He wanted her to scream. He wouldn't kill her quickly, she was sure of that. He would enjoy her pain.

She saw the little shallow dip in the land that she had walked around before. She clenched her fists and now, finally, she found that last little bit of extra strength that she needed. She took one, two, three steps—and she leaped. For an instant she feared she would fall short, and panic rose up like a wave. But then her feet reached the ground beyond—and at the same time, behind her, she heard a shout of surprise.

Mara skidded to a halt. She turned. Still full of fear, still trembling, she looked back the way she had come.

There was a terrible tortured bellow. It came from a hole in the ground—a deep, wide hole that had opened up where the shallow depression had been.

Cautiously, gasping for breath, still not quite daring to believe that she was safe, Mara ventured back. The bellowing was louder now and full of agony.

She hesitated, then took one last step and peered down.

Ten spears had been planted in a pit that had been dug during the night. The spears had been deeply embedded in the soil, with their points facing upward. And now six of them had impaled Graum.

His great weight had sent him plummeting down when the ground opened up under him, and now the cruel flints were working their way deeper into his flesh as he struggled to free himself. Mara saw one of the spearheads break through his belly, having pushed through him from behind. Blood started pulsing out, vivid red under the noonday sun.

Another spear pierced him, emerging through the side of his right arm. And another, poking through his abdomen.

Mara stared at the horrifying sight and she started shaking so much, she feared she could no longer stand. "Die!" she screamed at him. Her face was wet, she realized. She was crying. "Die, you horrible man!"

He looked up at her with eyes full of pain and fury. He tried to throw his flint knife at her, but his arm was impaled, and his muscles wouldn't obey him. The flint tumbled out of his hand and landed harmlessly beside him in the pit.

"There's more than one way," she shouted at him, "to kill a big, ugly beast." She waited a moment, and she saw the slow understanding in his eyes. He remembered, and maybe he even saw the justice of it.

He grimaced, clenching his teeth, trying to deprive her of the pleasure of his screams. His face contorted, his head fell back, and he closed his eyes.

She almost weakened then. Even now it seemed wrong for her to stand and watch a man die such a terrible death. But then she looked up and saw his people coming toward her. They were moving uncertainly, because it seemed inconceivable that the big man could have been outwitted by her. It must seem even more difficult to believe that she could have killed him.

Still, they had heard him scream. And she was standing alone on the plain now. They started moving more purposefully toward her, raising their spears.

Once again, Mara turned and ran. This time, though, she had no need to draw so deeply on her strength. She loped across the land, and she looked up and gave a shrill cry.

She no longer had any doubt that her people would respond. Even from their high hiding place, they would have been able to see Graum fall into the pit, and that alone would have given them fresh confidence.

Figures rose at the edge of the mesa. The men on the plain looked up and saw them, and they hesitated. Mara could imagine them judging the distance with their eyes and thinking that they must still be safe. But, of course, they were wrong.

The Lake People cast their spears—not with their bare hands, but with the bones that Mara had given them back when she had trained them in the village by the Great Lake. The spears flew out high and far. Impossibly far.

Graum's men shouted in surprise. Mara saw them

standing out there on the plain, and she felt like calling out to them: *Run, you fools!*

But they couldn't believe what they saw. They were too stunned, too confused. They bumped into one another. They backed away a few steps, but by the time they actually turned to run, it was too late.

The first wave of spears felled fully half of the men. The others stared down at their comrades, then looked back up at the mesa. Finally, now, they started fleeing—but another wave of spears was cutting through the air, and ten more men were screaming, falling down on the plain.

There were only six left now, scattering out from the scene of the massacre. More spears came raining down, and even now the men were still not out of range. Most of the spears fell wide, but two found their targets.

Mara shuddered. She felt suddenly overwhelmed—with relief, and with guilt. Some of the men out there were her own kin, and no matter what they had done, it still violated her deepest principles to cause their deaths.

She turned suddenly and paced back toward the hole in the ground where Graum had fallen. Along the way, she seized a spear that had fallen short. The smooth shaft in her hand added fuel to the determination which she felt.

She reached the edge of the pit and looked down into it. There was a deep pool of blood around Graum, but even so, he was still alive. He was grunting, struggling desperately to breathe.

"All this killing," she shouted down at him. "All this hate. All of it came because of you!"

Weakly, he opened his eyes.

Mara's fury crested. With an inarticulate cry, she cast her spear. The point struck him in the chest with such power, it plunged through him and into the ground below, piercing his heart.

Graum shouted in agony, and he died.

Chapter 45

Some of Graum's men were merely wounded. Mara had foreseen this, and she had decided beforehand what she must do. Clearly, the job had to be done while her people were still making their way down from the mesa. If she waited, and if Shani saw the situation, Mara knew what her sister would say—that any man might change, and it was wrong to kill. After all, Arin had served Graum, hadn't he? There could be others who would come to their senses, now that their leader was dead.

Mara knew how persuasive the argument would be, because she felt its power herself. And yet she had to resist it. These men had done far more than Arin had ever done; they had burned the village by the lake, and they had slain the innocent people who ran from the flames. They had pursued her, and they had tried to destroy the very last remnants of her tribe.

Mara was tempted to think that they would lose their killing lust now that Graum had gone. But at the same time, the survival of her people was at stake. There were so few left alive, the tribe might not survive if any more of them died.

So she went among the wounded men and she slew them. She tried not to look at their faces. She worked quickly, as if she were killing animals at the end of a hunt. One man actually got up and tried to run from her, with a spear trailing from his thigh. Weeping, she threw her own spear and brought him down.

Finally, while her people came to her across the plain, calling out in sorrow and dismay at all the bloodshed, Mara sank down on the ground. All the courage flew out of her, and she felt no stronger than a wounded bird.

She clutched herself and sobbed, overwhelmed by the horror of everything that had happened.

She left it to her people to cope with the grim business of burying their enemies. Excavating the sandy soil was easy enough—just as easy as it had been, the previous night, to dig the pit that Graum had plunged into.

Mara stood to one side, watching while Shani organized the villagers to tackle the grisly task. They started digging, and for a long while during the hot afternoon, the only sound was of bones and sticks and hands scooping the dirt away. No one spoke; no one looked up.

Mara felt sure that they must disapprove of what she had done, and they might even fear her a little for her ruthlessness—and her courage. After all, hadn't she stood alone against Graum, with no weapons to defend herself? After a while, she walked away and climbed to the top of the mesa. She sat alone there till the job was done.

She wondered what had happened to the four men who had managed to outrun the hail of spears. She was sure they wouldn't dare to come back after seeing Graum and all their companions killed. Perhaps, she thought, they would survive. Or perhaps, one day, she would find their bones out on the prairie.

As the afternoon turned into evening and the sky dimmed from blue to purple, the plain became lost in deepening grayness. But the mesa was high enough to catch the last golden light of the setting sun. It seemed as if it was suspended in space, a magic island amid a mysterious ocean of shadow. Maybe that was why Mara found herself feeling such affinity for the prairie. Its flat expanse reminded her of the lake where she had spent so many hours and days just daydreaming, staring out over the water.

She saw the Moon creeping above the horizon, raising its face toward her. *Thank you, Mother Moon,* she said inside her head. *Thank you for protecting me.* Had the Moon Spirit really looked after her? Mara didn't know, really, what to believe. All she knew was that she had reached inside herself for more strength than she'd ever imagined she could have, and she had found it waiting there. Lizel had been right, after all.

For a short time—less than two weeks, all told—her tribe had been entirely hers. She liked to think that she had led it wisely and safely. After all, her people were far more secure now than they had been before.

She heard them laboriously climbing up to join her, and she got to her feet, trying to prepare herself to meet them. Would they be thankful, or would they look at her askance, as if she was so different from them, the gulf could never be bridged? She found it impossible to guess.

They reached the top, one by one, and she greeted them. Some of them seemed somber; others had been crying. There were some who couldn't look her in the eyes at all. "Thank you," she said gently, "for your efforts. And thank you for defending me when I was alone down there on the plain."

Finally all of them had gathered around her. They glanced at one another, and at Shani, as if they had agreed beforehand that something needed to be said. And sure enough, it was Shani who stepped forward. "Sister," she said. "I must speak."

Mara felt weary, drained by everything that had happened, and she wasn't sure that she wanted to hear what her sister had to say. "Perhaps I can speak for you," she said. "Graum is dead, now. The task which I tackled is done. You gave me the right to lead this tribe, so long as our enemy was alive. And now that he is dead, the time has come for me to surrender the tribe to you, as we originally agreed."

There was a long silence. Mara had expected them to be relieved that she was surrendering her authority without even being asked to do so. She wondered why they still seemed uncomfortable.

"Sister—" Shani began.

"It's probably for the best," Mara interrupted her. "I saw last night, Shani, how you can bring everyone together in times of peace. You have a gift for it which I could never learn. You bring out people's gentleness, where Graum brought out only their cruelty and fear."

It was hard for her to speak the words, but now that

she had fought her final battle, she felt as if she had moved to a different state of being. She no longer felt angry or deprived. She had had her chance to prove herself, and she had demonstrated her strength, more than she would have believed possible. That made it easier for her to admit her weaknesses.

She spread her arms, taking in the score of people sitting on the rocky ground. "My people are your people now."

Shani glanced around at everyone who had gathered there. "This is very strange," she said, with a forced, awkward smile. "I never thought I would hear you speak this way."

Mara felt suddenly impatient. "You didn't expect me to behave graciously? But I gave my word. Surely you remember that."

"Mara." It was Arin speaking. "Mara, please. We admire you. We feel so much gratitude, we hardly know what to say."

The words stopped her. She had been retreating from everyone, she realized—feeling alienated from them and following a familiar emotional path that would ultimately lead her, once again, into bitterness and isolation. It was disconcerting to hear Arin speak. She blinked. Was he really speaking for all of them? She looked from one face to the next. To her surprise, she saw that people were nodding in agreement.

Mara looked at Shani. Shani was reaching out. "Sister, you saved us all," she said. She took Mara's hands. She squeezed them tightly, and she drew Mara close. "You were so brave, I would have never believed anyone could do such a thing. We owe you our lives." There was no mistaking the heartfelt emotion in her voice and in her eyes. "Down on the plain, as we buried the dead, people were saying that since you saved the tribe, it seems only right we should look to you, now, for guidance. And . . . I always listen to the wishes of the tribe. If you are the leader they desire, then my only choice is to obey their wishes."

Mara stared at her sister. She felt as if the world were shifting around her, rearranging the rules that she had always lived by. She swayed on her feet. "Shani, are you sure of what you're saying?"

Now it was Shani's turn to look pained. "Of course! Do you think I can't recognize what's in front of me? I told you long ago, Mara, that I serve my people and follow their will."

"Well." Mara looked at everyone again. Some of them were smiling at her now. They looked uneasy, but she realized this wasn't because they disapproved of her. They were ashamed of their own weakness, and they were in awe of her. She found a thickness in her throat, making it hard for her to speak. "I don't know what to say." She laughed uncomfortably. "I never expected this."

But then, suddenly, it was very clear to her. Once again she turned to Shani. "This is not my tribe," she said. "Nor is it yours; not anymore. We should do this between us, you and I. What I said just now is still true: You can do things that I can't do, in times of peace. But what you said was true, too. My judgment was best—in times of war."

Mara turned and pointed toward the edge of the mesa, across the darkened plain. "Look there. It's empty, now, for as far as we can see. There are just four scared men who once served Graum and are now running in fear of their lives. We're alone here and safe from harm."

She turned back to the rest of the villagers. "But it won't always be so. More people will come across the mountains from the North Lands. They'll find the valley which we used to think of as our own, and they'll make their homes there. They'll hunt the game, perhaps more fiercely than we used to, and in a few years, it'll grow scarce. Why, we already saw that beginning to happen. So people will move farther south, and one day they'll reach this prairie. Some of the newcomers will be peaceful—perhaps most of them. But there may be more men like Graum, who take joy and pride in bloodshed. And when that happens, we'll need to be prepared. We must always take steps to see that our new home here is better protected than our last." She paused and lowered her voice. "I'll be very glad—if you agree—to accept that task."

Shani smiled. It was truly a warm, open, welcoming smile. At the same time, her eyes were moist. With confusion, Mara realized that her sister was crying. "Of course," Shani said. "Of course, what you say is so. I am gentle; you are strong. Both are virtues. Both are needed."

She stepped forward, then, and embraced Mara, hugging her close.

Around them, the People of the Mesa, who had been the People of the Great Lake, shouted their approval.

There was a lot of singing after that. Everyone thanked Mara, one at a time, in their separate ways. They were still a little uneasy, and she could see that in their eyes. They still knew that she was different—more defiant, more determined than they could ever be. She seemed to have a special power inside her, and it scared them a little.

Now, though, they tried to reach across the gap that separated her from them. They touched her, they embraced her, and everyone promised to help her in any way they could to keep the tribe safe from harm.

Later, when the fire had burned down and the kind words had all been said, everyone lay down, content but exhausted, ready to sleep under the stars.

Arin came to Mara, and wordlessly he took her arm. She stood and followed him. She had half expected this, and she had been trying to decide how she should respond.

She went with him to the edge of the mesa, and they sat there together, looking out over the moonlit plain. There was no yellow point of light, tonight, marking an enemy camp. The vast panorama was silent and empty, washed silver-gray by the moonlight. This was their land now, Mara realized. Theirs to live in and use as they saw fit.

"I have something for you," Arin said as he sat beside her on the rocks. He reached inside his robe. "Here. I took this before we filled the pit where Graum lay."

Mara tried to see what he was giving her. It was hard and cold, gleaming in the light from the Moon. Then she realized what it was: Graum's knife, with which he had planned to kill her.

The touch of it suddenly unnerved her. She almost felt as if a piece of him had reached out to her from his grave. She shivered. Her immediate impulse was to hand it back or throw it over the side of the mesa—anything to rid herself of it.

But then she thought a little more, and she realized that she'd be foolish to cast the knife aside. "I won't use it," she said quietly. "At least, not in times of peace. It would make me seem too much like the man that we hated and feared. But it will have a purpose, all the same."

Arin watched her, waiting for her to go on.

She looked at him in the moonlight. "People respect me now," she said, "and they're painfully aware of the dangers that can threaten us. But as time passes, they may forget." She weighed the knife in her hand. "So I'll keep this as a symbol, a token to remind everyone of the time that our tribe was almost erased from the land." She placed her hand over his. "Thank you."

There was a long, uncomfortable silence. She remembered the days when Kormor had courted her. She had flirted with him, and he had stared at her so intensely, it had filled her with excitement even while she was afraid of what he might do. There was none of that now. Arin sat a discreet distance away, and she wasn't even sure what she wanted from him.

"You know," he said finally, "I used to envy Lomel for being so close to you."

"Yes, Arin." She waited, feeling a little apprehensive.

"I'm a quiet person," he said. "Like Lomel, I suppose. I'm not nearly as bold as a man like Kormor."

She reached out and put her arm around his shoulders. "Arin, I've learned a lot since I courted Kormor. It was foolish of me to think that a man who was so domineering would surrender himself to me."

He turned toward her, and she saw his face clearly in

the moonlight. "Then perhaps," he said, "you might want to pair with me one day."

There it was, stated so plainly that it caught her by surprise. She'd expected him to hint at it; she hadn't expected him to come right out and say it. She felt a little flustered. "I've . . . thought about it," she said.

"Really?" Now he was the one to sound surprised.

She studied his face. He looked quite different from Lomel, and yet somehow she saw Lomel in his features. Lomel was there in his eyes, the fullness of his lips, and his deeply serious expression. And as Mara looked at Arin's face, she realized that something had changed.

"Your forehead," she said. "It was badly burned when we ran through the flames in the narrow valley."

"Yes." He sounded puzzled.

Gently she touched the blistered skin. Some of it had already peeled away. "I think," she said, "the fire burned away your tattoo."

"Really?"

"I think so." Now that she was touching his face, she felt more relaxed with him. He was not the man she would have chosen. He was far too diffident. Yet he had proved his inner strength, and perhaps that was the strength that really counted. It was certainly the strength that Kormor had turned out to lack.

She stroked her finger down the line of his jaw, then quickly, impulsively, she kissed his cheek. "This is not a time to make choices, Arin," she said. "This is a time to be calm and quiet, and take some days to restore our strength and our peace of mind. But I will say, there must be some pairings here before too long. There are only a score of us, and we'll need to have many children if our tribe is going to flourish in this new land." She squeezed his hand. "So let's see what happens, you and I."

Quickly, then, she stood up. She had said more than enough—perhaps more than she should have. "I must rest now," she told him. "All my energy is gone. So I'll bid you good night, Arin."

"Good night," he called after her. His voice sounded a little wistful, but there was some pleasure in it, too.

Mara picked her way across the uneven rock. Everyone seemed to be asleep, now, and her own weariness reached up inside her, taking her strength away.

She found a spot under one of the stunted trees, and she lay down in some tough, wiry grass and curled her robe over her. She stared up at the benevolent face of the Moon as it shone down through the branches, and once again she gave silent thanks to the spirits that had guided her, helping her to serve and save the tribe that finally, she could think of as her own.

Author's Note

The events in this novel take place about ten thousand years ago. Almost all archaeologists now agree that at that time, the first human beings had entered North America through the area which we now think of as Alaska. The last of the ice ages had ended, glaciers were retreating from the Continental Divide, and the way was open for immigrants to move south in increasing numbers.

Evidence suggests that a great wave of Stone Age people spread from the north all the way into South America, devouring everything in their path. They almost certainly caused the extinction of species such as the mammoth, the mastodon, the llama, the ground sloth, and the horse (which is thought of as being quintessentially American, but was extinct in North and South America till the Spanish reintroduced it in the 1500s). Early peoples saw no reason to conserve resources. They would kill a whole herd of mammoths by stampeding them over a cliff, even though just one of the beasts would yield more meat than the tribe could consume.

It's conceivable, though, that a singular group of Stone Age humans could have been more enlightened. After all, intelligence had already evolved, and the men and women who lived ten thousand years ago almost certainly possessed a language. A wise leader could have laid down customs and practices designed to create harmony with the land and with other tribes. In this way, such group could have prefigured many of the customs that probably didn't appear elsewhere until thousands of years later, when depleted resources forced others to achieve a better balance with their environment in order to survive.

Unfortunately, a free, peaceful matriarchy of the kind described in this novel must face a terrible dilemma when it encounters outsiders who are more aggressive and less highly evolved. An egalitarian system which allows unprecedented freedoms will find it hard to survive under these circumstances unless it becomes as authoritarian and warlike as its adversaries—at which point, it has sacrificed the ideals that it was fighting to preserve. Even today, free societies face the same kind of problem.

For those who are interested in the location of the story, it commenses in the area which we now think of as Idaho. The subsequent trek takes our people south into Utah. Many of the customs of the Lake People prefigure those of tribes such as Blackfoot, Crow, and Mandans, which dwelled in the vicinity of the Rocky Mountains till the white settlers moved in and displaced them.

This is a work of fiction, but readers who have a more factual interest in early cultures, Native American tribes, and the environment of the West and Northwest might be interested in the following reference books. Although some titles may be hard to find at a general bookstore, most of them can be special ordered.

ORIGINS AND CUSTOMS OF NATIVE AMERICANS

The Great Journey
The Peopling of Ancient America
by Brian M. Fagan
Thames and Hudson, New York City

Book of the Eskimos
by Peter Freuchen
Fawcett Books, New York City

America's Fascinating Indian Heritage
James A. Maxwell, editor
Reader's Digest books, Pleasantville, New York

Indians of North America
by Harold E. Driver
The Univeristy of Chicago Press, Chicago, Illinois

North American Indians
by George Catlin
Penguin Books, New York City

George Catlin: 1796–1872
by Donna Mann
National Gallery of Art, Washington DC

My Life as an Indian
by J. W. Schultz
Fawcett Books, New York City

Recently Discovered Tales of Life Among the Indians
by James Willard Schultz
Mountain Press Publishing, Missoula, Montana

Indian Hunts and Indian Hunters of the Old West
by Dr. Frank C. Hibben
Safari Press, Long Beach, California

The Medicine Way: A Shamanic Path to Self Mastery
by Kenneth Meadows
Element Books, Rockport, Massachusetts

The Way of an Indian
by Frederic Remington
Memento Publications, Wilmington, Delaware

WILDLIFE AND ECOLOGY

After the Ice Age: The Return of Life to Glaciated North America
by E. C. Pielou
University of Chicago Press, Chicago, Illinois

Prehistoric Animals
by Daniel Cohen
Dell Books, New York City

Rocky Mountain Wildlife
by Susan C. Trudeau
Great Mountain West Supply Company, Salt Lake City, Utah

Idaho Handbook
by Bill Loftus
Moon Publications, Chico, California

The Audubon Society Field Guide to North American Trees
by Elbert L. Little
Alfred A. Knopf, New York City

Edible and Medicinal Plants of the Rocky Mountains and Neighbouring Territories
by Terry Willard Ph.D.
Wild Rose Books, Calgary, Alberta, Canada

Animal Tracking and Behavior
by Donald and Lillian Stokes
Little, Brown and Company, Boston, Massachusetts

SURVIVAL

Survival: Training Edition
Department of the Air Force, Washington, DC

Outdoor Survival
by Charles Platt
Franklin Watts, New York City

Survival with Style
by Brandford Angier
Vintage Books, New York City

The SAS Survival Handbook
by John Wiseman
Collins Harvil, London, England

ARCHAEOLOGY

Prehistory of the Americas
by Stuart J. Fiedel
Cambridge University Press, New York City

The Archaeology of North America
by Dean R. Snow
Chelsea House Publishers, New York City

ARTIFACTS

The Indian Tipi: Its History, Construction and Use
by Reginald and Gladys Laubin
Ballantine Books, New York City

The Art of Flint Knapping
by D. C. Waldorf
D. C. Waldorf and Valerine Waldorf

*Arrowheads & Stone Artifacts: A Practical Guide for the
Surface Collector & the Amateur Archaeologist*
by C. G. Yeager
Pruett Publishing Company, Boulder, Colorado